ATKINS AND PALMER

To [illegible]

Hope you enjoy

THE QUEEN OF CUPS MURDERS

[illegible]

GB WILLIAMS

Published by HanWill Publishing
Cover design by Deranged Doctor Designs

First Edition

ISBN Paperback: 978-1-7398427-6-5
ISBN eBook: 978-1-7398427-7-2

Note for Readers

If you don't speak Welsh, don't worry. There isn't much in this book and it's mostly translated within the text. The only thing that might be useful to you is to know that a single Welsh 'f' sounds like an English 'v', and the Welsh 'dd' sounds like the English 'th' (as in 'the' rather than 'thin'). So, when you see Dafydd, the Welsh equivalent to David, it's pronounced Dav-ith. However, mostly what you'll see is the shorter 'Daf'; read this as 'Dav'.

And just in case, Tom Bomber's surname is pronounced as Bom-ber not Bomb-er.

Prologue

He landed face down. Mud splattered. *What the hell?*

Weight slammed onto his back. Human weight. He scrambled to push himself up. Didn't work. Mud oozed and shifted under his hands, stole purchase. His hands slid away.

Two vicious fists grabbed his hair, controlled his head better than he could. His head was twisted, face slapped into cold, gloopy mud. The struggle to move became the struggle to breathe. Wet slop, stinking of earth and coal, clogged his mouth and nose.

The need for air dominated every trembling thought. He tried to swallow the foul, viscous liquid, but it choked him. He tried to spit it out; it had nowhere to go.

Forced down, pinned, his own strength served only to dig him deeper into the quagmire.

Stars went supernova in his eyes. No movement, no breath. Coughing and spluttering were impossible. No breath! Limbs of lead. Cotton wool for brains. Darkness beckoned.

One last push. The grip on his hair tightened. No oxygen. He couldn't survive.

Why?

Chapter 1

The gibbous moon looked wonky. Hardly an astronomical term, but it described Madoc's thoughts. Sitting alone, he watched the glow of the moon through the trees in the lightening blue. Maybe the Goddesses viewed his thinking about the future the same way — wonky.

The cold air carried the refreshing scent of damp earth and fresh-washed living pines. He wore only cargo pants; it was too cold to be skyclad. Aside from the biting temperature, remodelling the deconsecrated chapel behind him left splinters and sawdust everywhere. Those were hard enough on his feet. He wouldn't risk more sensitive body parts.

Atkins is a frosty-arsed bitch without an ounce of compassion. The words Becca had sneered on his last day working under her rang in his head. *Should suit you perfectly.*

Maybe it would. At least then his new DI would keep her distance. And at a distance she was less likely to spot what he didn't want anyone seeing.

His phone rang. But what surprised him most? That it was still in his pocket, that he had signal, or that someone was calling him at 04:37 a.m.?

He recognised the number and answered. "*Bore da, modryb* Maureen." Welsh was their second language, but Aunt Maureen preferred it, claimed it engendered a better sense of spiritual connection than the harsher English.

"*Beth sy'n bod gyda ti?*"

A good question. What was wrong with him? He should be asleep, but such peace had evaded him. That other sense would not rest quietly. "I'm not sure."

"Why not?" She switched to English because he had.

"Because I'm not." His uncertainties stretched before him longer than the night, which was nearly over. The next few days would change his life, but the positivity of the outcome was currently unseen. The woman he'd be working with worried him. Moving jobs was advancement and practicality. The bonus being it got him out of Cardiff. Back to his own local area. In all likelihood, nothing would change in real terms, he hoped. New location, new people. Same job. Well, the last training assignment for advancement in his job. A job full of challenge. A job he loved. Besides, today, his first day, was likely to be office based.

"So, why are you staring at a cold lump of wonky rock?"

Sensing the feelings of others clearly enough to echo them was Maureen's forte. "I like that lump of rock. And she's not wonky, she gibbous. Why are you even awake?"

"The spirits woke me."

What could Madoc say? Maureen was different. She had 'the gift'. Though his own weaker talent proved it was sometimes a curse.

"Why did they do that?" he asked.

"Something's happened, something bad," she said. "It's going to impact on you."

"Aunt Maureen, I'm a police officer. I deal with bad things every day. Can you be a little more specific?"

"No. You're watching Mother Moon. Contemplating." The lyrical quality of her voice danced down the line, then changed. "And drinking."

He looked at the empty bottle. "The two often go hand in hand."

"And often go hand in hand into a nosedive."

There it was again, that uncharming habit of pointing out his foibles. And the even more annoying habit of being right.

"All things are connected," he said. "As you often remind me."

He heard guttural annoyance.

"It was one beer, and I don't have to be at work for hours."

"*Twmffat twp.*"

The insult stung. The literal translation was 'stupid funnel', but it meant a great deal worse than that. Especially from her. "*Diolch yn fawr, anti.*"

This time he heard a tut. "You're being deliberately ignorant."

"Am I?" His eyes returned to the moon. The Goddess – or lump of rock, depending on viewpoint – didn't look impressed with him either. "Aunt Maureen, I love you, you know that, but I'm not like you. I don't see the future or get clear messages."

"But you do get a sense of things, uncommon things. You can hear them. Echoes of them."

That was true. He did get a sense of the departed, hazy and indistinct, but a sense. It had served him well in the past and he trusted it would in the future. As long as he kept it hidden. Showing the world, or more importantly, his colleagues, was dangerous, though. Losing his job wasn't an option, too much of his life depended on it. His son's face was clear in his mind.

"*Iawn, beth wyt ti moyn i fi 'neud?*" He asked what she wanted him to do.

"*Twmffat. Twp.*"

The line went dead.

Two words. Not the insult. The literal translation.

The moon looked down, matching Maureen's impatience. "Okay," he said. "Got it. I'm the lump being stupid. I'll go funnel."

Stomach churning, he returned inside. The reassuring scent switched to cut dry wood. Dawn was creeping in, granting enough light to see by. He avoided the various building materials and tools, going to the Welsh dresser placed in what would eventually be the kitchen. His hands weren't as steady as he'd like as he selected his preferred tarot deck, the clearest medium for messages for him. Unwrapping the protective velvet, he shuffled quickly. He wanted only one card, but fumbled it, caught it just before it hit the floor. Well, he hoped that wasn't a sign of things to come.

The Queen of Cups.

Upright or reversed?

Motherhood and abundance embodied. Spiritual. Creative. An ideal partner. Unless reversed, then it might become smothering, even martyrdom.

How did that relate to something bad? Was the card reversed after all?

So many possible interpretations. He'd take it as a good sign until life proved different. The card went back into the deck, then the velvet, and the amethyst on top.

Time for coffee, a shower, and his first day in a new role.

Chapter 2

"Ruth!"

Ruth Atkins had barely stepped through the door, her jacket only half off, and DCI Geraint Evans was already bellowing at her. Mind, being a big man, bellowing was his default. She just didn't know why he was bellowing at her this time.

"Did I actually do it?" she asked.

Geraint frowned, his caterpillar eyebrows meeting in the middle. Those brows were her barometer to his mood.

"Do what?" he asked.

Good question. *Oh, for heaven's sake. I'm a Detective Inspector. Time to stop being a wuss and get a grip.* "Whatever you're shouting at me for, sir?" Her chin rose as she shrugged her leather jacket back on. He couldn't know what was going on in her head.

"Sir?" The grey caterpillars stretched up towards Geraint's thick thatch of salt-and-pepper hair, heavy on the salt. "Guilty conscience, Ruth?"

"No." Maybe. "Sorry for being late?"

"It's barely one-minute-past, even I'm not that tight." His scrutiny sent a billion bugs squirming under her skin. The way he stepped closer could intimidate; his ex-prop-forward frame easily overshadowed her. Luckily, she'd known him long enough to be immune. Mostly. Though she'd known him so long the danger was he'd read her like a book. He thrust a buff file towards her. "Get up to the new housing development at Heolgerrig."

Oh no. A new case was the last thing she needed today.

"Take Jackson," he added.

"Sorry, Geraint, can't."

Geraint reared. His surprise surprised Ruth.

The door behind her opened but she wouldn't let that, or her boss's affront, stop her explanation. "Jackson's due in court later," she said. "Witness for the prosecution."

Geraint grunted, then turned his attention to the new entrant as Ruth checked the scant detail in the file. A robbery. Pallets of valuable goods taken, easy-to-fence items. What had been left behind was a whole lot more worrying.

"Ah, good. You're here at last," Geraint said to the newcomer.

Ruth focused on the file.

"Everyone," Geraint called. "This is Detective Sergeant Madoc Palmer. Madoc, this is everyone." A murmur of welcome rumbled around the room. "Welcome to the Major Crime Investigation Team. Now go with DI Ruth Atkins, here."

Ruth looked up. Palmer was taller than expected, over six feet. Strong features, honest, if guarded, brown eyes, short dark hair, clearly physically active outside work. It appeared some rumours about him might be true. She hoped to God others weren't. However good-looking he was, she needed him to be a good investigator. Sadly, he hadn't transferred up from Cardiff with much sense. He wore beige trousers. Even in a city they probably weren't a great idea. Had he expected the office day she'd been hoping for? He couldn't have predicted this case on his first day. Now, she could only hope he could hack it.

"Hi." She returned the file to Geraint. "Come on, then, DS Palmer. Work to do."

"Ruth." She paused at Geraint's call. "While you're out, try to impress on the lad my views on timekeeping."

"Yes, boss." The response was automatic as she moved on.

They had a job to do. *Follow procedure.* Worries were balled into a lump and cast aside. *Don't mention it, don't make it real.*

Signing out a car was routine, no thinking required. On autopilot, she grabbed a bag from the back of her own vehicle. She was driving, DS Palmer beside her, before she realised she had yet to speak to him properly. Poor bugger. The rudeness was unintentional. She just hadn't thought that … No, she just hadn't thought. Damn it, she was being unfair.

"Er, you don't mind me driving do you?"

"Of course not," he answered easily. As the junior officer, he expected to drive but wasn't bothered either way. Was this a test? Had she hoped to emasculate him? That would work on some.

She made a strange noise and lapsed back into silence.

The second he'd seen her, Madoc had known there was more to Ruth Atkins than reputation indicated. Those other senses told him her substance was more resonant with Pentacles or Wands than Cups. Perhaps she wasn't the Queen. He'd have to wait and see where she sat in the deck.

Physically, she was the opposite of his usual type, but there was something about her that called to him.

Her hands on the steering wheel were competent and confident. She was a skilful driver. Probably aced every police driving course she'd ever taken. He'd heard she'd aced every course ever. Little wonder people found her intimidating. If she discovered his abilities, she'd laugh him off the force. He couldn't let that happen.

He also couldn't seem to move his eyes from her hands. The overcast sky sent weak light glinting on the simple gold band around her ring finger as she turned the wheel. He wore one similar.

"So," he risked breaking the silence, "the new boss is a stickler for timekeeping?"

She nodded, concentrated on driving. "He wants us in on time to start briefings and assignments on time." She threw him a brief smile as she added, "And he's only new to you."

She's a pedant. Great.

"But we're missing this morning's briefing."

Her shrug communicated acceptance, not disinterest. "Cases take precedence. He'll catch us up later. Oh, and don't take the whole timekeeping thing badly. Geraint's just as keen we go home on time. He doesn't want us burning out."

Moments later, they approached the village of Heolgerrig. The housing development became immediately visible, the village itself just beyond. Panda cars and crime scene tape marked the cordon. Men in hi-vis vests swarmed the area. The difference between the police and the builders came down to hats: white hard hats or black helmets. And that there were a couple of women in police uniform.

Madoc checked the sky. Overcast with white clouds, no obvious threat of rain. No guarantee there, though.

"Right," Ruth said as she switched off the engine. "The site got broken into early this morning. Copper piping and plumbing supplies were stolen, along with a forklift."

It was good to know what they faced. "Okay." A glance at the site sent dark niggles crawling beneath his skin. Instinct screamed something was wrong, something that wasn't theft. Was this the something bad Maureen mentioned? For theft, he'd expect to sense the Seven of Swords. This was more like the Five of Wands, the midst of battle, competition. But who was in competition with whom? He had questions, only Ruth had already left the vehicle.

Out of the car, he found Ruth at the boot, changing her DMs for wellingtons from the bag she had grabbed. Of course. The building site would be churned mud after two days of persistent rain. He glanced at his polished black shoes.

"You might be able to get shoe covers from the CSIs."

"You might have warned me. I could've got my own boots." *Damn, shouldn't speak to a superior officer that way.*

She looked up at him. Was her smile amusement or approval? Both? "Do you keep wellies in the boot of your car?"

He swallowed; her direct gaze saw right through him. Unfortunately, the ground opening up was a lot less likely than the sky opening. The lightweight jacket he wore wouldn't save him from the rain any more than the shoe covers would keep him mud free. Whereas Ruth's outsized leather sports jacket would keep her dry. He'd have to rethink his workwear up here.

"I will in future."

Her grin notched up a little before she turned, closed the boot, and locked the car. Her ponytail bobbed down to her waist as she headed for the tape cordon. "Harris!" She called a uniformed officer's attention. The big guy turned and strode over.

As they neared the site, Madoc's impressions grew stronger. The senses tickled through him, whispering the perceptions from others. The more experienced officers were stoic, the less experienced clouded tension into the air. The builders milled around. They had mixed feelings on the inability to work – related to a question of pay as much as professionalism, judging by the grumbles. Clearly standing around in the cold and mud didn't please anyone.

"Hiya, Ruth," the constable said.

"Hiya. Constable John Harris meet DS Madoc Palmer."

"Ah, the new boy." The man eyed him up and down, which made Madoc feel about ten years old. "Pleasure to meet you, sir."

That 'sir' was going to take some getting used to.

"Don't suppose you've got a spare pair of wellies he might borrow?" Ruth asked as she ducked under the tape John held for her.

Having his DI speak for him chipped at Madoc's masculinity, but it proved Ruth wasn't entirely inconsiderate. She didn't seem frosty-arsed to him either. Day one, remember? Uncertainties were the only certainty at this point. He'd figure it out.

John's mouth twitched. "Size ten?"

"Eleven."

John shrugged. "I've got a pair of large nines."

"I'd struggle with nines." Madoc glanced at the site. Mud all the way. He could kiss goodbye to his shoes, the heavy canvas slacks, too, probably. Their work meant never knowing what they'd face in a day, but this he hadn't expected. However unsuitably dressed he was, he'd just have to tough it out. "I'll be fine. Thanks, though."

Ruth's raised eyebrows, her slightly parted lips suggested she was unconvinced. With a tiny shrug, she turned back to John. As she moved on, Madoc thanked John again and followed her under the cordon. The extended plastic scraped along his back. Should have ducked lower.

Ruth stood with another woman, this one carrying a blue ring binder. The crime scene manager. Ruth turned when he stepped up.

"Walk behind me," she instructed.

The perfunctory order didn't sit well with him. Nor did not being introduced to the other officer. Was the frosty-arsed bitch showing up? Ruth's steps were short and careful. He quickly realised that she was testing the ground with each footfall, not only to keep to the marked route, but to select the shallowest mud. It wouldn't stop him getting mucky, but she was trying to minimise it.

Heavy-duty chain-link fencing ringed the site. To his right, three flattened panels showed telltale tracks from the missing forklift. But they didn't head this way. Dissonance echoed through him. A sense of wrongness screamed in his head, in his veins. This wasn't about theft.

"So why is MCIT involved in a straightforward smash and grab?" Madoc asked as he stepped carefully after Ruth.

"Aside from it being a pretty major smash and grab?"

He saw the CSIs up ahead. "Erm, should we actually be on the crime scene if the CSIs are still here?"

Ruth stopped and smiled up at him. "Good application of procedural knowledge, Sergeant," she congratulated him. Then she pointed off to their right. "The goods and forklift were taken from over there." Two CSI personnel were working that crime scene. "We're not going anywhere near that. I have the crime scene manager's permission to approach this area because the CSIs have already processed what they can, but there is a marker beyond which we can't go."

"Hold on." He called her back when she started to turn. "The crime scene manager, what's her name?"

"Ah." A light blush coloured Ruth's cheeks. He shouldn't find it attractive, but he did. "If I could remember that, I would have introduced you."

She moved on. A chill unrelated to the temperature washed through him. The grave was cold indeed.

"This is about the dead man?"

Ruth stopped, and he stepped up behind her. She looked at him oddly.

"How did you know? How did you know it was a death, let alone a man?"

Shit. He shouldn't have spoken. Ruth's picking up on the oddity was impressive observation. Now he had to explain it away.

"I'm taller than you," he said. "I could see him before you would have." He pointed into the trench behind the line that limited their permitted approach. A makeshift grave from which lost life echoed. Madoc's senses whispered that this dead man needed a reason more vengeance for his death.

Ruth's eyes narrowed. He got the impression she realised something was odd, but not what. Then she broke eye contact to look into the trench. His lie hadn't convinced. His gut clenched.

The dead man revealed little at first glance. He was face down, his hair darkened by mud and damp. His clothes - checked shirt, cargo pants - befitted a man in the building trade. Two no-longer-white-clad CSIs were at either end of the trench, preparing to lift the body out to the matching pair on the far side of the three-foot-deep cutting. They gave off a mixed air of fascination, resignation, and the general desire to get away from the cold and wet. The rain had only stopped in the early hours. Now it darkened the mud and soaked the victim; it would be hell getting forensics off that.

Madoc caught himself. *That?* At what point did he start thinking of the dead as *that*? But in truth, the man was gone. All that remained was the shell and the surprised echo of an untimely end. Their job was to find out how and why. Caring too much about the victim as an individual could lead to personal issues best avoided, especially for someone like him.

"Meet Raymond Bevan," Ruth said. "His death is the major incident we're here to investigate."

The CSI by the victim's head looked up. "Hiya Ruth, how you doing?"

Madoc could see the man was about five-foot-three tall, but beyond that, he couldn't be sure. With the hood up and a mask on, only the man's eyes showed, and they were behind safety goggles and shadowed in the murk. The man's thickness of waist might be down to the clothes he had on under the coverall.

"Fine, Daf, absolutely fine. Any theories on what happened here?"

"Plenty." Daf looked at the other man in the trench. "On three."

The other man nodded. Daf counted, and together they heaved the body up to the side where another two CSIs took hold. As they took possession of the body, moving it to the waiting body bag, Daf and his assistant looked back at the trench floor. Before Ruth's feet lay a two-foot-square dry mat. The CSI who wasn't Daf reached over, wiped his gloved hands on blue absorbent paper torn from the roll, then took up the big camera with the industrial flash and documented the trench floor.

Daf turned to Ruth. "Possibilities include anything from an innocent trip and fall to someone smacked him over the head and pushed him down here. Apparently, this trench is in the wrong place and was due to be filled first thing this morning."

"Where's the guy's hard hat?" Ruth asked.

Daf shrugged. "Doesn't appear to have been wearing one."

"Does that weigh for either theory?"

"Nope," Daf said. "The pathologist will have to guide you there. Frankly, I don't hold out much hope for forensics here. The way this ground is, the traffic you get on a site like this, any evidence will largely be circumstantial if it's not on the body itself, and even then …"

Ruth nodded. "Even then, proving it's going to be a bugger."

"Finding it's going to be the bugger," said Not-Daf. Then he put the camera back on the dry mat and moved further down the trench to pull himself out from the pit.

Daf knelt, looking at the ground. Temperature readings to be done, he put one probe in where the body's waist had rested. It sank easily into the mud.

"Think you'll be able to estimate time of death?" Ruth asked.

As he studied the electronic readout, Daf moved the probe, took another reading. "Somewhere between seven p.m. yesterday when the site closed and five a.m. today when the body was found."

Ruth gave a small laugh. "Thanks, Daf. Real helpful."

Daf stood and passed the electronic thermometer up to Not-Daf. The two CSIs with the body were slipping away – literally slipping as they moved.

"What can I say?" Daf said. "Temperature degradation isn't an exact science, and these conditions won't help much. I think I heard someone say the robbery took place about four this morning, but I can't even guarantee the two incidents are related. It seems likely, but not certain."

"And certain is a big word to you."

Humour showed in the man's eyes twinkling and crinkling. "I'm a scientist. Of course, certainly is a big word." Daf looked at Madoc, properly looked. It was a little unnerving, like being a specimen in a jar. "Who's the new eye candy?"

"Daf!" Ruth's tone was light-hearted admonishment. "This is DS Madoc Palmer. Palmer, this is Dafydd Pugh." She pointed to the man in the trench then the one with the camera. "And this is Chris Daniels."

The photographer offered a silent wave as he worked.

Daf said, "See why you're calling him Palmer."

Madoc didn't. Geraint had been clear the team worked on a first name basis so her using his surname felt like a slight, though he sensed no animosity.

"Aye, well, with Ruth Madoc having lived a valley or two over, it would be good to avoid the obvious jokes."

Of course! Merging their names to get the comedy actress's name wasn't the worst comparison, but repeatedly hearing that 1980s holiday camp catchphrase 'hi-de-hi' would quickly grate.

"Oh, come on, Ruth, it's going to happen whatever you do. Suck it up." The friendly banter was batted back. As Daf stepped towards the higher ground where Chris had left the trench, his foot skidded out from under him. His arms went wide, clawed fingers tried to stop the fall. The unintelligible cry hit Madoc like a cold spot headache. The fleeting sense departed, the cold disappeared, as Dav splashed into the mud.

Thankfully, Daf was unhurt. Madoc caught Ruth's strangled-back chuckle. He leant over to look down at the prone man, kept his tone light. "As a scientist, what level of certainty would you give to your having deserved that?"

A raspberry blew beneath the mask. Daf floundered before rising.

"Daf?" Ruth asked, her tone serious. "What's that?"

Daf looked to where Ruth pointed. Madoc looked, too. Within the four-inch-wide burrow Daf's fingers had gouged, a smooth, round stone lay exposed. Only it wasn't a stone, and that prickling, nagging sensation Madoc had felt since they got here was stronger than ever. This was the wrong he had felt. The source of the cry.

Daf moved to the thing, leant down, and looked at it. "Frell."

"You been watching science fiction shows again?" Ruth asked as Daf started pushing mud away from the thing. The dripping brown back blocked Madoc's view, but he knew what Daf would uncover.

"The missus doesn't want me swearing around the kids. I'm trying to be a good boy." A good boy who threw a massive clump of mud to splash back into the trench. Daf straightened with a sigh and turned. "Chris, I need you to get more shots of this."

"Frell?" Madoc asked Ruth under his breath.

"Substitute swear word from a show Daf likes," she explained.

"*Farscape,* to be precise," Daf said.

"And he does like to be precise, our Daf." Ruth grinned.

As Chris took up the camera again, Daf stepped aside, revealing a mud-stained human skull. Four-to-six inches from ground level.

"That's shallow, even for a hasty grave," Ruth observed.

"Not necessarily," Madoc said. "Groundworks are likely to have changed the depth." He shrugged. "We'll have to get the site surveyor to tell us how."

"Whatever it was, your workload just doubled," Daf said.

Chapter 3

Yet another new case. Great. Not. Ruth kept the groan internal as she worked with Daf and others to outline an action plan for exhuming the second body. They had to include an archaeological team, because at this point, there was no way to determine how long the remains had been there. Still, the crime scene manager, whose name Ruth still couldn't recall, could oversee that. She made the call to advise Geraint.

Ruth was concerned about Madoc claiming he saw the body before she did. When he'd first mentioned it, they had to have been too far away for even his greater height to have revealed the body. She said nothing because she couldn't be sure. Daf wasn't the only who liked certainty. But there was something different about Madoc Palmer, something she couldn't define. And it wasn't because he was – she rejected the word gorgeous - attractive. She touched her left thumb to her wedding ring. Instant attractions faded, and she'd figure out Madoc given time. Right now, she had other things to concentrate on.

Ruth needed to speak to the site manager and get Madoc out of the muck. His shoes and trousers were ruined. She was impressed he hadn't uttered a syllable of complaint.

At twenty-nine, Madoc was two years her junior, and Ruth tried very hard not to judge him on the reputation that preceded him. He was annoyingly stereotypical: tall, dark, and, okay she'd admit it, gorgeous. Daf's eye candy comment didn't help. Their being farewelled with, "Hi-de-hi, campers!" grated. Though Daf was right: there was no way they could avoid it altogether. *Too great a gift from the Tedious Bastard Gods.*

Such considerations got pushed aside as she headed towards the builders skulking by the site entrance, sharing low opinions on procedures they obviously didn't understand.

"Who's in charge?" Ruth asked as they got closer.

"That'd be Andy Porter," said a hulking bloke with more neck rolls than one man had a right to.

"Thanks. Where's Andy Porter?"

"Site office." The man pointed to the first PortaKabin down the edge of the site.

Ruth nodded to him. "Thanks."

Aware that Madoc followed, she walked carefully across the flatter mud towards the PortaKabin. She guessed this route was usually hard-packed but recent rain had rectified that. Her foot slid beneath her. She skated four inches, arms spread for balance. Ruth willed herself to remain upright; she would not look the fool before her new DS. Besides, she was used to this – dead bodies tended to appear off the beaten track. Or in their own homes, of course. Or mangled in wrecked ca—

No! She would not go there.

At the cabin, the battered blue door proclaimed it to be the site office. She knocked twice, then tried the handle. The door opened and she went inside. The floor proved muddy boots were frequent visitors, so she didn't worry about her own. Split into three, this cabin offered offices left and right. They had entered the middle section. A desk stacked with papers stood before them, an empty seat behind it. As Ruth moved forward, Madoc stepped in, and two women appeared in the right-hand doorway. Both wore boots and hi-vis. One looked more construction-ready than the other. The younger-looking woman wore rougher, dirtier clothes.

"Andy Porter?"

"That would be me," the younger woman said.

Ruth raised her ID and warrant card. Madoc did likewise while she introduced them. "We need to speak with you about Raymond Bevan."

The woman nodded. "Just me or do you want Maggie, too?"

"Just you to start with." Ruth offered a small smile but looked at the older woman. "Are you Margaret Drake?"

The woman nodded. Again, it struck Ruth just how much cleaner this woman was than either Andy or — she checked — herself.

"You reported the incident?"

Maggie nodded. "I told the guy on the phone everything and went over it with another officer here."

"I'm sure you did, Mrs Drake. It's the unfortunate effect of the multi-layered structure of investigation. We often have to ask the same questions repeatedly, and I'm sorry, but you'll have to go through it again to give an official statement. We don't aim to upset or waste time, but we have to get to the truth and it's surprising the details that turn out to be important – things witnesses don't necessarily remember to say the first time we ask. It's the shock. I hope you don't mind us speaking to Ms Porter first, but if you've been through this twice already, I suspect you have a great deal of work to get back to."

Drake offered a tight smile and sharp glance, then she stepped out. Andy moved back and Ruth entered the office. Madoc shadowed her. Ruth heard the squelches. The grey-brown mud clinging to his shoes must have worked its way inside. Every step was the sound effect of the monster from the Black Lagoon. Life today seemed like that: dank and rotten, corrupted. It shouldn't. She'd worked murder cases before without feeling icky. Even with new partners. But today, she was off-kilter. Deep inside, she knew the imbalance was hers only.

She was no more ready for today than Palmer was for the terrain. She felt sorry for him, but it was one way to push him in at the deep end and see if he could swim. She wasn't keen on breaking in newbies. Far too many broke far too easily. Palmer was an adult, an experienced officer; she had to let him make his own choices, his own mistakes. Ruth glanced at him in her sweep of the dust-covered office. Phone in hand, he was poised and ready to record what was said.

"Excuse the mess," Andy said, indicating the many archive boxes around the room and on the chairs. "It's not usually this bad, but we're preparing for an audit regarding another site. A closed one. This is the only place Ray and I can get the work done. Well, could get the work done, now, I suppose."

They remained standing to talk. Ruth would write her notes up later. For now, she listened closely to what Andy said.

The site closed at seven last night, probably not on the dot. No, Andy hadn't checked her watch when she locked the gate. Raymond Bevan left. Definitely, she saw him go. Yes, he had his own keys. No, he was local, so walked to work. He kept his own hard hat at home, but spares were available from the stores. He would have had keys to get one. No idea why he hadn't worn one. The alarm sounded just after four; Andy got here just before five, met Maggie; the police arrived shortly after. The ditch had been dug in the wrong place because someone mis-aligned the drainage plans. It happened occasionally, but caught quick, it was no biggie this time. Of course, there were people on site who didn't like Raymond, as a human and as site supervisor, but she wasn't aware of any real enmity. Yes, she could give them Ray's wife's name - Pippa – and her telephone number and the family address. Uniformed officers already had that information and had gone to inform Pippa.

Ruth thanked the woman and explained what would happen next.

"What? Why can't we get back to work? I'm on a schedule here."

Nodding sympathetically, Ruth gave no quarter. "I understand. However, you're also on a crime scene, potentially a triple crime scene."

"Triple!" Andy frowned. "How is it a triple crime scene?"

"The break-in, and Ray's death — which we have to treat as suspicious. Then there's the human skull we just found buried by that trench. The only people working here today will be the forensics and archaeological teams. Gives you more time to prepare for the audit, though."

Two bodies certainly confused things, Madoc thought. Raymond had been surprised by his death. The other screamed inarticulate outrage. There was something feminine about the sense, though he couldn't define what.

Ruth had been so smooth with Andy and Maggie to separate them without offence. Once they'd finished with Andy, the way she'd handled Maggie, double-checking the facts, was simple and efficient. But something he saw in Maggie left him with an immovable conviction.

"I need a drink," Ruth muttered as they left the site.

Needing a drink before noon struck Madoc as worrying. Police officers with drinking problems were a cliché, but it happened. Ruth having a drinking problem seemed unlikely. Amidst all the spite he had heard poured on her, he had also heard accusations of her being teetotal – which made her needing a drink now a tad confusing. The whole morning had been confusing. He felt like something was trying to bore into his skull, while he was trying to push his attraction to his new superior officer out of it. He couldn't afford another mistake like Becca. Still, he had other concerns, more pressing ones about this case.

"What's wrong, Palmer?"

The surprise question snapped him back to the here and now. He noted the vehicle unlocking. How to play this?

Remember Biddy Small.

He could never forget the case he had resolved because he listened to his instincts, not his boss.

"You know how 90 per cent of the time, the murderer is either the person who found the body or the one who called it in?"

She nodded and got in the car. He did likewise. Naturally, she knew. She had a brain and more experience of murder cases than him.

"Maggie Drake both found the body and called it in."

Again, she nodded as she started the car. "True, but then Daf found the second body, and I called it in. Pretty sure neither of us had anything to do with that death."

"Which is where the other 10 per cent comes into play."

A grin played around her lips. He noticed she wore no makeup. She was all natural, with a clear complexion that didn't require cosmetic assistance.

"Also true, and something we will look at closely. Maggie's not top of my suspect list, but she's on it. Don't rush to an assumed result. We'll get the answer, for both cases."

That was fair. Maybe he was relying too heavily on his other sense. Though he feared the ridicule that would come from others discovering his methods, the past had taught him to trust his instincts. He simply had to keep his methods secret.

As Ruth found first gear, rain drops splatted the windscreen. "Timed that right." The drive was slow, the road badly potholed.

"'Ow fussy are you about your coffee?"

The question and the increased anglicisation of her accent surprised Madoc. "Sorry?"

"How fussy are you about your coffee? Like I said, I need a drink. Feel right parched. Do you prefer Costa, or you happy with a drive-through from Maccy Ds?"

Coffee. Of course. She was thirsty. She wanted a drink, not a *drink*. Ashamed he'd assumed the worst, he hung his head. He saw the bottom third of his trousers had turned a muddy grey, probably a permanent alteration. His socks squelched as he moved his toes. "A coffee would be good." It would help ground him after all he had sensed. He usually carried snacks but had forgot this morning. "Think a drive-through would be the best option right now."

She followed his eyeline, then focused back on the road. Again, no censure, just acceptance. "Yeah, sorry about that. Do you live locally, or have a change of clothes at the station?"

"I've a gym bag in my car. I've got spare clothes in there."

"Okay, then. Coffee to go and back to the station so you can clean up."

Inspector David Mannford in Cardiff had once forced him to do a full interview in sopping wet clothes after falling in a canal with the suspect. Said suspect had been given a warm drink and a change of clothes. Mannford had barely allowed Madoc the chance to run a towel over himself. Clearly, and thankfully, Ruth wasn't what he'd been told.

"Appreciate that, sir," he said.

"'Sir'?" She glanced at him as she waited at a roundabout.

He floundered. He hadn't meant to say it; it had just slipped out because Mannford accepted nothing else. She huffed, a small shrug under the leather. More acceptance.

"Been called worse."

Chapter 4

Concentration eluded Ruth. The nagging need to see a doctor had to be constantly pushed aside as she struggled to focus on paperwork.

Palmer walked in, towelling still-wet hair. What caught Ruth's attention was the way two other women in the open-plan office craned their necks to stare after him. Palmer wouldn't see because they were behind him, but Ruth saw all right. Ogling. Sickening. He wasn't an object, and they should know better.

"Hi, again."

She lifted her head, doubting she had quite got the scowl off her face. "Turn around."

He frowned. "Turn around?"

"It's a simple instruction."

Confusion filled his expression as he turned. The others pretended they hadn't been ogling like mad. Ruth looked over Palmer. The T-shirt hugged him from a good set of shoulders to an athletic waist. What had obviously caught the girls' attention was lower: his worn blue jeans cupped a beautifully proportioned backside in all the right ways. The view flowed too far down to a beaten pair of unbranded trainers. Oh God, now she was ogling, and double standards weren't good enough. "Hmm."

He turned to face her. "Problem?"

"Yeah." She sighed. "Don't wear jeans to work again. We try to project a professional image."

"Says the woman in an oversized T-shirt and coat?"

She deserved that. "It's my husband's coat. Or was until I adopted it. Okay, honestly, it's not the professional image that worries me as much as the way that pair were eyeing up your butt." She glared at the two women, who melted away. "And you of all people should get why I might try to hide these assets." She sat straighter, shoulders back and down, and wasn't in the least surprised when his eyeline dropped. "Don't really want a witness, suspect, or victim's first impression to be 'massive breasts'."

His eyes returned to hers. "No, of course not. Sorry, sir, I was out of line."

"Actually, the oglers were out of line. Me too for seeing why they did it. That's your desk." She pointed over her own file-strewn desk to the one backed against it. She returned to her report as he sat.

"Sorry I took so long."

She shrugged but didn't look up. "Gave me time to write up my notes." A noise drew attention behind her. She turned to find Geraint filling his office doorway.

"Ruth, Madoc."

A general titter circled the office. The temptation to tell them to stop was great, but was also the best way to ensure the nickname stuck. She ignored it and prayed Palmer would, too. Geraint twitched his head towards his office. Ruth stood and heard Palmer move. They headed inside.

After leaving Geraint's office, Madoc was unsure what to think. While he sensed nothing negative in the catch up for the missed briefing, Madoc was uncertain about everything, except Geraint being The Emperor of this deck. He mulled it over, without a satisfactory conclusion as he followed Ruth to the car park. Once they were in the pool car, he had to ask.

"Is he always like that?"

"Plain-spoken?" Ruth asked. "Thankfully, yes. Always know where you stand with Geraint. I like it."

"What happens if you get in his bad books?"

She smiled at him, a spark of humour showing, shooting dangerous desire through him. "Oh, don't do that. I pissed him off once. Barely spoke to me for two days and I got all the shitty jobs for the next month. Look, you're gonna take a few days to settle in. We've had wannabes in before who couldn't deal with me and Geraint, and frankly, I've kicked them over to Pete – DI Saunders – to see if they cope better with him. Some do, but most request, or are given, a transfer ASAP. I haven't handed you over because you're not showing any of the usual signs."

He frowned as she drove out of the station car park. "Usual signs?"

"Twitching." Her grin sparkled in her eyes, eyes of banded brown and green with a thin grey outline he noted, but it didn't last. A sign of sadness at her core. Everyone kept secrets, and it seemed the ones Ruth Atkins kept haunted her. A glance at his wedding ring made him wonder about his own secrets. Too soon to reveal them.

"Okay." Ruth surprised him with a forlorn sigh. "I'm not good at the whole mentoring, bringing people out of themselves thing, but if you're unsure about something, ask. Okay?"

He nodded. A million questions tumbled in his mind. One fell from his lips. "Are you married?"

Her features pinched, darkened. "Well, that doesn't bode well for your observational skills."

"I see your wedding ring. It's just …"

"Occupational hazard though it is, I am not divorced."

No. He knew that. But he suddenly wasn't ready to push for an update. "Any kids?" This one he wasn't sure of.

She took a tight-lipped breath. "One son." Annoyance bit in her tone. Her grip on the wheel was white-knuckled. He turned his head away.

"Sorry," she said a moment later. "I'm not comfortable talking about this sort of stuff. Family's … well, it's … complicated. I'm sure the rumour mill will fill you in eventually, but right now I don't … I … erm …" Her voice trailed away.

"You don't know if you can trust me yet," he said. "Makes sense."

"Think you can handle that? Or is this where you start twitching?"

He offered a small smile. "No twitching yet, sir. So, during the interview, shall I record like before?"

"Please. I've left my body cam in the office, do you have yours? You have been issued with a BWV, haven't you?"

BWV, or body worn video, were issued so everyone was clear what happened in various encounters. "Had to give my old one back when I moved division. Haven't had a new one yet."

"No worries. We'll get it sorted next time we're in the station. So, yeah, please take notes. I find it difficult to write *and* concentrate on what people are saying. How do you feel about driving?"

Being given a choice was a pleasant surprise. "I'm fine with it, sir." Perhaps he should stop calling her that.

"Okay then, you record the discussions, then you can drive back so I can start writing my notes up in the car."

He nodded. "Works for me."

"Good, because first, we need to go to the pub." She pulled away.

In the morning? No, that instant reaction was unjust.

"Which pub?" he asked as she negotiated a roundabout.

"The Earth Harp."

Madoc gaped at her. "Seriously?"

"Yep."

"That's a Flack's stronghold."

Her lips twisted upward. "You know the family then?"

Who didn't know the bloody Merthyr Mafia? The Flacks were not people he wanted to antagonise. No one in their right mind did. Police officers who tried failed badly - painfully. The Flack family patriarch was Griffith. He had six children – five boys and a girl. The eldest, Dylan, was the only one Madoc had met. Dylan had caused some trouble for Madoc's sister, Mary;

he'd wanted her, she hadn't wanted him. Nothing about the experience had been pleasant for the Palmer family. Then there was the Princess. The Flack daughter, real name Nia, was reportedly a total nightmare. Daddy's little princess was a widow twice over. Both deaths had been investigated, but with only one prosecution, a drunk American who'd entered the M4 down an exit ramp. The more suspicious second loss was a closed case the CPS said there was insufficient evidence to prosecute. Few people believed that. Madoc wasn't sure he believed *this*. Going into a Flack den? Naked bearbaiting was safer.

"I know them mostly by reputation. Which is why I'm wondering why you want to drink in one of their pubs."

"To tweak a nose."

She's crazy. No one tweaked Flack noses and lived. He swallowed. "Didn't think I'd joined a suicide squad."

"It's hardly that." She tutted. "Just remember not to react. It's Iolo that drinks here, and he'll take any excuse to attack."

If this was Iolo's stamping ground, she didn't need to know about his encounters with Dylan.

"I don't want this descending into a punch up. But don't worry." This time when she looked at him, that wicked sparkle shone in her eyes. "I'll protect you from the Big Bad."

Weirdly, he believed her.

Despite the angelic figure barely legible on the battered pub sign, there was little heavenly about The Earth Harp. The place was a nightmare, well known for violent disturbances. A place no copper with sense went. The sawdust on the floor wasn't exactly a recommendation. The darker patches could be spilt beer, urine, or blood – only CSI could tell. Probably without certainty, Madoc grouched internally. The wooden bar was ringed and scarred. Given the way Ruth reacted when she touched it, he guessed it was sticky, too. She ordered two cokes. Dread assailed Madoc.

The urge to protect Ruth was as much an external force as an internal instinct. But he had to remember she was a capable woman. He would only step in if it became necessary. He hoped it wouldn't.

"What're you doing in my pub?"

The dark demand came from a bald bloke sitting beside the open fire. That hearth and mantel looked designed for the Devil himself to arise from.

Madoc didn't recognise the man, but the sudden quiet indicated his authority. Iolo Flack. He bore a distinct resemblance to his older brother, Dylan, in that he looked like a muscle-bound he-man woman-hater. Iolo's ink didn't exactly engender trust, especially the prison tats. Madoc's guard came up.

His usual sense of the people around him reinforced how much trouble they would be in if the patrons in here turned against them. But there was more than that. Something else was pressing into his head, had been since he stepped into the station first thing. Something new.

Ruth's capable. A voice said.

Madoc's instincts screamed.

Oh, you're more of a girl than she is.

This voice was new. Unwelcome.

But she's more vulnerable than she'll admit.

The temptation to turn towards the voice almost overwhelmed him. Only instinct told him exactly where the voice was: in his head. He stood beside Ruth and desperately tried not to react visibly.

His heart hammered like a scared prisoner wanting out of the torture chamber of his rib cage. *Concentrate on the real.* He noted the unevenness of the sawdust under his shoes. The dingy lighting. The pockmarked bar. Nothing appealing to the touch. Except Ruth. Ruth appealed to his touch.

Protect her, don't perv on her.

Usually when he got messages, they were indistinct. Impressions not clarity. Outlines not details. He'd never had a voice speak to him. In his head. Clearly. With full sentences.

What did it mean? Why was this happening?

Adrenaline dried the back of his throat. It was an unwelcome, ill-timed development. Couldn't it have waited until he was alone?

No, you need to know now.

He swallowed. Ruth's eyes flicked to his and he saw something in those banded depths. Worry? Concern? Given her powers of observation, she might realise something was wrong. He could be in serious trouble. His future depended on his proving himself in this job.

Then don't make another mistake, however attracted you are.

That the voice was right made it all the more annoying.

Ruth glanced over to the man. "Well, hello to you, too, Iolo."

Then she turned casually to the drinks being placed before her. "Didn't know you'd become a landlord." She pushed one glass towards Madoc.

As dry as his throat was, Madoc couldn't drink without choking on his inner turmoil, which wouldn't look good.

Save her, the voice demanded.

Madoc tried desperately not to openly react to this unsettling new development. *She doesn't need saving,* he argued silently.

"It's my pub."

Ruth nodded thanks to the bartender as she accepted her change. "Says Green Hills Brewery out front." Ruth faced Madoc.

Over her head, Madoc saw the man rise and stomp towards them. Ruth's warning echoed in his head and in her eyes.

Iolo towered over Ruth – well, tried to – and he snarled at her. "I said, this is *my* pub."

She looked up calmly. "Yes, Iolo. I heard. But I would point out that the word 'pub' derives from the word 'public' because they let the public in. The public includes the police."

"I'm not having you harassing me while I'm having a drink."

"I've no intention of harassing you."

Ruth's comfort level amazed Madoc. He didn't dare even lift his glass for fear his shaking would give him away. Ruth, conversely, was relaxed, her grip on the glass secure but light, steady. She could be having tea with the vicar for all the stress on display.

"Technically, *you're* harassing *me*," Ruth pointed out lightly. "You came over to me. You're trying to intimidate me."

"I—"

"I'd advise caution," she cut across him. "Be careful what you say because, don't forget, I *am* a police officer and *do* have the power to arrest you for making threats of violence."

"I didn't!"

But he did step back.

"I know." She smiled broadly and sipped her coke.

"Why you 'ere, then?"

"I needed a drink. The café down the road has a zero-hygiene rating. This place got a four."

Her being oh-so-reasonable was annoying Iolo a treat. His breath huffed from his nostrils — hairy nostrils.

Like a bull preparing to charge.

That's insulting to bulls. Madoc found the odd interaction allowed him to release some tension.

"Why you even in here?" Iolo demanded.

"Police business," she said calmly.

"That's nothing to do with me."

"Never said it was."

"I din't nick nothing from that building site."

Ruth sipped again, grinned with her lips pressed together. Swallowed. "What building site?"

He scowled at her. "The one where they took all that copper pipe and plumbing stuff. Where they nicked the forklift and murdered that bloke."

No official statement had yet been made, and the news reports only carried the basic details. Building site, robbery, ongoing incident — no official mention of a death, let alone a murder. Ruth looked at Iolo. "I see."

"It's nothing to do with me."

"I see."

Iolo was going to bust a blood vessel if he got much more wound up. He obviously wanted an excuse to punch her. "I been 'ere all morning."

Ruth turned to the bartender, who moved out of punching distance. "All morning?"

The man nodded.

Ruth faced Iolo again. Then she got out her phone. "Hmm, no data signal." She put the phone back in her pocket and sipped again.

His lips compressed under piggy eyes. "I said, I din't do it."

"I heard." She paused. "Though you seem to know a lot about it for a bloke in a near-empty pub with no data signal." Ruth shrugged. "Still, you've been here all morning."

Iolo's fists balled, his face grew red. Oddly, the colour improved the tattoos on his thick neck. "Yeah. Exactly."

Even if he was telling the truth, it made no difference. The break-in happened at four a.m., and the pub opened at ten.

"How's your dad doing?" Ruth surprised everyone by asking. "Haven't seen him in ages."

Despite what people 'knew', it was impossible to prove Griffith Flack ran crime locally. Like his sons, Griffith was a muscular man. Unlike some of his sons, Griffith also worked the grey muscle between his ears. That said, you didn't piss off Griffith unless you enjoyed pain and suffering. This seemed likely to piss off Griffith.

"He's fine," Iolo stated.

"Good." Ruth drained the glass, put it on the bar. "Do give him my regards when you relay this conversation to him. In all its glorious detail."

As she stood away from the bar, she grinned like a barracuda. Uncertain what she was playing at, Madoc straightened with her.

"Especially the bit about what happened on the site," she added before she walked out casually.

Madoc moved to follow. Iolo stepped in his way. Madoc looked down several inches to the guy's hate-filled, piggy eyes. Iolo was twice his weight and punching him would be like punching a wall — being punched *by* him would be like a wrecking ball hit. So much for Ruth needing defending. Madoc remembered what he'd heard about Iolo's prison experience.

Madoc kept his voice low and leant in slightly, offered a cheeky grin. "What's wrong, big boy, you want to dance?"

Iolo paled and stepped aside.

Chapter 5

The woman who opened the Bevans' door was much older than Ruth had expected.

"Mrs Bevan?" she asked.

"Mrs Martin," the woman said. "And you are?"

Ruth showed her warrant card and made the introductions. Earlier, Ruth had contacted the officer sent to advise Mrs Bevan of her husband's death. He reported the usual denials, disbelief, the tears, and a neighbour coming round. This must be the neighbour. The older woman looked them over and curled her lip.

"Suppose you best come in then."

Not the worst invitation ever. Ruth stepped over the threshold into the front room, which had been knocked through to the back to enlarge the space. A corner sofa unit filled the front area, with a small two-seater facing it, narrow enough to give passage to the dining area behind and the kitchen at the rear of the house. Mrs Bevan stood from the sofa unit. At only five-foot-five, Ruth couldn't consider herself tall, but she felt giant compared to Pippa Bevan. She doubted the other woman would even reach five-foot. But for all that, Pippa was perfectly proportioned, a bit like Kylie Minogue.

They exchanged greetings, including permission to use first names. Condolences were given, tea offered and refused, and they were invited to sit. Ruth took one end of the smaller sofa, finding herself crowded when Madoc sat beside her. Like most men, he sat with a wide-legged stance. Unfortunately, so did she. That meant that on this small unit, their knees and calves touched. It was an intimacy too warm and too deep. To pull away would only create more tension. Besides, better this than Palmer standing. He would have loomed over them uncomfortably. Apparently unaffected, he readied his phone for recording, the South Wales Police badge prominent, and let her take the lead.

"I'm sorry we have to bother you at this difficult time." Ruth knew how difficult everything was for a new widow, and the evidence of Pippa's tears were in the bin of damp tissues and red-circled eyes. "I've read through the outline statement you gave my colleague earlier, and I'd like to double-check some points with you. Are you okay with that?"

Pippa nodded, gripped her hands in her lap. Mrs Martin put her hand over her friend's. Ruth felt the absence of such friendship in her life.

"You said the alarm went off shortly after four, around quarter-past, and Raymond left immediately?"

The older woman nodded. "That's right."

Ruth frowned; the problem obvious to her, given the time the alarm was cleared on site. "Immediately?"

Again, Pippa nodded.

Yes, to make the timings work, Raymond would have to have left immediately. Which logically didn't make sense. Ruth's frown deepened as she struggled to find a way to ask this delicately. "Why was he fully dressed that early in the morning?"

Pippa paused and swallowed; Ruth saw the lie coming.

"Ray's an insomniac. He gets up at all hours, dresses if he wants. I sleep like a log, so I have no idea what time he got up. But the call woke me, and Raymond left straight away."

Simple and easy. A practiced lie? What was being hidden?

"Did he contact you at all after he left?" Ruth asked.

Pippa shook her head.

"And you didn't think anything was wrong when he didn't come back?"

A head shake. "He'd been called to site, it's the other end of the village, and whatever he had to do would take time.

Besides, your men were knocking on my door barely an hour later. It wasn't like I had time to realise there was a problem."

Ruth nodded. "Excuse the question, but what were you doing between 04:15 and 05:20?"

"Oh, just pottering about the house. I usually get up at six, but the call left me wide awake, so I got up and did a few chores."

Ruth glanced around the room. Nothing needed doing, it was like a show house. She wished her own housekeeping were as meticulous. Then again, she didn't get up at four a.m. to clean.

"What's going to happen now?" Pippa asked.

Ruth concentrated on the widow. "We're going to follow every avenue of enquiry until we find out what happened to Raymond."

"You think the thieves killed my husband?"

It was a distinct possibility, but it didn't feel right. Like Mrs Bevan's answers. Spousal murder was common. Still, she was in no position to judge anyone else's marriage.

"We'll look into everything and let you know what we can." Which was likely to be a lot less than Mrs Bevan would like.

Ruth handed Madoc the keys as they approached the car. The brief contact reassured him as it demonstrated good faith. As soon as she clicked the seatbelt in, Ruth took out her phone and started filling in the notebook app they were all supposed to use.

"Back to the station?"

She shook her head without looking up.

"Please, not another nose tweak."

Stopping short, she tipped her chin up, better to face him. "Iolo didn't do this. It's not his thing. I tweaked that nose because it would quickly become obvious if he knew anything about it or not. And he did. And it still will."

He wasn't sure what to make of that.

"That I spoke to Iolo will get back to Griffith, and he'll react to that. It's *his* reaction that interests me."

By the Goddess, this was worrying. "His reactions have been known to put people in hospital."

The nod, like her tone, was reasonable. "Allegedly, but he's never been like that with me."

"Because you're a woman?" His mouth was running faster than his brain. The sexism screamed in his own ears. Nothing suggested he was inspiring her with confidence. Not the first day impression he'd hoped for.

"Nooo." She dragged the word out like she was talking to a five-year-old, and that felt like a fair assessment. "Griffith has never come after me because I don't go after him or his boys without good reason. I mean, we all know he's as bent as a nine-pound note. But so far, I've never actually been able to prove that. I've got used to him and his lawyer, so we get along with mutual mistrust. The lawyer, by the way, is Richard Steele, you're bound to encounter him at some point. But Griffith wouldn't come direct for me, and if he came for my family, I've made it absolutely clear that I'd visit the same ten times worse on his."

"How the hell did you manage that?"

The way her features tightened suggested nothing good. "I don't talk about it."

That was all very well, but if she had the Flacks worried, then the threat had to have been mighty awe-inspiring. Ruth was obviously not a woman to be underestimated.

She's still a woman.

That voice shivered the creeps through him. *Shut up.*

"Are you cold?" Ruth asked.

Damn, she was observant. "Not warmed up since the site, and the shower was cold. Where next?" he asked, since he was driving.

"The building site again, sorry. There's something I want to check with Maggie Drake."

He started the car and left her to concentrate on typing her notes as he pulled from the kerb and headed up the hill. Cars parked both sides of the road forced him to drive about two hundred metres before they thinned out enough for him to turn and head back towards the site. It didn't take long, Heolgerrig not being a big village. At least now he had trainers on; if these got muddy, it didn't matter. Also, the day had warmed up, so the ground was less soggy than it had been that morning. Though activity may have churned things up a bit. Time to put up and shut up.

People still crowded the site entrance. Fewer workers, more CSIs, not to mention a Transit van marked *Archaeologica Cymru*. Madoc guessed they were the guys in blue overalls. PC Harris greeted them.

"Still here, John?" Ruth voiced Madoc's thoughts.

"Back here," Harris clarified. "Ash asked me to cover a few extra hours, and a bit of overtime never hurts."

"Depends how much you've already done this month."

"Depends how close my silver wedding anniversary gets," Harris countered with a smile.

Ruth laughed. "You still keeping that blow-out from Jill?"

Harris' grin grew. "Yep."

Once they had moved past, Madoc leant towards Ruth. "Who's Ash?"

"Ashley Fallon, Head of Uniform for the Division."

"Inspector!" a female voice called.

Madoc only just avoided bumping into Ruth.

She turned and tipped her head to look at him. "Either don't walk so close or walk more to my side. Either side. Don't mind which." Then she switched her attention to the fast-approaching figure.

The caller was a slight woman, even in the full white overall and white wellies.

"Sorry, Inspector," she said. "Daf thought you'd want to know this." The young woman pushed back her hood, revealing spiky green hair.

"What happened to calling me Ruth?"

An impish grin showed teeth augmented with veneers to extend the incisors like a cat, or a vampire. "I like to remind the boys who's really in charge."

"Should I be insulted?" Madoc asked.

The woman looked him up and down. Not for the first time, Madoc understood objectification from the really unpleasant side. "Meeoow."

Pure primal desire. He wasn't attracted, she was too young and too alternative for his tastes. A Page. A messenger, disseminator of information, representative of intellect. Childlike in some respects. The Page of Swords. Not to mention, she was way too forward.

"Oh, come on, Ali Cat," Ruth cautioned. "Don't be like that. Ali, meet Palmer. Palmer, this is Alison Caterham, one of Daf's team. So, Ali, what did Daf want me to know?"

There was no sense of chastisement from the younger woman. She looked at Ruth evenly. "It's the archaeologists. They say it's not a historic burial."

"So, it really was a shallow grave?" Madoc asked.

"Looks like," Ali confirmed.

"Great," Ruth said. "Is it going to the Heath like the other body?"

Ali nodded. "Uh-huh. I'll confirm when we get it down there." She was back to looking at Madoc, preparing to say something.

"Anytime, Pussycat," he forestalled, seeing Ali blush as she turned away. Then he saw Ruth's expression, her raised eyebrows. That left him at a loss.

"The ground's drier," Ruth said as she turned towards the site office.

Uncertain how to take that, he quietly followed. She knew his reputation, he realised. He resented being talked about for his looks rather than his skills, but other people's gossip was beyond his control. Sometimes it was even fun to play up to.

You could try some honesty.

The voice in his head sent chills down his spine direct to his soul. It damn near tripped him.

Nope. He pushed the idea of honesty away. With Ruth, telling her the truth could go either way. He'd need to know her way better to be that honest.

In the office, Maggie Drake sat behind the desk facing them, on the phone. Her look stated they were the last people she wanted to see. Not an uncommon reaction. Ruth waited and Madoc said nothing. The phone slapped down harder than necessary.

"It's not easy to just stop a concrete pour, you know," Maggie snapped.

She got no response.

"What do you want?" Maggie said at least.

"Are you on the call list for the site alarm?" Ruth asked.

"No."

"Then how did you know there was a problem this morning?"

"I didn't," Maggie said. "Something woke my dog, then Kohl woke me. So, I got up and walked Kohl, came past, saw the flattened barrier, and came on site to have a look."

"You brought a dog on site with you?"

"No, I left him at the fence line. There's all sorts gets into the mud on sites. I wouldn't risk his paws."

"Where were you heading?"

"Usual place."

"Which is?" Ruth said impatiently.

Maggie tutted. "The waste ground off Upper Colliers Row."

That made sense, the waste ground would be a great space to let a dog run. Initial reports gave Drake's home address on the main road so heading from there to Upper Colliers Row would bring her right past the site.

"What time did you get here?"

The affront screamed in Maggie's straight spine and compressed lips. "A few minutes to five, possibly. I didn't check my watch. Not long before Andy arrived, though. A few minutes before I called you."

"What did you do between entering the site and making that call?"

Maggie's scowl demonstrated her underlying resentment at being questioned. "I had a look round for damage, saw Raymond. I think … that is, I may have stood staring in disbelief for a while, can't really remember. Shock, you know? Then I heard Andy and came to meet her. After that, I came in here and called the police."

"Called from that phone?" Ruth indicated the phone on the desk.

Maggie nodded.

"You unlocked the door to come in?"

"Yes."

"You brought the site keys out with you on an early morning dog walk?"

Maggie's eyes widened. The feeling of wrongness hit Madoc again.

"No." Maggie glowered at Ruth. "I used Andy's keys."

Ruth nodded. "When did you take the dog home?"

Maggie blinked at her. "Pardon?"

"You said you brought the dog down, but there's no mention of a dog in any of the reports I've seen. When did you take the dog home?"

"Oh, I …" Maggie struggled for words. "I nipped back after making the call, before the first police officer arrived."

That didn't feel right to Madoc. Something jarred in the timeline. Every word screeched on his nerves.

"Okay," Ruth said. "Thanks."

Ruth nodded to Maggie, turned to face Madoc, offered him a tight smile, and walked out of the cabin. She went to the car, stopping by the rear passenger door. He wasn't sure what the vibe was; Ruth gave no clue as to what she was thinking. Had she believed everything Maggie said? He unlocked the car. Ruth didn't move. Lacking certainty or direction, he reached down and opened the front passenger door. Her eyes flicked to it, to him. The deepening frown was a mark of confusion.

"Why'd you do that?"

A fool in hot water, he had no appropriate answer. "I thought that's what you were waiting for."

Her frown lessened but didn't disappear. "Not sure which of us that would make the most sexist, but no," Ruth said. "I was lost in thought and didn't hear you unlock the car. Just for reference, the only time I'd expect you to open a door for me, would be when my hands are full. And I'd do the same for you. It's a practicality thing. So, thanks for the thought, but the act was unnecessary."

He stood behind the door, facing her, arms folded along the top. "Okay. What thought stopped you?"

She kept her voice low to answer. "Does the timing work?"

The same doubt he'd had. "Possibly," he said. "I'd want to check all the statements, and how far up the road Mrs Drake lives from here, but it could work. Just."

Her frown disappeared. She almost smiled. Serious eyes softened a little. "Guess what you're doing when we get back, then."

She slid into the front seat. He closed the door.

Chapter 6

By the time they got back, someone had set up the incident board. It was almost as if each letter had been stamped, next to no variation in the letters, except in the top right-hand corner, where the last two letters were angled oddly. Someone short and not quite able to reach? The work was admirable and offered helpful clarity.

Though there were plenty of bodies around, not many MCIT team members. That meant they'd have peace to make notes and check the timeline.

At her desk, Ruth sat quietly, getting straight into the paperwork. She appeared to be all dedication to the job, but just as his reputation had preceded him, hers had reached him. The reality wasn't what he'd expected, but then, neither was a murder case on day one. Her refusal to talk about family struck him as odd, but he respected it. He understood they didn't know each other well enough to over-share. Besides, he wasn't telling her everything, either.

Time to get his head down. Work to do.

"What are you doing?"

Madoc looked up to see Ruth standing beside him. He realised she had left her desk a few minutes ago, but he hadn't consciously noted it. She frowned at his screen and placed a mug of coffee on his desk, standing to cradle her own in both hands.

"Are you doing a background check on Maggie Drake?"

There was little point in lying. "Yes, sir."

"Why?"

He had reasons but couldn't properly explain. "Gut instinct."

The frown didn't lesson when her focus switched to him. "Find anything?"

That was the annoying part. "Not so much as a parking ticket."

Ruth nodded. "Yeah, well, hate to break it to you, Palmer, but the vast majority of the population get through life without ever getting a police record."

"So, you're crystal clear then?"

"Nope." She admittedly easily. "No parking tickets, but two speeding fines, both along the same damn stretch of the M4 and both issued by Gwent Police." She sighed. "Look, gut instinct is valuable, but, at the moment, we've got no reason to suspect Margaret Drake of doing anything other than reporting the incident. Background checks on her will be on the actions list and will be done by a constable. You're here for the last part of your training to become a fully-fledged sergeant, so you need to think about moving on from things like background checks. Okay?"

He nodded. "Yes, sir."

"Good, because I don't want this turned into some kind of witch hunt."

The flinch was instinctual. That was the last thing he needed, the flinch or the witch hunt.

"Madoc?" she said softly. "There a problem?"

Damn her observation skills. "No, sir."

She returned to her desk, and he got back to the reports.

Unknown time passed before he heard the steady beat of feet approaching over the tapping of their keyboards. It seemed to take a while before Ruth noticed the shadow that had fallen over her desk. Casting such a shadow was no mean feat when the light was angling across her desk towards Geraint. A big man, powerful in body and rank. Ruth carried on typing while Madoc looked up, but all Geraint's focus was on her.

"All right, Geraint?" she asked after more heartbeats than Madoc felt comfortable with.

"A word. My office. Now."

She hit save. Madoc watched, curious if helpless. Grim-faced, Geraint waited at his office door.

"You, too, Palmer."

Oh dear. The precariousness of his position threatened to kick his knees from under him. A deep breath fortified him as he stood and joined Ruth before the big man's desk. Though he sat, Geraint didn't invite them to do so. Palmer's gut sank.

"Had a good day?" Geraint asked.

"Had better, had worse," Ruth said carefully.

"Enjoy the pub?"

Ruth's innocent look was quite impressive. "I'm unsure what you're getting at, boss."

Grey caterpillars crawled upwards. "Seriously?"

"Seriously," she said. "I needed a drink. I ordered two cokes; I drank mine but he—" She tipped her head towards Madoc. "—didn't touch his."

"So, no interrogating Iolo Flack?" Geraint's arms crossed.

This couldn't be a good sign.

"Nope. In fact, the only question I asked him was how his father is."

"Really?" Geraint asked.

Ruth nodded, but Madoc sensed she was less confident than she appeared. Geraint didn't look impressed.

"Now ask me if I had a good day," Geraint suggested.

"I'd rather not," Ruth said. "The way you're glowering, I'm pretty sure you haven't."

That Ruth faced their boss in a relaxed, open manner said a lot about her nerve. This was a relationship that worked, and not just a working relationship. So, what more was it?

"Not for the last hour, no," Geraint stated in a flat slate voice that would crush anyone fool enough to interrupt. "I just got a lecture from the Super. Richard Steele called demanding to know why Iolo Flack was being interrogated for a crime he did not commit, is not connected to, and hasn't been arrested for."

"He wasn't interrogated," Madoc risked, earning a pointed glare from Geraint. Madoc shut up. Geraint sharpened his focus on Ruth.

"That's typical Tricky-Dicky trying it on," she said.

"We have no record of speaking to Iolo Flack being an action in your investigation."

"Investiga*tions*."

Ruth's correction met stony silence. If she would stand up to the local mafia and the DCI alike, was she courageous or suicidal? Madoc chose courageous.

"I was thirsty, so I went for a drink. Iolo was there. He approached me in what I have to say was a rather aggressive manner. Something I can prove if you'd care to listen?"

The caterpillars slid down to crowd above Geraint's nose. "Prove?"

She nodded. "I had my phone on voice record. I recorded the whole thing."

"Play it."

Ruth had to return to her desk to get her phone. For a few seconds that felt like an eternity, Madoc stood awkwardly before Geraint. Then she played the recorded encounter. The quality wasn't brilliant, but if there was any harassment, it was of Ruth, not by her. When it finished, Geraint was rubbing his temples like his head ached.

"Put a copy of that on record," Geraint ordered. "It's probably inadmissible, but Professional Standards may want to listen to it."

Madoc's heart sank.

"The complaint has gone to them, has it?" Ruth asked.

"What choice did the Super have?"

Ruth sighed. "None, I suppose." She shrugged. "Oh, well. Just have to ride this one out."

Her phone made a noise. She glared at it, frowned.

"What is it?" Geraint asked.

"It's a text from Griffith Flack." She stared at her phone like it was a two-headed snake.

"What does it say?" Geraint prompted after a moment.

"I don't know without opening it."

Geraint's jaw clenched. "Then open it."

Ruth demurred. "If I open it, I'll have to do something about it. I won't be able to deny I know about it because the fact that I opened it will be recorded."

A typical modern irritant.

"Open it." Geraint ordered.

A screen press and the text opened. Madoc leant closer to see it.

"'Look to Tredegar. The Prices'," Ruth read.

"Tredegar?" Geraint repeated. "Conveniently in Gwent Police's area and not ours."

"Yeah. The question is, what do I do with that? Now I've had the tip off, I have to report it. Then I'd have to investigate it. That's time and cost I don't want. A distraction I don't need."

"You're sure it's just a distraction?" Geraint asked.

Ruth stopped to consider it. "Not really. I tweaked Iolo's nose because I expected to get a response from Griffith. But I'm not sure what this means. Griffith does tend to have his finger on the criminal pulse, so he might have something, or he might just want me to look somewhere other than at his family. Thing is, Iolo knew a lot about what happened on site before we released the facts. If he's involved, I suspect his involvement is only after the fact. There again, if he's not involved, even tangentially, why would they get Steele to get on to the Super? It feels like a local issue."

Geraint said nothing.

Nodding, Ruth let her body sag. "I'll note the tip off with Mike, and we'll take the advice seriously."

Geraint considered her. "How come Griffith Flack has your phone number?"

"Oh, he's had it ages. I told him to contact me any time, should he think of something useful. I believe that's even on the record, part of …" Her eyes narrowed as she thought back. "The Dalrooney theft. Three years ago."

"Good. Make sure you keep that noted."

Ruth nodded.

"Give Mike the tip and tell him to get someone to liaise. Probably come to nothing, but we have to show willing. Don't want to piss off the neighbours."

"Okay. We done?"

Now, Geraint turned to Madoc. No, apparently not.

"How could you be so stupid as to let her go into The Earth Harp to face Iolo Flack? Surely even you've heard of the family?"

"Of course, sir," he said evenly. "But I've only ever met Dylan, and that was about my sister."

"So, you defend a sister, but not a colleague?"

"Hang on," Ruth interrupted. "Where's this coming from? Palmer did everything bang on right. Iolo was spoiling for a fight. If Palmer had reacted, he'd've had one."

Geraint looked between the two of them. Madoc saw in Ruth's expression the same thing he saw in his mother when she was defending her kids. The image was a little uncomfortable – she was only two years older than him.

"You sure about that?"

"Geraint, it was my call. I'm the senior officer, remember. And moreover, are you aware just how sexist you're being right now?"

The desk phone rang. Geraint looked away. The old man's nod dismissed them, and they left the office.

"What happens now?" Madoc asked as they returned to their desks.

"We get back to work. The Super probably goes on thinking I'm an idiot. And I won't be getting another promotion any time soon." She shrugged. "You should be fine, though."

"Why wouldn't he be fine?" Detective Inspector Pete Saunders asked as he strolled in.

Ruth looked up and greeted the dapper figure. "Because I just got a complaint lodged against me. Palmer was with me when the incident in question happened."

"No one's going to uphold a complaint against you," Pete almost laughed. "Geraint wouldn't let them."

"But the Super would, and he's the one who took the complaint."

"That's not good. Do I want to know?" Pete asked.

Ruth shrugged. "I don't want to tell you."

"Spoilsport," Pete said as DS Jackson came in.

Ruth made the introductions, but then each went to their own work.

Madoc leant forward to speak more quietly to Ruth. "Why don't you sound more upset about promotion being cut off? Aren't you the youngest woman to make inspector in the force? Don't you want that trajectory to continue?"

"Yes and no. I was one of the youngest, and that's partly why I'm not bothered about putting off being a DCI. I enjoy what I do. All the management stuff that comes with the DCI role doesn't attract me. Not yet, anyway. Trajectory is less important than job satisfaction. Besides, right now, I've a tip off to report. You want to come and meet Mike?"

Ruth felt sick as she led the way to the writing room, which was really just another part of the open plan office. There was nothing to Iolo's claims, but getting your name anywhere near Professional Standards was never a good thing. Especially not if the message came straight via your own superintendent. Would Vaughan shop her? What was she thinking? He didn't have a choice. He had to. No point worrying about what she couldn't change.

"Mike." She called the attention of the man in uniform trousers and polo shirt. "Sergeant Mike Bates, meet DS Madoc Palmer."

The two men shook hands. Mike Bates was a very fit forty-something, and Madoc's other senses told him Bates understand the myriad links of who had to do what, like a spider amid an informational web.

"Palmer, Mike here is the best damn office manager I've ever worked with."

"Ahh, isn't that nice?" Mike said. "But she's only saying that because I'm the office manager she works with most."

"Well, there is that," she admitted with a broad grin. "Doesn't change the fact that he's good, too. Anyway, Mike, I've had a text from Griffith Flack."

Mike reacted with some surprise, wide eyes and expectant. She showed him the text and then told him about the recording of her encounter with Iolo.

"Yeah, I got your email with the sound file a few minutes ago. I'll log the Price tip off, but frankly, given the source, it's hardly trustworthy."

Ruth grinned. "Debatable. Look, I promised Geraint we'd take it seriously. Get someone to call the Gwent boys, they can run the wild goose chase and we can claim due diligence."

"Like that thinking," Mike allowed.

Chapter 7

As Ruth parked at home, the movement sensitive light over the garage came on. The only light on in the house was in Zach's bedroom. She couldn't face another argument. The day and her worries were too heavy. She sat in the driver's seat without the will or energy to move. She needed to talk to someone. She needed support.

No. She was a mother, she had responsibilities, others to support. She owed it to her son to do better than to give in to maudlin. Painting on a smile was too much, but she had to take care of body and soul – well, body at least – for both their sakes. She left the car, headed inside. The porch light switched on automatically so she could find her keys.

Inside, she locked the door, removed her shoes, and padded through to the kitchen. The slow cooker waited on the counter. She noticed it was turned to warm, something Zach must have done. But when she looked inside, she realised he hadn't taken anything. The chicken casserole didn't appeal to her, either. She put the lid back on and turned the cooker off. After collecting two plastic containers, she ladled the casserole into them and secured the lids. They'd have to stay out to cool down before they went into the fridge. She'd have to remember to come back down later and put them away. At least that sorted tomorrow's lunch.

Padding upstairs, she heard gunfire and bombs. Zach playing video games again. She should be furious. Yesterday she would have been furious. She moved to his door and knocked.

"What?"

That belligerent tone usually made her blood boil. Tonight, she was just too damned tired. "I've put the casserole into boxes. You'll have to warm it up in the microwave if you want some later."

"'Kay."

Was the 'o' too much to expect? This conversation was too much as she faced the still-closed door. But she had to do it.

"Have you done your homework?"

"Nothing's due tomorrow."

This was the point when she should launch into the speech about not leaving things to the last minute. But she didn't have the energy. Zach had heard it all too many times anyway. "Don't play your game too late."

No response. None expected, really.

"I'm going to bed."

Again, no response, but again, none expected. As she slouched across the open balcony, the dust between the banister spindles caught her eye. Pippa Bevan would never let her house get into such a mess.

Pippa Bevan didn't have a full-time, demanding job or a kid to worry about. She didn't pine her absent sex life. Ruth stepped into the master bedroom, closed the door and looked longingly at the king-sized bed.

Stripping and letting the clothes fall where they would, she padded over and crawled under the thick duvet.

Reaching to the side, she used the remote control to close the curtains. The bed was way too big to sleep in alone. The thousand thread count cotton sheets were cool. It would warm up, though it'd warm up quicker with two. The image of Madoc in here with her filled her head. The bed wouldn't be too big then. True, but the greater truth was, what she needed most was not a man to sleep with, but her best friend to talk to. If only that were possible.

The house was dark when Madoc stepped inside and threw the dead bolt. His only security. Of course, it was dark, there wasn't any electricity. Automatically, he reached for the torch hung by a loop beside the door. That beam allowed him to step safely over the various building supplies scattered around.

Tiredness ran through him. He'd nursed a shandy for an hour before he relaxed enough to enjoy the unexpected evening out with his new colleagues. It was so different from the last few years. He felt accepted, included. It was nice. He liked these people and hoped they liked him. Even Ruth, who had stayed for one soft drink only. Would they accept him so readily if they knew his truth?

There was no point in putting the lamp on. He just moved over to the back corner, the least draughty area. He undressed, hanging his clothes over the open rail to avoid the sawdust. He should have cracked on with the conversion tonight, but he was glad he'd forgone that. Team building was important. People were important. Connections needed to be established and maintained. Automatically, he reached back down to where he'd thrown his wallet and opened the back section to look at the picture there. His son. Osian. He couldn't wait to see the boy again. For his sake, Madoc hated that his marriage to Julia hadn't worked out, but staying in a marriage they both regretted wouldn't have done any of them any favours.

No, the divorce was the right option, even if he hadn't mentioned it in work. They didn't need to know his private business. Suddenly, he understood Ruth better.

Finally, he slipped thankfully into the sleeping bag on the single mattress and turned off the torch, leaving it in easy reach for the morning. As he lay back in the darkness, he couldn't help wondering if Ruth was okay. She wasn't the frosty-arsed bitch Becca had made out, but she could be prickly. There again, there were certain soft curves about her that—

You really shouldn't be thinking about that. Those.

The tone of parental censure didn't help. He knew he shouldn't think about Ruth and her curves, only he couldn't stop thinking about them. Lying alone on a single mattress, he wondered what it would be like to lay with her in a double bed.

She has a king-sized bed.

He told himself he wasn't fantasising about that when the phone rang. Caller ID said 'Julia'. He sat up to answer – she'd only call in an emergency.

It was definitely an emergency. "I'll be right over."

Chapter 8

"Oh, you're not taking yesterday's tardy comment too seriously, are you?" The worry dropped on Ruth when she stepped into the office. She was early and Palmer was already working.

She wondered how the team drinks went after she left last night. He did look a bit tired.

Today, he'd dressed in thick, hard-wearing, dark blue trousers; all-black, lightweight walking shoes; his shirt was ironed and clean, though there were folds from it being under the waterproof jacket now hung over his chair. He wore a tie.

"No, sir, and morning."

He really shouldn't have such a lovely smile, or at least, she shouldn't think it lovely. *You're tired, get a grip*. The effect he had on other women was one thing, but she couldn't let it affect her. She hung her leather coat over her chair and sat opposite the younger officer.

"My father-in-law had a heart attack last night," Madoc explained. "Thankfully, quite mild, but worrying, you know? So, I had to drop Osian off and figured I might as well come straight in," Madoc said.

Fair enough, but a little confusing. "Osian?"

"My son."

She hadn't known he had a son. But it hadn't been an affectation yesterday; she really didn't like talking about family in work. Now, she had to not ask about his family, despite having a million questions. Though her biggest question related to the nagging doubt that her own son would get to school on time. He was at an awkward age, and it was growing increasingly difficult to know what he'd do next. Thankfully he generally enjoyed school.

"Why can I smell burnt sage?" she asked.

For a second, he blanched. "No idea."

The reaction said differently. Maybe he wasn't a good cook, particularly after a night out. She shrugged it off. "Okay, tell me that tie's a clip-on."

He frowned at her. "No."

She frowned back. "Thought not." She turned back to her work.

"Does it matter? There's no requirement for it to be a clip-on."

"I know." She sighed as she looked him over. "You look fine, but so neat. I feel like a scruff." She looked down at her own boat neck blouse, casual trousers, and, though he couldn't see them, she wore DMs again.

"And what was it you said about my jeans yesterday?"

She clamped her lips shut. She deserved that.

"Besides, you look fine." He pulled off the tie. "Better?"

She nodded. "And if it helps, you still look smart."

"Thanks. I've been going through the timings and Maggie Drake's claims about the dog."

He hadn't had time to finish that when they'd got back yesterday. Another case had claimed their attention instead.

"Good. And?"

He passed over an A4 lined pad with all the timings on it. His handwriting was italic but neat and tidy, readable. The long, loopy nature of the 'g's and 'y's suggested sensuality. Graphology training seemed to have stuck with her despite her general distrust of the premise. She ran her eyes over the times and tried not to think about the writing, the writer, or the sensuality.

"And narrow as the timeframe is, it works." His dull tone echoed her own reaction. "There's a little slack, but Maggie said she wasn't entirely sure of the timings. She lives closer to the site than the Bevans and she has a dog, which she could have nipped home between calling us and the first responder arriving."

"Fair enough." Ruth passed the pad back. "Thanks for checking." As others started drifting in, she turned her attention to reviewing the Bevan case.

The morning briefing started on the dot. As usual. Geraint stood at the front and gave the usual rundown. He ended on a positive note.

"Jackson's court appearance yesterday helped secure a guilty verdict, but that's just one criminal off the streets. Still plenty more. Pete, update us on your current workload."

DI Pete Saunders was the same age as Geraint but appeared older. In the tall five-foot range, he was naturally thin, and a jogger, which had made his face gaunt. His number-two grey buzz cut didn't diminish his increasing bald patch. He had three years left till retirement, and Jackson was running a book on whether he'd make it. Ruth had a pound on 'to the day'.

"We're awaiting DNA for the Dynevor case, lab indicated another four days. Anomalies have been picked up between the statements of the two boys involved in the drag racing crash up on the Gurnos Road, so that's our primary focus today."

Pete Saunders had more than two cases on his desk, but there was only so much anyone could plan to do in a single day.

"Ruth?"

"The Geddings forensics were due yesterday, but haven't arrived, so that's to be chased. Mike put the word out with local scrap merchants for the supplies gone missing from Heolgerrig yesterday, but I want to follow that up with some calls and/or visits. I want to do a house-to-house for the Bevan case, and I'm hoping for some prelims on the two bodies."

Geraint nodded. "Ash has the house-to-house in hand, and the incident room's already taking calls," Geraint told her.

"Gethin's still off on the sick, so you may have to wait on the pathology."

Ruth shook her head once. "Tom's back, he texted me last night to say he'd take a look today. He'll start about ten."

"Good," Geraint said. "Well—"

"Hang on, sir," Ruth added. "One slight fly in the ointment. That tip off about the Prices? Turns out the family were seen in Merthyr on Monday night. Mike was reviewing CCTV for another case, spotted them in the background – no connection with the case Mike was on. We're liaising with the Gwent boys. Mike's covering the actions for now, but I'm monitoring it."

"Fair play." Geraint nodded. "Okay, people, we've got a lot to do, and few bodies to get it done. Go to."

The team moved away to work. Madoc followed Ruth back to their desks.

"How come Jackson and I are called by our surnames?"

She glanced up at him. "You know why with you, to avoid the jokes. Jackson's first name is Geoffrey, though he prefers Jeff. Thing is, when he first started, we already had a Jefferson and a Geoffrey, who both preferred to be called Jeff. Jefferson had to put up with being Jeff2, but Jeff3 wouldn't really clarify, would it? So, we called him Jackson, and though Jeff and Jeff2 are now gone, we're just all used to calling him Jackson now." She shrugged. "You know Gethin Nobel is Head of Forensic Pathology down at the Heath, right?"

Madoc nodded; he recognised the name from cases he'd worked in Cardiff. Also, everyone in South Wales knew the University Hospital of Wales was the largest in country and known as the Heath after the part of Cardiff it was in. It was also a teaching hospital and the place where police postmortems were completed. "And that Tom Bomber is likely to take over that position when Gethin retires."

Another not-too-distant event.

"So, what's your preference on workload order, sir?"

Being called 'sir' felt odd, but she kind of liked it, since only Palmer called her that. It showed she was just another colleague to Palmer. Which was good. She supposed. "First thing, I think I should introduce you to DCI Fallon."

Ruth looked pale as Madoc approached with two coffees. He was pretty sure he hadn't caused this. He maintained that it wasn't his fault. After checking parameters of the house-to-house with Ashley Fallon, she had chased for the Geddings forensics, only to have them passed to her in paper copy by a civilian admin while she was on the phone. Madoc had offered a smile to the middle-aged woman; the coy blushing, the come-hither smile, was not what he'd expected. Ruth had tutted, and the woman had scuttled away. His intention was not to encourage such interest.

Thank God Ruth wasn't like that. She treated him as a professional responsible for himself and his actions. She treated him as an equal, though of course they weren't. More worryingly right now, the vibes rolling off her carried a darker tone that he didn't understand.

"You okay?" He placed one coffee before her.

She looked up; revulsion showed in her eyes. She blinked, the revulsion dissipated, and she thanked him. "It's one of those reports you really wish you didn't have to read."

The Geddings case involved the body of a young woman found in the house of an old man, Jason Geddings. When police were called, they went in to find Geddings dead on the downstairs sitting room floor and a young woman dead upstairs on a bed.

"A heart attack killed Geddings," she said, indicating the papers. "Seems to be natural causes, given that he was seventy-eight and diagnosed with coronary artery disease. The girl died about six-to-eight days later. She'd been beaten, raped, and strangled. Not necessarily in that order."

"And not by Geddings, with that timeline," Madoc said as he took his own seat.

Ruth shook her head. "Can you imagine it? She's dragged into a house, there's a week-old corpse there, which presumably her attacker knew about. She's forced upstairs where she's raped and choked. Poor kid must've been terrified."

Any one of those factors was appalling on its own; together it was the act of a very disturbed individual. Little wonder Ruth looked sickened.

"So, now it's not just a case of tracing the victim's identity, we've got to trace a new killer, too?"

To his surprise she shook her head. "Semen found inside the body identifies the attacker as Dwayne Evans, forty-four. He's a repeat offender, been on the sex offenders register since he was eighteen, and was on our watch lists long before that. He lives up in Mountain Hare, two doors up from Geddings. Which is probably how he found out the house was unlocked. The appeals and photo circulation on the girl continues, though." With another sigh, she stood. "I'm going to tell Geraint, then we'll get the warrant and go arrest a scuzzball. Hopefully this time, the system will keep him out of circulation until his balls shrivel and he can't do this to any other woman."

"Think that's likely?"

Nothing in her body language suggested she did. "Having killed this time – which, by the way, is a first – and given the circumstances of the murder, I'd suggest it's more likely. But I don't hand out sentences any more than I make laws, so what happens in court is beyond my control and I try not to worry about it. You okay to deal with the scrap merchant calls?"

"Er, what about the postmortem?"

Ruth checked her watch. "Bugger." She considered a moment. "I'll speak to Geraint."

Madoc handed the squirming Dwayne Evans over to the Custody Sergeant with great satisfaction. And relief.

What they'd found in Evans' home churned Madoc's guts. He'd known enough horny teenage boys to be semi-used to scrunched, crusty tissues left after wank sessions, but Evans' entire flat was full of such waste. Not to mention evidence that he didn't always use a tissue. The retch-inducing salt and sweat stench attacked his nose and throat. Ruth appeared unaffected. Either she had no sense of smell or an enviable professional demeanour.

That he had ended up literally rolling in the mess only sickened him more. Evans had made a lunge for Ruth, and he'd stepped in. Evans was a scrapper, surprisingly strong – his fingers around Madoc's neck had nearly robbed him of breath and life. Thank God he'd taken off the tie.

Then Ruth had stepped in, grabbed Evans in a half-Nelson choke hold long enough to get Evans off Madoc and cuffed. The little shite continued kicking and swearing, calling curses down on them, finding some inventive descriptions for Ruth's breasts. Madoc was impressed Ruth hadn't responded. Many women would have retaliated, but Ruth did her job, used minimum necessary force, and let the rest slide.

Evans was now in a holding cell. He and his foul mouth were someone else's problem. Madoc wasn't looking forward to the interview, but there was paperwork to do first.

"I feel the need to scrub myself with bleach and wire wool," Ruth grumped as they headed to the office. "Guessing you feel much the same."

He did. "Thanks for getting him off me back there."

"It's my job," she stated. "Thanks for defending me. I like to think I can take care of myself, but given Evans' state, he'd probably have hurt me a lot more than he did you. How's your throat, by the way?"

"Sore, but I'll survive." They'd reached the first floor.

"Make sure you report to the medical officer and get it documented for the case file. It adds weight to the choking accusation."

He nodded. "You'll have to excuse me. I've got to go wash off again."

She nodded. "Me, too."

The paperwork seemed never-ending, but when Ruth looked up as Palmer approached, again rubbing his washed hair with a towel, she couldn't help but smile. He'd changed his shirt and, given the tissue she'd seen fall off him as they wrestled Evans into cuffs, she wasn't surprised.

The grin grew wider at his confusion.

"What?" he asked as he reached his desk.

"You've had to shower in work two days in a row. Jackson's already running a book on tomorrow making it three."

He looked over to the other DS in the team and Ruth twisted, too, in time to see Jackson pick up and wave his little yellow bets notebook.

"I didn't actually shower," Palmer announced.

"You had to wash up, including a hair wash, and change clothes, so it counts," Jackson laughed. "Keep this up and I'll be able to clean up, too."

Jackson returned to his work as Palmer sat. "Am I the station laughingstock?"

"Nah." She grinned at him. "You're just the new boy, and as hazings go, you're getting off easy. The duty solicitor is with Evans. We'll give them ten, interview the scrote, then a late lunch and we'll go down to meet Tom."

Chapter 9

Lunch refreshed Ruth before she drove, heading down the A470 to Cardiff, Palmer beside her.

Palmer was working out well, she thought. Clearly intelligent, worked methodically, was sensitive, accepting of others, and gallant. She wasn't used to gallantry. She was grateful he'd stopped Evans' attack. Yes, she'd controlled and cuffed the man, but if she'd been knocked down and strangled like Palmer, she wasn't sure she'd have bounced back as fast.

She was still finding her feet with him. Married with a son, that was common ground, but off limits. She'd seen the effect he had on women, and that could be useful, but his reputation for a roving eye – and hands – bothered her. It should obviously bother his wife more, but that was beyond her jurisdiction. She'd simply make sure that she wasn't party to his infidelities. Then there was the weirdness. The feeling that there was something, some secret she wasn't in on. She hadn't seen enough yet to ask, but when she did, she would.

"Palmer?" She broke the comfortable silence. "Can I ask you something personal?"

"Depends how personal."

She grinned. "Not that kind of personal." She indicated left and pulled into the slower lane to let the speed freak in the Audi approaching far too fast pass her. If she worried about every broken law, she'd spend her life chasing Audi drivers around these roads. "You know you're good looking, and I've already seen how one smile from you sends women weak-kneed."

His laugh was low and warm. "How are your knees?"

"Steady as a rock," she assured him. "My point is, Daf already called you eye-candy, and as insulting as that is, you kind of are. Sorry, but I'd have to be dead from the brain out not to have noticed. Have you any objection if I use it sometimes?"

His pause for thought was unnerving as she drew up at the red lights on entering Whitchurch.

"I guess not, if it helps." He didn't sound convinced. "Can't see how it'll help with Tom, though."

She grinned at that suggestion. "Me neither." They were moving again. "It wasn't an imminent proposal, just for future reference. Do you and Tom get on?"

"I've only met him twice, but yeah, we get on. I guess you've known him longer?"

She nodded. "A decade, roughly. It's the nature of investigating suspicious deaths, you get to know the pathologists."

He made an inarticulate noise of understanding. "So, you don't mind me filing away your admission of finding me physically attractive, then?"

She felt her cheeks burn. "As long as you understand that fishing for compliments isn't attractive."

"Of course, sir." This time he chuckled, and Ruth found it unexpectedly safe and comfortable.

The hospital was the usual parking nightmare. Ruth didn't even try to withhold the torrent of abuse when an idiot in a C2, who could barely see over the steering wheel, all but drove into the side of them. She was shaking as she pulled into a tight parking space.

"You okay?"

She looked at Palmer, swallowing the bile in her throat. "One too many road accidents. It's …" Unable to find the words, she closed her eyes, gripped the steering wheel, trying to push those images away. Losing a loved one in an accident was never easy, but she couldn't let it control her life. She certainly shouldn't let it impinge on her professional life. "Sorry."

"Don't be. You need a moment?"

She glanced at him, turned the other way, and judged the gap between her and the next car. "I think I need a can opener." She turned back to him. "You got enough room there?"

He checked. "Just about. It's not like there're any other spaces available."

The door clicked as he opened it and she opened hers, having to ease it against the next car to contort and squeeze out. Palmer had similar issues.

Both mortuary and pathology labs were on the ground floor at the Heath, and they stepped inside at three exactly. DC Catherine Davies was back in her day clothes, making notes and looking in the rudest health. How she managed that, Ruth was at a loss to know. She greeted Diane, the receptionist.

Catherine finished her notes and stood. Ruth made the introductions. They got a quick run through, and Ruth thanked Catherine for stepping in at short notice. By the time the official exchanges were done, Tom was waiting to greet them.

Even in blue scrubs with a pen tucked behind his ear, pushing his glasses to a slight skew, he still reminded Ruth of Harry Potter, for all the only thing he had in common with Daniel Radcliffe was brown hair. It was the glasses. He favoured small round glasses, and he looked so young, younger than her even though he was several years older.

"Hey, Ruth, Madoc." As he heard what he said, his grin grew.

"Don't you dare," Ruth warned.

"Best come through, then." They did, and he led them into the white and steel mortuary. "You want scrubs?"

"You're not planning on cutting anything open while we're here, are you?" Even she heard the dread in her tone.

His look showed amusement. "No, done with all that for today. Your minions and CSI have all the evidence, all bagged, tagged, and done in accordance with evidentiary rules."

"Cathy is great at all this stuff."

Tom's grin just grew. "Certainly better than you. At least with her I only have one splash zone to worry about."

The splash zone was the area over which bodily fluids could be projected during a postmortem. Mostly, it was unavoidable, but just occasionally, if the pathologist knew they could upset a rookie, or more especially an experienced inspector who didn't enjoy the experience, then they did it on purpose. Ruth gritted her teeth and indicated for Tom to lead on. She'd never actually thrown up in a PM. Felt like it pretty much every time, come close occasionally, but never done it. Yet.

They were in a room with two gurneys. A white sheet covered one and the body under it. The other was uncovered bones.

"So," Tom asked, "where shall we start?"

"With the Naked Lady," Palmer answered.

"Excuse me?" Ruth asked.

Palmer kicked himself. "Sorry. Just how I'd started thinking of them. The Drowned Man and the Naked Lady."

Ruth raised her brows. Literal and oddly fitting descriptions.

"Works for me," Tom said as he stepped up to the uncovered gurney, and Palmer moved closer. Ruth was already closer than she liked, but she had to show willing, so she stepped up.

"So, you got that this was a woman from the bones?" Ruth asked Tom.

"Of course. Gender differences show in the bones."

Ruth agreed even as she threw a querulous glance at Palmer. Everyone knew skeletons revealed biological gender, but this was the first official report, and the first sight he'd had of the skeleton as a whole. So how had Palmer known? "Any idea how long she'd been in the ground?"

"Given that there's no soft tissue left and Daf reported no sign of recent disturbance around the burial itself, I'd estimate at least five years. And yes, the bones do prove that this is a woman, but there were other indications." He moved to the side and tapped a computer screen to show images of evidence in situ and bagged. "These lay under the body."

Ruth and Madoc looked closely at the screen. A picture showed a layer of long straight fibres, dark and with solid blocks at one end.

"Hair extensions?" Ruth questioned.

"Yep," Tom agreed. "Then there's these." He moved to another set of images.

Ruth frowned as she studied them. "Gel bags?"

Tom nodded. "Basically, though they've been leaking for a while." Taking the pen from behind his ear, he pointed to the flatter of the two. "This one especially. That affected the soil around the bones, which is why you see the clumping on the in-situ photos. These are silicone breast implants."

"Really? That's good," Ruth said. "We can trace her identity from their serial numbers."

"Unfortunately not." Tom smiled at her. "The serial numbers aren't on the implants themselves, only in the implanter's records. You'd have to trace her identity to trace the serial number."

"Oh."

"It's all right." Tom smirked. "It's not like implants are something you need to know about." His eyeline slipped to Ruth's chest. She tried to downplay them, but double-Ds couldn't be completely hidden. "No extra padding needed in those fun bags."

Palmer made a strangled sound, then laughed along with Tom.

"Tom?" Ruth asked sweetly.

"Yes, dear?"

"Which of the handy implements would you most like me to beat the pair of you to death with?"

"Hmm." He was grinning under the mock consideration. "I'd recommend the bolt cutters I use for cutting ribs. Heavy enough for one-hit bludgeoning and long enough that even you could smack Madoc across the skull."

"Oh, so you're not just going to take the piss out of my breasts, now you're going to make a joke of my height, too?" She rolled her eyes but struggled to keep a straight face. Since Tom was only five-ten, a good pair of heels and she was just as tall at him. Though she couldn't remember the last time she'd worn heels. "I hope you don't say stuff like that to other women around here."

"Are you kidding?" Tom asked. "I'd be up before the board and on a sexual harassment training course if I did."

She couldn't resist. "You don't need training to know how to sexually harass a woman."

Tom shook his head and chuckled. "Oh, Ruth. Just as well we've known one another long enough not to take offence."

"Wouldn't be without you, dear. Now, the case." She looked at the skeletal remains. "Any indication of how our Naked Lady died?"

Tom denied it with a gesture. "No bone injuries, the only misalignments visible in Chris's pictures are those that decomposition and earth movement could explain. Whatever killed her was in the soft tissues and hasn't survived the test of time."

"Can you give us estimated height, weight, or age?"

"Height would have been in the region of 170–180 cm. Weight I can't guess, but not especially heavy. Maybe the around 60 kilo mark. The coronal suture hasn't fused yet and there's only partial fusion of the iliac crest, so she would have been between sixteen and twenty-four at time of death."

Ruth narrowed her eyes at him. "Sutures are in the skull and the crest being some part of the pelvis?"

He grinned at her. "Top of the class, Miss Atkins."

"Thank you, Professor Snape." Ruth offered a blatantly saccharine smile. "So, the only indication that this wasn't a natural death is that someone put her in a shallow grave?"

Tom nodded.

"Better than leaving her on a bed with another corpse downstairs," Palmer muttered.

Seeing Tom frown, Ruth explained, "The Geddings case."

"Ah, I'll have to catch up with that one. As for this one—" He pointed at the Naked Lady. "—nothing more I can tell you there."

"Nothing unique in the dental record?"

"Usual fillings, mostly amalgam, but one white top. I've arranged x-rays for matching purposes, but there's nothing so different that it'll help with identification. I have, however, taken a marrow sample from the femur, which should allow for a DNA match."

"Assuming we have her DNA on file," Palmer said.

"We normally have for mispers gone in suspicious circumstances. There's one more thing." Ruth stopped Tom when he moved towards the other gurney. "You liked the Naked Lady description. Was that because she lacked skin, or lacked clothes?"

Tom looked at her. "*If*," he stressed the word, "she was dressed when put in the ground, any natural fibres – like cotton – could well have rotted away by now."

Ruth nodded. "But no metal zips or plastic buttons? Were any fastenings found in the excavation?"

Though he was shaking his head, Tom stepped to the side and the clipboard he had there. He ran through the manifest of what he'd been sent. "Nope."

"Not even a hook and eye from a bra?"

"Not that I received," Tom reported.

Ruth refused to acknowledge that Palmer was running two fingers over the skull. She wasn't overly comfortable with the way his touch seemed so gentle, intimate. His eyes looked distant and his face paled. He leant more heavily on the gurney.

"Palmer," she asked softly, "are you okay?"

He nodded guiltily but standing entirely on his own two feet again seemed to take effort. "Fine."

Ruth frowned. What was with him? Then she turned to Tom, whose nose was firmly pointed towards the notes in his hand. Had he seen anything?

"Looks like some of the excavated material was taken directly to forensics, so they may have something I don't. I only had the implants and extensions because they'd become intertwined with the ribs and vertebra."

Tom put the clipboard down as he moved to the other gurney, and Palmer moved with him. Ruth stayed put. Old bones were so much easier to deal with than dead flesh. It had always bothered her, that she had to see the wrong human laid out—*Don't think about it.* The struggle was real, but she would get through this.

Tom carefully pulled the white sheet back and twisted his head to look down at the dead man's face. Raymond Bevan was a blocky sort, hard hewn from the land, salt of the earth and not much sweetness in his features.

"What is that line across his face?" Palmer asked. There was a blotchy red line from his forehead to his chin, it covered half his nose.

"That's livor mortis. The collection of blood at the lowest parts of the body," Tom explained.

Ruth frowned. "I didn't think he'd been on the ground long enough for that."

"Starts after about twenty minutes, gets visible at about two hours. It's only on half the face as you don't get livor mortis where the body is touching the ground, which compresses the capillaries, so the blood can't go into them. Yet our Drowned Man here was face down in mud, has mud in his nostrils, mouth, throat, and lungs, and still, he has livor mortis."

"Meaning?" Palmer asked.

Tom shrugged. "My guess, from the state of what was in his airways, is that someone held him down, then – and this is a total guess – I'd say the head was pulled up, the killer checking life had been extinguished, and then lay or possibly dropped the head down again."

"Someone held him down?" Ruth asked.

Tom looked across at her and nodded, then he glanced at Palmer. "Take his hips and help me roll him on his side."

Glad she wasn't having to do that, Ruth watched and swallowed bile as the two men moved the body. Two areas of bruising, one on each shoulder blade, were obvious even to her.

"The rounded, vaguely triangular shape of the marks suggests knees to me," Tom said. "If Madoc were to pull the sheet down further, you'd see two similar, but wider, marks on his buttocks. They indicate flat-soled shoes. Not clear enough to distinguish a tread pattern. There'll be photos in the report." With a nod to Palmer, Tom eased the man onto his back. "There's more bruising on the back of the head, suggesting sustained pressure put on that spot."

"Are you saying someone jumped on his back once he was in the ditch and held his head in the mud to drown him?"

"Yep." Tom covered the man again. "I'd also say, from the measurement between the knees and the toe tip, that your murderer was in the 160 cm range, give or take. Actual height depends what angle the ankles were at as they sat on the man. What I can't tell you is why he landed face first in that ditch. There are no additional physical signs of assault. If he was pushed, it wasn't hard enough to leave an impact mark."

"Can you even be sure that he died in the ditch and wasn't put in it after?"

"Can't be 100 per cent sure, because the soil across that site is all likely to be the same, but the soil in his lungs matched the soil around the Naked Lady, so I'd say it's more likely than not that he died where he was found."

"Thanks."

"Oh, actually, there's one more thing you might find useful. The hair extensions."

"They were originally blonde, like the girl," Palmer said.

Tom frowned at Madoc. For a moment, the younger man seemed panicked. "How did you know?"

"There's coal in the soil," Palmer said as if grasping at straws. "After five years or more, that will have dyed the fibres."

"Hmm," Tom murmured. "Ruth, I think he just jumped to the top of the class."

Chapter 10

As Madoc followed Ruth from the mortuary, the urge to tell her what he'd seen was great, but he wasn't ready for that. The risk was too high. He needed this job.

*Just be honest with her.*

He pulled a small snack bar from his pocket, unsure he could be *that* honest with a colleague. He'd tried it once and been ridiculed. The oblique digs were one reason he'd wanted away from Cardiff. He took a needed bite of the bar. Sugar to replenish the energy his abilities often took from him.

Ruth stepped outside and took a deep breath, a soul-deep refresh.

Maybe he could start this from a different angle. He swallowed the mouthful.

"PMs aren't fun, are they?" he said as he stepped to her side.

"No," she agreed. "But you got to have a laugh with Tom."

"And you didn't give as good as you got?"

That brought out a big smile. "Yeah, well." She took a breath. "Where did you get that from?" She looked at the bar in his hand.

"My pocket. I need something to settle my stomach after what happened in there."

She nodded, but did she take it at face value?

"I've never been too great with them, postmortems," she said. "But recently, they've got more difficult."

Time to take the risk. "Can I ask a personal question?"

"Hmm." Her glance was assessing. "Can I hit you if it's too personal?"

He grinned. "I'm pretty sure hitting a colleague is gross misconduct, but I'll allow it this time."

She nodded as they meandered back to the car. "Okay then. Ask."

"Your … erm, driving …"

"You don't like it?" she asked as the question lost its way.

"No problem with it, sir. It's just that … your reaction to that idiot pulling out without looking. Justified, but a little extreme."

"Okay." There was affront in that tone, but she was controlling it. "Not actually hearing a personal question yet."

"Is it because of what happened to your husband?"

She stopped. He didn't realise, took another step, and had to turn back. In the sun, she was white as a sheet. "Ruth?"

Swallowing hard, she looked up at him again. "The grapevine never fails, does it?"

"Not often," he admitted. "I don't always trust it, but, well, that kind of news, it shocks people into talking. And given what happened to … I'm sorry, I just realised I don't even know his name."

For a second, he thought she was fainting, then he realised she was just sinking down to the bench he hadn't noticed beside the path. He sat angled towards her.

"Paul." The name seemed to rip from some wound deep inside her. "His name was Paul."

She was struggling. The pain zinged from her like static. It was in her voice. A scream that rent the air with its silence.

"As for what happened …" Her voice trailed off. "What do you know already?"

"Not much," he admitted. "RTC. I never read the case file. It wasn't my place."

Her breath shuddered. She swallowed again. "It was Christmas before last. White van man was playing with his phone instead of watching the road. He failed to take the curve in the road, smacked into the car in front of Paul. Paul did an emergency stop. The Forensic Crash Investigation Unit believe he stopped in time to avoid a secondary collision."

The words were technically neutral, but they echoed suffering. It pricked at his skin.

"The articulated lorry behind didn't."

He didn't want to imagine what that would have done to the car Paul Atkins had been in.

"Worst thing was, I almost saw it. I certainly heard it. I was seconds behind. I called it in. I parked across the two lanes, put the hazards on. Had the phone to my ear and was giving details as I rushed from my car. I saw the lorry driver; he was horrified but uninjured. As was the stumbling white van man. And the driver he'd hit. Then I saw the Merc." She took a shuddering breath, looking to the sky, begging for help with a need she couldn't name. "I don't think he died instantly. It's a dreadful thought, but I think he saw m—"

This time she stopped, articulation beyond her reach. Scrunching her eyes shut only made the tears overflow. She hunched in on herself. Her hands were gripping the front edge of the bench. He shifted closer, dared to put his hand on her shoulder.

"That's not a dreadful thought," he said softly. "What husband wouldn't want his wife to be the last thing he saw?"

She allowed a sob to escape, but turned her head away from him, steadied her breathing, and her hands moved up to her face, wiping her eyes as she sniffed. "Oh God, I don't talk about this. Even before the accident, I didn't like talking about my family in work. How is it I keep finding myself talking to you about them?" She finally turned to him, eyes red and welling.

He smiled at her. "Coz I'm easy to talk to?" he suggested. "And because whatever else you might have heard, I don't spread gossip."

She nodded. "Thank you. There's something else about the crash you should know. White van man – I could name him, but I try to depersonalise him. They breathalysed him at the scene.

He blew thirty-eight. By the time he got to the station, and blew again – which he made sure he dragged out as long as possible – he was on thirty-four. The lorry driver was at twenty-nine. Both officially not drunk-driving. That's why I didn't have an alcoholic drink last night. I've always thought the legal limit for alcohol when driving should be zero, and that was before two 'not drunk' men killed my husband."

Sounded perfectly reasonable to Madoc.

"So, yes, what happened to Paul is why I did, do, and probably always will, overreact to bad driving. It's why I have no tolerance for drink-driving. And it's why I struggle with PMs. You see, there still had to be an official identification. Geraint offered to do it, but I insisted. Geraint came with, but … Tom and Gethin did a wonderful job. Paul almost looked like he was just asleep, but … not. You know? On account of his being dead. But …" She paused, controlling her breath again. "The problem now is that every time a white sheet gets turned down, the face I see is Paul's, regardless. It's only an instant, but it's there."

Madoc nodded. It all made perfect sense. It pleased him that she was back to her normal self. Or at least, her normal professional self. Reluctantly, he took his hand away.

"Can I ask you something?" she said.

He nodded.

"What the hell were you doing when you stroked that skull?"

Damn it.

What did you expect? that annoying voice in his head asked. **She's a good detective, observant, of course she saw.**

"Come on, Palmer. I know you're hiding something from me. If you don't tell me, I'll …"

And thus, his fears were given voice. "You'll what?"

Her lips pursed. "Oh, I don't bloody know. But I know you're up to something. If you don't tell me, I'll have to assume it's something nefarious. Hopefully not necromantic. But something that … Oh, I don't know. Just tell me what's going on."

The world froze over. Each breath spiked with ice shards. If he told her, he could lose his job. If he didn't tell her, he could lose his job.

Exactly. So you might as well tell her.

Oh, shut up.

"Come on, Palmer. This is your one chance."

One chance to keep his job. He had to take the risk. He also had to lick his lips before he could speak. "Did you ever hear about Biddy Small?"

"No, but I'm not asking about her. I want to know what happened in there, and I want you to be honest."

"I am being." He pushed back his hair, swallowed the bile in his throat. "But to be honest, I have to tell you about Biddy first. To make you understand. If I can."

He had still been on probation, out with a constable of seven years' experience. Walking the beat had grown increasingly rare over the years, but then they had. An anonymous white van pulled too fast down the street, forcing them to rush across the road. His colleague had shouted after the vehicle to no avail. They heard someone hammering on a door, calling out, and went to investigate. The neighbour claimed to have heard a worrying clatter, something heavy falling down the stairs. Now she couldn't get an answer. Since that constituted good cause, they checked the windows - old wooden sash windows that opened with a squeal of resistance. Madoc had entered the property.

"I found Biddy at the foot of her stairs," he said. "Obviously dead, but I checked for breath – you know, procedure. And then I knew it hadn't been an accident. My partner called it in, and no one listened to my certainty that someone else had been there, that it wasn't just a fall. I was overruled. Then the family came down. They claimed things were missing from the house, valuables. They accused us, but that was just their grief talking. I knew then that I had to find out who had been in Biddy's house. I investigated in my own time. What I found was a rogue trader. He'd ripped off and stolen from several older people in the area. He still had some of Biddy's items when I caught him. When pushed, he admitted Biddy had confronted him at the top of the stairs. He'd already grabbed what he wanted and pushed her aside. Pushed her off balance. He ran down, she'd tried to follow, but still off-balance, she'd fallen. Her death wasn't natural, and her family needed to know that."

Ruth was watching him closely now, curious. "That sounds like you have very good instincts, but …"

Now the lump in his throat threatened to choke him.

Her frown didn't disappear. "It's more than that, isn't it? Whatever it is, it's more than instinct."

Damn, she was perceptive. He looked directly at her. "Do you have a faith?"

"Yes." She paused. "No. Sort of. I don't know if there's a name for this. I believe in God, I just don't believe in religion."

That was good. That meant she was more open to the supernatural than many. "That's either Deism or Agnostic Theism, not sure. The thing is that, in my view, there's more to life than what we can see and touch and hear. Sometimes I get … indications of stuff. Messages, if you like. I don't exactly talk to the dead."

Don't you?

Shut up.

"My Aunt Maureen keeps telling me I could if I wanted to. But I don't." That last was more for the voice than her.

"Aunt Maureen sounds like fun."

Her sardonic tone made him laugh. "She is, actually. Once you get past the incense, the multi-coloured clothing, and her penchant to use tiny bells for jewellery and adornments. As a kid, I remember thinking she always came in with angel bells. Anyway, Maureen is a psychic, makes a living from it. She's a bit Marmite, though, people love her or hate her. Never an okay.

Generally speaking, I believe in cosmic harmony," he told her. "I get people. Sometimes more than I want to. I sense things."

You're weird.

Says you? Go away.

"You sense things?" Disbelief weighted her tone.

His heart pounded as he looked at her. How was she going to take this? Would he still have a job tomorrow? Well, he'd have the job, she couldn't get him fired for this, but the laughter and discreditation could make work impossible.

Inquisitiveness marked her interest rather than contempt. "Then I was right. You did know about Raymond Bevan before I told you. Before you could have seen him?"

Dangerous territory, but he'd come this far. "I felt his … surprise at being dead. He wasn't sure how it had happened."

She blinked as she tried to process that. "So, he wasn't conscious when he drowned?"

"Oh no, no I don't mean that. He was aware of what physically happened to him, he knew he was dead. It was more the sense that he was struggling with how he could suddenly be dead when he hadn't expected it. But that knowing he was dead is why I don't get any clear message from him. He'd gone over."

"Gone over?"

"To the other side. Passed over, crossed the veil. I'm not sure what you'd call it."

"Okay, but what about her in there?"

"It felt like the right thing to do. Sometimes physical contact intensifies the connection."

"You looked unsteady on your feet, like you might pass out."

She really was observant. "Sometimes, when I just get messages, it's an emotional burst that I pick up, like the radio going from easy listening to an unexpected blast of heavy metal."

Her smile was short-lived. "I like heavy metal."

Why didn't that surprise him?

"Are you," she asked, her voice low, full of curiosity, "desperately trying not to tell me you're psychic, too?"

"Not quite." He could just leave it there and be done with it, but if he was finally going to admit this to someone on the force, he might as well say it all. "I get things sometimes, but it's inconsistent. The messages are generally hazy indicators. Or a certainty without evidence. I'm not about to read your aura or preside at a seance. I'm not a medium."

"Guessing that's Maureen's territory?" she asked.

He smiled. "Well, yeah."

"And the snacking? That something to do with it all?"

Observant and logical. No wonder she was good at the job. "After a, er, moment, I find eating or drinking helps. Are you going to tell the others about this?"

His phone started ringing.

The way she broke eye contact rammed a fist into his throat. She'd taken things well, on the surface at least. But could she accept it? Would she tell everyone else? What would they say? Had he just handed another senior female officer the gift to force him out?

The phone rang on.

"You'd best answer that," Ruth said, standing.

Madoc let her go as he reached for his phone. He could only pray she didn't crucify him with her new knowledge.

Chapter 11

Ruth stepped away and took a deep draw of fresh air. As fresh as air got in a city, next to a busy dual carriageway, with people crawling their cars around looking for that elusive parking space. Still, carbon monoxide beat gore and viscera. She couldn't wait to get home and have a long soak in a hot bath. She needed time to adjust to Palmer's revelations. Police officers were ridiculed for using psychics – what would happen to one who *was* a psychic? God, what a mess. Maybe necrophilia would have been better. She wished she'd never asked now.

Madoc took the phone call. He said they'd be there in an hour.

Ruth frowned. Be where?

"That was Andy Porter," Palmer reported after he ended the call. "We need to visit Heolgerrig. She said it was important. I can go on my own if you've got to get home."

The soak in the bath would wait. "We'll go together." They got into the car, Madoc driving this time. "Andy didn't say what she needed to talk to us about?"

"No."

"Weird. Though, in fairness, not the weirdest part of today."

Rush hour on the A470 meant it took fifty-eight minutes and a fair amount of frustration to reach the site. Once there, Ruth could see that the site as a crime scene had been closed down. The CSI team had been crawling over everything yesterday and today, but with the conditions and improbability of finding more, they had, according to the text Ruth received while they travelled, released the site about half an hour ago. Someone with a digger was already filling in the trench where Raymond's body had been found. Ruth wondered how superstitious the builders would be about working here now, or how the eventual homeowner would react to discovering that their house stood over what had once been a shallow grave. Parked outside, Ruth looked at Palmer.

He pointed across the road. "Did you notice that?"

"The big gold Bentley parked badly over the way? Yeah, I noticed it. As nice an area as Heolgerrig is, wouldn't be surprised if that gets keyed the way the driver couldn't be bothered to decide which side of the road to park." The car was a clear foot from the pavement.

Since the weather had cleared up, the ground appeared dryer. Ruth looked at Palmer. "My DMs can cope with the mud no problem. Your shoes gonna be okay?"

"Have to be. Still don't have any wellies on me. A factor I shall have to take care of. I'll stick some in the car when I get home tonight."

"Well, that should guarantee we won't need them, then." The sardonic tone said it all.

On site, Ruth was relieved to see pallets had been laid out as a path to the office.

They heard raised voices as they approached the office cabin. Ruth didn't bother knocking, simply stepped in to find Maggie scowling behind her desk. The voices were male and female: Andy Porter and a man she didn't recognise.

The voices stopped as soon as Ruth stepped into the office. The man wore a charcoal suit with a silver-grey tie in a Windsor knot. He did not look happy as he checked records on his laptop.

"Get out. You've no right to be in here," he snapped.

Ruth just looked at him, then slowly she pulled out her warrant card.

"I'm Detective Inspector Ruth Atkins."

The man's face froze.

"Do you want to try that greeting again?" she asked.

"This is Martin Wainwright," Andy said. "Shalestones' chief accountant. I called him just before I called you."

"Something you shouldn't have done." He glared at Andy.

"And why's that, Mr Wainwright?"

The suspicious brown eyes turned back to her. "Because we're not sure there's anything to report. That's what I'm here to check."

"Well, I'm sure Detective Sergeant Palmer here can help you with that one."

Wainwright's lip curled. "Only a properly qualified accountant would understand."

"Lucky I've a degree in accounting, then," Palmer said, moving to stand beside Wainwright, who was looking less than happy with each new development. "Where would you like to start?"

The accountant pressed his lips together. Palmer could deal with his resistance. Ruth turned to Andy and stepped closer, separating them from the two men. "What did you see?"

The site manager's eyes flicked to Wainwright. "Probably nothing." Resentment and dejection warred in her tone.

"Okay, that happens, but I'm here now, so happy to listen."

Andy paused before answering. "As I mentioned, we've been preparing for an audit. It was Raymond's site, and I was asked to review the files with him and prepare everything. It was only a small development – six houses out in West Llanelli – but they were large five-bedroom luxury homes. A one-off development. The idea was to use as much reclaimed material as possible while also installing solar panels, a shared wind turbine, and ensuring the houses were as energy efficient as possible. When working that design, you need to be in contact with multiple reclamation yards."

Ruth's stomach sank even as she encouraged Andy to go on.

"In these houses, there were twelve bathrooms – well, there were technically thirty, but twelve with actual baths. But according to the paperwork, we received and paid for eighteen baths."

"I'm guessing 50 per cent breakage is a higher rate than normal?"

Andy nodded. "It wasn't just the baths, though they were what jumped out at me first. There's also way more wooden panelling than the houses used, enough banister rails for stairs to the moon. Well, okay, about fourteen stories when we only had to go up nine."

Ruth ran that through quickly. "Half the houses had a second floor?"

Again, Andy nodded. "The thing is, it was a luxury development, and a trial of some new ways of working, which is why the site is being audited. As a business, we expected it to be costly, but profits should be high. With all the over-purchasing and no on-sales or evidence of returns and refunds, the profits aren't as high as they should have been."

Ruth nodded. "Okay. That's disappointing, but I don't see what makes it a police matter."

"Shalestones doesn't just build new buildings. Sometimes, we take down old ones. We use reclamation specialists for that, too. It's often the same people we buy from. Raymond was site manager, oversaw all on-site day-to-day activities, as he did with many sites. I've wondered about things before, but this, after what's happened, really made me think. You asked me if Raymond had any enemies, and honestly, I don't know of any. But if he was doing something dodgy, then there's a chance something could have been going on with a supplier that I don't know about."

The cold in Ruth's gut solidified to concrete. "I've heard bungs can be rife in the construction industry."

"Not in our company," Wainwright declared.

"Okay." Ruth kept her attention on Andy. "Can you give me the suppliers' names? I can at least speak with them about their view of Raymond."

"I'll give you a list."

As Andy reached for something on the desk, Ruth looked at Palmer. He straightened from where he was talking to Wainwright.

"Technically, there's no evidence of wrongdoing. The deliveries outweigh the requirements, but not the orders. The orders, the delivery notes, the invoices, they all follow through," Palmer explained. "However, were I in Mr Wainwright's position, I'd be asking some awkward questions internally."

"You see?" the accountant told Ruth. "Nothing here for you to get involved in."

"Probably not," Ruth agreed as she took the list from Andy. A quick scan confirmed her dread. "Okay, is there any way you can check which baths were actually used and identify who supplied the excess?"

"We can do that," Andy agreed.

"But it's an internal matter," Wainwright again underlined the point. "Your attention is not required."

Ruth pinned him with a hard glare. "Mr Wainwright, the more people tell me I'm not needed, the more I find that is exactly where my focus should be."

The man said nothing.

"Right," Ruth said. "I agree that at this point, there doesn't seem to be anything for us to be concerned about. But Andy was right to call us. We have to investigate every avenue for potential action against Raymond Bevan." Ruth turned back to Andy. "Thank you, Andy, and if you think of anything else, however minor, please let us know."

Madoc got into the car; Ruth had taken the keys from him to drive. She waited until both doors were closed before she turned the air blue. Four-letter Anglo-Saxon words were common enough, but this was an absolute avalanche of them. Sensing

Ruth had grown increasingly tense while on site hadn't prepared him for this.

"Ruth?"

Releasing a last expletive, she faced him again.

"Sensing something might have upset you a little, sir?"

The huffed breath wasn't directed at him, just in his general direction.

"Did I do something wrong?" Madoc asked.

Surprise widened her features. "Good God, no. Why would you even think that?"

Because, according to Inspector Mannford, doing something wrong was his forte.

"This is the problem." She passed over the paper Andy Porter had given her and checked her watch.

The reclamation specialists. Madoc cast his eyes over the suppliers, couldn't see any problem.

"Merthyr Architectural Salvage," she said, dark-toned. "Would you like to take a wild stab in the dark at just who owns that?"

This couldn't be good. "Not Iolo Flack?"

"No." She started the car. "Griffith Flack."

Yep, that four-letter Anglo-Saxon word covered it.

"You need to get home?" she asked.

"I'm okay for a couple more hours."

"Not sure we'll get the overtime, mind."

He shrugged. "I'm okay with that."

Face set tight and grim, Ruth moved the car into the road and headed north. They turned off the A470 to the A465, then off at Cefn Coed, through Trefechan, where council houses gave way to country lanes until they reached Vaynor. An empty country road until Ruth took a turning marked 'Private' and stopped before an electronic gate. Ruth rolled up to the gate and wound down her window to press the intercom. Eventually, a tinny voice answered.

"I'd like to speak to Griffith Flack. It's Detective Inspector Atkins."

What came back was crackly and gruff but could just about be made out as a response that Griffith wasn't home. Movement behind their car caught Madoc's eye, and he looked back to see a solid black Range Rover pull up behind them. The man behind the wheel was just as solid, though a hell of a lot whiter.

Ruth spoke to the telecom again. "Griffith just pulled up behind—"

The buzz told them the gates were opening.

Ruth's window rose smoothly as the gate pulled back. Atkins pulled forward – the Range Rover way too close – then she drove around the large oval at the centre of the drive. The Range Rover parked before the house, and they all got out.

This was Madoc's first meeting with Griffith Flack. The man was shorter than he'd expected, squat and solid, no hair, lots of muscle, but he looked more naturally built than Iolo. And there were fewer tattoos. The word 'villain' echoed in Madoc's head just to look at the man. He carried today's *South Wales Echo* under his arm.

"Inspector Atkins."

His manner and tone were polite, unobjectionable. Madoc sensed no hostility, but the man had power and authority, the courage to bend the world to his will. The King of Swords. They closed the gap between them.

"Mr Flack."

Griffith stopped. "*Mr* Flack? Should I be calling Steele?"

Ruth didn't stop, and Madoc kept a pace behind and to the side. "Oh God, Griffith, please don't. However, if you insist on wasting your time and mine, and paying through the nose for a service you don't really need, feel free."

Ruth stopped and waited, then Griffith relented.

"You'd best come in then. Who's your lanky companion?" Griffith looked closer. "Wait, are you one of the Palmer boys?"

"Detective Sergeant Madoc Palmer," Ruth said. "Meet Griffith Flack, local entrepreneur."

Surprisingly, Griffith offered a hand. Madoc stepped forward to shake. Prepared to get his hand crunched, Madoc found instead a firm grip without overt control. An undertone thrummed through, whispering 'don't mess with me, boy'. Madoc had absolutely no intention of doing so. The shake separated, and the warning left him. A few moments later, they were led into the massive house and met in the hall by another nearly hairless muscle-bound man. This one, Madoc recognised. The eldest son, who had been the problem for his sister.

"Palmer." The man nodded.

"Dylan," Madoc returned, not knowing what else to say.

"Why am I not surprised you're a copper?" The sneer was insult and provocation.

The great temptation was to point out that Dylan wasn't quite as dumb as he looked, but Madoc resisted.

"Dylan." The paternal rebuke was mild. "Go stick the kettle on. I could do with a cuppa, and I'm sure our guests wouldn't say no."

They said nothing, not being given the option.

"Guests," Dylan sneered as he moved away.

Griffith led them through into a massive lounge. A 70-inch TV filled the wall in front of a sofa Madoc reckoned was wider than his entire home. There was a massive thick oak dining table big enough for at least twelve beside the wide bifold doors that led out into a manicured garden. Who said crime didn't pay?

Griffith waved them to sit, and Ruth did, though a slight flick of her eyes communicated that she wanted Madoc to stay standing. Griffith glanced up and then at Ruth.

"He too tall to bend?"

"I just want him ready to help Dylan." Ruth relaxed back and looked at Griffith. "I got your text. Wondered what you meant by it."

The big man shrugged. "That you should look to Tredegar and the Prices. Not your jurisdiction, but I'm sure you've heard of them."

Just as Gwent Police had heard of the Flack family.

"Is this a general direction or a specific one?" Ruth asked. "Are you accusing them of something?"

Griffith appeared as relaxed as Ruth. "What would I have to accuse them of? I keep my deals legit."

Madoc wondered if anyone believed that.

"I see. So, no specifics?"

Griffith shook his head.

"I'll just pass it on to Gwent then. Let them deal."

The way Griffith's face tightened suggested he wasn't happy with that.

"I just need to ask you about Raymond Bevan."

Griffith frowned. "Don't know the guy."

"Nice try." Ruth smiled gently. "But come on, Griffith, we don't lie to each other. Bevan's name has been plastered all over the afternoon papers, and you did business with him through the Merthyr Architectural Salvage."

Griffith smiled and leant back on the sofa. "I'm not hands on with all my businesses."

"Of course not, you're not Superman," Ruth said easily. "But Merthyr Architectural Salvage was the first business you set up alone without your father's help, and I know it holds a special place in your heart."

"Added to which, I've seen the contacts between you and Shalestone. Ones Mr Bevan signed," Madoc said, to feel less like a spare part. "The last with both signatures was only four months ago." While checking for returns, Wainwright had shown him the PDF receipts.

Griffith gave Madoc a hard stare, calculated to intimidate. It partially worked. Then Griffith refocused on Ruth. "Is he accusing me of something?"

"Only of knowing Raymond Bevan. You did know him, didn't you?"

Griffith confirmed it.

"And you worked with him on the West Llanelli development Shalestones finished about three months ago?"

Again, the agreement. "What of it?"

"How would you describe Raymond Bevan as a person?"

Now Griffith frowned. "In what way?"

Ruth shrugged. "Any way. I'm trying to get a feel for who he was."

"Why?"

"He's unexpectedly dead. I have to find out why and at whose hand."

"Not ours," Dylan proclaimed as he stomped in with a tray.

Madoc noted there was a teapot, small milk jug, sugar bowl, a big mug labelled 'World's Best Dad', and a tiny porcelain cup and saucer. Just the one.

Dylan put the tray on a low coffee table that was well beyond Ruth's or Griffith's reach. Dylan took the mug and passed it to his father. There was no move to pour tea or pass a cup to Ruth. Dylan looked so pleased with himself. Griffith not so much.

"Why come to us first?"

Ruth focused on Griffith. "We didn't. We've been speaking to his wife, his colleagues, his neighbours, lots of people. But now we have a list of business contacts. You're on it and it's late in the day, you were closest, and I'd like to get home at some point tonight. So, what can you tell me about Raymond Bevan?"

"Actually, not that much." Griffith sipped his tea, looked pointedly at the untouched cup on the tray. "You're not thirsty?"

"Only for information. We don't want to take up any more of your valuable time than we have to. Now, Raymond?"

Griffith took a deep breath. "A business contact. We've met a few times, most often on the West Llanelli site you mentioned. He ordered, we supplied." Griffith considered her squarely. "Other than the poor man being dead, is there anything to suggest an issue?"

Ruth didn't move. Palmer thought it was like watching a poker match with everything at stake, but no chips on the table. "How did you find him as a person?"

"Nothing special," Griffith said.

Ruth waited, Griffith said nothing more. "Come on. You're a man who's always got his ear to the ground."

Griffith inclined his head in acknowledgement.

"And you know people. Is there anyone you would suggest might be closer to Raymond Bevan, someone who might be of interest in the current situation?"

Griffith paused before answering. "Harries Salvage in Aberdare changed hands nearly a year ago now. The new owners are more insular than the old ones. I don't know how straight they are. Then there's the Ferraris."

"Ferraris?" Ruth asked. "The bakers?"

Griffith shook his head. "Same name, totally different lot. This lot came up from Cardiff a few years back. They work Cantref Reclamation. I'm not pointing fingers mind; I know nothing about their dealings with Bevan or Shalestones. It's not my business to, but they're the ones I'd look at. Besides, Bevan was always on the lookout for a good deal. Didn't always know when he was well off."

"There's lots like that," Dylan added.

Ruth smiled up at him. "Indeed there are." She sighed and stood. "And I've got a number to go see."

She looked down at Griffith. "Thank you for your time, Griffith. Appreciate that."

She took a step away, paused. "Oh yeah, just so you know. Thanks to Steele's call yesterday—"

Griffith frowned. "What call? I didn't instruct him to call."

She shrugged. "Then I guess Iolo must have. Anyway–"

Now Griffith was on his feet, his bulk attempting to intimidate. "Why would Iolo do that?"

"Didn't Iolo tell you? I dropped into The Earth Harp yesterday, and he had Steele phone my superintendent to make a complaint that I was harassing him. I wasn't, but that will all come out in the investigation."

"About time someone dobbed you in."

The look Griffith shot Dylan cowed the son.

"Why are they investigating? What?"

Ruth looked so innocent; Madoc could hardly believe it.

"It's procedure, Griffith. Someone makes a complaint about an officer, the complaint goes to the Professional Standards, and they investigate. They're already going through every note I ever made about Iolo. And you."

Madoc hadn't been aware of that.

"They're looking for anything that can substantiate the claim. When they can't find anything, which they won't, then they'll start going through Iolo's claims. With a fine-tooth comb, just to see what they can come up with. All standard procedure. I'm sure you understand and will do everything possible to cooperate with my colleagues. We'll see ourselves out."

"Ruth?"

She looked back as they headed towards the door. "Griffith?"

"Can the complaint be withdrawn?"

She frowned. "Actually, I don't know. Never been in this situation before. But if it can, I'd suggest the best way would be to reverse the call that started it all. Have Steele call the Super and see what they can work out."

The tight face and flared nostrils suggested Iolo was far from Griffith's favourite child in that moment.

"And you'll try the Prices? You know, just in case."

Ruth nodded. "All in hand already. Thanks." She inclined her head just once and walked out casually.

Madoc didn't say a word until they were back on the road. Ruth had handed him the keys to the pool car. In silence, she was making her notes.

"Did that actually do any good?" He wasn't sure one way or the other.

"Not for the Bevan case, no. The Ferraris aren't on Shalestones' list, though Harries are. Still, it told us something."

All Madoc had learnt was that Ruth was gutsier than he'd imagined.

"Okay," she sighed. "It told *me* something."

"I'm sorry, but what? I guess something about the Tredegar Prices?"

"It sure is," she said as she finished a note. "Remember, I know the Flacks better than you, on a business level, anyway. Griffith wants control, so it makes sense for him to try using us to put the Prices out of action. That tells me there is something about the Prices I need to look at now, but I don't think it relates to our current investigation. However, if Bevan was on the take, which now seems possible, then he was probably dealing with people who didn't want to be compromised. They might have a reason to kill him. Especially if something on the reclaimed goods was about to come up. Maybe Iolo just got himself in trouble with his dad for no reason, or for a very good one. Or it could still be a robbery gone wrong."

That was the worst thing about these jobs: too many possibilities and not enough evidence.

"Are Professional Standards really investigating you?"

She shrugged. "Preliminary at most. I haven't had a yellow slip yet, and they can't go too far without that. Oh, bugger!"

"What?"

"Dwayne Evans. We need that interview done."

Chapter 12

May was proving to be a squib. At least the late night had been productive. Ignoring counsel advice, Dwayne had confessed all, including way too much detail on how it felt to choke the girl, whose name he neither knew nor cared about.

Ruth had taken everything with Dwayne Evans in her stride, even his rape threats. Things Dwayne had said that made Madoc want to pummel him, she'd just brushed aside. She was strong, yes, but not the frosty-arsed bitch he'd been warned of.

Madoc shook the damp from his coat as he stepped into the office to see Ruth sitting at her desk, staring at the whiteboard. Her hair was back in the long ponytail which hung down the chair back. She wore no makeup – perhaps she never did. He'd estimate her white shirt to be at least two sizes too big, and it was a man's cut. Another choice to hide herself? Or to keep her husband close? Her black trousers were nothing out of the ordinary, and her matt DMs looked comfortable, practical, and smart.

The start of their working relationship had developed his appreciation for straight talk, however uncomfortable. He felt a bit wrong-footed that she hadn't reacted to his being honest with her, but he didn't know if or how to ask about it further.

He moved to his desk and said good morning. There was a long pause before she muttered a response. She hadn't blinked, staring at that board.

He looked at it. The Drowned Man and the Naked Lady. The board was divided into two: on one side, pictures of Raymond Bevan and the listed details of his death. Names and avenues of interest filled up the space. On the other side was the name Jane Doe, with pictures of the empty skull and the two evidence bags from Tom. Nothing else. Madoc saw two stories, two lost souls who needed help. Their tales needed telling.

He noted the serious expression on Ruth's face. What did she see?

"Palmer," Ruth didn't even look away from the boards. "Ali called. She went through Dwayne's apartment yesterday."

An unenviable job.

"Found trophies. Unmatched stuff. Go down, match 'em. After the briefing. I'll check mispers for our Naked Lady."

Her voice was distant, like she wasn't even there. And she was giving him the active task rather than the boring trawl. She didn't treat him the way he was used to. But the point of the job change was to gain his sergeant's stripes, take on more responsibility. It was good but left him curious. He heard someone else come into the room. As he moved to speak to Ruth, Jackson tapped him on the upper arm, and his head motion pulled Madoc away from his desk, out of Ruth's earshot.

"That's full-on thinking mode." Jackson kept his voice low. "She sort of goes … somewhere else when she's like that. If she talks to you, great. Otherwise, it's best to leave her alone."

"Okay," Madoc whispered. It was odd to be on the other side of someone else's going somewhere. "Thanks for the heads-up."

Jackson frowned, glanced between Ruth and Madoc. There was definitely something there. Jackson was worried.

They all worry about her. She worries about them. It's part of being the team they are.

For a tough woman, she certainly brought out men's protective instincts, including his own.

"Everything okay between you two?" Jackson asked.

Madoc nodded. "Yeah. Why? Has Ruth indicated otherwise?" Paranoia had to be pushed down. He needed this job to work. Desperately. For himself, his ambitions. For Osian. But if Ruth told others his truth, how would things be then?

Snowflake.

Jackson shook his head, thankfully.

See? It's all teamwork here.

When Jackson moved to his desk, Madoc returned to his own, to the ever-present admin. Ruth had her hands steepled and at her face, her thumbs under her chin and her nose resting on her index and middle fingers. 'Somewhere else' seemed to have her in its grip. He wondered again who the voice in his head was, but again, got no answer when he asked.

The slap as her hands hit her thighs as she turned to face her desk, and therefore him, made him jump.

"Yesterday."

He froze and looked at her. "Yeees?"

Her eyes, those concentric rings of brown and green looked at him with the full keenness of her intellect. "You had a gut feeling that the timings were off."

"I did," he admitted. He still thought there was something wrong; he just couldn't figure out what. "I've gone over it twice, and it all worked out. Roughly."

"Then why does it still feel wrong?"

Good to know they were attuned on that. Maybe, if she trusted her instincts, she would trust his. "Someone's lying?"

Her hand waved that aside. "Someone's always lying. To the point where I assume everyone's always lying."

"Occupational hazard?"

"Actually, I had that one before I joined the police." Sadness touched her tone. She glanced from the things on her desk to the board and shook her head with a sigh. "This is going to bug me all day."

The morning briefing was clear and concise. Madoc was starting to like Geraint's style. What he didn't like was the distance Ruth seemed away from him today. She was upset. Had he done something wrong? Nope, he was sure she'd tell him if he had. Only she wasn't looking either him or Geraint in the eye. Then Superintendent Vaughan stepped in unannounced.

"Forgive the interruption. This is important."

As they stood together, Madoc heard Ruth swallow.

"Something rather unprecedented has occurred."

The entire room stood or sat in rapt attention.

"I have received a telephone call from Richard Steele. He called me to tell me that information he provided on Tuesday was incorrect."

Mutters and looks of disbelief ran around the group.

"Apparently, he was mistaken in raising a complaint against a member of this team, and apologised profusely for any difficulty his misinformation may have caused."

"Apologised?" Geraint sat down in disbelief. "Tricky Dicky actually apologised?"

Vaughan was nearly smiling. "Profusely." Now the Super turned to Ruth. "I have no idea how you caused this miraculous turnabout, but I've spoken to Professional Standards, and they are happy to close the case, given that they didn't believe it anyway."

Ruth was white when Madoc turned to her. She was focused on Vaughan. "Good. Great. Thank you, sir."

Vaughan nodded and turned to leave. "There are doughnuts in the kitchen area, I suggest getting to them quick before other gannets finish them off."

The hush in the room turned to a muttering in the Super's wake.

"Go on, then, go get the good stuff," Geraint said.

Most rushed out, but Madoc was too worried about the lack of reaction from Ruth.

"You two, too." Geraint was standing now.

Ruth sagged and released a big breath. Madoc noticed she still wasn't looking at their DCI.

"Ruth?"

"I can't … I mean … I …"

"Yeah," Geraint agreed. "I think we're all a little in shock."

"It is shocking," Madoc said. "Steele doesn't seem the apologetic type."

"No," Ruth said at last. "Still, there are doughnuts."

Madoc smiled at her. "Doughnuts are always welcome."

Ruth stood, and he followed. "Wait till Geraint brings in Liz's Welsh cakes, they're to die for!" They were all walking back to their desks, but Geraint took Ruth by the arm and gently pulled her into his office. It was only segregated by windowed partitions, so Madoc easily saw the odd look Ruth threw in his direction after a question from Geraint.

What were they saying? Would she tell all? *Please, Ruth, don't tell him.* Worrying as it was, Madoc had a job to do.

Geraint closing the door wasn't a good sign. If this was anything but private, he'd have spoken to her in the main office. Ruth felt her stomach spasm.

"Is there a problem, Geraint?" Ruth asked, hearing the worry in her own tone.

"Take a seat."

That was a 'yes', then. At his repeated indication, she sat.

"What's got you all withdrawn this morning?"

She couldn't help frowning. "Am I? Sorry, didn't notice."

"Ruth."

Of course, he knew her too well to let it go. "Motherhood. This case. Lots of stuff."

"That lacks a certain specificity."

She looked away. She could tell him the truth, the symptoms, but until she got an actual answer, she didn't feel she could. Of course, she couldn't get an answer without seeing a doctor.

"Is it Palmer?" Geraint asked.

She glanced out to the office, where the man in question was gathering what he needed to go to the lab. Caught his eye.

The connection was like an electric jolt. Now, there was a problem. Yesterday's revelations sat congealed against her awareness. What he'd told her yesterday …

No. That wasn't for this conversation. Besides, as far as she could see, it wasn't getting in the way of the job, so she didn't need to report it. He left. She looked back to Geraint.

"No, Palmer's fine." Her reaction to him was far more questionable. Inappropriate and poor timing, too.

"Is he not working out?"

The ground before her might hide bear traps. She met Geraint's gaze squarely. He was always straight with her; she just had to be the same with him.

"It's day three, Geraint, give the guy a break."

"You've broken officers in less time."

This was, unfortunately, true. "They weren't up to the job. Palmer is. Or at least, he has been so far. You know he proved competent as a constable. He's passed all the knowledge. And, to be fair, it's day three out of the year he's got for his on-the-job sergeant training. It's a bit early to write him off. Why are you asking? You haven't with any other incomers we've had."

"Your change of demeanour."

Damn it, she didn't need this. She wanted — needed — work to be normal. She hung her head. "I'm sorry. That's just me, lots on my mind. Besides, if you were really worried about me, you'd have drawn the blinds and offered a Penderyn by now." The Penderyn in question was a local whisky she'd given him a while back that he'd never taken home.

Now Geraint looked a little uncomfortable. "I've been hearing things about the lad. Things I don't like."

Not good.

"Like what?"

"Like he's a womaniser."

That was a relief. "Well, yeah, I'd heard that before he moved up. But you picked him. How did you not hear these things before?"

Geraint sighed and looked away. "I thought they were just vicious rumours, given the source."

"A certain Cardiff DCI?" she asked.

He nodded. "Don't think she wanted him appointed."

Really not good. If Palmer hadn't got a position in the next four months, he would have lost his chance for promotion. "He wouldn't have been the first quietly blocked that way. But why are you worrying now?"

"I got a call from Diane, from the Heath. Said that he was commenting on your …" He stumbled over the word and vaguely gestured with his hand towards her.

"Breasts? Tits? Boobies? There are lots of words for them Geraint, and I'm sure you've used most at one point or another," she said. "Probably copped a feel at a good few in your time, too."

"Only Liz's." Geraint had the good grace to flush but kept eye contact. "Well, since I met her, anyway. But that's not the point. His commenting on your breasts is inappropriate."

Her own feelings about her breasts had moved beyond indifferent acceptance when she'd found the lump two weeks ago. She really should see a doctor. But she couldn't discuss it. With anyone. "It was neither meant nor taken maliciously. Besides, it wasn't actually Palmer who made the comment. It was Tom, and you know his schoolyard humour. But that can't be all that prompted this conversation. What else?"

His smile was grudging admiration. "Ash tells me John Harris reported an exchange with Alison Caterham."

Ruth frowned. "Well, yeah, but it was nothing more than banter. Palmer just gave as good as he got. And I can't think of anything I've seen between Palmer and any of the uniform girls to give Ash any concern. Except that Bethan was up here ogling Palmer's arse when he was wearing jeans. But that's Bethan's issue, not Palmer's. Doreen became all coquettish when Palmer smiled a greeting, but again, Doreen's fault, not Palmer's. From what I've seen, if anyone has a right to complain about sexual harassment, it would be Palmer."

Geraint leant forward. "So, he's not put a foot wrong with you?"

Ruth rolled her eyes, almost wishing Palmer would. She told herself to get a grip. She tried not to think how she could do with getting a grip on a man, too.

"If you think he's that stupid, why did you agree to take him on?"

"Should I take that as a 'no'?"

She pulled in a breath to push down her rising irritation. "Palmer's not put a foot wrong, no. In fact, I haven't seen anything of the reputation that preceded him. He's intelligent and capable, he's also proved surprising considerate."

"Like when he got between you and Dwayne?"

"Yeah," she agreed. "Dwayne would have flattened me. Palmer kept him controlled."

"Palmer wasn't being sexist?"

"I would have said he recognised that as a taller, stronger individual he was better suited to the fight than I was."

"And that's it?"

"Yes." Ruth forced her bunching muscles to relax. She was stressed enough; she couldn't take much more. "Look, Geraint, I've treated Palmer exactly as I have the others, in as much as you can ever treat different people the same. He knows about Paul because of the grapevine. I admitted having a son."

"But not details?"

She shook her head. If she told Palmer that truth, she might just slip up and tell it all: admit to the irritation in her left breast that caused stomach acid to churn. "Point is, I'm not sure what your concern is. Palmer's been fine around me. Schoolboy humour is how Tom deals with what he does. It kind of helps me, too. Palmer joining in was fine. They got short shrift all the same, mind. Did Diane tell you I threatened to bludgeon them both to death? No? Well, there you go. So, here's the deal. If I have any issue with Palmer's behaviour or if he fails to do his job, then you'll be the first to know. Okay?"

Geraint nodded. "Okay."

"Then are you going to tell me what's really got you rattled? Because nothing you've said so far explains it."

"And nothing you've said so far explains your lack of reaction to Vaughan's announcement."

"I'm tired. Didn't sleep well last night. Zach's acting out, I'm …" No, mustn't say it. "I'm worried. About him. I can't …"

"Not having had kids myself, I can only sympathise. I can, however, tell you that, from what I understand, every parent goes through this at some point."

"All kids have to grow up," she admitted. "And you sidestepped the issue. What's eating you, Geraint?"

He licked his lips. "Phone call from Moira Williams."

Ruth hung her head, took a breath to steady herself. Moira was Sian's mother, and Sian Williams was an emotive topic. It highlighted how unsafe any woman could be. That turned Geraint ever more protective of her. That, in turn, had made him question Palmer's behaviour. But now the older issue was in the open, she had to face it. However painful.

"Any change?"

Geraint shook his head. "That was Moira's question, too."

Ruth scrubbed her face with her hands. "I haven't given up on the case. I will get the bastard who attacked her."

Chapter 13

The room was five feet square and contained one table and one chair. A hard plastic chair. Five minutes and Madoc was already uncomfortable. He faced a box of evidence bags from Dwayne Evans' house. This would not be a joyous task. He set up the laptop, found Wi-Fi, used VPN, and got into the police system. A few logins later and he was ready to search for unsolved rapes and sexual assaults.

As required with evidence, he was mindful of potential contamination, so as well as leaving things in their evidence bags, he pulled on latex gloves. Even as he filled out the evidence chain paperwork.

The stench registered as he pulled the box towards him. This wasn't about smell, though that was there, too. The vile nature of the man had imbued everything he touched with the reek of depravity. Madoc started the extremely unpleasant task.

He checked every item against the manifest as he pulled each bag from the box. Trawling through a rapist's trophies was not Madoc's idea of fun, but it was possible that something here could link Dwayne to another case and help close another woman's darkest hour. If that were possible.

He laid the items before him. Eclectic and grim. He started with the last item on the manifest: pink lace panties, size 28. It was obvious, even through the evidence bag, that these had had an owner - one who clearly wasn't Dwayne, or very good at wiping. A search only returned one potential match – something to move forward.

Taking each item, working through the manifest one line at a time, and returning each evidence bag as he finished with it, he worked through the items, noting any potential connections. There weren't many. Sometimes his gifts could help, but not always. At least so far, they hadn't been a hindrance.

The next item was a business card. He looked it over. Nothing obviously special about it, though it resonated with importance, and he'd learnt to trust such feelings. The only likely prints on it would be the card owner's and Dwayne's. The card advertised Queen Ree and a website address that told him exactly what kind of kingdom she ruled. Madoc noted it and suggested getting the tech guys to check Dwayne's internet use.

He focused on the next evidence bag. Thank God they were all bagged. He felt dirty just looking at this stuff; touching it would be gross. He'd walked into brothels and crack dens that were less objectionable than Dwayne's home. Remembering rolling in that muck to save Ruth made him want to go scrub down again. A ridiculous feeling, but one he couldn't push away.

"Having fun there?"

Madoc shifted to face the woman who now stood in the doorway. Today Ali Cat was ginger. She'd done something with her makeup, some eyeliner effect that added to the fangs to give a very soft feline effect.

"Hi Ali," he said as he slipped the evidence bag back into the box. "How do you get your hair to be such different colours so quickly?"

"Food colouring on bleach."

"Oh." Not what he'd expected.

"Also, non-permanent, non-chemical dyes. Less harmful chemicals, anyway, no ammonia. Except the bleach, that's never good for the environment."

Not really the discussion he'd expected or wanted. "Okay. What can I do for you?"

"Well," she said, as she closed the door and moved closer to run her hand up his arm. "It's more what I can do for you."

Her tone and actions made her intent clear. There was something uniquely unsexy about overtly sexual come-ons.

"No offence, Ali. You're a lovely girl and all, but you know." He held up his hand and pointed to his wedding ring.

"I heard that doesn't stop you."

His smile broadened. "I suspect you have, and if you want to add to those rumours, go ahead. Doesn't make them true."

"Oh." Ali slumped back to prop herself against the table. "Is it me? Something I did?"

"Someone else."

Go on, admit who. Dare ya.

Madoc pushed the voice away and sat back. "My wife."

"Oh."

Yeah, okay, she has kind of scarred you for life.

"And it's me," Madoc said. "Ali, you're attractive and smart. Why you feel the need to throw yourself at me, I'm not sure. I'm also not looking for extramarital encounters right now, let alone anything more … complicated."

"Well, I wasn't offering strings."

He smiled at that. "Great. Then when I am looking for sex without strings, I'll call you."

Unexpectedly swift, she offered him a card. "Make sure you do."

With a laugh, he took the card and slipped it into his jacket pocket.

"But I can't just duck straight back out. I've got a reputation to uphold."

His eyebrow rose as he looked at her. "Ali Cat by name, alley cat by nature?"

Her smile exposed the veneer fangs. "Something like that."

"You shouldn't belittle yourself so. You know how gossipy the Valleys are. You're worth more than that, and you should know it. Make other people know it. Still, if you tell the world I'm one more conquest, I've no objection. But in the meantime, you can help me with this lot." He nodded to the box.

"What about your reputation?"

"That's all it is," he pointed out. "I know the truth."

"You must have a very understanding wife," Ali said. "So, how can I help?"

"You can start by pulling up this website." He passed her the business card as he reached for the next item on the manifest.

She moved to the nearby thin client terminal and logged in. Her fingers flew over the keyboard and the website loaded as he studied a lock of hair. There was only one way to get a decent DNA sample from hair.

"Damn. No follicle."

Ali glanced at him. "We don't actually need one these days. Latest DNA tests can get a reading from the hair itself. Add it to the list of things you want us to do." She looked back at the screen. "Loaded."

At Ali's announcement, Madoc looked at the screen. What he wasn't expecting was the buxom black-haired beauty on screen. "Who's she?"

Ali looked at him. "That's your Queen Ree."

"Oh. Right."

"What were you expecting?"

He frowned. "Not sure. Dwayne's got a rap sheet as long as your arm for sexual assault, and he doesn't seem to have a type, but for some reason, I expected a blonde."

"Breathing and female," Ali said. "That's his type, and with the latest case, breathing is questionable."

"Nice," Madoc said. "Any chance of a cuppa? Two sugars, please."

It was a relief that Madoc had gone before Ruth left Geraint's office. She had lots to think about. She'd put Madoc's reputation to the back of her mind. She didn't need that rearing its head now. The Sian thing didn't help. Nor did her own head screaming about the Big C – a Pandora's Box never to be opened lightly.

She sighed, slumped at her desk, put her head in her hands. She closed her eyes and controlled her breathing. *The Drowned Man and the Naked Lady. Focus on them, focus on the problems you can solve.*

"Can't be that bad, can it?" Mike asked. She heard him sit in the chair at the desk beside her.

"Yep." She wasn't ready to open her eyes just yet. "What can I do for you?" she asked on the next out breath. Only then did she open her eyes and give him her attention.

"It's what I've done for you. Two things, neither of them great news. Sid had a chat with that Mrs Martin. You were right, she is a curtain twitcher, but she saw nothing useful, and there's no evidence Pippa Bevan left the house to follow Raymond to the site."

"Not great, but kind of what I expected. What was the second thing?"

"The Prices."

She didn't suppress a groan.

"Barry and Arwel," he said, naming the two brothers. "Like I said, they were in Merthyr on Monday night."

Only they'd previously discounted the men. If Mike was here, he had something new to worry about. She so didn't need another possibility to sift through.

"They came over for a mate's birthday bash," Mike said. "They were at a private function until after midnight in the Gwesty Keen – you know, the hotel in town?"

She nodded.

"They booked a taxi home but weren't there when it arrived."

That wasn't good news. "Please tell me Barry and Arwel are both alive and accounted for. Two dead bodies to start the month are quite enough."

Emotions warred on Mike's face, but finally he grinned. "Yeah, they're both safe and well."

Her eyes narrowed. "You were considering telling me otherwise then, weren't you?"

"Considering it, yeah, but like you said, two corpses are enough. I don't deserve to be the third." His grin made his eyes shine. "Barry and Arwel remember being at the hotel until about one in the morning, but remember nothing before about six Tuesday morning, when the newsagent whose door front they'd collapsed against opened up."

"At six? That sounds late for a newsagent. What about his morning delivery?"

"Goes to a back entrance. CCTV being checked now to see if we can confirm their movements."

Atkins nodded. "Okay. Anything else that could indicate their involvement?"

Mike shook his head. "But our friends in Gwent are keeping an eye on them and looking out for the stolen goods. Where's boy wonder?"

"Treforest. Well, Treforest Industrial Estate. He's gone down to go through Dwayne's trophies. See if that can tell us anything more."

"Rather him than me."

"Why do you think I sent Palmer? Meanwhile, I'm going to trawl missing persons for any likely Naked Lady candidates."

"Oh, didn't I tell you? I've already got Karen trawling for those. She's found about twenty possibilities and was still going when I last spoke to her."

"I'll come across and see if I can't help whittle that down."

Eventually, they worked it down to eight likely subjects, then Karen did the leg work to fetch the paperwork. Ruth had received six files. After the relatively recent relocation to these purpose-built premises, that was a good hit rate. It proved most files were in accessible order, and the others might take a little longer, but Ruth had the computer records, that was enough for now. At her desk, she read through the details, mapping with red spots where the girls had lived, where they were last seen, and where the people that reported them missing lived, then and now. Once done, it looked like Merthyr had measles.

Two images filled the monitor. Six others were spread in two rows on her desk. Eight blonde women – well, six natural blondes and two bleach addicts. Two mentions of hair extensions, one of breast enlargements. Such details were often not mentioned, because no one expects to have to identify a body from non-organic remains years after a disappearance.

Lesley Grant – Extensions

Diane Davies – Neither

Jane Madson – Neither

Katy Nightingale – Extensions

Seren Rosser – Neither

Amanda "Mandy" Stanford – Implants

Belinda Taylor – Neither listed but judging by the photo, boobs enough to float the wreck of the Titanic

Mair Thorne – Neither

These girls ranged from sixteen to twenty-four at time of disappearance. *Just kids.* That thought made Ruth feel incredibly old. She ran her hands over her face. What would she do if her Zach went missing? Tear up South Wales and probably do no good. Drive him further away, most likely. Some discord was inevitable, but please God, the worst never happened. Current troubles were growing pains. The pain growing in her breast was ignored.

Ruth heard the door open. She looked up to watch Palmer coming across the office. He looked less comfortable with the world than he had that morning. He was also carrying a thin folder.

"Palmer! Get in here."

Geraint's shout made Ruth jump and killed her greeting. She turned to see Geraint in his office door, lips crushed in an angry white line. Raging eyes turned on her.

"You, too."

Obedience was the only option. "What did you do?" she hissed to Palmer as he neared her.

"My job."

Together, they stepped into Geraint's office and faced the man. He was so agitated he couldn't even sit. Ruth carefully closed the door.

"Geraint?" she prompted when the set jaw and compressed lips didn't move. She was glad the fury in those eyes, the drawn-together caterpillar brows, were focused on Palmer.

When his gaze switched to her, Ruth's flinch was unavoidable.

"I just had a very uncomfortable conversation with Jacqueline Thomas."

That explained the poor temper. Talking to Jacqueline – 'no, you can't call me Jacky' – Thomas was usually a total pain in the backside.

"Did you send him down to the lab alone to go through the Dwayne Evans evidence?"

She frowned slightly, not sure where this was going. "I did."

"Why?"

Her spine stiffened. "Because trophies from Evans' other victims had to be checked against any outstanding cases. I sent Palmer to do those checks."

"Why on his own?"

"Because I was trawling records looking for our Naked Lady. Evidence checks are a fairly standard job for a sergeant. Besides, he's a big boy—" Geraint reared at the phrase. "—he can cope."

"Yes, I hear he *is* a big boy. According to Mrs Thomas, she overheard two colleagues talking about it. Saying that DS Palmer here is a very big boy. And was having sexual congress with one of those women! In the office."

She tamped down the instant reaction to defend him, recognising that she didn't know him well, and she'd already defended him once today. Something she didn't doubt Geraint also recalled.

"Ali?" Ruth demanded.

Geraint nodded.

She pulled her mobile from her pocket, called up a number and dialled.

"What are you up to?"

She looked at Geraint, threw a scowl at Palmer, then returned to her boss as the phone rang on. "Evidence gathering." She waited another moment and heard the overly cheerful greeting. "Ali, how are things?"

"Good, why?"

"Did you have an exciting morning?"

There was a pause on the line. "What have you heard?"

"What have you said?"

"I might have said Palmer was a big boy."

Ruth tried not to grind her teeth. "Really?"

"Well, he is very tall."

She glanced across, judged how far up she had to look. "Possibly over six foot. What else did you say?"

"Oh, erm, you're not sounding even vaguely amused."

"I am not finding anything about this even vaguely amusing. What have you done?"

Ali sighed. "Oh, crap. I was bragging to Sharon." The more serious tone proved Ali was getting the point. The next was mumbled. "She's been in my face about her fella for a while and I wanted a little payback. It wasn't serious, Madoc said he didn't mind what I said."

Tension in her jaw and head was vice-like. The rise of her temper had to be battled down.

"What exactly *did* you say?"

"Wasn't all that much, really, just hints and implications. You know, just … stuff. I didn't actually say we'd had sex, but I didn't deny it, either. It really wasn't anything much, and it's not like anything actually happened."

"You sure about that?"

"Absolutely." The dejection was clear. "Madoc made it clear he's not interested. And I only told Sharon, I swear."

"Problem is, Jacqueline overheard and called Geraint." The expletives were colourful and heartfelt. "The story got here before Palmer."

"Oh, shit. I'm really sorry. I'll call Geraint, apologise. Tell him nothing happened. Tell Palmer I'm sorry, too. Didn't think it would go like that."

"I'll talk to Geraint, but you'd damn well better clear it up at your end. And next time, try a little discretion, eh?" She ended the call, and glared up at first Palmer, then Geraint, though she tried to tone down the glare.

"Apparently, Ali made some implications to irritate Sharon. I'm guessing that's Sharon Willis, who has been nothing but a right cow to all unmarried women since she got engaged. Ali says that while nothing actually happened, pretty boy Palmer here was prat enough to tell her she could tell anyone anything she liked."

Ruth judged the overall annoyance level in the room hadn't lessened, simply transferred from Geraint to her. Now they both turned to Palmer. His jaw was clenched, and the high colour in his cheeks suggested he wasn't unaffected.

"I did my job and did not act inappropriately towards any female."

"And we all know that truth and rumour don't necessarily match," Geraint snapped. "You really were a prat to let Ali say whatever she wanted. That one's got a hell of a reputation, and yours isn't much better." Geraint turned to Ruth. "I'll keep him off report, but you'd better make sure Ali does her part, too. And from now on, you don't let him *anywhere* where there's a chance of him being on his own with any female member of staff, or suspect, or witness, understand?"

The problem was fairly obvious. "When you say any—"

He leant forward, virtually growling. "I mean any."

"Oh, do I not count?"

"Of course not!"

Ruth reared. "Well, thank you!" Storming out of the boss's office really wasn't the done thing and was especially not a good example for Palmer right now. "So, if there's nothing more, sir, we'll get out of your hair."

She moved to the door.

"Ruth, I didn't mean it like that."

"Of course you bloody did!"

Chapter 14

If Ruth was trying for a calm exit, she missed by a mile. Anger thrummed from her. Noting Geraint still had his head hung, and having nothing he could usefully say, Madoc followed his DI.

"Ruth?" Palmer said softly.

"Not. A. Word." She threw the growl over her shoulder as she slung herself into the chair.

He'd really messed up this time. He had to make this right. How? He stopped beside her desk, desperate to re-establish their connection. Words escaped him as she worked on her computer, each key stroke heavier than necessary.

"I-"

"Look," she grated. "Learn what's good for you right now and shut up."

Rage boiled in her eyes. He'd rarely seen anyone so angry. He felt the pain behind the rage. For Geraint's comment to hurt that much, there had to be more to their relationship.

"I'll tell you when you're safe to speak. Understand?"

Judging from his scant experience, she meant that. For now, he'd have to suck it up, despite his resentment. She stood up, switching off the computer. Tension showed in her posture. She was trying to keep boiling emotions from exploding out. He hoped her home life allowed her an outlet. Storing up that much angst could get toxic.

She pulled on her oversized leather jacket, gathered up the files from her desk and stepped forward. "Follow me." With only a momentary pause by the printer, she led him down to the car park.

The car she headed for was a black Lexus, the one she'd taken the boots from on Tuesday. This must be her car. A very swanky car for a DI's salary; had her husband's death left her that well set up? Ruth unlocked the car remotely, got in. Only when he was in the passenger seat beside her, pulling on his seat belt, did she dump her files on his lap with his own. The car interior was grey leather, the dash and steering wheel covered with all the toys. Very plush. He had the luxury of ample leg room, which was a bonus given his height. The engine purred with quiet power. She pulled out competently and safely, which was a definite bonus given her obvious temper. He wasn't sure where they were going and didn't want to be the target she loosed that temper on.

She drove up to Penydarren and pulled into a side road, where she parked and turned off the engine. Hands on the wheel, she stared straight ahead. "You're safe to speak now."

He looked at her white-knuckled grip. "You sure?"

She released her grip and stretched out her fingers. Two knuckles cracked.

"Are you pissed off with me, Ali, or Geraint?"

"Yes."

The snap wasn't helpful. He watched her close her eyes. For a second, she hung her head. He knew she was struggling emotionally. Not good. He and Geraint had both spoken thoughtlessly, but damn Ali and her motormouth.

Ruth drew in a deep breath, forcing herself upright. She expelled the lungful carefully, her tension flowing out with the air to dissipate. Only when done did she look at him again. "Right. You can start with your version of what happened."

"I looked through the items collected from Dwayne's house and tried to match them with open cases. Ali came in, made a proposition which I refused. But yes, I did tell her she could say what she wanted. It never occurred to me it would go straight to Geraint's ears."

She sighed. "Even if it hadn't got to Geraint that quick, it would have got to him. Look, you came up here preceded by a reputation, one I've ignored because I've seen no evidence of you womanising. And I don't want to see any. Get it?"

As Geraint had said, truth and rumour weren't always the same. What she was really doing was telling him she didn't want him messing around in the station, with anyone, including her. "Got it."

"Good. Your private life is your business, don't make me make it mine. And yes, I am aware how unfriendly that sounds, and it's not meant to be. I just prefer not to hear about the bed-hopping that happens."

Again, he nodded. She called it as she saw it. "Can I risk a question that might verge on the personal?"

Her eyes narrowed as she scrutinised him. "You still agree I can hit you if it's too personal?"

That brought a wry smile. "Sure."

"Okay then."

"Why did what Geraint said hurt you so much? He didn't mean it the way it came out."

Those eyes swung away from him, but not before he caught another glimpse of the vulnerable girl inside her. She hung her head in silence again. There was more to her relationship with Geraint than the professional, but how personal did it get? How was he supposed to break down this new barrier? "You're considering hitting me right now, aren't you?"

Finally, a small smile appeared on her lips. "A little, but probably not for the reasons you think."

"You don't know what I think."

"True." She nodded but struggled to face him.

This made little sense. She told him not to have a relationship in the station, but had she had one with Geraint?

The way she swallowed suggested a lump in her throat.

"Can't be that difficult, surely?"

"Can."

He saw it was. What could make relationships so problematic for her?

She sighed. "Look, I'm not comfortable talking about my private life, but this you probably do need to know. Most know it anyway. I met Geraint when I was twenty, a well-wet-behind-the-ears constable. Met Pete the same time, too. I was brought into CID because I had a vague connection with someone they were investigating. Someone who wouldn't know I was a police officer. The case was satisfactorily closed, and Geraint made sure I stayed in CID as we were then. Geraint's seen me through all the roughest moments of my career, and life since. In many ways, he's more a dad to me than my own father. So, for him to say something that negates me, hurts. Like hell. That probably sounds stupid."

"It really doesn't. It explains a lot." A father-daughter relationship made so much more sense than a questionable affair. "Thank you for being honest. But why didn't you just ask me what happened? Why phone Ali?"

"Because that girl's a gob-almighty. And she's still young enough not to comprehend how dangerous her loose lips can be. If I screamed and swore down the line at her, I'd be in line for a slap on the wrist. If I dressed you down in front of Geraint, there's a risk of a real reprimand. For both of us. I had to get the information direct from source to ensure that it wasn't coloured by worries of job security. Besides—"

The way she cut herself off told him he wouldn't like what he was about to hear. "Besides?"

Betrayal flashed momentarily in her eyes. "I trusted you," she said. "Then it looked like you'd let me down and I didn't want to deal with you while that disappointed."

He hadn't meant to let her down. At least her disappointment confirmed their working connection, so it wasn't all bad.

She took another breath. "Now, you came back with a file, so show me how little right I have to be disappointed in you."

From the driver's seat, she watched Palmer pick the file he'd been carrying since returning. They should have done this at the station, but after what had happened, they couldn't have stayed. The car was as good as anywhere, it wasn't like there were any pedestrians on the street. He opened it to show five printed pages, photocopies of things he expected to identify a victim by. Details, at this point, weren't important, so he flicked through them.

"Necklace, a lock of hair, a calling card, panties, and a dress ring." He closed the folder again. "Ali agreed to check the necklace, hair, panties, and ring for DNA. The hair and panties shouldn't prove problematic in that regard, but the jewellery might. Ali was more hopeful on the necklace but warned that there's a good chance that, if Dwayne was playing with his trophies, he's effectively obliterated any usable trace of the original owner."

"Let's hope this all pans out. That's possibly five cases sorted." Ruth nodded. "What's the calling card?"

"It's for a cam-girl service. Lush Ladies generally, and a Queen Ree in particular."

Now, Ruth was frowning, confused rather than annoyed. "We know Dwayne uses that kind of site. So what?"

The way Palmer drew his lips together and didn't quite meet her eye worried her. New teams were always an adjustment, but that adjustment would be difficult given the constant impression that he was withholding on her.

He shrugged. "It just seemed important."

She frowned at him. "Gut instinct?"

"Err, yeah."

Did that mean it was more his… other instincts? She wasn't ready to deal with that yet. "Okay," she said. "The other files are the missing women who meet the criteria Tom gave us.

Or mostly, anyway." It was possible to just reach out and take the files, but that might mean touching his thigh and some things were just too close to the surface right now. She couldn't afford another mistake for a good-looking man. Thankfully, Palmer opened the top file.

"Diane Davies," Ruth said. "Nineteen when last seen six years ago."

His eyes scanned the file. "Neither hair extensions, nor implants mentioned."

"No," she agreed. "The search didn't return any cases reporting both."

He turned to the next file.

"Lesley Grant, twenty-three when she went missing seven years ago." Ruth said. "Hair extensions under the bleach, so I thought her a likely candidate."

He moved to the next file.

"Mair Thorne. Went missing age nineteen, fifteen years ago."

When he didn't move on, but continued to study the photo, Ruth looked at him. A handsome profile even when frowning. It was obvious why women threw themselves at him; she was working hard not to. She glanced at his left hand. That helped. "Another instinct?"

He didn't stop frowning. "Not really."

"Oh," Ruth said. "Still, next one."

"No, wait."

He passed her the folder, Mair's photograph uppermost. "Look at that."

She did so, though she saw nothing new. This time, he found the folder he'd brought from the lab and withdraw the image of the necklace from Dwayne's trophy collections to hold beside Mair's photograph - in which she was wearing a necklace. Ruth's eyes switched between the two. They were very similar.

"What do you think?" he asked.

She wasn't sure. "I think this is a distinct possibility, and it needs following up. But the pictures are taken at different angles, leaving room for uncertainty. I'd want to see the necklace itself, maybe show it to Mair's parents. We need certainty."

"Now you sound like Daf."

She smiled at Palmer. "Daf's good, and rarely wrong." She folded the file shut again. "Right, we'll follow up on the necklace before we speak to the Thorne family. In that lot, we also have Seren Rosser and Katy Nightingale. Katy is listed as having extensions, but Seren neither."

He looked through the last three files, then picked out one. "I think we should start with this one." He said it with a surprisingly dark conviction.

Ruth read the file. "Seren Rosser, aged twenty-two when she disappeared. Listed as neither having hair extensions nor breast implants. Though the photos suggest both are possible." The photos were a posed headshot and a supposedly candid full body image, which was far too primped and preened to *be* candid. "Why her?"

When he didn't answer, she scowled at him. "Palmer?"

"Gut instinct."

That again. She wasn't ready to ask if this was another Biddy Small case. "Okay, well, gut instinct can be valuable, but right now we're going to see Amanda Stanford's folks."

"Why her?" Palmer asked as he looked for her file.

"Because," Ruth explained as he scanned the details, "Mandy's file says hair extensions, and she's got the kind of perky chest in that picture that suggests push-up bra at minimum, boob job possible. And I worked out the best route to take to visit five of the families. And we're parked three doors down from where the Stanfords now live."

Palmer nodded and smiled. "All particularly good reasons to look at that case first. One question: why are there only five families on your route?"

"The Rossers are divorced, they were before Seren disappeared. Mr Rosser moved to Spain to shack up with an Iberian goddess before the signatures were dry, and I don't fancy a trip to Cardiff to see Mrs Rosser this afternoon. Jane Madson was an orphan, no family to visit. And Belinda Taylor disappeared while staying with her boyfriend, and he's not left a forwarding address, but her family lives in Bangor. I'll get North Wales Police to liaise with them if necessary. So, we'll visit the Stanfords now, 'cause we're here, then cut the others, go back to the labs in Treforest, which is at least a little closer than Cardiff, though the A470'll be a 'mare on the way back. There, we'll see if we can sort out anything about the necklace. Then we'll go ask that scroat Dwayne about Mair, in case he can tell us what happened to her. By the time that's all done, the day'll probably be over, and we've an action plan ready for tomorrow to see the four families we cut – though, given your instinct, maybe I'll redo the route to start with Mrs Rosser."

Madoc blinked at her.

She grinned. "Want me to go over it again?"

"No, sir. It was just the most concise and decisive action plan I've heard thrown together in two seconds. Ever."

"I'll take that as a compliment."

Palmer smile back. "It was meant as one. I'll just have to make sure I listen to every word or there's a good chance I'll miss something vital."

"If it's vital, do you think I'd let you miss it?"

Chapter 15

The Stanfords visit achieved precisely nothing, except to rake up memories best left alone. Mr Stanford hadn't been at home, and his wife had indicated that the call would have severely upset him. Ruth didn't mention the skeleton they'd found. She didn't have to, given the news reports, but she left a card in case the Stanfords needed to get in touch.

"Want me to drive to Treforest?" Madoc asked as they approached the car.

"Want you to, yes," Ruth said, pulling the keys from her pocket. "But this is my car and you're not insured to drive it, so practically, no. I'll get that sorted at some point."

They got in the car and she started the engine, but paused to switch on her phone's Bluetooth. Then she was pulling out of the tight terrace.

"Phone."

Madoc reached for his, then realised she was talking to the car. It beeped in response, a computerised voice asked who she would like to call. "CSI Dave." As the voice said it was calling CSI Dave, Ruth glanced at Madoc. The question must have been plastered on his face. "Damn thing can't cope with Dafydd Pugh, so I found a name it could deal with."

He kept his laugh small and quiet as Daf answered.

"Hi Daf, it's Ruth. I'm on my way down. Palmer found something of potential interest relating to the Dwayne Evans case. Are Ali, Sharon, and Jacqueline still in?"

"They are, and they're all acting odd. I was about to call them in and read them the riot act."

"Put it off till I get there, would you? I've a line or two I'd like to add."

"What's going on, Ruth?"

Ruth looked grim. "I'll explain when I get there. See you in twenty." She pressed a button on the steering wheel to end the call.

Madoc's heart sank. This would not be fun. When her phone rang a few minutes later, Ruth answered with a button on the wheel.

"Hey, Ruth," Mike Bates's voice came through. "Just a heads up, the forklift stolen from the Heolgerrig building site has turned up. It was abandoned over by Bute Town."

Ruth groaned. "Well, I suppose at least that's in Gwent's area. Who was liaising with them?"

"Cathy Davies. Geraint thought she could do with liaison experience that doesn't involve a trip to the morgue."

It was gentle, as rebukes went. Ruth's grip on the wheel tightened. Given the day she was having, Madoc doubted she needed another prod.

"Good idea," Ruth said neutrally. "Cathy's good. The more experience she can get the better. Is this linked to the Prices at all?"

"Not clear, as yet. It's on neighbouring land to theirs. Could be something or nothing."

"True," Ruth agreed.

"Cathy's primed to check it, though."

"Great. Thanks, Mike. Well, since you seem to have that under control, could you have a look at something else for me?"

"If I can," the disembodied voice said.

"I think we're pretty much up on timings for keeping Dwayne Evans in holding. Thing is, Madoc's found some stuff in his trophies that I want to ask Dwayne Evans about – relates to the Mair Thorne case. Can you see if you can get me an extension for questioning before he gets transferred?"

"We're a bit tight for that, but I'll give it a shot. What do you need? Six, twelve, or another twenty-four?"

Ruth considered it. "I can do it in six if I absolutely have to, but I'd prefer ten. He's not getting bail, anyway, is he?"

"No. Magistrate flipped at that suggestion. No, he'll either be here or prison. But I'll get you at least ten."

"You really think the stuff I've found can be useful?" Madoc asked after the call ended.

"Of course."

That was a relief. Having his work respected was a welcome change. He really had been under Mannford too long.

The labs were just off the A470 at Caerphilly. There were similar industrial estates everywhere, anonymous, lacking in soul, and woefully short of parking spaces.

The building they entered didn't look any different from the rest, but inside was. The entry was like most, a reception before you could get through to the main building. Jacqueline Thomas looked up from the reception desk and Ruth wondered where the receptionist was. The office manager scowled at Palmer the second she saw him. "I don't think he should be here."

"Tough," Ruth responded and focused on Daf as he came through the connecting door.

"Hi, Ruth, have you both signed in?"

As they did so, Daf was very clear with Jacqueline that she was to fetch someone else to cover the front desk and join them in the boardroom as a matter of urgency.

Jacqueline disappeared into the main building.

"How bad is this going to be?" Daf asked, holding the office door for them.

"I'm going to tear them off a strip. What you do after that is up to you," Ruth said softly as she headed through, thanking Daf for holding the door and heading for the boardroom. This time, Madoc had a chance to look around, seeing the outer door to the clean rooms and labs, the lockers and lab coats. He wouldn't ever see more than that because he didn't need to and couldn't risk contaminating evidence. That was a world he didn't inhabit and didn't want to. This open office area was for report writing and general admin.

"Ali, Sharon," Daf called the women's attention. "Boardroom. Now."

The boardroom was another smallish office with an oval table and six chairs, which didn't live up to its title. Daf walked to the head of the table, pulled himself up to his full five-foot-three and crossed his arms. Ruth, too, moved behind the table so she could face the others coming in. Madoc stood beside her. The three women entered, shrouded in uncertainty. Jacqueline scowled at Palmer, Sharon sneered, and Ali was too embarrassed to look at anyone.

"Right, who wants to start?" Daf asked.

Apparently, no one. Silence strained everyone in the room. Ruth took a deep breath, deliberately audible, and fixed her gaze on Ali. The younger woman shifted her weight then faced Daf.

"I may have inferred to Sharon that something happened between me and Madoc when he was here earlier." Her voice was a flood of regret. "Though I didn't actually state that anything happened." She added. "I didn't say it *didn't*, either." Ali hung her head. "Sorry."

Sharon folded her arms and tipped up her chin. "Well, I did nothing wrong. Ali's the liar."

"I didn't actually lie."

No one responded.

"Well, I certainly didn't," Jacqueline asserted. "I only reported what they represented to me."

"No one actually *represented* anything to you though, did they?" Ali said.

Jacqueline crossed her arms and looked away.

"I see," Daf said. Then he turned to Ruth. "Anything you'd like to add, Ruth?"

Ruth was looking at the other three women like she might rip their heads off. They would not get away lightly. "I cannot believe—" She enunciated each word with the careful restraint indicative of barely controlled rage. "—how incredibly stupid three supposedly intelligent women can be. It's difficult enough to get a half-decent DS. Now there's a risk I could lose him because a gob-almighty, a braggart, and a gossip don't know when to stop flapping their gums."

Sharon, who had been smiling and lording it over the other two, turned to Ruth, her face falling. "I haven't done anything."

Ruth pinned the younger woman with the kind of steely gaze a drill sergeant would quake beneath. "You are, in fact, the root cause of all this. For the last four months you've done nothing but rag on every unmarried woman in the room. You go on and on about your fiancé like he's God's gift. He may be, but that's no reason to make other women feel bad for not having the same. It was inevitable that someone would try to get their own back. I, for one, do not think it's fair that right now the one person paying for all this nonsense is Palmer, the one person who is not to blame."

The weight of that claim hung in the air.

An unintelligible huff came from across the way, and Ruth focused on Jacqueline. "Oh, don't you play holier than thou with me, madam," Ruth told the older woman. "You took a half-heard innuendo and tried to destroy a career with it."

"The problem," Daf said quietly, drawing all attention to him, "is that our jobs are not just about science, they are about evidence gathering. The touchy nature of the legal process means that just about anything can become prejudicial. I can't afford to run a business where the people who use our services can't trust us to keep their information confidential."

He looked at each of his employees in turn. Eventually, each looked away, realising the trouble they were in.

"The three of you are a disappointment," Daf said. "Now, get out of here. Take the rest of the day off to think about the damage you could have done. I don't want any of you back in here till morning."

The trio bristled, suddenly worried about their jobs.

"Go on," Daf said. "Get out."

They did.

The silence in their wake was worrying. This all seemed a touch heavy-handed to Madoc.

"What are you going to do?" Ruth asked softly.

Daf shrugged. "Depends how much contrition I see tomorrow."

"None of them deserves to lose their job over this."

Madoc was glad Ruth's statement echoed his own feelings.

Daf glanced out through the transparent partition to see Ali, last to leave, look back, nearly in tears. Madoc's heart went out to the poor girl.

"Don't worry," Daf said at last. "I won't sack any of them. They're all too good at what they do. My worry is that this is hardly the first such incident and I'm sick of the sniping. With luck, this'll teach them all a lesson." He looked up at Madoc, then back at Ruth. "How much trouble did it cause your end?"

"Thankfully, very little. As long as Jacqueline doesn't complain to anyone else, Geraint should be able to keep it under wraps. Or at least, unofficial."

Daf nodded. "Good." He turned his attention to his last remaining visible staff member, who looked rather confused about the mass exodus. Daf signalled him forward and Chris brought the Dwayne Evans box. "You said you wanted something from this?"

"Thanks," Ruth said and nodded Madoc forward.

"You get dirty yet?"

Jackson's question caught Madoc off guard when he answered his mobile. He would have to put up with this for a while yet. "No, nor will I, just for you to make a profit."

"Oh, good, I make more if you don't shower. Well, technically the Police Benevolent Fund does. All proceeds go to them. Anyway, is there a problem with Ruth's phone?"

That threw him. "No, but it hasn't rung, and she's driving."

Ruth glanced at the phone in the cradle. "Sorry, it's on silent and not Bluetoothed."

"Hear that?" Madoc asked. Jackson had. "What do you need to tell her?"

"We've had a call from Dowlais Scrap Metal. They've been offered the type of copper piping stolen from Heolgerrig."

Madoc relayed the information.

"Who?" Ruth asked as she negotiated traffic.

"Do we have a name on the sellers?" Madoc clarified.

"The Jameses."

"Jameses," Madoc told Ruth.

She frowned across at him. "Alan and …?"

Madoc played go-between to get the answer. "Timmy."

"Jesus, he's just a kid."

"Jackson says they've got a warrant, going to arrest them now. Do you want an interview?"

Ruth's eyes narrowed as she studied the road and considered the idea. "Yes."

"Yes."

Jackson clicked the phone off.

Chapter 16

Ruth rushed into the station, worrying whether Mike had got that extension or not. She reached the MCIT area to find Pete there, chatting with Mike. Thankfully, Geraint wasn't around – his earlier comment still rankled. She wasn't sure how to deal with it, with him. She was already feeling less than a woman without additional evidence.

"Hey," she breathed.

"Did you just run up the stairs?" Pete asked.

"Pretty much."

"Well, sit down," Mike said. "I got the extension for Dwayne. We were just talking about how to approach the Jameses' interviews."

As she grabbed the chair from Jackson's desk and sat down, Ruth was aware that Pete looked behind her and motioned wordlessly for Madoc to join them.

"Where's Geraint?"

"Meeting with brass. You just missed him."

"Shame," Ruth lied and ignored the look Mike and Pete exchanged.

"First off, given the timings involved," Mike said, "you two need to sort out Dwayne first."

Ruth nodded. Madoc stood at the periphery of her eyeline, which suited her fine.

"Jackson can lead with Alan and then you—" His look switched to Ruth. "—can lead with Timmy."

"Sorry about that," Jackson said as he re-joined them. "What did I miss?"

Jackson pushed Ruth back down when she shifted to give him his seat and he perched instead on his desk as Pete repeated and continued. "Alan's asked for a duty solicitor, who has yet to arrive, but Timmy's waived the right. However, Dwayne's solicitor, Jacobs, has arrived, and he looks bloody knackered." He fixed on Ruth. "You may be able to take advantage of that."

"Probably won't need to," Ruth said. "Dwayne's not got the sense to be a 'no comment' man. Anyone got anything useful on Timmy?"

Jackson picked up a file. "He's fourteen, been cautioned twice, linked to several minor offences, but nothing proven. He's definitely a chip off the old block from Alan."

Ruth nodded. "Right, well, let me deal with scumbag number one, then if you get anything from Alan that I can use against Timmy, let me know."

There was something incredibly degenerate about the way Dwayne looked at her that made Ruth want to punch the man. That hateful, base presumption that a man had the right to force his desires on a woman, or indeed another man, made her sick.

She and Madoc sat across from Dwayne and the disinterested duty solicitor, or more likely the knackered-and-desperate-to-go-home-not-paid-enough-for-this-shite duty solicitor, Adam Jacobs. Jacobs had been called out at two o'clock that morning for a domestic abuser. They all knew that Dwayne was about to spend a long time in prison for what he'd done in Geddings' home. Now, they just had to find out about Mair Thorne.

All formalities observed, Ruth was hopeful of gaining a confession. She reached under the open top the file before Palmer and slipped out the clear evidence bag containing the necklace they'd collected from the lab. She slipped it across the table. For the benefit of the tape, Madoc reported that DI Atkins was showing the suspect the evidence, with its official number and description.

"Never seen it before," Dwayne said after barely a glance.

"It was found in your house."

He shrugged. "Maybe a girlfriend left it."

Ruth raised her eyebrows. "Dwayne, no woman's voluntarily set foot in your house since the housing association moved you there."

"You did."

"To arrest you," Ruth pointed out. "Tell me about the necklace."

"Nothing to tell." He wouldn't meet her eye.

"How did it get into your house?"

"Dunno."

She sighed and glanced at Jacobs. "Mr Evans, by stating that you don't know how this necklace got into your home, you are denying responsibility. If we later prove that you *do* know how this necklace came into your possession, then we will have proven you a liar, and that will not look good in court. Do you understand, Mr Evans?"

"S'pose."

Ruth just about controlled the urge to roll her eyes. She paused for a beat. "Mr Evans, how did this necklace come to be in your home?"

He glared belligerently at her. "You planted it under my mattress."

She wouldn't touch his mattress if her life depended on it. To be fair, her life – or at least, her health – probably depended on *not* touching his mattress. Her good peripheral vision also reassured her that Madoc hadn't notably reacted to Evans' obvious slip, and neither had the solicitor.

"Why do you think it was under the mattress?"

Dwayne's eyes darted around. "You said."

"No," Madoc said lightly, "we didn't."

"Sergeant Palmer, I believe you have the forensics report there. Can you confirm where the necklace was found in Mr Evans' house?"

He made a careful production of opening the file and dragging his finger down the page. "Ah, here we are. Necklace, silver-coloured metal, dove-shaped," he read out. "Retrieved from the only bedroom, under the mattress in a cutaway space in the divan."

"Since you knew before I did where this necklace was, shall we try this again?" Ruth asked. "How did the necklace come into your possession, Dwayne?"

"No comment."

That was the first sign of intelligence so far. "Why keep it in your bed?"

"No comment."

This was going to get elongated if she didn't do something about it, and she wanted to get home at a decent hour tonight. She'd promised Zach. Still, this wasn't the first time Ruth had had the misfortune to deal with Dwayne, and she'd accidentally discovered a way to loosen his tongue.

"Where did you get the necklace, Dwayne?" As she asked, she stood.

"Going somewhere, Inspector?" the solicitor asked.

"Nah, just going to boil if I don't take this jacket off," she said. It was warm in the room, mostly because she'd considered this tactic and told the station manager to increase the temperature – not wildly, just enough to be classed as warm. She was a little too aware that Palmer was watching as she took off the heavy leather jacket. She didn't have to jut out her chest to focus attention. Her chest jutted on its own, minimiser bra notwithstanding. Dwayne's interest was totally expected. Casually, she dropped the jacket on her chair back and sat down, adjusting her shirt collar to fall forward a little more. She sat just as she had before. "You didn't answer the question, Dwayne. Where did you get the necklace?"

"Dunno," he sneered, then folded his arms and sat back.

She sighed and crossed her arms, leaning back in a mirroring action. "Why keep it under your bed?"

Dwayne shrugged and looked away.

Time to use the big guns. Arms still crossed, ache in left breast ignored, Ruth leant forwards, elbows on the table, shoulders up, well aware that this pushed her breasts up and forward. Just as she was aware only a hint of cleavage could show under her boat neck blouse. No one could accuse her of entrapment. But Dwayne didn't need much. His eyes fell on her chest, brightened, and his hands disappeared under the table. She refused to think why.

"Why'd you keep the necklace, Dwayne?"

"Cuz." He was virtually drooling, eyes fixed and glazing.

"Come on, Dwayne, I'm interested. Where'd you get the necklace?"

"Dunno."

His hand moved more than Ruth wanted. She sighed and sat back; he stilled and whimpered at losing the view. "If you want to keep me interested, Dwayne, you'll have to give me more than that. I'm only interested in the truth."

He looked sullen. "Got it off some bird."

"Some bird?" Ruth asked and took a photo from the folder, placed it before Dwayne and sat forward again, her arms crossed. "This bird?"

"DI Atkins is showing Mr Evans a photograph of Mair Thorne."

Was that accusation in Palmer's tone? Or her own paranoia?

"Oh, yeah." The breathy response could have been for the way Dwayne looked at Mair or Ruth, it was hard to tell.

"Take a long look, Mr Evans," Ruth said neutrally, normally. "Take a long, hard look." His arm was moving again. "Do you recognise this woman?" She tapped the photo.

Dwayne looked down. "Oh, yeah, I shagged that. Squealed like a pig, that one."

Disgust churned Ruth's stomach. "Dwayne, are you telling me that you recognise this young lady and that you had consensual sex with her?"

"Nah." His breath rasped. "I held her down and fucked her. Tight and dry she was. Ugh," he struggled to breathe.

The duty solicitor shifted uncomfortably.

"Hurt her bad I di-urgh!"

"Mr Evans!" Jacobs said, standing.

Ruth sat back, took a disgusted breath, smelling the additional salty mess in the room. "Please sit down, Mr Jacobs. I believe Mr Evans has more to tell us."

"I believe Mr Evans needs a moment."

She believed he'd just had one, but saying so wouldn't help and would get caught on tape. "Mr Jacobs, sit down and do your job, let me do mine." The man sat. She focused on Dwayne. "Dwayne, do you remember meeting this young lady?"

Dwayne slumped back now, a beatific smile on his face. "No lady, that one. Dressed like a slut. Skirt to her arse and boobs pushed up. Not much tit, but enough. Acted like a virgin and screamed and screamed. She was right tasty."

"When and where, Dwayne?"

"Years ago. She was on a bus. We got off together."

Together or at the same time? Ruth would check on that later, but while he was in this talkative mood, she would make the most of it. "Got off where?"

"Thomastown."

Mair had lived in Thomastown. "Then what?"

"Took her into the bushes, shagged her. That necklace came off in my hand. I like things coming off in my hand." Dwayne laughed at his own joke.

No one else did.

"When I was done, she ran off. Kept looking over her shoulder, so I chased her. Just to scare her some."

Ruth felt sick. The poor girl. "Where did you chase her to?"

Dwayne shrugged. "Dun't matter."

"Yes, Dwayne, it does matter," Ruth sighed. "It matters because this young lady has disappeared. You might be the last person to have seen her alive."

"I fucked her; I didn't kill her."

"You raped her, Dwayne. Just like you raped the others before her, like Jodie Carter, Tracey Connelly. And then there's the girl you killed in Geddings' place. It's not a big stretch to conclude that you might have killed before. It would be easy to frame that argument for a jury. You'd be facing two murder charges, then. Is that what you want? Double the time in jail?"

"I didn't touch her." He flicked the picture back towards Ruth.

She stopped it flying off the table and turned it back to Dwayne. "You just said you raped her."

"Yeah, well, sex is sex, innit? I didn't kill her. She run off."

"Her name was Mair." The use of past tense bothered Ruth. There was always a good chance that someone missing for any length of time was dead, but she tried not to think that way until she had some evidence of it. But there again, Dwayne may just have given her the evidence she needed. "Mair Thorne. She was nineteen years old. And you raped her."

Dwayne just looked at Ruth. The afterglow had subsided. Now he just looked belligerent. "I'll fucking rape you."

Ruth didn't react. "Where did you chase her to?"

"Dunno, she ran across the road."

Ruth was familiar with Thomastown. When she'd first joined the police in the area, she'd made it her business to explore all areas of Merthyr Tydfil. To memorise the geography. Even the areas she wouldn't want to venture into otherwise. Though Thomastown wasn't the worst area. "Away from the rec rather than through it?"

Dwayne shrugged again. "Probably."

"Yes or no, Dwayne. Which is it?"

He thought about it. "Yes."

"Did you see where she went?"

"Nah."

"What happened to her, Dwayne?"

He shrugged. "Dunno. She ran across the road. Scrambled over the fence and up the rise. I couldn't be bothered anymore. I just went home."

"You went home?"

"Where else did you expect me to go?"

"Well, that was disgusting," Madoc said as they climbed the stairs to the office.

"Yeah, I feel like I need to scour my skin," Ruth agreed. "Wire wool and bleach." She'd pulled her jacket on as soon as they'd finished the interview. She shrugged into it, shoulders up and forward as if to hide inside it. Suddenly, she stopped and turned around to face him. "You are talking about Dwayne, right?"

Because she was two steps above him, he had to look a little way up. "Of course." That didn't appear to give her any relief. "Technically, I don't think anyone can say anything about what you did. Other than you played him like a fiddle."

"Yeah." Her curled top lip suggested that she wasn't impressed with herself. "I've known Dwayne too long. He makes me sick, but I know how to push his buttons. And we did get a full confession to another rape. If CPS will accept it is another matter. Right now, I just want to go home and scrub myself till there's nothing left. Guess if you play in the sewer, you end up stinking like shit."

Madoc caught her elbow as she turned away, pulled her attention back to him. "Before, you suggested using me as eye-candy, but that's what you did to yourself."

If she was trying to frame a response, she failed.

"You did nothing wrong, Ruth. You didn't break any standard of behaviour. So, you shouldn't feel bad. Like you said, you got another confession, that takes us closer to finding out what really happened to Mair and our Naked Lady."

She smiled. "Thank you, but it's not great to know that I just used—" She glanced down. "—my God-given gifts to trip a man into committing an act of self-satisfaction that fried his brain enough to confess to rape. It makes me feel as degenerate as him. And I'm guessing that you can't have enjoyed the experience much either."

"Not really," he admitted. "Never been in the room with another man while he … sorted himself out before. Not pleasant."

"No."

"Surprised Jacobs didn't stop him."

"I'm not. Jacobs has been on call for the last three nights and he's been called in on every one. I doubt he's had more than two hours kip a night. Besides, he's represented Dwayne before. And even the defender of lost causes will realise there's no winning with some people."

Chapter 17

Ten minutes later, Ruth and Palmer were back in the interview room opposite Timmy James, who had refused a solicitor. Clarence Scott from Social Services had been provided as an appropriate adult. Jackson and whoever he'd found to sit in with him were still with Alan James, Timmy's father. Looking across at the spotty teenager, Ruth figured that with a father like Alan, who spent as much time inside as out, Timmy really didn't stand much chance in life.

Palmer had recited the protocol for the tapes and now Ruth looked at Timmy.

"Timmy, how old are you?"

For a second, he just glowered. "Old enough."

"Old enough for what?" Ruth asked evenly.

"For a good shag. Want one old lady?"

Ruth just watched him. Timmy lost a certain amount of his bravado. "Do you see that?" She pointed over her shoulder to the dark round lens. She watched as Timmy looked directly at the camera.

"So?"

"So, everything you say and do is being recorded. If necessary, it can be played back for the court. Do you understand that?"

Timmy shrugged. "So?"

"So, you're fourteen. In this country you are considered at the age of criminal responsibility from ten years old. That means you are responsible for your actions. And, perversely, still too young for a legal shag. Now, your father is currently in another interview room with a duty solicitor. Are you sure you don't want legal representation?"

"Don't need no brief." Timmy sat back, looked sideways at Scott. "Nor no babysitter."

"Mr Scott is here as your necessary appropriate adult."

"What if I say he's not appropriate?"

"Why would you say that?"

"I reckon my dad's the real appropriate adult." Timmy's lip curled.

Ruth took a calming breath. "Not in a case where the parent in question is potentially involved in the acts to be discussed under caution. So, if you don't agree to Mr Scott as an appropriate adult, we could return you to the cells and lock you up for a few more hours while another appropriate adult – one who isn't your father – can be called. Which probably won't be till morning. Of course, if you're thinking about using up the twenty-four hours holding time you think I'm restricted to, please be aware that your efforts to delay the process only increase the likelihood of my being able to get a judge to sign off on a holding extension, especially when I put the case to the judge that this isn't just a robbery, but also a murder."

Timmy's sneer slid off his face. His eyes widened until the frown clamped them down. "We robbed the site. Didn't kill no one."

"That's good to hear, but we have to go through this step by step. Why don't you start with what you did early Tuesday morning?"

Timmy looked at Mr Scott.

"Go on, Timmy. The more honest you are, the better it will be for you."

Timmy said nothing.

"Your loyalty is commendable," Ruth said. "Thing is, I've questioned your father before, and in all cases his tactic has been to show contrition and give up his accomplices quick. He thinks that's the best way to get a reduced sentence."

Timmy looked at her, eyes uncertain. Then he looked at Scott.

"All I can advise you is tell the truth or say 'no comment'."

Ruth allowed that to sink in. Timmy bit his lip. This was, impressively, Timmy's first time in a police interview, and the kid clearly wasn't sure what to do. She let him stew.

"Timmy, Mr Scott, I'm sorry, I need a moment here. Interview suspended at—" She checked her watch. "—16:38."

Palmer switched off the tape.

"If you gentlemen wouldn't mind waiting here a few minutes, I won't be long."

An hour later, Timmy, having sung for his supper, was back in the custody suite, and Jackson was grilling Alan James with the facts Timmy had shared.

"That was a good tactic, delaying like that," Palmer said as they headed back to the office.

Ruth grinned up at him. "Wasn't a tactic, I needed a pee. Though it gave Timmy time to consider his options. He caved quick enough when I got back."

"Aside from the delay, I think you tipped him over the edge when you reassured him that his dad 'would be so proud his little boy turned into some hard man's bitch inside'. The kid went white."

"Yeah, feel a bit guilty about that. But I figured an image of what he might have to fear might help loosen his tongue."

"It worked."

"True. Shame he didn't know anything about either the Prices or the Flacks."

"I think he knew something about the Flacks."

"Yeah, well, pretty much every criminal in Merthyr area knows something about the Flacks. Even if it's just 'don't bloody mess with them'. So, get the tape to the incident room, one of the reader receivers can deal with it as an action tomorrow." She checked her watch; they were well past clocking off time. "Once you've done that, nothing stopping you heading home for the night. I'm going to check my inbox, then clock off. See you tomorrow."

Chapter 18

"I hate you!"

Zach's bedroom door slammed in Ruth's face. She staggered back. It hadn't been a physical blow, except to the door frame, but it felt like it. To have her only child declare such hate with such venom was too much. She could cope with any scumbag in work, but couldn't handle her own child? What was wrong with her?

You're a failure as a mother, that's what's wrong with you.

As she staggered to her own bedroom, Ruth controlled the sob, tried to ignore the critical inner voice that told her the things guaranteed to hurt her most. The bath was a necessity, she stank and felt disgusting after the day she'd had.

She set the bath running and sat on its edge, letting tears fall and wondering what she could possibly do to make things right. Then she heard a tentative knock on her bedroom door.

"Mum?"

She smiled at the fact that her son, like her, used the anglicised pronunciation. She stood and wiped her eyes, going to the door to open it and see her son, already taller than her, looking shame faced.

"I didn't mean it." Clearly, he'd been crying, too. "I don't hate you."

"Oh, love." She reached up and pulled him into a big hug. "I know that, sweetheart." But hearing it still hurt. She guided him into the room, and they sat together on the edge of the bed. Paul would have hated that when a perfectly good chaise lounge sat by the window.

"It's just that all the other boys are playing games."

She nodded. Peer pressure. Oh boy, did she remember how difficult that could get. "I know."

"I can't just completely stop playing."

"I don't want you to completely stop playing." This was the part of the argument that was difficult to make him see. "God, I've spent enough on those consoles and games for you, I'd feel really pissed off if you never played them. All I'm asking you to do is de-prioritise them and do your homework first. I'm your mother, it's my job to try to bring you up right, and make sure you get a good education. I can't stand by and do nothing while your work slips because you're spending too much time playing games."

"But I beat Jeong Chan yesterday."

He could be talking a different language for all she understood. "I have no idea who that is, but I'm guessing you consider that an achievement?"

"Jeong Chan is from Korea. He's a player."

Did that have a different meaning in teenage linguistics?

"He won a million dollars at last year's *Call of Duty* playoffs."

Her jaw dropped. "There are playoffs where you can win serious money at this stuff?"

"Yeah. Esports, world champs, loads of them."

"Oh. Did not know that."

He grinned, very much like his father in that moment. "So, you'll let me play?"

"I told you, I'm not trying to stop you playing. I'm only asking you to do your homework first."

His shoulders fell and he rolled his eyes.

"It's important, Zach. You need to do well in your exams next year, so you can go on to A-levels and then uni."

"What if I don't want to go to uni? Father didn't."

The instant red mist got pushed away. "Do you really want to model your life on a man who thinks the pinnacle of sophistication is pouring a can of Tennent's Extra into a glass before parking his butt in front of a 60-inch TV to watch women's beach volleyball?"

Zach shook his head. Even he saw the pitfalls of his father's lifestyle. Ruth still struggled to believe that she'd slept with him. She blamed youth, inexperience, and whoever spiked the bloody punch. Which was probably the scuzzball himself.

"You didn't get a degree, either," Zach argued.

There was an indisputable truth.

"No, I didn't. Because I didn't have a choice. Hold on, I've got to go turn off the taps." She did, and she was glad to see Zach still waiting when she turned back. "Zach, you're not stupid. You know I'm thirty-one years old and you're fifteen. You therefore know that I had you when I was sixteen. And when you look at where our birthdays are, you don't have to be a genius to figure out I was fifteen when I got pregnant." These were facts she'd never hidden from him. Just from other people. "Uni wasn't an option for me. That's what I want for you. The option to do what you want, to study what and where you want. We have this wonderful, comfortable home because of Paul, and your dad did study. He got not only a degree, but two, plus a Master's and a PhD. He worked hard, he grafted to build his business, and he was real generous to bring us into his life and share all of this with us. I am grateful every day for Paul and what he's given us. If it weren't for him, you might have grown up in a one-room squat with a drawer for a cot, and that's assuming Social Services didn't take you away from me." She moved up and hugged her son. She'd fight to the death to make sure no one ever did that. It was a big part of the reason she'd accepted Paul's proposal. "Seriously, Zach. I just want to see you reach the full potential your dad and I see in you. Paul and I only want the best for you, whatever your father says."

She was so glad that Zach understood that while scuzzball Darren Jones was his biological father, Paul Atkins had always been his real dad.

"Mum?"

"Zach."

"I know I was a mistake—"

She pushed him up to look at her. "You were never that!"

"You can't say I was planned!"

"Well, no."

"You do love me, though, don't you? You don't wish you'd never had me?"

"Oh, Zach!" Her heart could break just hearing that question. "I love you more than I'll ever have words to tell you, and I always will."

"Even when I'm being a bastard about games."

She half laughed to see the cheeky grin growing on his face. That was definitely more her than either his father or dad. "Well, you should very glad that, thanks to your dad, you're not, technically, a bastard because you were born in wedlock, but you need to remember this if nothing else: I'll always love you. And always means always."

She pulled him into a fierce hug, a tactile attempt to make him understand.

"Mum?" His voice was muffled in her shoulder.

"Yes, love?"

"You stink." He pulled back. "Go have a bath."

She laughed as he left, carefully closing the door behind him. In the bathroom, she turned the hot tap back on, then after emptying her pockets on the side, she stripped, her clothes going straight into the laundry basket. The mirror over the sink told its own story. Dark smudges underlined her eyes. Then she raised her arm, twisting to see the lump on her breast. If anything, it looked bigger, redder. She put her arm down.

Always means always.

If she wanted to be around for always for Zach, she had to get that seen to.

Stepping into the bath, she still hoped and prayed that it really wasn't anything to worry about, but that didn't stop her worrying.

Okay, if worst came to worst, and it was cancer, it wasn't a death sentence. She might have to have a mastectomy. Possibly a double mastectomy. To be fair, that might be a good idea anyway, she was getting a bad back with the weight. She'd be fine. She just had to get it checked out.

The phone ringing made her jump, splashing water over the side of the bath. She recognised the ring tone: Geraint calling from his home phone. But she couldn't deal with him, not tonight. She'd been through the emotional wringer too much today.

Madoc looked around the conversion, feeling satisfied. He had running water in the bathroom, which amounted to a flushing toilet and a standpipe, but at least he wouldn't have to go to his parents to wash anymore. The electrician had been in during the day and completed all the basic wiring, so now he just had to get all the drywall and plastering done before they came back to do the final finish. He had no idea how long that would take.

To the faint accompaniment of the generator in the storeroom behind the thick stone wall, and in the harsh glare of the site lights, he changed from day clothes to a boiler suit. He wanted to get the walls up in what would be the bathroom. Once he had a fully functional bathroom, he'd get to the kitchen, and the rest would be relatively simple. He'd done the stud frame wall, the services were in, so what he had to do now was install the drywall and insulation. The headache started as he began measuring up. He could hardly see before he got to the drywall, and that was not a good sign. He didn't want wavy walls.

He sat on the closed toilet lid and looked around. It was tiny. The en suite in the house he'd shared with Julia was bigger than this, but at least this was his own. Looking around, he wondered yet again if there was anything he could have done differently, a way to pack more in. But the original chapel had comprised a covered porch, a small outside storeroom, and the oblong of the chapel itself. There wasn't room for more than one double bedroom and a small shower room. The cost of putting a mezzanine in had stopped the idea of a second bedroom. Something Julia was pleased about. It ensured Madoc couldn't claim full time custody of Osian. What Julia failed to see was that, as much as Madoc would love to have his son live with him, given Madoc's job it was impractical. No, he understood as well as his ex-wife that it was better for Osian to live with her. Given how much happier Julia seemed since he'd moved out, he had begun to wonder if that was what Julia had been after all along: a son without the complications of a husband.

The headache was getting worse. He closed his eyes, rested his head in his hands, and realised whose screaming he could hear. The question was, what was he going to do about it?

Phone her.

The voice was insistent, but after the day they'd had, he wasn't at all sure Ruth would appreciate a call.

With a sigh, he stood and moved to the Welsh dresser. He shifted the amethyst, unwrapped the deck, and shuffled. To call or not to call. Then he lay a card: the Eight of Wands. Beneath that, side by side, he lay the King of Swords and the Three of Swords. Well, that was fairly clear. Meanings of the Eight of Wands included fast communication. And Swords were all about the intellect and words, literately containing the word 'word'. In the first choice position to call Ruth was the King of Swords, who often represented someone stand-offish or cut off, who only wanted to work with facts. Someone very much like Ruth. The second choice, not to call her, was the Three of Swords. Not a good card, as it represented heartache. So, if he called her, he'd probably get short shrift. If he didn't, was that heartache for him or her?

He packed up the deck. Better short shrift than wondering all night.

"Hello?"

She sounded curious, didn't recognise who was calling, which seemed off. Then he remembered he hadn't had cause to call her, so she wouldn't necessarily have his number yet.

"Hi," he said. "It's Madoc."

"Oh shit, are we needed in work?"

"No, nothing like that," he assured her quickly. "You okay? You sound odd."

"Echoey?"

"Yeah."

"I'm in the bath."

He swallowed. Her naked in warm soapy water was not the image he needed in his head during this conversation.

"What's the matter, then?" she asked. "If this isn't about work, why are you calling?"

Bloody good question. Nothing for it but to be honest. "You know I said I get vibes off people?"

"Yes."

"I can hear you screaming all the way over here." There was no response. What could she say to that? What could he say? "What are you struggling with?" Still nothing. "Ruth?" She didn't answer. "Are you still there?"

"Yeah."

When she said nothing more, he asked again. "Are you okay?"

She took her time to answer. "Yeah."

"Remember how you said people always lie?"

Her huff sounded loud in his ear. "I'm not okay, but it's personal. I'll try to tone down the rage."

"It's not rage." He was sure of that. "I just want you to understand, you can talk to me if you need to."

Another long pause. "No." she said. "Sorry. I mean, thank you, but no. I don't need to talk."

A more obvious lie was unlikely. "Okay, but if you can't talk to me, talk to someone."

Still no reply. He wondered if she had anyone to talk to. Her husband was dead. Her son was a child. She seemed estranged from her family. Geraint was a substitute father, but he was also her boss, so that limited things a bit. Who did she have?

"Well, you've got my number now. Call whenever."

Silence greeted that.

"I, er, I suppose I should go."

"Yeah."

He moved the phone from his ear.

"Madoc!"

Her voice called him back. He pressed the phone back to his ear. "I'm here."

"Thanks." Her voice was tinged with tears.

She disconnected.

Chapter 19

"I'm disappointed in you."

Ruth blinked as she reached her desk the next morning and turned to see Jackson at his own. It had been a tough night – she hadn't slept – but she smiled by way of a greeting. "You're not the first person to say that, but any particular reason in this instance?"

Jackson's face split into a broad grin. "You didn't get Palmer wet yesterday. I was hoping he'd run out of clothes soon."

Ruth grinned in response. "Well, if I ever have occasion to be up in Cyfartha Park with him, I'll order him to jump in the lake. See if we can get that Colin Firth/Mr Darcy moment."

Jackson's brow rose at the idea. "Now that I'd like to see."

It was an inviting image indeed. Ruth had to push it away. "Whatever would Nigel say?"

"Phwoar?"

They both laughed at that. Jackson and his husband would both appreciate Palmer's aesthetics without ever causing the other a moment's worry. It was the kind of secure relationship everyone, no matter what their sexuality, wanted to find. In that way Jackson was the object of much envy around the station.

"Who won the bet, by the way?"

"Pete. He figured you'd give Palmer a lecture about professional standards, and he wouldn't dare do anything stupid."

Ruth frowned. "Not sure that paints me in a great light."

"Well, Doreen reckoned you'd give Palmer a lecture about professional standards, and he'd be so unnerved that he couldn't help tripping up again."

That brought out a small, self-loathing chuckle. "Not sure that paints either of us in a good light." And after yesterday's interview with Dwayne Evans, she really wasn't sure of her own professional standards - whatever Palmer said. "Besides, no lecture was given."

"What was Geraint on the warpath about yesterday?"

"What have you heard?" No one else had been here when it happened.

Jackson laughed. "Oh, don't play that game with me, Inspector. I sit your side of the table, remember?"

She did. "Just a storm in a teacup."

"Least said, soonest mended?"

She smiled. "Exactly." The smile slid off her face as her jacket slipped from her shoulders. "I think I need more coffee."

Returning with the coffee, Ruth stared at the whiteboard again, her lips compressed, eyes narrowed. She scanned the board but returned repeatedly to the picture of bones in the ground that Chris had sent. The office was filling up now. She sipped her coffee and tried to make sense of it all. Someone moved up beside her, stood at her left shoulder.

"Why weren't there any clothes?" the man said.

"Morning, Palmer," she said without looking at him. "There may have been. There are a number of ways that a woman can dress without obvious fastenings. Only they aren't often used by women with large or augmented breasts. Except that if you look at fashion pictures from back then, there were a fair few Lycra stretch dresses, which were better without undies. Only – and I'd need to check it with Daf – I think we would find Lycra fibres even after five years. My thought processes really aren't helping much this morning."

His small laugh was a low rumble at her ear. "Clearly, you know more than me about women's fashion. We'll find something that makes sense."

She hoped so. "Also depends on the material her clothes were made from. Could well have rotted away faster than normal with the petrification of decomposition." That was something unpleasant to consider. "Or," Ruth added, "she could just have been buried naked."

Madoc smiled. "Occam's Razor. In two competing theories take the one with the least assumptions. Same with the shoes."

"Not necessarily." Ruth continued looking at the board. "If she was killed elsewhere and taken to the field to be buried, then she could have lost the shoes during transfer, or the killer may have kept them as trophies. If she was killed in the field, it's possible that she kicked them off to run away from her attacker. After this amount of time, anything left topside would be long gone."

"And thus, we've no connection at all to the killer."

"Not forensically, but forensics aren't everything. Police have been catching killers without forensics for a long time." She picked up a file and handed it over. "Seren Rosser's file. I've skimmed it, but you should read it in detail before we head out."

"Ruth, I want a word with you before you go."

This wasn't the way briefings usually ended, but today's had been noticeably icier than usual.

"Sir."

Geraint refocused on Palmer as Ruth ignored the looks she got from the rest of the team as they filed out. "You can manage on your own for five minutes, can't you, lad?"

Palmer nodded and, like the others, returned to his desk. Geraint closed the door and the blinds. She and Geraint hadn't been alone since the insult had been dealt. She didn't expect this to be a fun experience. She would not be the first to speak, though, just in case.

"You didn't answer your phone when I called last night."

"I was in the bath."

"I know. I called Zach. He told me you two had an argument."

Ruth tried to shrug it off. "It happens."

"Of course, it happens. Parents always end up clashing with their kids at some point. He said it was his fault, he started it, and that you two had, in fact, made up."

"Yeah." She remained worried, though. Not sure what the next encounter would bring.

"If you, or he, needs a break, he can come stay with Liz and I for a bit."

"Thanks, sir, but I hope it won't come to that."

"Sir? You're still pissed off with me, aren't you?"

She shouldn't be. It wasn't fair. "Bit."

He smiled. "You know what you sound like, don't you?"

"Belligerent teenager?"

"Yep." He stood over her, big and imposing, arms crossed and features darkly set. "What I meant when I said you didn't count as a female was that I completely trust you. I know you won't fall for the charms of the likes of Madoc Palmer." Geraint moved over and put his arm around her shoulders, kissed her hair. "I'm actually a little worried that you've got to the stage where you'll not fall for anybody's charms."

She sighed and leant into him. "I've just been stressed lately. Paul's birthday, a call from his mum." Palmer's revelations still worried her. Then there was the other spectre she wouldn't mention. "Arguing with Zach. That kid's so wilful."

"Takes after his mother."

She laughed at that. "Did he tell you what we clashed over?"

"He did."

"Do you think I'm being unreasonable?"

"No idea. Do you think you're being unreasonable?"

"Overall, no. But you know what the incel indoctrination briefings say. It's difficult to figure out how best to handle that. I worry." And if the worst came to the worst – no! She couldn't allow herself to think that way, not yet.

"Of course, you worry. Christ, even I worry."

She sighed. "But I probably was unreasonable last night."

"You know what to do, then."

"Yeah, grovel to my own son for forgiveness."

"Can't be as awkward as a DCI grovelling for an inspector's forgiveness, trust me."

She laughed at that. "If you think that was grovelling, Geraint, you've got another think coming."

Chapter 20

"Right, Seren Rosser," Ruth said as she parallel parked in a tight space between two other cars that Madoc wouldn't have even attempted.

Madoc had read the Rosser file, concentrating on the events when Seren was last seen. On 16 May, the twenty-two-year-old was last seen by her mother, Wendy. Mother and daughter had said goodnight at 19:45, before Wendy, a nurse on night shift, left for work. Seren was due to go to Cardiff for a screen test early the following morning, leaving before Wendy was due home. Seren had left her mother a note saying next time she saw her, she'd be on her way to stardom. There wasn't much else. Several unconfirmed claims of sightings, including one of her getting into a blue car with a partial reg that was never matched. It really wasn't much.

But Madoc knew it was Seren Rosser they had found. Ruth still hadn't mentioned what he'd said of his gift, not even last night when he'd mentioned vibes. Was she just playing along, waiting for him to slip up? No. That wasn't her. He took comfort in the lack of ridicule.

Wedmore Street, Grangetown, wasn't anything special, but it wasn't bad, either. Tightly packed terrace houses that opened straight onto the street, built deep enough to be spacious inside, especially if modernised. Rather than come all this way on the off-chance, Ruth had called ahead to confirm Mrs Rosser, now a Marie Curie Nurse, would be home that morning.

Like her daughter, Wendy Rosser was a natural blonde, and naturally slim. If Wendy's thin hair was anything to go by, Seren used extensions more to plump the hair than elongate it.

They were invited into a warm, cluttered home that spoke of comfortable nights in cwtched up on the sofa with a good book or the TV on. They almost sank into the over-stuffed sofa, and Wendy looked crowded in the chair opposite, one covered with cushions and throws. She looked nervous, wide eyes verging on tears. Thin, veined hands wrung together on her lap.

"I take it this is about Seren? Have you re-opened the case?"

Ruth took the lead. "We review all unsolved cases every few years, just in case something new is spotted."

"Is this about the body found in Heolgerrig?" Wendy asked. "We lived that way. Which you probably know. Of course, you know, you—"

"Mrs Rosser?" Ruth interrupted softly.

"I'm sorry."

"No need to apologise, I just don't want us to get too far ahead of ourselves. There are many things to check first."

The air suggested that both women were carefully trying to rein themselves in and not excite skittishness in the other.

"So, do you have something new to tell me?" Wendy said. "Something good?"

The hope in her tone pulled at Madoc's gut. The worst part of unsolved crimes, especially missing persons cases, was the hope that there might still be good news, and the nagging suspicion that there couldn't be.

"Actually, at the moment, it's just more questions," Ruth said.

Mixed emotions formed an uncertain expression on Wendy's features as she invited Ruth to go on.

"Reading the notes from the original case file, I believe that the last time you saw Seren, she was heading to Cardiff for a screen test?"

Wendy confirmed it. "That was the plan. She was in the running for casting for the series *Valleys View*. It was to be a reality show, like. Young boys and girls and how they led their lives in the valleys. They seemed extremely impressed with her down there. I really thought she'd get through to selection. Would have given her career such a boost."

"I don't remember that series," Madoc said.

"I'm not surprised," Wendy said. "There was another similar thing before, *The Valleys.* It didn't get good viewing figures, so even though the first episode of *Valley View* was filmed, I don't think it ever aired, and it definitely got cancelled."

Ruth nodded. Madoc had no idea what Ruth's opinion of reality TV might be. Somehow, he doubted she'd be a devotee.

"I see," said Ruth. "But all that came later. When she prepared for the casting, she would have wanted to put her best foot forward, yes?"

"Naturally."

"Would that have included getting hair extensions?"

Wendy frowned briefly. "Yes, she had them done when the interview process started. Why?"

"It wasn't in the missing person's report," Ruth said. "Are there any other details that might have been left out?"

Wendy looked at Ruth closely. "What have you found?"

"Wendy ..." It was unlike Ruth to falter.

"You've found something. I recognise that tone. It's the tone people use when they have bad news they don't want to give a loved one. I hear it all the time with patients. They tell me what their oncologist told them, and then can't tell their family. It's that tone. You've got that tone." As she spoke, Wendy's voice grew higher pitched. Her hands were moving, covering her face, pushing back her hair, the worry paling her paper-thin skin.

"Wendy," Ruth said. "I'm sorry my tone upset you, that wasn't the intention. We haven't found anything conclusive, but there are new leads."

"Something about hair extensions?" Wendy asked. "Why ask about that? What can it possibly matter if she was wearing hair extensions when she disappeared? She wouldn't be wearing them today."

"I understand that, Wendy, but I still have to ask the questions. Did your daughter have any other work done to enhance her appearance before the show?"

The already deep frown lines on Wendy's forehead drew deeper. "Do you mean the boob job?"

"Are you telling me that Seren had had breast augmentation surgery?" Ruth asked neutrally.

Wendy confirmed it.

As awful as this potentially was, especially for Wendy Rosser, Madoc felt the thrill of confirmation. They had identified their Naked Lady. But now it was time for that most awful of jobs, telling a family member that they might have found the body of a missing loved one.

"Wendy, when you moved down here, did you bring anything of Seren's with you?"

"Everything. Why? Oh my God, you're looking for DNA evidence." Tears welled over in Wendy's eyes. "You think she's dead. She can't be dead. Not my Seren."

"I hope not, Wendy. Really, I do, but we need to prove that one way or another."

"It's her dad's fault."

As Wendy railed about Mr Rosser, Ruth looked to Madoc, mouthed the words 'family liaison' to him, then indicated the door. Stepping outside, he took a gulp of city air that reminded him why he'd transferred from Cardiff to Merthyr. He made the call.

Wendy was still ranting when he stepped back inside.

"Mutilation, that's all it was. Body mutilation."

For one horrific moment, images of violent mutilation flashed before his eyes. Then he remembered the situation and guessed Wendy was not a fan of breast augmentation.

"I understand that point of view, Wendy."

Says the woman who would never need breast enlargement.

Tell me who you are or shut up. Unexpectedly, the voice shut up.

"Do you have anything that might hold Seren's DNA? A hairbrush, or even a toothbrush?"

"I have everything upstairs."

"Would you mind getting something for us?"

Wendy nodded and disappeared from the room. Ruth looked at Madoc. "Local FLO will be with us in ten, but it can take more than that just to get from the city centre."

Ruth nodded in acknowledgement.

Ten minutes of awkward silence passed and still Wendy didn't reappear. They were both getting antsy. Ruth moved to the foot of the stairs.

"Wendy? Is everything all right up there?"

Madoc stood behind Ruth, unable to see up the stairs. He still heard the sniff.

"I'm okay." The voice and the words didn't match.

"Do you need a hand?"

Some noise was choked off. "Please."

Ruth went up the stairs and Madoc followed. The stairs twisted at the top to a landing with three doors. The middle door stood open, and inside, Wendy was crumpled on the floor, leaning against the wall, a cardboard packing box beside her.

"I didn't unpack it. I couldn't." She sniffed as she looked to Ruth. "It was hard enough packing it up."

Ruth nodded through the banister towards Wendy. "I understand. It's difficult." She went the rest of the way upstairs, but a hand flick ordered Madoc to stay back. Which was when he heard the knocking at the front door.

He didn't recognise the young woman on the doorstep, but she showed her warrant card and introduced herself as Deborah.

"DI Ruth Atkins is upstairs with Wendy Rosser. She's crying. Rosser, not—"

"Yeah, I guessed that." Deborah nodded as she stepped inside, and Madoc closed the door behind her. Deborah looked up the stairs, then looked back to him.

"Go put the kettle on. Tea really is helpful in these situations."

As Palmer drove, Ruth made her notes and spoke only to tell him go to the Heath. Ruth quit writing notes and made a phone call, asking to speak to Tom.

As ever, the hospital car park was rammed, so they had to trawl the place and wait for someone to leave. Ruth received a text as Palmer reversed into the spot.

"Hmm."

"Bad news?" Palmer asked.

"Well, it ain't good. I'll drive when we leave." Her phone beeped again. Another message. "Tom says he'll meet us in Y Gegin."

Y Gegin was Welsh for 'The Kitchen' and was the name of the recently refurbished canteen. When they reached the cafeteria, there were several tables where staff in uniform or blue scrubs sat or slumped at various stages of alertness. Even a cursory glance could correlate exhaustion with coffee mug size. Tom, in scrubs, was near the windows.

"Rabbit food? At this hour?" Ruth greeted. Tom had muesli with fruit and what Madoc assumed was yogurt. The smell of bacon hung in the air.

"I just autopsied a diabetic who died on the way into the hospital. He had a massive heart attack even as the paramedics were doing everything in their power to keep him alive. While the death certificate will state cause of death as myocardial infarction, obesity and type 2 diabetes will be stated as contributory factors. My brain is screaming that he basically ate himself to death. So, excuse me while I choose the healthy alternative."

"And now I never want to eat ever again," Ruth said as she sat down.

"You've nothing to worry about," Tom stated as he looked her over.

"What about drinking?" Palmer asked. "Either of you want a coffee?"

Tom indicated the orange juice was enough.

"Mint tea would be good." Smiling up at him was too easy, and the smile that flashed back was just too delicious.

As Madoc turned away, Ruth focused back on Tom, who was grinning around his food. Her eyes narrowed. "What?"

"You like him."

"He's a good officer."

Tom swallowed, and the grin got bigger. "You fancy him."

"He's married."

"Yeah," Tom nodded. "That is a bit of bugger. Still, you're allowed to fancy without touching."

"Gee, thanks." She smiled. "How's your love life?"

"I'm sure you could spice it up."

"Would you like to develop a contusion on your tibia?"

"Only donkeys kick shins under tables," Tom said. "Or ill-bred DIs." He grinned as he swung his legs out of reach and the table clattered at her strike.

There was something so innately youthful and fun about the serious man behind the round glasses that Ruth couldn't help grinning back at him. They'd been friends so long, it was doubtful they could really offend one another.

"So, what's up?" Tom asked.

"Maybe I just couldn't keep away from you any longer, lover."

Tom nearly choked on the husky voice, and she felt Palmer pause as he returned with the drinks. They turned to Palmer, whose smile struck Ruth as a touch uncomfortable when he placed her tea and sat with his own flat white coffee.

"Actually, I came to ask about the Naked Lady," Ruth said as she blew across the steam coming out the cup. "I forgot to ask when we were here before, and I haven't seen your official report yet."

"I have submitted it," Tom said.

"Don't get defensive, I wasn't criticising. It's just that we've been busy, and I haven't even looked for it yet. Since we were passing, I thought I'd drop in and ask you directly. Have you had time to send samples off for DNA testing yet?"

"I have."

"Great. I think we've found our girl, though." Ruth opened the file and showed Tom the Seren Rosser photographs. "What do you think? See anything there that suggests this *isn't* our Naked Lady?"

As he chewed more muesli, Tom looked over the headshot. He moved it for a better look and revealed the full portrait below. Another spoonful of muesli and he looked over the second photograph. He swallowed again and put the photographs back in the folder.

"Nothing there that would obviously rule her out, but dental records and DNA will tell you."

Ruth nodded. "As long as there's no point of exclusion, that's all I wanted to check. Thanks."

Chapter 21

Ruth turned the car into the street, carefully checking numbers and wondering what it cost to live here. The house they were looking for had a wide driveway to take at least four cars. She pulled in. The 1970s house sprawled across its self-build plot, dormer extensions and all. She cut the engine and, for a moment, they just sat looking at the building.

"And why are we here?" Palmer asked.

"Because of that text I received." Ruth said. "Ali lives here."

"Are CSIs paid more than I think?"

"Ali lives with her parents. You know what the market's like today. Getting on the property ladder's difficult."

"All too well."

She just caught Palmer's answer as she opened the car door and got out. The smooth tarmac led up to a wide front door that needed a little TLC. Ruth knocked and waited. Nothing happened. There was a bell on the side. Ruth tried that, only to be disgusted with a terrible jingle that was both unpleasantly expected and worryingly reassuring. An older woman answered.

"Mrs Caterham?"

The older, greyer version of a long-haired Ali looked at them with doubting eyes. "Yes?"

"Is Alison at home?" Ruth felt like she'd been transported back to those awkward early teenage years.

Mrs Caterham lifted her jaw a little. "She's not feeling well."

"Well, luckily, I may just have the cure. Can we come in and speak with her?"

Mrs Caterham looked between Ruth and Palmer. Looked like she would refuse.

"Let me introduce myself," Ruth said, moving to display her warrant card. "I'm Detective Inspector Ruth Atkins, this is Detective Sergeant Madoc Palmer. We need to speak with your daughter, and I don't like being made to feel like a schoolkid asking if a friend can come out to play. Besides, Ali's twenty-three and really should know better than to behave like a sulky teenager. Now, will you let us in, or do I have to go to some stupid extreme to get your daughter to buck her ideas up?"

Apparently, this mother recognised the authority of a mother more than the authority of the police. Which was just as well, given the police really didn't have authority here. Mrs Caterham stepped back. Ruth stepped in and Palmer followed.

There was something old fashioned about the decoration. It was all in good condition, but the stripped wallpaper under a dado rail and single colour – beige, not magnolia – above was all rather last century. As they followed Mrs Caterham up to the first floor, things seemed to step back another decade, despite the thick carpeting that suggested recent renewal. Then they walked up an additional staircase that was clearly an extension into the roof space. At the top, they stepped onto a small landing to face a room bearing a name plate marked 'Alison', one that might have suited a pre-teen.

"Alison, sweetheart," Mrs Caterham called through.

"Go away." The muffled voice sounded incredibly young.

Mrs Caterham tried again. "Some friends to see you."

"I don't have any friends."

Ruth looked heavenward. She didn't like stroppy teenagers when they were teenagers.

Mrs Caterham looked apologetically at Ruth.

"Let me handle this," Ruth said.

"Would you like a cup of tea?"

Ruth shook her head. "Thank you, no." She didn't want Mrs Caterham to come up again. "Just leave us to it."

Mrs Caterham nodded and left. Ruth made sure she was gone before she signalled Palmer to stay outside. Then she opened the door and walked in. A quick glance showed a hedgehog-shaped doorstop to one side. With a little effort, she pushed it into place to prop open the door. "Hiya."

"Thought Mum said a friend had come to see me."

"If I'm not a friend, what am I?" Ruth asked as she sat on the stool by the dressing table. Ali sat up on the bed, hugging a large stuffed Stitch plushy. Her hair was now a dirty-looking bleached colour. She wore no makeup, and the sparkle was absent from her eyes.

"The woman who's angry at me for nearly costing her her DS."

"That was yesterday. Besides, Madoc's still here. Well, out there." He popped his head around the door and waved. Ali just hung her head. Ruth signalled him back, and he disappeared from view. "Why aren't you in work?"

"Daf dun't want me there."

"Why'd he text me, then?"

Ali shrugged and hid her face against Stitch's oversized head.

"He's worried about you, you ninny. You didn't answer his call. He thought you might have called me if not him." Ruth took a moment to look around the room. The roof dictated the overall A-shape, but the conversion was well done, and there was none of that too-cold-in-winter, too-hot-in-summer feel about this place. Unfortunately, it looked like a teenager's room. Or maybe a tweenager's. Pink carpet, toys all over, fairy lights around the white metal bedhead. It was a wide single bed, luxury for a little girl, but not the double a grown woman might want to share with a lover. Only the DVD rack showed some adult tastes. Ruth looked at the posters on the sloped ceiling. Bands she didn't recognise and retro movie posters.

"Well, at least you're more Bela than Edward," Ruth commented.

Ali turned to her, frowning. Ruth pointed to the black and white reproduction of the 1931 *Dracula* movie poster. "Bela Lugosi, not that *Twilight* stuff."

"Dracula's a monster. He's supposed to be terrifying, not sparkly."

"Couldn't agree more. Know what else is terrifying?"

"You in a rage?"

Ruth shrugged. "Yeah, well, there is that. But it's really horrifying when you see a friend lose their sparkle."

Ali turned away.

"And bloody annoying when you see someone with talent throw it all away in a tantrum."

"I'm not in a tantrum."

"Sulk, then."

"I'm not sulking."

"Really?" Ruth said. "You're sat on your bed, in a room most teenagers would find too twee, hugging a toy from a movie that came out when you were, what, pre-school? Were you even born then?"

Ali shifted, hung her head, and set the Stitch aside.

"Right now, you should be in work, doing your job. Making a valuable contribution and being a responsible adult. Moreover, it's a job I need you to do. Couldn't have closed the Jones-Howard case without your analysis, could I?"

Ali glanced at her from under her lashes. "I can't go back after what I did."

"Why not? Jacqueline and Sharon both have."

"Well, of course they have, they didn't cause this trouble."

Ruth tutted. "Oh no you don't, you don't get to play the 'poor me' card. Yes, this is partly your fault, but it's partly theirs, too. The difference is that they are so busy telling themselves it's all your fault that they can't even comprehend their own portion of the blame. But that doesn't mean that you have to take on all of it. You don't even get to take on a full third, because Palmer has to shoulder some responsibility for telling you you could say whatever you liked. Like a prat."

"Thanks, sir."

Ruth smiled at the sardonic tone from the hall. "See? He knows he's at fault, too, but he still turned up for work. Hell, stretch it, and it's partly my fault for sending a handsome man un-forewarned into your lair."

"Lair?"

"Well, you're the one with the vampire obsession."

Ali glanced up at the posters. "Saw them when I was little. Always thought they were fascinating. Vampires. Like a medical problem to be solved. Severe anaemia or something."

"Is that where your interest in the sciences comes from?"

Ali nodded.

"Hmm. Unusual root, but okay. Look, this is bugging me, so I have to ask: when did you last decorate?"

"I never have. This was Mam's choice. It hasn't been redecorated since the conversion. The only change I've made is putting up the posters, and even they're years old."

Ruth looked at them again. They clearly were. She considered Ali, a young woman crushed by the little girl she had been at home. "You need to get back to work."

"I can't face them."

"Why not?"

"I was stupid."

"Yes, you were. But giving up the job you love because you're embarrassed would just compound the stupidity."

"I'll get another job." Ali's chin jutted with the declaration.

"Not in Wales you won't. There aren't any other criminal forensics labs here. Unless you actually come work for the Police and move to Bridgend. Otherwise, you'd have to move to England, and you've said you don't want to do that. Come on, I need you back doing your job."

That made Ali frown. "Why?"

"Why?" Ruth laughed. "Because I've got two dead bodies found in the same location, clearly dead for different reasons and at different times, so that's two killers to find and not a lot to go on. I need everything forensics can give me to build a case. Then there's the whole disgusting Dwayne Evans case to contend with. We're always pushed for budget and time, and if I don't get the forensics done, then the CPS call it circumstantial and the bad guys get away. Isn't that why you like movies like *The Fugitive* and *Hot Fuzz*?" She named two of the DVDs she'd recognised. "Because the good guys win? Hell, even in *Dracula*, Van Helsing and Quincey do what needs to be done. Good beats evil."

"Who's Quincey?" Ali asked.

That flummoxed Ruth for a second. "The American in the book that helps kill Dracula but dies. Tends to get ignored in the films. If it makes you feel any better, there was a *Quincy ME*, an America TV series about a medical examiner, but I think that makes me feel even older, and judging by the weird look you're giving me, remains beyond your age range. Which is fair. It was above mine, too. Still, my point is, you have a sense of right and wrong. Do you really think what you're doing now is the right thing?"

Ali sighed. "Is DCI Evans annoyed with me?"

"Doubt it. It was my arse got kicked, not yours. Not even Palmer's."

"Madoc wouldn't even speak when he was in the office yesterday," Ali said.

"Because I told him not to."

"And he'd rather lurk out there than step inside now."

"Because I told him to," Ruth said.

Ali frowned at her. "Why?"

"Because this is your bedroom and there enough rumours flying around already."

"Oh please, I'm not a child."

"Then stop acting like one. Go to work."

Ali's jaw dropped, but a squeak was all that came out. Ruth challenged her with a look.

"You don't give quarter, do you?" Ali grumbled.

"I don't let promising careers go to waste, either," Ruth said easily. "You're good at what you do, Ali. I see that. Daf sees that. You've got see it, too. You have the sense of humour to see you through both the sometimes-intense horror of a crime scene and the intense boredom of processing drudgery." Ruth stood. "Your choice, of course. Now, we have to go."

"Ruth!"

Ruth paused and looked back at Ali.

"Thanks."

She nodded once, then turned away. Palmer didn't say a word as he followed her back through the house.

"Is she coming down?" Mrs Caterham asked as they stepped into the foyer. "Is she going to stop acting like a child?"

"Hopefully," Ruth said. "But if you want her to stop acting like a child, stop treating her like one. Let her grow up, and for God's sake, let her redecorate that room."

Palmer followed Ruth out. Only when the door was shut did he speak.

"So, that was you not being very good with the mentoring thing, was it?"

She threw him the keys. "Shut up and drive."

Ruth directed Madoc to Thomastown, which left him feeling the fool. He was grateful that Ruth didn't imply any deficiency. For all he was Merthyr born and bred, sort of, he didn't know this area. Queen's Road was a nice, quiet suburban road with the rec ground on one side and some nice semis on the other. As they moved along, he saw the housing give way to a two-foot stone wall with rails above, and beyond that a grassed area opened up and he saw a stone circle.

"Park on the pavement by yur."

It wasn't like Ruth so sound quite so Welsh. He frowned. There were no double yellows or parking restrictions, but this didn't seem like a great place to park. Still, with flat grass beyond, he wouldn't be blocking the way.

"Don't worry, we won't be long," Ruth assured him as she stepped from the car.

He left the vehicle, making sure it locked. Like a puppy knowing no better, he trailed after Ruth to where she stopped by a lamppost.

That explained nothing. "Why here?"

"This is where the bus used to stop."

"Really?"

She smiled up at his doubt. "Yes, really. It changed a few years ago, the locals got up in arms about it. A punch-up started; three middle-aged idiots arrested. They were the armchair warrior type but that day they became street brawlers."

"You know the area well for a bluebird." It was a reference to the emblem of the Cardiff City Football Club.

"I hate football," she said.

"Clearly not enough to not know what I'm talking about."

She shrugged. "You can't hate what you don't know. And for a Merthyr boy, born and bred, you don't know this area as well as I'd expect."

"Technically, I was born and bred in Cefn Coed, I just came to Merthyr for school, and that was in Bishop Hedley, not here."

She looked surprised. "You're Roman Catholic?"

With a grin he shook his head. "My mum is. And reckoned it was the better school."

She nodded. "I'd probably agree with her, if I didn't—"

"Didn't what?"

She pulled in a breath. "Didn't hold certain prejudices about priests and choir boys. Anyway, I made it my business to learn as much about the town as I could when I started policing it. But I must admit, I checked the map for this location when I was looking through Mair's file."

"Never hurts to be prepared." He looked across at the white-painted railings in the hedge that bordered the Rec. "So, you reckon Mair Thorne got off the bus here, Dwayne Evans followed, and he dragged her in there?"

Ruth nodded. "Seems likely."

"There's not much cover."

"Dwayne's more worried about getting his rocks off than discovery or discretion. According to the file, Mair's mates said she was blasted. Mair got on the Thomastown bus while her mates all took the Dowlais bus. By the time the bus got here, it would have been dark, not that many walkers left in the park. If she was that drunk, even Dwayne, unsubtle as he is, might not have registered till too late and he wouldn't have taken long with the deed."

"But he said she screamed. Someone would have heard …" His voice trailed off as he looked around. The other side of the road and all the edge of the recreation ground. The nearest houses this side were three streetlamps away. Streetlamps were generally 30 metres apart, so that was roughly 90 metres from the gate. "No one in their homes would have heard."

"No," Ruth agreed with a sigh, then turned around. She moved to the wall.

Madoc realised it was a taller than his original assessment, three feet high, made of capping stone, and topped with a one-foot-high railing. The once-green paint had flaked away from the iron rails. "Wouldn't be any problem getting over this."

"Says the tall guy."

Sometimes he forgot things weren't as easy for shorter people. He judged Ruth against the wall. "You'd clear that easy enough."

"I'd clear it," she agreed, "but not easily. But there again, I'm wearing flat shoes and trousers, not to mention that I'm sober. Mair was drunk, wore a mini skirt, a boob tube under a chiffon blouse, and high-heeled boots. Also, she was only five-three."

Madoc nodded. "That would make things more difficult. But not impossible."

"Especially if you're trying to get away from the man who just raped you."

She nodded and looked around again. "So, why didn't Mair just run across the rec and home?" Ruth pointed back to the rec grounds. "There's a path that connects to Danyparc Road, where Mair lived. That's why she used this bus stop. Why run this way?"

"She was drunk, doubtless in shock, probably disorientated. If Dwayne was between her and home, maybe she just ran from him. Ran anywhere."

"Possible."

"What used to be up there?" Madoc tipped his head towards the rise behind the wall. There was only six-foot wire fencing up there now.

"Erm, I'm not sure. I think there was something there when I was a PC, but I can't tell you what. Not sure what it was or when it closed or when it got flattened."

"What if it were in the process of being flattened? Could Mair have got in and been crushed with the buildings?"

Ruth turned and looked up the rise with him, considering the idea. "Is that another gut instinct?"

"Just an idea."

"Hmm." She considered for a few heartbeats. "It's possible I suppose, but you'd hope someone would have spotted her remains and reported it." Only no remains had ever been found of Mair. "Someone's going to have to check out what happened to those buildings and when." She turned to face him, a grin on her face.

He knew what was coming. It was his own fault.

"Wanna guess what you're doing when we get back?"

Chapter 22

Geraint's hand clamped over Ruth's as she sat at her desk.

"Stop it."

Only then did Ruth realise she'd been tapping her fingers and, judging by the looks she was getting from Palmer and Geraint, she had been irritating them for a while.

"What's the problem?" Geraint asked.

Ruth sighed. "Too many open ends."

"Like?"

"Why didn't Seren Rosser's mispers team take a DNA sample? What really happened to Mair Thorne? How am I going to tell her parents about what Dwayne said? Why does the timeline Maggie Drake gave us feel wrong? Why does insomnia not explain Raymond Bevan being dressed at four a.m.? Why does no one from the production company of *Valleys View* seem to be around to answer questions? What the hell happened to Seren's clothes and shoes?"

"So basically, this is just the middle-of-a-case, more-questions-than-answers morass?" Geraint asked.

Ruth huffed out her frustrations. "Basically."

"So, what are you doing to find those answers?"

"I've got samples from Wendy Rosser for DNA analysis and we're matching them against the samples Tom sent the lab. Palmer's working his hypothesis for Mair. I'm prevaricating on the Thornes until I've got something decent to tell them. I'm reading and re-reading all the statements about Tuesday morning and hoping something will jump out at me. I'm intending to speak to Pippa Bevan shortly, and then catch Maggie Drake at home after work for more questions. Apparently, TV and film crews are freelance and frequently move around. Mike's emailed those we can trace from the production company, there were a couple on file. And I'm still wondering why that body was naked and shoeless."

Geraint nodded. "Sitting here doing nothing, then?"

She rolled her eyes.

"You know these things are never as straightforward as we'd like, but you are making progress."

"Not as fast as I should be. Forty-eight hours is all it usually takes to find a killer, and we're well beyond that."

"The Naked Lady was never going to be an instant closer."

"Raymond Bevan should be."

"And you've got plans to sort that. If you're going to Drake's after work, that puts you on overtime."

"If it's a problem, I won't book it."

"Don't be stupid, book it. And don't forget, you've got the backing of not only Palmer here, but the whole team, particularly Mike's team, too. Tell them specifically what hours you're looking at and see what they come up with for a timeline."

"Already have, and their answers match Palmer's."

"That's good. Now all you have to do is be the genius who sees what they've missed."

That made her smile, and she looked down at Geraint's hand still over hers. Dry and warm. He believed in her abilities, he always had. He squeezed her hand in silent support, then stood upright. "Just no more tapping."

She nodded. He left. She looked across at Palmer.

"You should have told me I was annoying you."

"Called your name twice. Geraint heard, saw you ignore me, then stopped you."

She closed her eyes. "Sorry."

"'Sokay. What were you getting stuck into?"

"The timeline." She opened her eyes. "Something is wrong with it."

"Gut instinct?"

Her eyes narrowed. "No. There's something I've heard or seen that I only registered subconsciously. It will come to me, but right now, it's just a distant nag."

This time when Ruth knocked, Pippa Bevan answered the door and let them in.

"On your own?" Ruth asked as they returned to the living room and took up much the same positions as before.

Pippa looked stronger already, less the pale grieving widow. Had that been an act for Mrs Martin?

"I'd like to go over why your husband was up at four a.m."

"I told you, he suffered with insomnia."

"I remember, Pippa. My husband suffered insomnia in the past," she lied. "But he just stayed in bed. Sometimes restlessly and he ended up waking me."

Pippa nodded. "That's why Ray started getting up. So as not to wake me. He was being thoughtful, really."

"Tidy. And what did he do when he got up?"

Pippa's gaze slipped away. She shrugged. "Read a book, watched TV."

She was lying. Ruth wasn't sure whether to call her on it. "Neither activity requires dressing."

Pippa didn't respond other than to look away.

"What was he doing Tuesday morning?"

"I don't know."

"Pippa?" If there was one thing being a mother rather than a police officer had taught her, it was how to innocently request with an undertone of accusation.

The older woman leant forward, elbows on knees, and hung her head. "I don't know what he was doing."

"Pippa." Palmer surprised Ruth by shifting to sit next to Pippa as he spoke. "If you know anything, tell us. It may help."

Pippa's face crumpled; tears flowed. "He was in his study." She leant against Palmer, her head on his chest. "On one of his girly sites." Palmer looked incredibly uncomfortable as he glanced at Ruth.

She rolled her eyes and mimed patting Pippa on the shoulder. What she saw was the least natural attempt at comfort ever.

Ruth moved over and gently pulled Pippa to sit. "Sorry, Pippa, I can't have you scaring my young DS here." That made her feel old.

The woman looked from Ruth to Palmer and back again. "Sorry, but it's almost a relief to say it. This doesn't have to come out in the investigation, does it? I can't face what the neighbours will say."

A murdered husband was okay, but not one who watched porn? Ruth wondered sometimes if she would ever understand people.

"It'll only come out if it's relevant to the investigation. But I do need to know about your husband's habits, and I will need to have his computer checked out."

"Best come upstairs, then."

Ruth frowned as the woman stood and led the way. Palmer looked for Ruth's lead, and she nodded to have him follow. Pippa led them to the second bedroom at the rear. It had a single bed, but the obvious feature of the room was its desk and computer. The shelves of files suggested Raymond worked in here. And there on the side was his Shalestone hard hat.

"This is where he used to do it."

Ruth indicated Palmer should take control of the laptop. He looked back at Ruth, his eyes wide in an expression that said the last thing he wanted to do was look at another man's porn habits. It certainly wasn't the sort of thing *she* wanted to look through. Relenting, Palmer stepped past Pippa, pulled the seat back, and opened the laptop. The screen lit up. Clearly, Raymond hadn't closed it down before he'd left.

"Do you have the password?"

Pippa shook her head. "There isn't one. It's only me and Ray, and I don't judge."

Ruth wondered about that as Palmer hit return and the screen saver became the desktop, Chrome open on a sex site, or more specifically, a cam-girl site. No actual sex. The frozen image showed an empty bed, and the informative pop-up stated they required a new deposit for more time with Queen Ree.

"Ray sits there and watches," Pippa said. "I think he's got a favourite, but I don't know who. I don't–didn't ask. This was his thing. Private."

Ruth studied her. "But you were aware of it?"

Pippa nodded. "Not at first, but I walked in one evening at the wrong moment. He was deeply sorry. After the surprise wore off, I realised I didn't mind."

"No?"

She looked at Ruth and shook her head. "No."

Ruth considered the woman. There were no indications of children in the house – it was tidier than a show home and just as sterile. Ruth wondered how she'd feel to discover her husband was watching porn on the internet. Unfortunately, the word that came to mind was 'relieved'. She tried again, wondering how she'd feel on discovering her husband used porn sites if she had a *normal* marriage. Shock made sense. But not minding? She could imagine women going ballistic over stuff like this. "Why not?"

Palmer glanced at her, his surprise at the rude question was clear in his wide eyes. Ruth wondered if her cheeks coloured with her embarrassment; they certainly heated. The question had slipped out.

Pale-faced Pippa looked away and then up. "Do you have children, Inspector Atkins?"

"A son," she confirmed.

"I don't. I can't."

Pippa looked into the middle distance. Ruth watched her closely. "A few years after Ray and I married, and I still hadn't become pregnant, I went to the doctors. They planned a battery of tests, but they only got to the ultrasound. They found I was riddled with fibroids. Any attempt to have children was likely to kill me as well as the child." Pippa's voice trailed off in mourning. Again, she looked up at Ruth. "Under the doctor's recommendation, I had a full hysterectomy at twenty-five. Ray was so good about it all, so loving. He never had a bad word for me. He was very patient. Surgery like that takes a some recovering from. When I was told all was good, when we could, you know, be together again, we were, but I found no pleasure in it. That's hard on a man. To have those urges when his wife doesn't."

Ruth knew it wasn't easy the other way around either.

"For a while, we tried. There was a little pain, but then … things got better, more comfortable. Ray and I would spend our time together. We enjoyed being together, doing things together. We were good friends as well as husband and wife."

Ruth sympathised with the older woman. "Sounds nice."

Pippa's own smile broadened. "It was, it really was. Ray was always so considerate and charming, and we had a good life. We laughed together, talked, cuddled, kissed. Everything but sex, and even that occasionally, when I could. We found ways – lubricants, positions. It's what you do when you love someone. You find ways. That's what Ray's watching was. His way to fulfil his needs without pushing me to do something I couldn't manage. Without cheating on me."

The idea put a lump in Ruth's throat. It wasn't an arrangement she felt marriage should include, but apparently, it had worked for the Bevans. Pippa loved Raymond. Did Raymond love Pippa? Was this the whole story? What was Raymond's view? Did Pippa love Raymond to death?

"Mrs Bevan, I'm sorry, but we have to confiscate this laptop and look into your husband's internet dealings."

She frowned. "But why? I've just told you."

"I appreciate that, Mrs Bevan, but pornography and blackmail often go hand in hand. There's a chance someone already knows about Ray's interests, and we have to check for that."

"But people will find out!"

People usually found out. "I'm sorry, but we have to check every potential avenue. I'm also going to need you to come to the station and put all this on record formally."

"But it was just a robbery gone wrong."

Chapter 23

The interview room was on the ground floor. This one didn't have windows, just air conditioning set low. The fixed table sat at the centre of the room, attached to the back wall, with the dual tape deck and a fixed video camera on the wall. The chairs were new, but the hard grey plastic ensured they wouldn't be comfortable for long. Ruth pointed Mrs Bevan to the far side of the table, where the camera would have the best view of her.

"Do I need a lawyer?" Pippa asked.

"You don't need one, but if you want one, I don't mind waiting, though the delay may raise concern with your neighbours," Ruth said and sat opposite Pippa. She gave Pippa time to comment. When she didn't, Ruth pressed the machine to record, then stated case number, persons present, date, and time.

"Mrs Bevan, this is a formal interview, but only to establish and record the facts as you perceive them. You are here voluntarily. If you feel you would like legal representation, that is your choice, and we can wait, but you don't *need* legal representation. You're here as a witness, not a suspect, hence no caution has been given. Are you prepared to proceed on these grounds?"

Pippa nodded.

"Would you mind verbalising that for the tape? The tape, by the way, is just so we get a clear record of all that passes in this room. So, are you willing to proceed on stated grounds?"

"I am." The voice was small.

"Thank you, Mrs Bevan. Would you prefer we called you Pippa?"

She sighed slightly. "I would, actually. Would you mind?"

"No, that's no problem, Pippa. Some people just prefer us to be more formal than others. Okay, so we need to go through what happened Tuesday morning, the first. But just to double-check, did you and your husband go to bed together on Monday evening?"

Pippa nodded again.

"For the tape, please, Pippa."

Her swallow was audible. "Yes. Yes, we did. We watched some catch-up TV, that Dara Ó Briain's quiz show thing." Pippa fell silent, drifting away.

"He's good, isn't he?" Palmer said softly.

Pippa refocused on him, had to think about what he'd said, then gave a small smile and nodded again. "A favourite of mine and Ray's. Anyway, we watched a few episodes, then headed to bed around half ten. I think Ray fell asleep first, which is unusual, but happens sometimes when he had a busy day, and Mondays were always busy. So, all was perfectly normal." Her voice drifted off, lost in the memory and the shock of sudden loss.

"Pippa?" Palmer's voice was soft when he spoke, and Ruth dropped her eyes to the table to hide her reaction to that gentle tone. "Tell us about Tuesday morning."

Pippa took a deep breath. Her thin hands appeared over the lip of the table, pulling at a white cotton handkerchief, apparently more habit than need. "The alarm call came through around four that morning. About a quarter past, I think. Ray answered the call at the extension in the second bedroom. I was just sitting up when he came in. He sat for a moment on the bed, said he had to pop down to the site. Then he left. I got up, did some cleaning."

"Pippa?" Ruth asked as the other woman's voice drifted away. "Do you have a clock in your bedroom?"

Both Pippa and Madoc looked at her like she was crazy. Then Pippa's look softened.

"No, actually. Why do you ask?"

"You said that the alarm call woke you at four-fifteen, that Raymond came in, told you what was going on, and left immediately?"

"That's right."

"If you don't have a clock in your bedroom, how do you know it was four-fifteen?"

Pippa frowned. She tried to speak, stopped. "I'm not sure. But I know I take around fifteen minutes to dress and do my hair, and I was downstairs at half past."

"So, it's possible that you have the time a little wrong? That Ray may have left earlier than you realised."

She frowned. "I suppose so. Five or ten minutes, perhaps. No more. Why does it matter?"

"It matters because we have to establish a timeline as exactly as possible," Ruth said. "So, it could have been a little earlier than four-fifteen when Ray left, but you were up and dressed by half four. And then you did some cleaning?"

Pippa nodded again; Ruth pointed to the tape.

"Yes. Yes, I was cleaning when your young officer turned up and told me about Ray. He seemed young. Was he?"

Ruth smiled, thinking about Sid. "Not that young. Though I suppose young depends on perspective. He's older and more experienced than he looks."

"I see. That explains it, then."

"Explains what, Pippa?"

"Just that he was genuinely nice. Broke the news gently, so considerate. Not that I have any other experience with such news being delivered but, you know …"

"I do know, Pippa," Ruth agreed softly. "And thank you. I'll be sure to thank Constable Jones properly when I see him. What happened after that?"

"Mrs Martin came over. She may have known before I did."

That sharpened Ruth's interest. "What makes you think that?"

Pippa shrugged. "She was at my door very quickly. Mind you, she is such a curtain twitcher. She was probably just being nosey."

Ruth would ask Mike to check with Mrs Martin again, see why she was up so early. "You say Ray popped in to let you know he was leaving. What exactly did he say?"

Thinking back, Pippa considered it. "'Alarm's gone off at the site. I'm going to pop down, shouldn't be long. See you later. Love you.'"

"The last thing he said was that he loved you?" Ruth asked gently.

Pippa nodded, made an affirmative noise. "He always does—did. We always did. 'Love you' is always the last thing we say – said to each other. Just in case." Her voice was cracking now. "Just in case it's the last thing we ever say to each other." Now, the tears came.

"And that's the memory you should hold on to."

"Yes. Sorry." She sniffed into the hanky. "I'm sorry."

"No need to apologise." Ruth hated this bit. "Do you fancy a cup of tea? I fancy a cup of tea." She was just about to stand and go get one when she realised that would leave Palmer alone with a female witness and Geraint would kick her arse for that. She looked to Palmer.

"I'll go."

She felt uncomfortable without Palmer in the room. Give her attacking nonces over crying women any day. Pippa took the time to calm herself, eternal moments that attempted to crush Ruth with her own awkwardness. Then Pippa turned red eyes to look up at Ruth.

"I'm sorry, I shouldn't have done that."

"It's fine. Normal. I'm sorry there's nothing I can do to help."

"Do you deal with murder cases often?"

"I've dealt with my share over the years. It's never nice," Ruth told her. "That the last thing you and Ray said to each other was 'love you', now that's nice."

"Yeah." Pippa braved a smile. "He was a good man. I guess that's difficult for you to believe, knowing that he used those sites, but he was a good man. A faithful husband."

The door opened and Palmer returned with a small plate of biscuits. "Jane said she'd bring the teas in a minute; she was looking for sugar."

Jane Smart was the FLO on this case. And sugar was always going missing from their small kitchen area, though every wing had its own kitchen. She suspected the cybercrime boys were pilfering supplies. They were always jonesing on coffees. She nodded and quietly thanked him before turning back to Pippa.

"Now, you said Ray left immediately he got the call. So, he was dressed at four in the morning?"

"That's right."

"What was he wearing?"

Pippa blinked at her. "Sorry?"

"What was Ray wearing? Tuesday morning, when he left."

Pippa shrugged. "Work clothes."

Ruth looked up. "But what clothes? Exactly?"

Pippa's eyes widened. "I'm not sure. I didn't get a good look."

"Didn't you?"

"No."

Ruth stopped as the door opened and Jane, a woman comfortably rounded with middle age, came in with a tray of four teas. She smiled up at the older woman and explained for the tape what was happening. Jane looked at Ruth darkly as she distributed the teas and sat with Pippa.

"Pippa's not under caution, Inspector Atkins."

"Of course not, sorry. Just a matter of habit." Ruth turned back to Pippa. "Sorry. You said originally that you didn't go back to sleep after the alarm, because you were too awake, so you got up as Ray left the house?"

Pippa stirred some sugar into her tea. "That's right."

"And a few minutes ago, you said before he left, he came in and sat on the bed. That's a fairly clear view, Pippa. What was he wearing?"

Pippa looked away, frowning as she considered the question. "I think he was wearing a black T-shirt, a blue and black checked shirt, and cargo pants. He often wears the company sweatshirt to work, but he wasn't wearing it that morning. At least, not when he left the bedroom."

The only inconsistency Ruth saw was that the T-shirt had actually been navy blue. Which was good, because if the clothes he died in were those he'd left the house in, there was nothing to make her question the timeline again. So why did it still niggle her?

"Okay, do you have any idea what time Ray actually got up?"

Pippa shook her head. "Sorry, I was fast asleep. We went to bed about half ten. I woke at four or quarter past, not sure now. I'd slept so well I didn't want to carry on sleeping."

"How did you know he'd been at his computer that morning if you only saw him when he told you he was going to site?"

Pippa looked into her tea. She glanced nervously at Palmer, then her eyes slid back to her tea. "I knew."

"How?"

This time when her eyes moved it was to glare momentarily at Ruth. "Because I could see he had an erection."

Chapter 24

"Tell me what you see." The woman had a strangely hypnotic voice. Melodic, gentle.

Madoc considered before he answered. "It's all a bit … well … frayed around the edges."

"Early days yet," she said softly.

"I see …" Madoc focused, struggled for a description. "There are silver shapes. Symbols."

Her voice encouraged him on.

"They're distorted. Unnatural looking. Upside-down."

She huffed. "You're describing what you see *through* the crystal ball, not in it." Her tone was harsher now. "You're describing the runes on my cloth, aren't you?"

He couldn't help grinning as the overhead light came on. "Sorry, Aunt Maureen, I couldn't help myself." He blinked at the white light above them. It threw the previously soft, attractive room into stark relief. Maureen was busy huffing out candles. "Wasn't that bulb lilac when I came in?"

"Yes?"

"How?"

"Magic," she snapped.

Raised, disbelieving brows questioned her.

She showed the controller. "Colour-changing, remote-controlled bulb. Now stop changing the subject. You came here tonight because you wanted to know about contacting the spirits."

"Something you've been nagging me to do for years," Madoc reminded her.

"Because I know you could do it if you'd only take the craft seriously."

"I'm sorry, Aunt Maureen, but crystal balls just don't float my boat."

"They aren't supposed to *float your boat.* They are supposed to connect you to the other side, transport you to new visions of the world."

"Transport? Like on a boat?" Madoc asked. "That floats?"

Maureen's eyes narrowed.

It's not like you need that kind of help, anyway.

Maureen's eyes eased in surprise. Then they widened. "Are you hearing voices?"

"I'm not crazy." Though Madoc was beginning to wonder.

"No, no, of course you're not, *bach.* I didn't mean that. But some spirit just spoke to you, didn't they?"

The temptation to deny it was strong, but he had come here for help. "Yeah."

"How do you hear them?"

Uncertain what the question meant, Madoc couldn't answer.

"Is it like a shout or a whisper? Close or far? Clear or static-y?"

"As if he's stood right beside me, talking clearly."

"It's a him?"

Madoc nodded.

"Who is he?"

Madoc shrugged.

"Haven't you asked him?"

"Several times."

I told you. You need to work it out.

"Apparently, I've got to work it out."

Well, you are a detective, aren't you?

"Oh, shut up."

Maureen gasped.

"Sorry, not you," Madoc assured her. "Him." Who he had to find a name for. A temporary one, at least. "In absence of anything better, I'll call him my passenger."

Not sure I like that.

Give me something better, then.

He didn't.

"When did you first hear him?" Maureen asked.

"Tuesday."

"The first? You first day at the new job?"

He nodded.

"Are you working on a murder? Could he be the victim?"

"Yes and no. We're working on two murders."

Nice use of the inclusive, well done.

Madoc ignored the voice. "But the man who died, while surprised to have died that way, knew he was dead, so he moved on. All I got was the echo of his surprise. This voice came in a little time after."

"Is he helpful?"

"Sometimes." Madoc decided against saying the voice was a better life coach than a work mentor.

Thanks. I think.

"Are you suffering any side effects?"

The question surprised Madoc. "Side effects?"

"Headaches? Nausea? Tiredness?"

You're hearing voices, not pregnant.

"He's getting to be a proverbial pain in the neck, but no, no side effects."

"And he's not intruding on your life?"

I could.

"Not yet. And he better not start."

Spoilsport.

Maureen grinned. "That last was for him, wasn't it?"

Squirming was an option. Madoc avoided it. Just. "Yeah."

"Then I'm not sure what help you think I can give. You seem to have it under control."

Yeah, right.

"If only." Madoc dragged his hands through his hair. "I …" This was harder than expected. "It's … I'm worried, okay? Part of the reason I've been reluctant to come over here and talk to you about talking to spirits is because I've been hearing them for years."

"Really?"

"Not clear like this guy, but I get impressions, insight."

"Oh, that's wonderful." Maureen clapped her hands, tinkling. Which was to say that the various little bells on her blouse made a sound. "Simply marvellous. Hang on." She ran from the room in a rainbow of flowing fabrics, clouds of incense, and a wind of chimes.

Not the reaction Madoc had hoped for. Uncomfortable that he was alone in Maureen's reading room, or more accurately the garage her husband had converted into her reading room to avoid having her clients in the house. Madoc got up and followed Maureen. Beyond the reading room, the house was a normal semi. Though with Maureen's personality, it was predictably more eccentrically and colourfully decorated than most.

He found Maureen scrabbling around in the sideboard at the back of the open lounge-diner. The man on the sofa reacted to the sudden activity by looking around his paper, knowing better than to ask. He wore jeans and an old cable-knit jumper that looked far too thick and warm for May.

"Hiya, Uncle Andrew."

"Hiya, butt. What's put the priest amongst the infidels with her?" He nodded to his still searching wife.

"The boy's hearing voices," Maureen said without pause.

Heat flooded Madoc's cheeks. Uncle Andrew married into the family and loved Maureen to distraction. He accepted all her eccentricities, while maintaining a healthy scepticism. He looked at Madoc squarely.

"Welcome to the freak show." Then he went back behind his paper.

"Ha!" Maureen stood, a notebook and pen in one hand. "Haven't had to use this in a while."

Madoc noted with some concern that his name was marked on the front cover.

"Let's go back—"

"Actually, can we sit in here?" Madoc glanced at the dining table. "Would you mind? I think I've had enough of the incense in the reading room. Do you mind, Uncle Andrew?"

"There's coffee in the machine," Andrew said from behind the paper. "I put it on when I saw you coming. Should be done nice by now. And while you're there, you can pour one for me."

The eyeroll this time was Maureen's. She indicated Madoc should sit, left the notebook, and went to the kitchen. Madoc opened the book. Dated entries, starting from when he would have been a baby, noting his spiritual development.

"God, it's like finding your own CIA dossier."

"Oh, the CIA have nothing on Maureen," Andrew said, lowering one corner of the paper to look at Madoc. "Don't feel special, she's got one of those on all the kids in the family. She just has more to write about you than the rest."

That didn't make him feel any better.

Maureen came in with an oversized mug which she took to her husband, exchanging it for a kiss. Then she returned to the dining table and offered a standard sized mug to Madoc, but only once she'd put a coaster out. Maureen herself didn't drink coffee. The closest she came was nettle tea, something Madoc considered an abomination.

She retrieved her notebook and turned to the last entry. It finished near the bottom of the page, so Madoc didn't have the opportunity to see what the previous entry was as Maureen turned the page and started writing.

Then the questions came. When did he start hearing things? What did he hear? How often? Was there any common trigger? Questions bombarded him. It was worse than being interrogated.

"Like I said," Andrew said as he stood up, "the CIA have nothing on her. Are you staying for dinner?"

"Of course, he's staying for dinner," Maureen asserted. "The pie's plenty big enough for three. Just do more vegies than normal. And why would the CIA have anything on me?"

Andrew just grinned.

"Actually, I can't stay," Madoc tried.

Dear God, are you Welsh or not? You're in a family home. The woman of the house is going to feed you. Whether you want it or not.

"I need to get on with the plasterboarding at home."

"I'll drop over after work tomorrow," Andrew said. "The two of us will get it done together much quicker than you could alone. We'll easily catch up on one missed evening of solo plasterboarding."

To be honest, Madoc had been wondering how he was going to manage to hold and nail the big boards on his own. Besides, Andrew was a dab hand at DIY – Maureen's reading room was just one example.

"If you're sure?"

"Of course he's sure," Maureen said. "Besides, we could be some time with this."

Madoc threw a thank you after his uncle as the man headed for the kitchen, and Maureen started with more questions.

"So, you're sure this man you're hearing isn't the victim? Of the murder you're investigating?"

"Yes."

Well, not of the murder you're investigating.

Madoc turned to the side, as if he could stare at the man who had spoken.

"Madoc?" Maureen called him back. "What did he say?"

Turning just his head, he faced his aunt again. "He said he's not the victim of the murder I'm investigating. Inferring that he was the victim of another murder."

Well done, Sherlock.

"Help or cut the sarcasm." Madoc grouched aloud.

"She is trying to help," Andrew said from the kitchen. "Be nice."

"It's all right, love," Maureen called back. "He wasn't talking to me."

Madoc was grateful she understood, but he had to be more careful not to answer aloud. That could get awkward.

That could get you locked up. Nice comfy cell for one. Well, two with your 'passenger'.

Madoc clenched his jaw.

Okay, I'll rein it back. But you know, your uncle's right: she is trying to help.

Maureen frowned slightly. "Hmm, perhaps that's his unfinished business."

"His what?"

"Unfinished business."

When she didn't go on, and didn't start throwing more questions, Madoc finally got to ask the question he'd come here to get an answer for. "Where do they come from? The voices?"

"Your guess is as good as mine."

Not helpful. "What do you mean?"

"I mean I don't know. No one does. There are plenty of theories. The collective conscious. The collective unconscious. Alternative dimensions. The afterlife. Purgatory. The Akashic Field."

"But if I don't know where it comes from, how can I stop it?"

You can't.

"Why would you want to?" Maureen asked.

"Well, what if I want ...?" Oh, how did he say this to his aunt?

You want to charm the snake? Spank the monkey?

He had to ignore the voice. "What if I want some ... private time?"

Uncle Andrew guffawing in the kitchen didn't help.

Maureen looked confused then she smiled. "You've got a girlfriend!"

"Well, no."

You do have a colleague you spend an awful lot of time thinking about.

"But I live in hope." Madoc did his best to push the voice to the back of his mind.

"I don't know," Maureen said. "Ask your passenger to step off the train for a while?"

The man was guffawing in his head. **You could try that, but …**

Great, now he was getting cheek from a dead man. "I'm not sure that's going to work."

"Well, firstly, be sure. You're the one in control, remember. You're the living human, he's just a memory."

I'm a damn sight more than that.

Madoc ignored him.

"Okay. Well, I think you know what to do. The thing is, this man has found a way to talk to you. He's probably been looking for someone to talk to since he passed. Which may have been a very long time ago." She stopped to look away and consider. "Or it might have been Monday." She shrugged. "You could ask him."

Given the passenger's penchant for sarcasm, Madoc doubted it would help. "Guess that's something I'll have to find out when I work out who he is."

You're catching on, Sherlock.

Madoc ignored him.

Maureen sat and considered. Madoc didn't know what she was thinking, so held his silence.

Look, if you're going to sulk and ignore me, I promise I'll give you space if you're with a woman.

Mentally, he thanked the man, and wondered if he could give him space when he wanted to, why he couldn't just give him space always.

You'll figure that out as well.

Madoc wasn't convinced.

"You know," Maureen said eventually, "I think he's already told you what to do to get rid of him. You need to find out who he is. Then you need to find out who killed him. Once that person is brought to justice, his unfinished business will be finished. Maybe he'll go then."

It's as good a theory as any.

Given that tone, Madoc didn't think his passenger believed Maureen any more than he did.

Chapter 25

The atmosphere in the station – well, the MCIT part of it – felt different this morning. Strained. Madoc forced himself not to sigh as he looked up. When he'd walked in, Ruth was in full-on thinking mode again. She'd absently thrown him a greeting, but otherwise acted like he didn't exist.

Madoc wasn't sure what had happened with Ruth, but it was clearly more than just this investigation. The screaming had settled down, but it was still there. She was still worried about something she wasn't talking about.

He'd noticed the change in her during the little time they'd been together after that interview with Pippa. Her thoughts had turned inward. So much so, she'd put off visiting Maggie Drake.

He mulled over what had been said, about Pippa and her marriage, but couldn't see any obvious issues. Even the cards had failed to enlighten him. There was just too much he didn't know about her and her life. All he really knew was that she was a widow with a son. He could imagine her running about after a toddler and laughing. Though she was only just thirty-one, laughter lines had etched around her eyes. There was a liveliness about her that showed a tendency towards laughter. He looked forward to the day he heard that laughter. As long as it wasn't pointed at him. So, what had triggered her? Pippa's husband using cam-girl sites? Had there been an issue between Ruth and her husband? It was hardly unusual for married officers, as he knew from bitter experience. Still, if she wasn't about to open up to him, there wasn't much he could do to help.

Just be there for her, his passenger said. **But don't push it, or she'll shut you out.**

Ruth stood looking at the board again. Concentrated on the Drowned Man this time. Raymond Bevan. All the details they had were up there. He still wasn't sure who put the boards together, but whoever it was, they had good, clear handwriting. They'd even redone Ruth's scrawl from yesterday. Her handwriting was perfectly legible cursive, but scrappy compared to the rest. He looked back to Ruth. Totally absorbed in what she was frowning at. Oddly, it reminded him of the way Maureen looked when going into a trance.

Give her time.

I may not have much.

She's just deep in thought.

He hoped his passenger was right.

"What aren't you seeing?" Madoc asked.

She turned to him. Her blinking signified she was coming back from wherever to reality. Her frown deepened, then she turned her head towards the DCI's office. Madoc looked, too. Geraint was inside, signing off papers. The door wide open. Madoc checked his watch. The briefing was due to start in five minutes.

"Geraint?" Ruth called through. "Can I borrow you a second?"

The older man looked up through the transparent top part of the partition. "Why?"

"I need a male point of view."

That stabbed Madoc to the core; what did she think he was?

Chopped liver.

He ignored that.

Only saying what you were thinking.

Madoc clenched his jaw and pushed the passenger away.

Geraint's thick eyebrows drew together. "You've got Palmer, ask him."

Tension gathered across Ruth's shoulders. "That would not be a safe choice, boss."

Now Madoc really worried, even as she turned to other male colleagues whose interest had been piqued by the odd exchange. Jackson was smirking. "Pete, Jackson, can I borrow you two, too?"

"Four male points of view?" Geraint asked, equally curious as he left his office and they all moved to stand around Ruth. It was the first time Madoc had really appreciated how short she was now she stood surrounded by taller men. "You tend to think in a more masculine way, so I'm curious why you need to ask multiple men a question."

Even her ears were red with the blush.

Oddly cute, isn't it?

Yes, it was, but he shouldn't think such things.

"I have to call for multiple men and, in each other's company, because if I asked you one at a time, there're all sorts of accusations could be thrown my way."

Geraint folded his arms, took a wide-legged stance, and looked down at Ruth with a broad smile on his face. "Should I be worried?"

"Possibly." Ruth hung her head, hid her face. "I am."

"Embarrassed to ask and worried about the fallout?" Jackson laughed. "What happened to your balls, Ruth? You always had more than the rest of us."

She glared up at Jackson. "The problem isn't my not having balls. The problem is I don't have a penis, so I have to ask."

The four men gaped at her in stunned silence.

"Look," she said, "we've all seen Dwayne Evans, probably more than any of us would like, and he's always in joggers, so he can easily get his cock out and play with it." She looked around the group.

Madoc was painfully aware that the men were all studiously not looking at each other.

"Good, looks like I'm not the only one uncomfortable with this conversation. Anyway, the question I don't want to ask is this." She pointed to the pictures on the board. "Raymond Bevan was wearing cargo pants. If you were getting up at stupid o'clock in the morning to go watch some girl flaunting it on screen, the point of which I'm presuming is to have a wank, would you get dressed in cargo pants? Come to that, would you bother getting dressed at all?"

If ever there was a question Madoc less wanted to be asked, let alone answer, he couldn't think what it would be.

"Should I take it from the awkward silence that no one wants to answer my question?"

"Preeeetty much," Jackson said.

"It depends," Pete said evenly. "How loose were the cargo pants? How big was his dick?"

All four of them turned to Pete, standing tall and thin, booted and suited, starched as an Edwardian. Strait-laced and respectable, Pete Saunders was the last person in this group Madoc had expected to answer. His tone was straightforward and reasonable, yet discussing such intimate matters felt out of place from him.

"Consider this: your assumption may be incorrect," Pete continued. "All we know for certain is that Raymond Bevan connected to a cam-girl site. He might not have been looking for release that morning. He could have just been gathering ideas for later use. A deposit in the spank bank, if you will. If he was going in for the full masturbatory experience, how he's dressed is simply a matter of choice. Personally, I wouldn't have seen the need to dress at all. Too much potential for mess. But we're all different. As for those trousers, cargo pants are a reasonably loose design. Clearly, he could get a hand in to urinate, so getting his penis out to play with shouldn't be a problem. Practically, as long as the zipper doesn't nip—" Three men involuntarily winced at the idea of zippers catching sensitive flesh. "—then there's no obstruction to doing the deed however he dressed. It's all down to taste. He might have liked it that way." Pete shrugged and looked at Ruth, who looked back, lips parted and expression stunned. "Does that help?"

"Actually, yes. That's been bugging me, but you just made sense of it. Thanks, Pete."

Ruth and Pete both turned away, as natural as could be. Ruth sat at her own desk, and Madoc glanced up to not quite look at Geraint or Jackson. They each slipped silently away as if that conversation hadn't just happened.

"I wanna catch Mike before we go," Ruth told Madoc after the briefing. "I assume Drake is working today. Did you bring boots with you for going on site?"

"I did, sir," he said.

He followed her to the incident room.

Mike greeted Ruth with a smile. "Hiya. How's business?"

"Complex, much like yours. Anything new?" Ruth asked.

"As it happens, yes." Mike's sombre tone suggested nothing good. "We've got a possible ID for the Geddings girl. Tentative at the moment, but I'm getting details for cross matching. I'll confirm when we're clearer and bring you details. And we've spoken to Dwayne again. You were right about Miss Size 28, Loren Baxter. She's also identified him in a line up. So, well done, that's another case closed. Congratulations."

"Don't congratulate me, that was all Madoc." Ruth said. "Anything on the Bevan case?"

"We've tracked down a couple more production staff from *Valleys View*, waiting on responses. There's the usual million-and-one callers claiming that they saw way more than they could have. Of course, Lee Glyndwr called, another confession."

"Sorry," Madoc frowned. "Lee Glyndwr?"

Mike nodded. "That's what he calls himself. Real name's Bradley Walters. He calls and confesses to just about every crime we have. Gets especially inventive with the murders. We've spent some time looking into him, but he's just a lonely bloke. Poor guy was brain damaged in a motorcycle accident in his early twenties. I think he just wants to talk, and if we've got someone with five minutes to spare, I'll send 'em up to just check on him."

"Lives up on the Gurnos?" Madoc asked. "Aged probably thirty-nine, forty?"

Mike nodded. "You know him?"

"Sort of. One of my older brothers used to be into his bikes. He had a mate called Bradley Walters. I remember when the accident happened. My brother gave up the bikes shortly after, much to Mam's relief. I hadn't realised that Brad had been so affected by it. Shame. I remember him being a good bloke when I was a kid."

"Happens. Sorry."

"Bad news is never fun to hear," Ruth said. "Oh, and while I think of it, Pippa Bevan said Sid was good when delivering the bad news."

Madoc watched the other two in silence. Clearly, they were long-standing friends, he hoped he'd have as good a relationship with them in time.

"I'll let him know," Mike said. "He's good with women like that."

"Yeah." Ruth grinned. "It's the innocent look. He even makes me want to mother him when he starts, and I've seen him mooning while three sheets to the wind."

Now Mike laughed. "That was a good night."

"What you remember of it."

"Well, we can't all be teetotallers."

You're jealous!

Of their professional relationship only, Madoc thought back to his passenger.

Lie to yourself, not to me.

Then the voice was gone.

"Can you be professional?" Ruth asked Mike with fake sweetness.

Mike matched her. "Can you?"

Her grin broadened. "Only if I have to."

It wasn't jealousy, Madoc decided. It was awkwardness. He felt he was intruding. Ruth had been here a long time, and he was a newbie. It was natural her ties to these people would be close. He'd find his fit in time.

"Oh, just for you to be aware, there's nothing we can link to the Flacks regarding the robbery. Neither of the James boys gave us anything. However, one of the builders' statements says that when they were stopped from going on site, he wandered up to The Earth Harp as soon as they opened."

"So that's like as not how Iolo found out?"

"Exactly," Mike nodded. "And as far as we can tell, there's no link to the Prices, either. They were just drunk as skunks and missed their taxi."

Ruth nodded. "Thanks for checking."

"I saw your request for information on the dead space opposite Thomastown Recreation Ground," Mike said. "That flattened area off Queen's Road?"

"Christ, that was quick," Ruth said. "Do you read everything that comes through?"

"God no, I'd never get through it all. Besides, that's what we hire reader-receivers for. No, the address just caught my eye. See, I've lived around here long enough to know it was a school," Mike said. "Originally it was the Queen's Road Secondary School, then it became the Ysgol Santes Tudful Primary, a Welsh-medium school. It closed in 2009, demolished between August and September 2010."

"And Mair Thorne went missing …?"

"September 16th, 2010." Madoc was glad to add something to the conversation.

Ruth nodded.

"So, if she ran from Dwayne and headed across the road, she could have jumped the fence, got up to the demolition site, and then what?" Madoc wondered aloud. "Hid? Too afraid to come out?"

"It's possible." Ruth nodded. "She wasn't wearing much, she'd be in shock after the rape, terrified of Dwayne coming back. Even sober, that's a dangerous mix, and according to the reports, Mair had left sober way behind in Cardiff. That's a recipe for hypothermia."

"God, what a way to go," Mike said.

"But then what?" Madoc asked. "Her body got dragged away with the rubble? Should we try and find out where the rubble was taken?"

There was little chance of anything being left or findable now. Ruth looked to Mike.

He rolled his eyes. "I'll add it to the Actions List."

They hadn't got out of the station door before a call from Geraint diverted them to another case, which meant they didn't get to the Heolgerrig site until early afternoon. The wellies saved their shoes, though they weren't on site long.

"Sorry," Andy told them. "Maggie's not in today. She booked annual leave weeks ago. Though she didn't go away as planned, she's still taking the time. You'll probably find her at home."

The door to 32 Heolgerrig was uPVC with two panels of glass in the upper section. The tops of each panel sloped up towards the centre point. It made the door look sad, like a puppy about to cry.

"Can puppies cry?"

"Sorry, sir?"

For a second, Ruth frowned up at Palmer. "Sorry?"

"You said something about puppies?"

"Oh, sorry. Random thought. Sometimes they just spill out." She leant up and knocked on the door.

"What was the thought?"

"Can puppies cry?" Something sounded behind the door. "Apparently, Labradors can bark." Another sound, claws scratched on plastic, and they saw the black face of a dog bobbing between the two glass panels, trying to get a view of their visitors. "And it's a jumper. Great."

A figure appeared behind the door. Maggie Drake.

"You don't like dogs?" Palmer asked.

"Not ones that jump all over me." She ground the answer out as the door started to open and Maggie appeared, bent over as she held the dog back. At least the dog was friendly, judging by the open mouth and lolling tongue in the dumb-looking face. Maggie's hold suggested it was also ill-trained and likely annoying. "Hello, Mrs Drake. Would you mind if we came in for a quick chat?"

Maggie scowled back. "And if I do?"

Ruth shrugged easily. "I'll insist on you coming down to the police station for a much longer formal chat. Will you invite us in, or do I have to invite you out?"

Maggie's already sour look curdled. She held back the dog by its collar, even as its tail wagged wildly, thumping the wall. "You'd better come in, then. Come on back, Kohl."

They moved in, struggling a little around the dog. Palmer flinched when it shoved its muzzle into his groin. Maggie closed the front door and let the dog go. The animal wound its way between and around them. Ruth gave it a quick head rub to guide it away.

"Not working today, then?" Ruth started.

"I booked the day off ages ago," Maggie said. "I intended to go to London, but the trip got cancelled."

"That's a shame," Ruth offered, thinking the exact opposite.

"People get sick." Maggie shrugged. "Go on through." She pointed to the relevant door.

The sitting room was neat and comfortable. The biggest central chair stood like a throne at the heart of the furniture arrangement. It was covered in a throw, which was covered in dog hair. It was obvious who ruled the roost. Maggie sat on the arm of that chair. The dog jumped up and curled around to lick its privates.

Nice, Ruth thought.

Maggie didn't offer her or Palmer a seat. That made life easier for Ruth - it would have been rude to refuse, but the idea of sitting among the amount of dog hair in the room wasn't inviting.

On the mantel and wall, there were various pictures of a young girl with black hair. It was odd for a Celtic country, the Celts being famed for their red hair, but Wales had a lot of people with black hair. Ruth guessed it was from the influx of Italians, many of whom had settled in the Rhondda. Several families made great ice cream - or *gelato* - around the country. 'Drake' wasn't an Italian-sounding name, but that didn't mean there wasn't Italian blood somewhere in the line. In the pictures, the girl grew up to become busty and attractive. A bit of a stunner, really.

"Is this your daughter?" Ruth asked as neutrally as she could.

"Yes, that's my darling. Rhiamon." Maggie's voice was softer than Ruth had heard it before. A doting mother.

"Does she still live with you?" It seemed unlikely.

"No, she's in London now. That's where I was going, to see her. Beauty was always her way forward. Works as a model, catalogue stuff and shows. Did Fashion Week in Milan a few weeks ago. Makes great money. Of course, she has to live in London, so it's costly, too. She's breaking into commercials now, did one for some department store in Kent recently. I haven't seen it myself, would love to. Of course, it's only shown in the southeast. No point advertising up here for a store that's only down there."

"No, I suppose not." Ruth also supposed that if Rhiamon really wanted to, she could have got a copy for her mother. Maybe the devotion only went one way. Ruth nodded as she turned away from the photographs and focused on Maggie. "I was wondering if you'd explain a few additional things for me. You're the site secretary for the Heolgerrig site, right?"

Maggie nodded.

"So, it's a temporary job?"

"Of course not. I've worked for Shalestone Homes for seventeen, nearly eighteen years now. I just move with each new site. Sometimes I work two or three sites at the same time. Could be anywhere in the South Wales area. If we need additional help, I employ temps, oversee their work."

"Must be nice, then, working this close to home for a change."

"It is," Maggie said, petting the dog.

"So how long have you lived in Heolgerrig?"

"In the village, all my life. In this house, the last thirty-ish years. We moved here just after Rhiamon was born."

"We?" Palmer asked.

It seemed like an odd question to Ruth, but she'd let it pass.

"Me and Rhiamon. Oliver, too, at first."

"Oliver?"

Again, Ruth allowed Palmer the question.

"My husband. Ex-husband. He's long gone now. Back to England. I'm better off without him, he was the selfish type. You hear about it, but never think the man you pick is going to be that way, like."

Ruth frowned. "What way?"

Maggie looked up. "So selfish. You wouldn't understand."

"Try me."

Maggie's look was dark. A thin white line appeared around her pressed lips. "When Rhiamon was born, Oliver got jealous of the time I spent with her. She was a helpless little baby. Needed me for everything. I had to change her, to feed her. He didn't even like that I breastfed her. But it's the best. That's what all the doctors said, I was only doing the best for my baby. Looking after her the way a mother is meant to. I was all she had in the world, and Oliver was jealous of that. Said I was obsessed, said I was ignoring him. Selfish. Then he buggered off with some bimbo. He was the selfish one."

Ruth watched the other woman. There was such zealotry in Maggie's manner, Ruth knew this was the heart of Maggie's psyche. Maggie was about as average a woman as Ruth had ever met – nothing special, nothing extra-good, nor extra-bad. All the photos were of Rhiamon, the girl who wasn't here, so Maggie had made sure the girl could never leave. She looked, then, at the way Maggie petted her dog, set up the house to make it the centre of her world. The Dedicated Servant. Maggie gave love like worship, and she wanted it back. The kind of unconditional love a mother got from a baby; an owner got from a dog. Ruth pitied the woman.

"So, you've lived here all your life?"

Maggie nodded. "As I just said."

"Raymond Bevan was a local, too. How long have you known him?"

Maggie looked back down at the dog.

"A fair few years. I met him after I started with Shalestone Homes. He was already there, a civil engineer. He wasn't a site manager then." She looked up at Ruth. "What's your point?"

"Just trying to establish how well you knew him. Hold on a second, I thought Andy Porter was site manager here."

"She is," Maggie confirmed. "The original supervisor was Owain Long, but his wife got a job in Aberdeen, so they moved up there. Bevan was between sites, so he took over as supervisor."

"I see. How would you describe your relationship with Raymond Bevan?"

"We were colleagues. Neighbours, I suppose, if you stretch the definition. We worked on the same sites a few times. Occasionally shared a car. But not friends, like. I'm not keen on men like that."

"Men like what?" Ruth asked.

Maggie shrugged. "Like him. Selfish. Puts himself before his wife. She's never been allowed to be who she could have been."

Ruth glanced to Palmer. He was getting all this recorded. She wondered if he understood what Maggie meant any better than she did.

"I'm sorry, I don't understand. What do you mean by that?"

"Well, he was selfish. Couldn't even give his wife a baby, and she always wanted one."

Not exactly the case, but … "So, you two didn't get along?"

"We were colleagues. That's all."

"Not friends?"

"No."

"Had you ever been?"

"Not really."

"And with Pippa Bevan?"

Maggie frowned at her. "Not really. Does it matter?"

"You said that you knew Pippa Bevan always wanted to have children. That's the kind of confidence shared between friends. So, how do you know that?"

"I know Pippa. I hear things. In the village. Everyone knows she wanted kids, but Bevan couldn't deliver. Too busy using those pervert sites."

Ruth wouldn't correct Maggie. It wasn't Raymond's fault Pippa didn't have children.

"When you say 'pervert sites' …?" Ruth left the question hanging.

"You know," Maggie said. "That kind of site." She looked oddly at Palmer. "Men-only sites."

"Can you be a little more specific about what sites you're referring to, please?"

Maggie's lips pursed, and she covered Kohl's ears. "Porn sites."

Given Pippa's wish for the neighbours not to know about that, Ruth had to ask. "What makes you think Raymond was using such sites?"

Maggie's look conveyed judgement and disapproval. "He—" she licked her lips. "He's just the type, isn't he?"

"Is he?" Ruth asked. "What type is that?"

"Selfish."

Ruth wondered if Maggie had any idea how blinkered and ignorant she sounded. How circular her arguments were.

"Why give his wife a child when he could–" Again she covered the dog's ears. "–self-pleasure over someone else's daughter?"

"How do you know this?" Madoc said.

"Well, I …"

Ruth waited, nothing more materialised. "So, this is just speculation on your part?"

"Well, I didn't sit down and help him …" She glanced at Kohl. "Do stuff like that."

"No," Ruth said. "I don't suppose so. Let's get back to Tuesday morning …"

Chapter 26

"Sir?"

Ruth looked at Madoc as they returned to the car.

"I know it's not really in the caseload, but would you mind going to the Gurnos?"

"Gurnos?" Ruth frowned. "What for?" Her shoulders sagged. "Bradley Walters?"

He nodded. "Do you mind?" He felt awkward just asking. "I'm sorry, it's been playing on my mind."

She pulled out into the traffic and shook her head. "It's fine."

Now she'd agreed, Madoc was unsure what to say or do. There was no plan, simply the absolute certainty that he had to go see Bradley. He wasn't sure why.

"Were you good friends?" Ruth asked as they crossed the town entering the outer limits of the Gurnos.

"No, not at all. He was a mate of my older brother's. I've not seen him since the accident. I know when Francis saw him after the crash, it freaked him the hell out. That was when he got rid of his motorbike."

"Do you know what happened? To Bradley?" Ruth asked.

"Not really. Only that it was a crash on Llangynidr Moor."

She concentrated on the road as she spoke. "I remember his claims were investigated, several times, but years ago now. At one point he claimed responsibility for a missing nine-year-old girl. The team took that very seriously. From what I remember, you're right. The crash was up on Llangynidr Moor. A motorist saw his bike and stopped to investigate. Found Bradley in a ditch. The motorist called three nines. There was no obvious reason for the crash. According to Gwent, Llangynidr Moor being their territory, there was no indication of any other vehicle, person, or animal involved. So, no one really knows what happened. Can't remember who interviewed him, but I remember the briefing when it was discussed."

"Have you met Brad?"

She answered with a head-shake as she slowed to avoid teenagers having a kick about in the road. "I only know the name because he calls every time we open an incident room. Confesses to everything. Adamant he killed some kid."

They crawled up the road of featureless grey-rendered 1970s homes.

"It's that one there." Madoc pointed, and Ruth found a parking space a few doors down.

The white uPVC door had a cracked window taped with black duct tape. Madoc knew the area wasn't the best. Brad's dad had lost his job years ago and had not been able to find work after. Mrs Walters had worked three jobs to keep the roof over their heads and food on the table. It must be difficult to keep on top of things if they were surviving hand to mouth. Ruth indicated for him to go first. There was a doorbell, but tape covered that, too, so Madoc knocked.

It was only a few moments later when the door opened wide. The face behind wasn't quite the one Madoc remembered. It was still recognisably Brad, but his nose bent to the right and his left cheek and eye socket had been flattened, the eyebrow was half gone, and the skin was rough with scarring. He must have been wearing an open-face helmet that hadn't done its job. The first look was scowling and ready for a fight. With kids, judging by the angle of Brad's eyes. Then he looked at the taller man, and that belligerence melted away.

"It's little Frankie's little brother!" Only the unscarred right side of his face grinned. "Maddy!"

It was a long time since anyone had called Madoc that. He wasn't expecting it any more than he was expecting to have Brad throw his arms around his shoulders and hug him tight, slapping him on the back.

"Maddy, butt." Brad stepped back and looked up. "Long time, no see. Come in. Come in."

Madoc looked at Ruth, who was struggling not to grin too widely. How soon would his old nickname get around the station?

Brad looked at Ruth. "This your girlfriend?"

"No, it's …"

"She's a looker," Brad jumped in. "Great honkers."

Mortified, Madoc had to ignore his passenger's guffaws. He remembered Brad with Francis, as teenagers. Of course, they'd been interested in girls and breasts, but he didn't remember Brad being so crude about it. Perhaps, since the accident, he'd lost the filters that usually govern social interaction. At forty years old, Brad wasn't likely to get away with teenage antics anymore. A glance at Ruth didn't show any sign of the blush he felt burning his own cheeks.

She regarded him squarely, spoke calmly. "Perhaps we should step inside?"

Nodding and feeling like a fool, Madoc took the first step over the threshold and into the house. Built in the 70s, the house was open-plan and updated; the Walters family must have modernised, or the council, possibly. They stepped straight into the front room, and the smell of sweat, curry, and beer. The sofa and chairs were a woven beige fabric. The arms had worn through. There were grease marks where heads would rest, and a bin full of cans and snack wrappers beside it. Brad was living like a teenager – well, almost, aside from the fact that all the cans and wrappers were actually in the bin and not just discarded where they fell.

Brad stepped in after closing the door to face Madoc. He wore that goofy one-sided grin as he turned off the TV. Then he gazed around the room before turning back to Madoc. The grin slipped away, his head hung, and he looked at his left hand, which Madoc saw now was badly scarred and missing the little finger.

"Sorry." The man's voice was full of regret, uncertainty. "I tried, but it's difficult to hold on. Now Dad's gone, and Mam, well …" Brad stopped. The left hand went down, and he looked up at Madoc again. Some of the lucidity drained from his eyes as he grinned again. "So, to what do I owe this pleasure, butt? Why you come and see the old Bradster?"

Bradster. Another name Madoc hadn't heard in years. The name Brad had always called himself, not liking the full Bradley. "I wanted to see how you were doing," Madoc said. He could see that the answer was 'not great'. "Make sure you're getting the help you need."

Brad nodded. "Yeah, the Marie Curie Nurse comes in for Dad. Does a bit. You know?"

Guilt assailed Madoc. Brad was wrong. The nurses wouldn't come anymore. Mr Walters had passed on years ago. Francis had attended the funeral. Madoc wasn't sure about Mrs Walters. Was she still alive? This one visit wouldn't be enough. He and Francis would have to keep a check on Brad more regularly. But Brad was looking at Ruth. He saw her offer an uncertain smile and look up at him. Her uncertainty unnerved him. Total professional around that creep Dwayne Evans, easy camaraderie around others, but here, in a social setting, she was uncertain? He clearly had a lot to learn about his new colleague.

"Great hooters, girl," Brad said, virtually drooling. His hands came up as he moved a step forward. "Can I—?"

"No!" Madoc was a lot sharper than he intended and Brad stopped like a child who'd just been slapped.

"You said she wasn't yours." Petulance. "If she's not yours, I can have her."

"But I am his," Ruth surprised Madoc by saying and she stepped closer to him, put her arm around his waist. The other hand patted his chest. It was the easiest thing in the world to put his arm around her and pull her close. The seven-inch height difference meant that she fit easily against him. And yes, those great hooters pressed against him, and he knew exactly why Brad was reaching out. He was tempted.

Easy, tiger.

"We're partners," Ruth said.

Partners, of course. The truth hidden as a lie. *Work partners. Remember, work partners.* Even though, from this angle, he could look straight down the open button of her top and see-

Off limits, pal. She's just doing this to stop Brad assaulting a police officer.

"Look, Brad," Madoc tried again, not letting go of Ruth, and she seemed content to stay close. "I heard that you've been making calls to the police. Confessing that you killed someone."

Brad's face, the right side at least, contorted. There was very real self-loathing and regret, and so, so much pain. "I did. I killed her."

"No, Bradley, you didn't," Madoc said. For all he tried to be soothing, he felt and heard the catch in his throat. This was more difficult than he'd expected. This wasn't the man that the boy he had known was supposed to grow into. Ruth's hand rubbed his back in mute support.

"You haven't killed anyone, Brad."

But Brad covered his face with his hands and sank onto the aged sofa. "I did," he sobbed. "I killed that kid."

The statement hit like a shockwave. Then Ruth pulled away from Madoc to sit next to Brad. Madoc could almost see the girl's white face.

"Brad?" Ruth was so gentle. "Brad?"

Finally, the older man turned up to face her, the grey in his once-blond hair catching the light.

"Who do you think you killed?" Ruth asked.

"The kid." Heavy tears rolled down from his eyes. "She was just stood there. In the road. I didn't see her."

But Madoc could.

Brad sobbed again. "I tried to stop, but there wasn't time." He breath shook as he spoke. "She just appeared there. She did. I didn't see until it was too late." He wailed as he hid his face in his hands again. "I killed her." The phrase came through the tears, heart wrenching and painfilled.

Madoc didn't know what to do.

"It's okay," Ruth said gently. "Brad, you didn't kill anyone."

"But she was right there! In the middle of road."

"You didn't hit her," Ruth's soft voice seemed to get through to Brad. "You missed. You swerved, and you missed."

"No," Brad shook his head. "There wasn't time. I must have hit her."

"But you didn't." This time Ruth stroked back the overlong hair and caught Brad's attention. "There was no one hurt that night but you."

Brad looked at her at last, uncovered his face. "But what if I knocked the kid off the road?"

She shook her head. "You didn't. It was only you at the crash site. Brad, I promise, if anyone else had been hurt that night, I'd tell you. But they weren't."

Madoc heard a key in the front door. As Ruth soothed Brad, Madoc turned to see the small, wiry frame of an older woman come into the house, heavy shopping bags in her hand. She gaped at him, startled into immobility. Her jaw slackened at the sight of the woman sitting with her son on the sofa.

"Mrs Walters?" Madoc said quietly as he stepped up, leaning down to help the woman with her shopping. "I'm Detective Sergeant Madoc Palmer—"

"Oh my God," she paled. "What's happened?"

"Nothing bad," Madoc assured her softly, surprised by the weight of the bags as he took the full heft of them. "Shall I take these to the kitchen for you? We can talk in there."

Mrs Walter nodded and pointed the way.

"He's not been the same since the accident," Mrs Walter said after Madoc explained their presence. "Swears there was a kid in the road, that he must have hit her, killed her. But there was nothing there. The police investigated. There were skid marks from the sudden breaking, but the only blood was Bradley's, and the only vehicle was his bike."

Madoc nodded.

"His dad used to tease him. Poor thing. He said, Mr Walters that is, that Bradley must have seen *Mair Merch Farw*. It was a wee bit nasty, but I think the cancer got to his head sometimes. That and his not being able get work after Hoover laid him off."

The closing of the Hoover factory in 2009 had been the death of industrial employers in the town, and its loss still reverberated, though the regeneration of the area was at least offering opportunities for the younger generation.

They could hear that the sobbing had subsided and risked going through to the sitting room again. Ruth still sat beside Bradley, but he was sitting up now, no longer crying. Ruth looked up when Madoc cleared his throat.

"Oh hi, Mam," Brad sounded like a child now, a carefree teenager.

Ruth stood. "Hello, Mrs Walters."

"Oh, you dun' have to be so formal with Mam," Bradley said, standing. "This is Ruth. She's Madoc's girlfriend."

Madoc saw the move of Bradley's hand, and he suspected Ruth did, too, when she stepped away from him.

"Partner," Ruth emphasised to Mrs Walter.

The older woman nodded as Bradley joked how they were 'so modern' using that terminology.

"We should go," Ruth said.

"Aw, don't go yet," Brad said. "Have a cuppa. And a biscuit." He looked to his mam. "You got any of that drizzle cake left?"

Mrs Walters smiled at her son, then threw an apologetic look at Madoc and Ruth. "I think your friends need to go now, love."

Madoc said 'bye' and led Ruth to the door.

"You can't go without a kiss!"

Brad's shout stopped Madoc in his steps, swinging around to face Brad, take him on. Ruth bumped into him at the sudden halt. Brad was grinning, ignoring his mother's scolds.

"I'm not kissing you, Brad," Ruth laughed, and tried to move Madoc on.

"Not me, him." Now Brad was laughing.

Madoc stared down at Ruth, his brain sparking ideas and refusing to function rationally, to find them a way out of this.

Don't even think about it.

Ruth rolled her eyes. Mrs Walter told Brad to stop and let them go, only Brad was getting agitated.

"It's okay." Ruth waved Mrs Walters down.

Then she turned to Madoc, stretched up on tiptoe.

Don't do it.

His passenger's warning was needless. Madoc was too damn nervous to do anything. He looked down at her, so close their breath mingled. She'd shifted to put her head between them and the Walters. The pause was killing him. Internally he was begging her to kiss him, scolding himself to do nothing.

A quick dry kiss pressed onto his cheek, and she moved away.

He could breathe again.

Chapter 27

"Thank you," Madoc said as he drove back towards the station.

"What for?" Ruth asked.

"Being so gentle with Bradley. He's not the man I knew."

Ruth sighed. "I doubt he was ever the man you knew, given how young you would have been when you last saw him. Moreover, I doubt he's the man he was meant to be after that accident."

"True." Madoc said. "But also, thanks for figuring out how to appease him while not …"

"Not what?" she said. "Doing something so stupid as actually kissing you? I'd really like to keep my job, thanks, and putting the moves on a younger, lower-ranking officer wouldn't exactly be conducive with that."

No, but plenty of people, of all genders, got away with it. He wasn't sure why kissing him would be so stupid though.

Because it could cost her her job, his passenger reminded him. **Not to mention the fact that she's not sure she could stop at kissing.**

Oh, don't be ridiculous. Nice thought though it was. *You can't know what she thinks.*

I know what you think. And I know you like her. Way more than you should on so short an acquaintance.

Madoc turned to hide his face from Ruth. His passenger had a point.

Look, all I'm saying is that she's trying to keep your relationship professional. You need to do the same.

Yes, he did, because he wanted – needed – to keep this job.

"Er, Inspector?"

Ruth turned from the knackered-looking woman in the mirror to the young woman at her side. They were both washing their hands in the ladies'.

"Excuse me but …"

Ruth frowned then. Palmer wasn't twitching, but she might be. Maybe she'd take some leave when this case was over; she clearly needed it. Not to mention a visit to the doctors. But that was for another time. For now, she had to be professional as she flicked water off her fingers and left them dripping over the sink, missing the days when they had had paper towels rather than ear-bursting air blowers. "Yes, Constable?"

"I think, ma'am, that I've … that is …"

Clearly, the young woman was having trouble getting the thought sorted. "Hold on." Ruth ducked into a cubicle and grabbed a load of toilet paper to dry her hands. "Right, let's start by you reminding me of your name. I hate just calling people Constable all the time."

"Oh, it's Constable Jefferies, ma'am. Rita Jefferies."

Ruth also hated being called 'ma'am'. It made her feel old. But a lot of things were doing that recently. "Okay, Rita, what do I need to know?"

"Well, it's just that I saw in the Seren Rosser file that she was going down to screen test for *Valleys View* on the day she disappeared."

Ruth nodded. "Yeah, that's right."

"Well, you were so interested in that timeline about Maggie Drake, that, just out of curiosity, I stuck her name in Google to see what came out. Her daughter is Rhiamon Drake, and until about the time same Seren went missing, all Maggie's Facebook news was about Rhiamon and how she was going to be a brilliant famous actor, the next Catherine Zeta-Jones."

"Okay." Ruth wasn't that impressed, but then she'd rather read a book than watch TV.

Rita swallowed before she continued. "There's a post that says Rhiamon was up for a screen test on a 'reality TV show that would put South Wales on the map as much as Essex.'"

That made no sense to Ruth. "Essex? Why Essex?"

Rita's look was equal incomprehension. "Essex," the woman said. "You know, *TOWIE*."

"*TOWIE*?" Ruth's frown deepened. "Oh! You mean that *The Only Way Is Essex* thing? Wasn't that some TV show?"

Rita's eyes suggested she didn't understand how anyone could not know. "It's a reality show, or at least it was. Not sure if it's still on. Anyway, it occurred to me that *Valleys View* might be the show that Maggie was referring to." Rita shrugged. "It's nothing, I suppose."

More than likely. "It's nothing obvious, but it is a potential connection. You never know where that sort of thing might lead."

"Yeah, it's just …"

This was the bit of mentoring and man-management that Ruth hated most: trying to encourage younger, lower-ranking officers to risk being wrong.

"Look, Rita, whatever it is, just tell me. It probably wouldn't be weighing on your mind if it were really nothing."

"I also found out that Culverhouse Cross banned Maggie Drake from their site."

"Just Maggie, or Rhiamon as well?"

"Just Maggie."

"Interesting."

The frown could have been confusion or annoyance at the animal hair Rita was picking off her own uniform arm. "Why's that interesting?"

"It means Maggie was the problem, but Rhiamon had potential," Ruth explained. Just about the opposite view people had of her and her mother. "Okay. So, see if you can find out why Maggie was banned. Don't put any great priority on it – best it'll do is illustrate Maggie's character – but add it to the list of actions. Also, add finding out where the screen test for *Valleys View* was done. All I have at the moment is Cardiff."

"Yes, ma'am."

Ruth nodded. "Right, well, it's past clocking off. I'm knackered and I'm going home." She'd got as far as the door when she stopped. The dog hairs from Maggie's place were still on some of her clothes.

No. Could it be? She turned again to the constable.

"Rita?"

"Ma'am?"

"Could you check something else for me?"

"Of course."

"Good. I think I've just realised what it is about the timeline that's bothering me. Maggie said she nipped home with the dog, Kohl, but the dog hasn't appeared in any statement I've seen. But there should be more than I've seen from the house-to-house. Can you check to see if anyone else mentioned the dog or Maggie leaving the site after calling us. Anything that fills those questionable minutes."

Rita nodded and Ruth turned to go, then turned back again.

"Not necessarily tonight, though, eh? I suspect it's past your clocking off time, too."

Madoc headed for the office. There were notes he wanted to write up before going home. He was also going to check that damn timeline again – it nagged constantly. Ruth had dropped him off, booked the pool car back in, and bid him a cursory goodnight. He worried about her. She was growing more insular. It wasn't affecting her performance as a police officer, but it was definitely influencing their fledgling working relationship.

Given it was after six now, he was surprised to see Geraint still at his desk. The man pulled him in with a movement of his greying head.

"Where's Ruth?" Geraint asked as Madoc stepped into the doorway.

"Gone straight home, sir."

The grey head nodded. "Good, she needs some rest."

Madoc frowned. "Something I should be aware of?"

Geraint just shook his head.

"Really? Because—" He cut himself off at Geraint's sharp look.

Geraint looked away first, closed the file he had been working on, and focused on Madoc. "Because what?"

"She said something about how she's been known to make newbies twitch."

She's uncommonly hard on herself.

Madoc agreed but noted Geraint's nod.

"Well, I'm not twitching. Is she?"

Geraint considered before he answered. "She's not. I might be."

"Because of Ali?"

Geraint nodded.

Madoc look at the ceiling, begging Mother Moon for guidance. "I'm sorry. That was my mistake. I'll do better in the future."

"You'd better." He wasn't sure what to make of Geraint's scrutiny.

"Is she dropping the ball with work at all?" the DCI asked. It was clear this man had a deep affection for Ruth.

"No, sir, of course not. Can't imagine her doing that. But I kind of got the impression of something being wrong."

Again, the pause and consideration before Geraint answered. "Parenting issues, that's all. But you know how difficult they can be."

He did. Osian kept him busy, though he'd prefer to be busier in that arena. He glanced at the gold band on his left hand. "But she seems ..." He struggled to find the words. "Too quiet, tired."

"Pale too," Geraint added. "Wonder if she's coming down with something? I'll speak to her." When he refocused on Madoc, Madoc felt pinned. "What have you told her about your situation?"

"Only that I have a son."

"Not that you're divorced?"

Madoc held up his left hand, showing his wedding ring. "This still offers some small protection."

"You know you don't need that protection with Ruth."

"Does she trust me?" Madoc needed to know. "Professionally if not personally?"

Those caterpillars huddled up for a conflab. "I'd say so. She's been complimentary about your work. I'm sure the personal trust will build. Just give her a little time. After all, she comes to work to work."

That struck a negative chord. "Sounds like running away."

"Does she strike you as the kind who runs from anything?"

"No." That was laughable.

"Exactly." Geraint leaned back. "How are you finding working with her?"

"Good." Madoc nodded. "I like that she's straight with me. But I know she's holding back. Maybe it is just parenting issues, but it feels like more. She is okay, isn't she? I think the threat of the Professional Standards worried her a bit."

"That should worry any officer worth their salt. The vaguest hint of that sort of thing can blight a career, and she's too good for it."

"Totally."

Geraint considered him with a shrew gaze. "What's your coping mechanism?"

The truth was not something he generally revealed, but Geraint had already proved he respected the privacy of his staff. And as they were the only ones in the office, he'd risk it. "Yoga."

Geraint's look was surprised amusement. "Not a rugby man, then?"

He shrugged. "I'll attend a match or two, but I'm not a great fan. And before you ask, same with football."

"Yoga keeps you fit, does it?"

"No, the running, squash, and kickboxing does that. Yoga keeps me calm and flexible enough not to feel the pain of the running, squash, and kickboxing."

Geraint nodded. "How're the cases going?"

"Ruth's good."

"I know. That wasn't the question."

"Pippa admitted that the oddity at the start of the timeline could be because she doesn't have a clock in the bedroom."

"Who doesn't have a clock in the bedroom?" Geraint asked. "For the alarm if nothing else?"

"Well, I don't. I just use the alarm on my phone. But in Raymond's case, he was an insomniac. His doctor advised removing the clock so he couldn't watch the hours drag by. Instead, he used his watch alarm to wake him, and Pippa doesn't need an alarm because she doesn't work."

Geraint huffed a laugh. "All so prosaic when you lay it out like that."

"Yeah, there's something odd in the timeline of the death, but we can't find what. There's nothing to indicate the Jameses were involved in Bevan's death, and no other enemies have come to light. We think we've solved one of the missing girls cases our Naked Lady could have been. And that trawl through Dwayne Evans' trophies may have moved another on. Forensics are doing the DNA tests to confirm if the second body is Seren Rosser or not. No new leads on why she might be dead, but I'm going to do a thorough review of her file tomorrow."

"You do realise tomorrow's Saturday?"

Yeah, and he still needed to put up some plaster board. "You realise murder takes precedence?"

Geraint grinned. "Now you sound like Ruth. Did she tell you to come in tomorrow?"

"We didn't discuss it," he admitted. "But I'm just going to go through a few things. I want to …" He wasn't sure how to express the need he felt. "I want to get things right. Be professional. I want to impress her."

This time, Geraint chuckled. "Glad she's made a good impression on you. Just watch out for the overtime; budgets and all that."

"You're working late."

The senior officer made an odd noise and turned back to his file. Madoc was effectively dismissed.

Though Madoc had many questions, now wasn't the time to ask. Instead, he sat at his desk, and quickly wrote up his notes.

Even as he packed up and drove home, he was thinking about what he had seen. The image of that girl on the Lush Ladies site. It nagged at him, but he couldn't see why.

He was grateful to get home and find Andrew waiting. The drywall went up quickly and well.

Chapter 28

The idea had come to Madoc during the night.

Can't imagine why.

He ignored his passenger. Before he could act on his idea, he needed approval, and because of how yesterday ended, he didn't even know if Ruth would be in today. He had to show his abilities in the job or he risked losing it. Whoever was in as senior officer, he'd have to convince them his idea would help. So, he had to be logical. Even with Ruth, he couldn't just say it was gut instinct again, couldn't tell her he'd had a dream, or she'd definitely think him a flake. No, he had to supply a good, reasoned argument as to why the idea was worthwhile. He had to find the evidence to point them in this odd direction. He also wanted to look into Bradley's accident. That name, *Mair Merch Farw*, was scratching at his consciousness.

He bounded up the stairs, ready to start the day, to find what he needed to impress Ruth on Monday.

The view stopped him short.

Ruth was at her desk.

How early had she arrived? How difficult were her parenting difficulties?

She looked up as he approached, nodded in greeting, and focused back on her files. She signed something off, closed the file, and put it to the side.

"Morning."

He was sitting now but returned the greeting as he switched on his computer. With Ruth in, he wasn't sure he could research Bradley's case after all. Yet his conscience pricked. He couldn't forsake the study. He had the data, and there was no question of anyone else being involved, but the rest would have to wait.

Ruth's mobile rang. She glanced at it, frowned, and answered. "What?"

The tone was harsh. She clearly knew her caller and didn't like whoever it was. He didn't hear the response, but he saw the colour drain from her face.

"He was ready and waiting when I left. Maybe you should have been on time."

More listening, the male voice on the other end of the line getting louder.

"All fucking right!" Ruth all but shouted. "I'll see what I can find out." She was swearing again as she ended that call and started another. Her fingers drummed hard on the desk as she waited. Finally, the answer apparently came. "Zach." The snap was hard, she closed her eyes, taking a deep breath. "Sorry, babe. Your father just called. Where are you?"

She listened, and Madoc tried to work as if he wasn't straining to hear every word.

"Zach, sweetheart. I totally get it, but you have to see him. He's your father."

That made little sense. Ruth was a widow, so why would she be having trouble getting her son to see his father?

Her husband and his father aren't the same man, dumbass.

His passenger was really grating, and the lack of identity grated as much.

"Not till you're sixteen at least." Ruth said, the listened. "Well, I'm sorry, but you're just going to have to suck it up for now."

More argument, then Madoc vaguely made out a whine from Zach. He realised if Ruth was prepared to leave the boy home to wait for someone, then he must be older than Madoc thought. Eleven or twelve? That meant Ruth had him very young.

"Look, right now all I can tell you is that there will be a mass of legal wrangling if you don't go see your father. But we'll talk more when you're home on Sunday, okay? Please, Zach, I can't be worrying about you all day. I mean, I will anyway, but … you know what I mean. Please, love, just spend the weekend with your father as arranged." There was some pause. "I bet he'll let you play video games longer than I do." Again, she listened. "Well, let's face it, he can't be as bad as I am."

Madoc heard a distant laugh.

"Okay, love. I get it. But you'll go today, yeah?" Her relief was palpable. "Yes. We'll talk when you're home tomorrow. I promise. Love you."

She sighed, switched off the phone, and shot him a warning glare. "Don't ask. Don't repeat."

Clear enough. "Okay."

Ruth returned her attention to the files as he started pulling together the information he needed, though he was still processing what he'd heard. He wasn't even standing up, but he felt he was walking on eggshells. A quick glance around assured him there were few staff in today, weekends always being quieter.

"Ruth?" he asked quietly.

"Yeah?"

"You okay?"

She looked up. Sighed. "Yeah. I'm fine."

"Good." He wasn't convinced, but he had to keep it professional. Taking up a file, he stood and moved around to sit at the file-covered desk beside her. There were fewer files than on Tuesday. She was frowning slightly at him. He had to make his case well. "I've got a suggestion and I doubt you're gonna like it."

"Well …" She looked heavenward, perhaps for inspiration. "Maybe the best thing for both of us is for you to just say it."

"The thing is—" He swallowed his nerves. "—I think we should head down to the Lush Ladies studio."

The frown deepened. "Why?"

"It's kind of …" Dare he? He internally cringed even as the words came out. "Gut instinct."

"Really?" Her sardonic look tripped down his body. "You sure this instinct isn't coming from a few inches lower?"

"Yes, sir, I am." His cheeks burnt. "That's not really what you think of me, is it?"

"No, but hey, if you light up a neon sign saying 'kick me', there's a bloody good chance I will." She sighed. "Look, I'm sorry. That's my life right now: overreact, then have to apologise."

That didn't sound good. Didn't sound like just parenting issues, either. It helped explain her reaction to Geraint earlier in the week, though. And internally, she was still screaming. However, he mustn't pry.

Oh, go on. I want to know.

She faced him directly again, that odd mix of strength and vulnerability. "Okay, then. Can I just check?" She kept her voice low not to carry. "Is this one of your *instincts*?"

"Sort of."

Her sigh left him wondering how she was adjusting to knowing. "Madoc, no disrespect intended, but I need a better reason than that."

He nodded. "Raymond Bevan used Lush Ladies on the morning he died."

"Okay," she said, sitting back. "But so what? Why do we need to go there?"

"'Cos of this." Madoc opened the Evans file and pulled out a screenshot of a woman captioned as 'Queen Ree'. Ruth frowned at the picture, blinked, then looked closer.

"Is that Maggie Drake's daughter?"

"She could be," Madoc confirmed.

For a moment, the image in Ruth's hand dropped. She turned her head slightly. Oddly, he thought she was looking at the board for Seren Rosser. He couldn't make out why.

"She certainly looks like the pictures in Maggie's house," he pushed. "But Maggie told us her daughter was living in London working as a model. Catalogue stuff, she said. Some advert, only shown on southeast stations."

Ruth was nodding, her lip twisted like she was biting the inside. "She also said Rhiamon did Fashion Week in Milan a few weeks ago."

Madoc didn't understand. "So?"

"I looked it up," Ruth explained. "Milan Fashion Weeks are in February and September/October. Given that it's now May, that's rather more than a few weeks away."

"True, but people misrepresent dates a lot. You think she lied?"

"Either that or her daughter lied to her. Did you get an address for Lush Ladies?"

"Yeah, they're based at a site in Newport."

"Newport?" She didn't sound too happy. "Under Gwent Police jurisdiction."

"Yeah, but–"

He cut off when she raised her hand. "That's a way to go without very good reason." Again, her eyes twitched up behind him. "We could just call the company and ask for details of Raymond's activity."

"We could," Madoc agreed, trying to push down his disappointment and the concerns in his own head. "Everything all right, sir? Things I can't ask about aside?"

She frowned as she returned her gaze to him. "Yes, everything is okay. It's just that I spoke to Rita before I left yesterday."

"Rita?"

"Constable Jefferies. Works in Mike's team."

"Oh, of course, yes. Sorry."

She shrugged. "You're new, you can't take in everyone's names that quick. Anyway, she thinks Rhiamon Drake might have been up for a place on *Valleys View,* just like Seren."

Now Madoc's stomach churned. "That's a bit of a coincidence."

"Isn't it? That means I've got questions for Rhiamon Drake." Again, her focus flicked up to the board.

"Sir?"

Tension clouded her eyes as she met his gaze. What was bothering her? Would she tell him if he asked?

"This is all a bit tenuous," she said.

For all he agreed, he didn't want to.

"So, why does it feel like the right direction to go?" she asked.

That was the very point that had caught him out. "I checked the action list," Madoc said. "Rhiamon's name is on the list of people of interest. Despite what her mother said, she lives in Newport, not London."

Now those brows moved up in surprise. "Impressive," she said. "Christ, even I don't lie to my mother about where I live."

There was so much to unpack in that statement that Madoc didn't know where to start.

On your own time, not now.

Steel returned to Ruth's eyes. The barrier between work and home.

"Right," she said. "I'll make a call first – after all, we are encroaching on Gwent's territory, but it shouldn't be a problem. Do you reckon Lush Ladies will be working today?"

"Why not? More men not working on a weekend may well mean more punters for them. Besides, it's an internet site, potential for customers all over the world. The day and hour may be irrelevant."

After spending some time discussing the best approach when they arrived in Newport, they headed out. Ruth drove the Lexus, not a pool car. Madoc wasn't sure how he felt about her doing all the driving. On the one hand, it was great – less pressure on him, but he felt slightly emasculated. And this car! It was luxury indeed compared to the much rougher ride of his old Defender. He stretched his legs out just because he could. The A470 and M4 had been nicely quiet, but by the time they reached the rise into Newport, the road was clogging, showing how the world was waking and going shopping, a more leisurely Saturday start.

"It's nice up here," Ruth said, pulling into the secluded cul-de-sac. "Every house has at least three bedrooms, up to five, I believe. Minimum half-million price tag."

Madoc could see what they were paying for, too. Every house was detached, with a decent front garden and a generous space between the buildings. All the houses had a driveway and a garage for at least one car, some two. He'd seen new estates in Cardiff with houses of the same or similar design, probably the same developer.

There was no movement from within the house of interest as they approached.

Without instruction, Madoc took the lead, his long legs eating up the short drive. He slowed his pace, suddenly realising what he was doing. He turned to look back at Ruth. Her brows were up, her lips slightly twisted, her eyes sparkled with sardonic amusement.

"In a hurry, Sergeant?"

"Sorry, sir."

She shrugged as she walked past him. "Not a problem."

There was a doorbell evident, but the ring was muted, not to mention an annoying tinny version of a classic he couldn't name. The uPVC door stood as a clean, neat guard. The fan window at the top of the door gave little view of what was inside. Madoc stretched up on tiptoe to look through - nothing. They waited in heavy silence. No response. Ruth rang again. Again, no response.

Stepping back, Ruth looked up. He looked, too. The windows were closed, and there were no lights on. Not that any were needed at this time of day. Madoc found Ruth looking up at him. He returned her gaze and shrugged.

"Try knocking," she suggested as she stepped to the side of the house. There was a gateway between the house and the double garage that led to the back garden.

Madoc knocked but shifted to see Ruth stretch up and feel for the latch that gave and allowed her to step through to the back of the house. He turned back to the door. Nothing to see. He heard a hammering at the back door. Ruth didn't take prisoners. He stepped onto the featureless lawn and looked through the front window. Vertical blinds hung at an angle; he couldn't see anything of use.

Ruth re-appeared.

"Anything?" Palmer asked.

Her initial answer was a head shake. "Big back garden. Shrubs still have last year's woody growth, not flowering well. Lawn's lush but could do with a mow. Presumably Rhiamon isn't an avid gardener. Couldn't see anyone or anything inside, though. All the windows are closed and no answer when I knocked. Doors are locked."

"Should we be worried?"

Another head shake. "Not yet. It probably doesn't mean much. Rhiamon's a young woman, could be staying with friends, whatever. Might even be out shopping. Or maybe she actually is sick, like her mum said. What?"

She must have seen him frown.

"You said mum, not mam," he pointed out. "That's not a Cardiff thing."

She shrugged. "It's a having-an-English-mother thing. We've got contact numbers for Rhiamon, right?"

"We do."

"Okay, we'll phone her at some point, then. Maybe try later. If that doesn't work, I'll ask Gwent to do a call round." She headed for the car. Madoc followed.

Chapter 29

Ruth pulled up by the industrial unit that was clearly marked LL Productions. Madoc looked around at the industrial units as he stepped from the car. The estate was decades old, and it showed. They weren't far from the Newport Transporter Bridge. The road was dark and wet from overnight rain, emphasising the fact that the drains needed a good clear out.

"Not what I was expecting," he said as he turned to Ruth.

"Location doesn't surprise me." Ruth locked the car. "Neither do they, but they do annoy me." She pointed to three sports cars, two Porsches and a Lotus. Nice cars. None over three years old.

"Annoy? Why?"

"Because I kind of fancy having a Porsche."

He looked over the Lexus. An ES. Takumi version, last year's model. Metallic black. With all the optional extras. The HUD display was like a science fiction set. It was well out of his price bracket, well beyond the pockets of most police inspectors, too. If she could afford this, she could afford a Porsche.

"Also, because I'm conflicted about how I view the sex industry." Ruth said. "On the one hand, I am disgusted that men objectify women in a way that means this sort of thing can happen. I also think that some of it, like this cam-girl stuff, is at least to some extent consensual, and better this than there being a rapist in every shadow. Part of me congratulates these girls on making money while they can. Let them rip off the tossers. Closely followed by the worry of what's going to happen to the girls later in life. After all, there's a time limit on how long this career can last."

Madoc understood every point, even shared some of the conflicts, but was aware he had a different perspective. There were no simple answers for the oldest of professions. Tech had just given it new options. "Not sure age is a barrier anymore. Pretty sure I've heard there's a seventy-odd-year-old dominatrix still working in the UK."

Ruth apparently didn't know how to respond to that and headed towards the building. It stood in grey steel-cladding, paint peeling on the exposed stretches. Not seedy, but not salubrious. Average and easily overlooked. Perhaps that was best, in this line of work. Ruth tried the door and found it locked. She pressed bell on the side.

"Did you hear anything?" Madoc asked.

"No, but if this is a broadcasting location, the bell probably puts on a light rather than ringing a bell," Ruth suggested. "Wouldn't want to put the punters off their stroke."

His appreciation for her dark humour growing, Madoc tried to control his smile as the door opened to reveal a woman in a smart silk blouse and casual slacks. There wasn't a grey hair on her head but the thickening of her waist, lines around her eyes, and scragginess of her neck all suggested she was into middle age. Keen eyes surveyed him critically and got curious, then she returned her attention to Ruth.

"Yes?"

"Hi, I'm Detective Inspector Ruth Atkins." She displayed her warrant card. "This is Detective Sergeant Madoc Palmer. May we have a word?"

"Everything here is perfectly legal."

They knew that, though it was a tight-run thing.

"Good, but that's not actually why we're here," Ruth said easily. "Can we come in and talk?"

The woman paused, appeared reluctant, then stepped back. Madoc let Ruth go first but didn't miss the way the other woman assessed him.

You're the eye-candy, his passenger reminded him. **Maybe now would be a good time to use that.**

"Hi." He smiled as the woman closed the door. "Sorry, I didn't catch your name."

"Gwyneth," she said. "Gwyneth Davis, no e."

"You're the owner?" He'd done his research. "I was expecting someone older with all you've achieved."

Gwyneth smiled at him then returned her attention to Ruth. "Is that charm or smarm?"

Ruth easily met the older woman's eye. "I think he was going for charm. To be honest, I expected you to be older, too, but then expectations can be so dangerous. Where would you prefer to have this discussion?"

"Will here do?" Gwyneth raised her hand towards the corner sofa unit opposite the reception desk.

Partitioned off from the rest of the unit, this area gave no indication of what went on inside. In fact, it looked like the blandest reception Madoc had ever stepped into. There wasn't even a plastic pot plant.

Ruth indicated her acceptance by taking a seat, a flick of her eyes calling him to heel to sit beside her, as Gwyneth took the far end of the grey stretch of armless seats.

"Your site has come up in connection with two of our investigations," Ruth said.

"You're not the local vice squad." Gwyneth showed her age with that remark.

"No, we're not vice – which, by the way, is not a term we use anymore. We're from South Wales Police, not Gwent, based out of Merthyr."

Gwyneth looked unconcerned. "Okay, well, we are on the internet so anyone can login to our service."

"As long as they have a credit card."

"Would you deny us a living, Inspector?"

"No, not at all. That is part of why we wanted to talk to you. From what I understand, any user of your site must login and register a credit card before they can see anything of interest, is that right?"

"Generally. However, there are some brief clips of the girls that can be viewed for free. PG-rated, of course, and a client would have to at least part-register to see those."

"Part-register?"

"Name, email, no card details at that point. Just creates a very basic user account."

"Okay, so how does it work with charges? Do you record time spent viewing videos, or charge for however many watches?"

Madoc cringed internally; Gwyneth grinned.

"You really don't know how this works, do you, Inspector?"

Ruth's small shrug showed no embarrassment at the fact. "No, not my area of interest."

Gwyneth turned to Madoc. "What about you? Is this your area of interest?"

The woman stood before he could think of a safe answer.

"Come with me," Gwyneth said to them both. "Let me show you how it works."

She moved to an interior door, pressing a sequence of buttons to release the lock. They moved into a cross between a warehouse and a control room, though it was cleaner and neater than the last CCTV control room Madoc had been in. There was a bank of monitors along one wall. A dozen of them looked at rooms, bedrooms, three of them occupied. Madoc tried not to look at those. Then he glanced over the other monitors with their readouts of activities.

"Are these your staff's bedrooms or sets here?" Ruth asked.

"Sets here. I've heard of girls working from home being traced to their actual locations via IP addresses and being attacked there. Here we have some security. If any random came here looking for trouble, we'd batten down the hatches and call the police. I only opened the door direct to you two because

Drew called to forewarn me a couple of officers would be calling today. He didn't say more than that, mind."

Drew. DS Andrew Creak, Gwent Police, who Ruth had called to keep the neighbours happy before they came down here.

"He didn't know more than that," Ruth admitted. "Okay, so some man–"

"They're not all men," Gwyneth said.

Ruth stopped. "Right, of course. Sorry, I wasn't thinking. Okay, so some punter logs in, presumably you have their cards on record – then what? They select the girl they want to see?"

"Yes. The girls tend to have regular hours when they are available, but sometimes a client will arrange specific times with them."

Ruth looked confused. "Right, I'm clearly missing something. Are you saying that this is all live? No videos, just women in those sets doing what they do for whoever is watching?"

Gwyneth nodded. "Essentially, yes. Just to clear it up, customers log in, pick the room or girl they are interested in, and get the feed from that camera. For a higher charge, the client can book a solo viewing. They can also chat with the girls, ask them to do things. The girls can comply if they want, or not if they don't. Sometimes, they can charge extra, or if the client is taking things too far, they can put them on a time out. If clients get really bad, we can block them, but thankfully, I haven't had to do that often. The client gets what they want, the girls only have to go as far as they're comfortable. Everyone's safe."

"Sounds …" Ruth searched for the word, but her phone interrupted. She frowned when she saw the display. "Excuse me."

As Ruth moved away, Madoc moved closer to Gwyneth. "You say the clients can chat with the girls. How? Do you have audio?"

"We broadcast audio, but the clients' chat comes in as text." Gwyneth pointed to screen six and there at the bottom, in nearly illiterate text, was a client request coming through. Clearly, this was a man who didn't type, possibly not one-handed anyway, and what he requested wasn't anything original or shocking. Madoc decided it was time to look away from the screens.

"So, the girls know who's watching?"

"They know the client by their avatar name, but they don't know who the client is IRL."

"IRL?" Madoc asked.

Gwyneth raised a brow. "In real life."

"'Course, sorry." Thankfully, it was cold, so his embarrassment was less obvious. "Are these like instant messages, then? Sent, read, and gone?"

"More like direct messages. We keep a record for a month, just in case someone escalates dangerously. Longer if we think there's a need."

"And the girls all work from here?"

"Not all, no. We have girls who prefer to work from other locations, but all broadcasts come through us so they can't be traced elsewhere."

"You really do do everything to keep your staff safe, don't you? Mind if I ask why?"

"Good business," Gwyneth answered. "When I started in glamour modelling, trust me, I saw and did – and was forced into – things that I didn't want, didn't enjoy. So, when I got some money behind me to start this place, I wanted to take care of my girls the way no one took care of me. I don't tie these girls into anything. They do the times they choose. My only insistence is that, if they promise a session, they attend it, and it's a one-shot deal. They miss one promised time and they're out."

"Seems tough," he said. Though, when she was taking as much care of them as she was, it was worth it for the right girls. A damn sight safer than lurking on street corners, though those girls and these probably weren't the same sort. He glanced at Ruth. Whoever she was talking to, the tight body language suggested it wasn't a fun call. Madoc focused back on Gwyneth.

"It is tough, but I've had girls who've used this as income whilst at university. Means they didn't have to work long hours that pulled them away from their studies and they didn't have massive debt as they go out into the real world."

A side of the industry many forgot, but he could imagine it coming back to destroy careers later. Still, not his problem.

"You have one client, name of Raymond Bevan. Any chance we can get a printout of any conversations he had in the last month?"

Gwyneth looked uncertain. "What about client confidentiality?"

"Raymond Bevan died Tuesday morning in suspicious circumstances," Madoc explained. "We're trying to understand who he was, what his last movements were."

"You mean the guy in the papers? The one in the ditch?"

The inaccuracy of reporting, Madoc silently lamented. "Close enough."

"Have you got a warrant?"

"No, but getting one shouldn't be a problem. We know that he was on the Lush Ladies site Tuesday morning, but not when he logged in or out." He glanced at Ruth. Eye-candy to bad cop. "Look, if we have to get a warrant, she'll get annoyed. Then she'll look at your business closer than any of us want. Raymond Bevan is our only interest right now, no hint of fault with you or Lush Ladies."

Gwyneth still didn't look happy. "Give me a moment." She drew up a login screen on the computer. He didn't watch her fingers; he didn't need to know. Instead, he glanced across the room. He did wonder what had left Ruth so pale.

"Hmm."

The odd noise brought his attention back to Gwyneth. "What is it?"

"His avatar name. So typical. 'Mr Big Tool'. Like anyone this end believes that kind of tripe. But there are loads like it."

He dreaded to think what Dwayne Evans called himself. Wanker Extraordinaire, perhaps? "Come on now, we must account for the male ego."

She tipped her head up to look at him. It wasn't a comfortable gaze.

"Well, in our own little minds, anyway," he grumbled.

"Yeah, well." She returned her attention to the screen. "Most men think this is six inches." She held up a hand, thumb and forefinger about three inches apart. He felt shorter than that on behalf of every male on the planet.

"Can you give us a list of his activity? Exactly when he logged in and out, any messages he sent?" he asked.

"There're no flags on his account to suggest a problem."

"Good. I'd still like a report to demonstrate that we've been thorough."

"You'll have to give me a minute to compile the report."

Madoc thanked her as he heard Ruth bid her caller goodbye. She took a deep breath, and let it out slow and controlled before she moved towards them. He stepped away from Gwyneth.

"Problem?" Madoc asked quietly.

Her response was non-committal. "What's going on?"

Madoc explained.

As the printer started spitting out pages, Gwyneth turned to them. "You said that the company had come up in two cases. What was the other one?"

"Known sex offender," Madoc said.

"Can you share a name? I can look up his details and usage if you need," Gwyneth offered.

Ruth nodded her release.

"It's Dwayne Evans," Madoc supplied.

More tapping on the keyboard. "Oh yeah, 'Big Boyo 200'." Gwyneth tutted. "We had an issue with this guy a while back. We got stops on his card as he maxed out. But he's no trouble, no warning flags from any of the girls. In fact, some of them love him. We have a minimum payment system here, and he gets off really quick, so they have less to do for the same amount of money." Gwyneth's frown deepened. "That's interesting. Both accounts show a preference for Queen Ree."

"We found Queen Ree's business card in Dwayne's personal effects."

Gwyneth nodded. "Probably how he found the site."

"Was she chatting with either of them Tuesday morning?" Madoc asked when Ruth didn't.

A few keystrokes later and Gwyneth answered. "Yes, she was chatting to Mr Big Tool, but Big Boyo had been and gone much earlier after chatting with Suzi Wong."

Clearly another false name. "On Tuesday," Madoc asked, "did Queen Ree leave after Mr Big Tool signed off?"

"Hope not." Gwyneth checked. "No, she was here until six. With other clients. Don't think I should give you their details."

"No problem," he assured her. "Can you confirm Queen Ree's real name?"

Those keen eyes shifted between them.

"We believe her to be one Rhiamon Drake," Madoc said.

Gwyneth confirmed it.

"Address?"

Gwyneth had to check, but it was the same address they had on file.

"That's a very pleasant area," Madoc said. "She must be raking it in here."

Gwyneth shrugged. "She's earning nicely, but for a place up there, I'd say she's either overstretched herself or has another income stream I'm not aware of."

"Is she working today?"

"Not today, no. Ree works nights mostly. Comes in around 11 p.m., works till 6 a.m. Monday to Thursday. It's a popular time, so she always has lots of clients. That's how she's earning so much. Sometimes she comes in on weekday afternoons, usually only for an hour or two for one-to-one clients. Her choice."

"Any changes in the last few weeks?"

"Nothing major. Though she has had a few additional one-to-ones, but they often clump, then a client drifts off. She's not implicated in anything, is she?"

Madoc offered what he hoped was a reassuring smile. "Not that we know about. As I said, we're just trying to verify the timeline on Raymond Bevan's last day."

"Well, good luck with that," Gwyneth offered as she passed over the printout.

Chapter 30

Ruth sat in the driver's seat and gripped the steering wheel tight. The phone call had not been easy. She didn't want to deal with that at the best of times, certainly not while she was working. Maybe she shouldn't be working on a Saturday. But Zach was with his father – at least, she assumed he was from the lack of secondary calls. The question was, what to do about the latest call?

"We're not going to go far if you don't start the engine."

Twisting just her neck, she looked at Palmer beside her. Had to stop and figure out what he was saying.

"Are you really okay?" He looked genuinely concerned.

She neither wanted nor needed his concern. "Don't fancy driving through Newport town centre on a Saturday. Just thinking about the best route," she lied.

Palmer shrugged. "Either to the train station and up, or out to the M4 and back in at High Cross. Neither choice stands out as being that much better than the other."

"True." She still didn't start the car.

"Do you want to tell me about the call?"

"Later." She looked at the papers in his hand as she finally started the softly purring engine. "Does that register the time of Raymond's last conversation with Queen Ree?"

He riffled through as she pulled easily away.

"Ended at 04:07 Tuesday morning."

"Good match." Ruth sighed. She didn't need the traffic through town on a Saturday. She liked her car without scratches, a thing too many other drivers didn't seem concerned about. Still, the address in Ridgeway was quiet, nice, suburban, not the sort of place you'd expect to find a sex worker – or maybe it was. She clearly knew nothing about the online sex industry. Even Gwyneth thought Rhiamon was making money some other way to afford that house.

As Ruth reached the address, another car was pulling onto Rhiamon Drake's drive and the door across the double garage was opening. Ruth pulled up to the curb behind.

"You take the lead," she said.

"Yes, sir." Palmer was quick out of the car.

Watching the slow rise of the garage door, Ruth spotted a second car, a dark green one. Palmer was showing the driver his warrant card. The garage door reversed direction.

At least the driver was taking note. But there was still a fear that they might pull back without notice. She'd heard dreadful tales of some unaccountable driver actions when faced with the police. But now the driver's door opened, and a woman stepped out. Finally, Ruth stopped the engine and opened the door, having to relax back when she found she'd forgotten to release the seatbelt. With deliberate care, she closed the door and made sure to lock the car.

The female driver looked at Ruth with disdain.

Palmer introduced them. Ruth automatically displayed her warrant card.

Rhiamon was dressed all in black, in leggings and a baggy jumper. Ruth saw Rhiamon's hair was only shoulder length. The mounded beehive seen on Queen Ree must be a hair piece.

The younger woman led them to the front door. The beeping spoke of a house alarm that she stepped in and disarmed, inside what Ruth assumed to be a cloakroom.

Rhiamon grumbled as she opened the door wider. "I suppose you'd best come in. But take your shoes off."

"No," Ruth said and stepped in, though she did wipe her feet.

"Wipe your feet properly, then."

Ruth stopped doing so.

They stepped into the hall, all white walls and woodwork. Rhiamon pointed to their right to a sitting room. A massive corner sofa dominated the room, though the 60-inch TV on the wall gave it a run for its money. Other than those two pieces, there was nothing. The walls, ceiling, even the carpet was white. Little wonder Rhiamon wanted them to wipe their feet. In the unremitting white, the only colour was black: the TV and the owner.

Ruth stood quietly at the side of the room while Rhiamon sprawled and watched them indolently. Palmer explained their interest. The way Rhiamon's eyes roved over him was assessing. Ruth knew what the other woman was thinking. Gorgeous specimen of a man: tall, good looking, fit, probably good in the sack. Ruth's own thought struck her as odd. There was no guarantee that someone who looked that good *was* that good. Her mind was wandering.

Focus.

She had to pay attention, despite the phone call replaying on a loop in her mind. Those echoes demanded her attention, dragging her back to what had happened. It took control of her head, took her heart to the pain, to her worst failure.

Concentrate. You missed the conversation.

"Yeah, I know who you mean. He claimed he knew me, but I don't remember him. It doesn't help, of course, that all I see is a fake name on the screen. I've no idea who he is."

Palmer reached into his pocket and retrieved a photograph, moving closer to Rhiamon and sitting near her on the wide expanse of sofa. The woman studied the picture, was clearly searching her memory. But nothing.

"Sorry, no." Rhiamon passed the picture back. "I don't remember him, but from what he said, he knows Mam. What with him being her generation and them living in the same stupid village. You might have more luck talking to her. It's likely she knows him."

More than likely, given that they worked together. The thought made Ruth stop. It begged another question, which brought her back to the here and now.

"When did you last talk to your mother?" Palmer asked, before Ruth could even formulate the question.

Get your head in the game, woman.

"Last Sunday," Rhiamon said. "We usually talk early Sunday afternoon. After lunch."

Six days ago. Another conversation with another mother had thrown Ruth off her game. It had been over six months since Ruth had spoken to her own mother. Though 'spoken to' might be a stretch. They had attended the same show at the New Theatre in Cardiff. She'd greeted her mother, her mother had snubbed her.

"Do you know who your mother works for?"

"'Course I do. What's that got to do with anything?"

Palmer wordlessly pressed the point.

Rhiamon huffed. "Shalestone Homes. She does their site admin. Moves sites, trains people." This time she shrugged. "Not exactly brain surgery."

Neither's your job.

Ruth just about kept the words internalised. But she found the question she needed to ask. "When you say you talked to your mother, did you actually *talk*?"

Rhiamon frowned at her. "Well, how else do you communicate down the phone?"

"There is a difference between talking and just speaking," Palmer saved Ruth from explaining. And screaming. "I've known women who can speak for hours and never say a word of value."

"Oh yeah, I see what you mean," Rhiamon admitted. "I guess we speak a lot. We talk, but we don't say a whole heap. It's not like there's much to say. She's got a dead-end job she's been doing for the best part of twenty years. She might change location, but the job doesn't change. There's nothing new ever going on with her. Not even with Khol, and that damn dog is everything to her. She doesn't seem to have a life of her own. Never did. It was all me and Dad, but he buggered off and I grew up. Despite her best efforts." Bitterness tainted every word, and somehow Ruth remained unconvinced by any of it.

"And what about your life?" Palmer asked. "How much do you really tell her? Your mother said you were living in London, doing commercials and catalogue shots, even Fashion Week in Milan."

Now she had seen her, it was clear to Ruth that Rhiamon was nowhere near being a catwalk model. Rhiamon had a great shape, but she wasn't tall enough or skinny enough for high fashion.

"Well, I did move to London," Rhiamon said. "I was doing commercials and I do catalogue shoots now and then, just not the kind my mam would ever look through. I did go to Milan a few weeks back, for a holiday."

"When did you move to London?" Ruth asked.

Rhiamon's features tightened as she looked up. "Ten years ago."

"Why?"

"Because I wanted to."

Not overly helpful.

"When did you tell your mother not to come to London to visit you this weekend?"

Rhiamon's look soured, increasing her likeness to Maggie. "I texted her on Wednesday. Said I wasn't feeling well."

"Why?"

"Because the flat I usually use wasn't available. Does it matter?"

"Not really." Ruth looked to Palmer. He was getting better results, and she shouldn't impede that.

"You've been registered at this address for a few years now," Palmer said softly. "Why doesn't your mother know that?"

Rhiamon hung her head, colour creeping up her cheeks. Ruth understood better than most how difficult mother-daughter relationships could be, but she did not understand this one.

"If Mam knew I was back in Wales, she'd insist I move back home. But I don't want to live in the back of beyond. And I don't want her constantly looking over my shoulder. Or worse yet, she might insist on coming and living with me."

While feeling affronted on behalf of all Merthyr residents, Ruth both understood and figured there would be enough room for Maggie here. This had to be a four-bed house at least. Black dog hairs on all this white might be an issue, though.

Rhiamon was still talking. "You've got no idea what it's like to have a mother who thinks you have star quality. All my life she's been pushing me. She wanted me to have dance lessons, but I have two left feet. I was tortured by the girls who had talent. She wanted me to go to drama school, so I did that, enjoyed it. She was constantly taking me to auditions, photo shoots where I was good, but never the best. Mam never understood that I wasn't good enough for what she wanted me to do. There were loads of things I could have done, but she said they were beneath me. They weren't, they were beneath *her*. So, she kept me away from what I could have done well and forced me into stuff where I could only be average at best. She wanted me in films, but the producers she shoved me in front of all said the same thing: the only way I'd be a film star was on adult only movies. Mam heard that once and threw a total fit. So embarrassing. Can you imagine how she'd react to finding out that I touch myself for men for a living? She'd kill knowing that!"

"I understand," Palmer said smoothly.

"You won't tell her, will you?"

Now Palmer looked to Ruth for a response.

"I can't see how that would help anyone," Ruth said. "However, I can't guarantee it won't get out." She only wished she could, but the police were humans, too, and humans made mistakes.

"What happened between the two of you?" Palmer's gentle question drew Rhiamon's attention to him. The woman was attracted, and Palmer was making the most of that. Odd. She'd expect someone doing what Rhiamon did for a living to be more cynical, immune to such a man. Still, it was working, and she wouldn't interfere.

"The two of us?"

"You and your mam? Loads of people I encounter barely keep in touch with their parents, but you said you and your mam call every Sunday. Yet you can't stand her to know you live so close?"

Rhiamon looked down and shrugged. "We had a falling out. She'd been such a pushy stage mom that I started seeing casting guys rolling their eyes, turning and walking away when they saw us. She got banned from Culverhouse Cross Studios. I could go, but she wasn't allowed. That pissed her off. I can't say I enjoyed it either, but I found alternatives."

"Like moving to London?"

"It's where the action is."

Ruth couldn't argue with that. Even though she'd grown up in Cardiff, which had way more opportunities than most of the region, many of her friends and family had hankered for life in the English capital. "Were you still here when *Valleys View* started casting?" Ruth asked.

Rhiamon looked up at her, paused. "Yes, I was. Why?"

"Did you apply?" Ruth asked. "Culverhouse Cross Studios are BBC, aren't they? You shouldn't have had any issue with an independent production."

"No. Well. I didn't, not really."

"So, you did apply?"

Again, Ruth got that tight-lipped assessment. "Yes, I applied. Most people I knew did. Didn't you? You look about the right age, upper age limit maybe."

Cheeky cow. "Not my thing."

"No, it was all young, lusty, and prepared to make a fool of yourself." Rhiamon looked Ruth up and down. "Somehow, Sergeant, that doesn't look like your kind of thing."

"It's not, and I'm the inspector. He's the sergeant."

Rhiamon looked back to Palmer. "She's your boss?"

"Yep. Sometimes, I even have to salute her."

Rhiamon's smile twisted. She looked back at Ruth. "So, you get to play the dominatrix?"

"So," Palmer said, saving Ruth from answering, "to sum up. You knew your client, Mr Big Tool. You're aware he was someone who lived in your home village, but you don't remember him from your past, or recognise him from the photo. And the name Raymond Bevan doesn't mean anything to you?"

"Sounds about right." Rhiamon nodded.

Palmer looked to Ruth.

"How far did you get with *Valleys View*?" Ruth asked.

"Quite a way," Rhiamon admitted. "But not to the last round."

"Did you do a screen test in Cardiff for it?"

Rhiamon's look darkened. "Several."

"Did you meet any of the other applicants?"

Rhiamon didn't look half so comfortable now. "Some. They interviewed us in batches. I think it was batches of ten. Not always the same people."

"Did you meet Seren Rosser?" Ruth asked.

The pause was too studied to be natural. "Don't remember the name."

Ruth pulled her phone from her pocket and brought up the image she'd transferred earlier for precisely this purpose. Filling the screen with Seren's image, she focussed it in on the blonde's smiling face. "This was Seren then." She held out the phone to Rhiamon.

In a show of attention, Rhiamon sat forward and looked hard at the screen. "Maybe," she said. "I mean, she's not that distinctive from bottle blondes everywhere, so maybe. Can't remember her clearly, though."

Ruth didn't believe the other woman and wondered if Rhiamon was a better actress than she gave herself credit for. "Do you remember when you attended the various interviews for the show? The dates? The times?"

Her shrug was more disinterest than nonchalance. "Not really. It was more than a decade ago."

"Well, think on it. If you recall the date, or anything about Seren, let me know." She took a card from her pocket. "Here's my number."

Rhiamon looked up at Palmer. "Can't I have your number?"

"Inspector Atkins is leading the investigation." A slight exaggeration; technically Geraint was SIO.

Rhiamon reluctantly took the card.

"Though, we're usually together," Ruth added. She saw the flicker of jealousy in the other woman's eyes. "Sometimes he has to answer my phone."

This time she saw the calculation in Rhiamon's eyes. The woman wasn't telling them the whole truth, but at this point, Ruth wasn't sure what that meant. She also wasn't sure there was anything more to go through. Rhiamon was the one person they knew couldn't have killed Raymond Bevan. She looked to Palmer, nodded once. Palmer stood.

"Thanks for your time, Miss Drake. We appreciate it."

Rhiamon stood, too, reached for Palmer's hand, and held it for far too long. "Come back any time. I'm sure I can make time for you."

Chapter 31

First to the car, Ruth waited without a word until Palmer was safely belted in before she pulled away. It wasn't far to the High Cross junction with the M4. Thankfully, Palmer said nothing as he read through the printout Gwyneth had given him. His head rose, expression quizzical as Ruth pulled off at junction 29.

"I did nothing to encourage her," he said.

"You didn't have to."

The silence fell heavily again. Traffic moved slowly towards Cardiff city.

"Just because I'm curious," he said after a moment, and she dreaded what was coming, "how can you afford a car like this?"

Not what she had been expecting, but easier to deal with. "I'm a woman of means."

He fell back into silence, even as she pulled off the A48M and headed into the Heath hospital. Thankfully, he was no more talkative as she crawled around looking for a parking space, which she only found on the second sweep.

Once she parked, she found she had to unclench her fingers to let go of the steering wheel. "Leave the file in the glove compartment."

She marched inside, dreading and appreciating Palmer's presence. He was making this easy by not asking. The lift opened to disgorge a family taking home a young boy with a plastered leg.

The door took a long time to close, and the lift had never been the fastest.

It didn't matter if she tried to forget. Sian Williams was always lurking in Ruth's mind.

Sian had come to the station four years ago. She'd spent time on probation in Bridgend, but finished said probation in Merthyr, where a permanent placement had come up. Ruth wasn't overly sociable, but she and Sian had hit it off immediately. Ruth had never had a friend like Sian before or since. Someone she could be completely open with, someone she trusted. She believed Sian felt the same.

That was why she knew something was seriously wrong the second Sian clammed up.

Ruth closed her eyes; it was like it was all happening again.

The smell of the locker room, sweaty shoes, too much deodorant, damp things not drying out. Something forgotten and probably best not re-discovered.

Sian's locker was a couple down from Ruth's and on the top row, while Ruth's had been on the bottom. Ruth knelt to put her work shoes away, swapping for low-heeled court shoes to feel vaguely feminine again. Sian walked in. She was down to her shirt, her jumper slumped over her shoulder, hanging like her general expression. When Sian wouldn't look her in the eye, Ruth knew something was wrong. Luckily, she also knew she didn't have to rush home; a text would sort out any issues.

"Fancy a drink?"

Sian had just gone to her locker and opened it, shaking her head.

"Sian? What's wrong?"

"Nothing." The way she fussed in her locker, which wasn't a habit of Sian's, told Ruth that was a lie. She stood up and moved closer, leaning on the lockers to speak to her friend.

"Sian, talk to me."

Pulling herself together was a visible effort, and when she had, the taller woman turned to Ruth, and it was absolute and obvious that the shutters were down. It was the first time in their relationship there had been any barrier between them.

"Is that an order, Inspector?"

Ruth frowned. "Of course not, it's just a friend's request." She reached out and put a hand on Sian's arm. The taller woman flinched. "What on earth has happened?"

"Nothing."

"Bull." Ruth stood clear of the lockers. "Look, Sian, I'm here for you, whatever happens. I hope you know that. If you don't want to talk right now, that's okay, but you know I'll support you. You have my number. Call me. Any time."

Sian had called three days later. She'd called in tears with absolutely no idea where to turn or what to do. Ruth had been at her side within twenty minutes. They'd put a statement together, everything documented. She had done everything she'd known how to do to support Sian.

Four days after that, they had the evidence they needed to go to Professional Standards. The complaint of sexual harassment was taken seriously. Very seriously. Especially when it turned out that Sian was not the first to raise an issue. Plus she had actual evidence.

The officer who'd forgotten that treating female officers like dolly birds was so last century had lost his job. He'd also sworn that it was a female conspiracy because Sian wasn't up to the job and Ruth was so short and ugly, she couldn't get any if she tried.

He'd left, but five weeks later, Ruth had gone round to check on Sian and found her raped and badly beaten in the alley behind the younger woman's flat. In a panic, Ruth had called three nines and done everything that the call responder had advised until the paramedics got there to take over. Ruth, despite her tears, had documented everything she could, advised the first constables on the scene what they needed to do. The paramedics were loading Sian into an ambulance when the crime scene manager and the CSIs arrived. She'd done what she could to give the most accurate information, but she could barely see for crying. Daf had called Geraint, and he'd appeared out of nowhere to hug Ruth, stop her from shaking, and then they'd gone to the hospital together.

That was two years ago. Sian was still in the hospital. The beautiful, vibrant young woman who had had such a promising career ahead of her was withering in a persistent vegetative state.

Ruth had gone after the ex-officer with such a vengeance, it was amazing she had kept her job. The worst thing was the rug had been pulled out from under her feet by Daf. He had found that the DNA from the semen found inside Sian's body wasn't a match to the expelled copper they all suspected. It didn't match their suspect, and worse yet, it didn't match any other sample on the national register. They'd followed every potential line of enquiry, got samples from suspects, relatives, neighbours, and everyone they could who was close to any line of enquiry.

No match.

There *still* wasn't a match. And there wasn't any other line of enquiry for her to follow. Every lead was tapped out.

Ruth had never felt so useless in her whole career. At least, not until what had happened four months after that.

Lead feet dragged through treacle. Thick molasses suckered her back. How could Ruth want to be there and dread it at the same time? This time, she wasn't alone. Palmer was here, a distant fragment of humanity, yet it gave her the strength to go on. Besides, this was Palmer. He had to know, assuming he didn't already.

At the nurses' station, Ruth and the nurse on duty exchanged nods but not words, a frequent encounter. As Ruth reached for the door handle, she took a breath and swallowed. Then she stepped into the evidence of her own inadequacy.

Inside the room, the only sound was the beep from the monitors. On the bed lay the tall figure of Sian Williams. The beautiful woman who had so easily become her friend was gone. This body breathed for itself, the heart beat slow and steady, the lungs drew air in and out. The blood pumped, the body clung on, but only survived thanks to intravenous nutrition. A breathing cadaver, hydrated but shrunken, skeletal. The hand lay limp on the bedspread. Half afraid to touch her, Ruth stepped forward and took the unresponsive hand in one of hers. Cool, but human warm.

The door closed softly behind her, not normal for the closure on that door. This time warmth stood at her back. She shouldn't appreciate it, but she did. The solid and reassuring presence of another human being. Someone who hadn't been involved.

"Madoc," she said softly, "meet Sian Williams."

"Hello, Sian. Pleasure to meet you."

Ruth smiled but stopped Madoc's hand when he reached for Sian. She wasn't ready to know what he sensed, just in case he sensed nothing.

"Sian, this is Madoc Palmer." The catch in her voice was obvious. "Now, if you want a reason to open your eyes, Madoc Palmer is it. He's exactly the sort you always liked. Tall, intelligent, hot." Her voice caught.

"She fancies me really," Madoc told Sian. "Just too proud to say it. Too much the superior officer."

"Yeah, well. Madoc's working with me right now, so there's another reason you should wake up. All those warnings you could give the poor boy. Advise him against …"

She felt his hand come up to her shoulder, a small reassuring squeeze. His touch was support. Her head tipped slightly towards him. "Do you know Sian's story?"

"I remember the case from the papers. It was much talked of. I heard about the way you pursued her attacker."

"Not, as it turns out, her attacker."

"Not him, no. He got what he deserved though." Madoc spoke softly, respectfully. "I've also heard that the case is still open and that you investigate anything that comes up. That you won't close the case until you find who did this."

"No. Never. Whoever did this will answer for it."

Again, that reassuring squeeze. The warmth behind her was so welcome, she found herself leaning against it. Madoc sharing his strength. It was good. It was dangerous. Worse than the jeans. Or the way her lips had burnt for just kissing him on the check. She schooled herself to grow up, be professional.

"I believe you," Palmer said. "Don't you, Sian? If any part of Ruth's reputation is right, she won't give up until she gets a result."

He carried on talking to Sian, a normal if one-sided conversation. Quite a flattering conversation, too. She hadn't realised how much Palmer had picked up.

"Keeps lots to herself, which makes conversation difficult."

"Hey," Ruth said.

"It's okay. Respect for preference will be given." Palmer looked back to Sian. "Bet she talked more freely with you. I'm quite jealous, so I'm looking forward to the day you come round and look at me to tell me all Ruth's little secrets. I'd say dirty little secrets, but I have the feeling she's too uptight for that."

That comment stung. She dug her elbow into his side, lightly, and he gave a small humph of mock pain.

"Right, that's it. He's corrupted this visit enough. I'll be back soon, Sian. And I'll tell your mum you looked lovely." Ruth stepped forward and kissed Sian's dry forehead.

Chapter 32

The condition Sian was in, Madoc suspected recovery was unlikely. The big question was whether Ruth would recover. It had clearly hit her hard. Compounded with guilt that she hadn't found her friend's attacker. The connection between the two women had been palpable, as had Ruth's pain. Now, Ruth had sunk into silence. He worried she might drown in her emotions but didn't know how to help buoy her.

Perhaps he should have offered to drive, given her a minor break. Admittedly, it was more because he'd love to drive this car. It purred like a cat and cradled like a feather bed, until she put her foot down. Then, it roared like a tiger. The power felt like rocket boost. There again, there was the insurance issue. She pulled off for the Coryton Interchange.

"Er, Ruth? I think you're in the wrong lane."

"I'm in the wrong lane for going to Merthyr." No attempt to change lanes followed the admission.

"Where are we going, then?"

"The Village." She named the hotel on the side of the junction's roundabout. "They do a good bar meal. Unless there's somewhere else you'd rather eat? You've better local knowledge than me."

"The Village is fine." Besides, the lights had just turned green.

The turning off the roundabout snaked into the car park of the hotel complex. Parking space abounded.

"Shall I bring the printouts?" Madoc asked before they got out.

"Not unless you want us both to be pulled up on a disciplinary for risking investigative materials in the public domain. Leave them in the glove compartment, it locks when the car does."

It was lunchtime, but they got drinks from the bar and ordered quickly enough. A two-seat table by the window was free, and they took it.

"Thanks."

Madoc frowned at Ruth's gratitude. "You bought lunch," he pointed out. She had insisted.

"For Sian."

"You hardly have to thank me for that." Though it pleased him that she had. "No one should have to suffer as she has. It's not easy for her friends and family, either."

"But—"

His shrug stopped her. "I get it. You don't need any emotional support from me."

Her lips parted ready to deny him. Yet something in the way she averted her eyes screamed how much she did need his support, or *someone's* support. The way she had leant on him communicated more than she realised.

She was having parenting issues. Her son's father was shouting down the phone at her. Her husband was dead. And her best friend was in a coma. Who was there for her? Only Geraint that he knew of.

"Thing is, sometimes you'll get my support anyway, welcome or not. That's what colleagues are for."

Her lips compressed. Her eyes closed, and when she looked back up at him, it was an effort, an act of courage.

"That's what *friends* are for. Colleagues are supposed to keep me on track, on the case."

"Can't I be both?"

Excess moisture pooled in her eyes. She blinked it away. "Sian was both."

Was that it? Her barrier between work and home, friends and colleagues, was because she'd been close to Sian and lost her? It was a risky move, but he had to do it. A stretch of his arm allowed him to cover her hand with his.

"What happened to Sian wasn't your fault."

For the shortest moment, he felt her quake. Then, she dragged in a breath, got herself under control. He pulled his hand back. What she needed right now was for him to be professional.

"Besides, you have no problem staying on track."

She looked around. No one seemed in the least bit interested in them, but they were in a public place, and someone might overhear. "Have you read anything interesting recently?"

It took a moment to realise what she was asking. "I've been giving a new genre a try."

"Really, what genre?"

"Porn."

Her brows rose. "Are you seriously telling me you've never read porn before?"

"Well, it's not really something I feel in need of."

"Lucky you. I read porn. Well, soft porn."

He refused to dwell on that comment. Did she really read porn, or was she just saying that to cover the conversation that they weren't allowed to have in public? "Mills and Boon type porn?" he asked.

"If you think I mean steamy romance, you've clearly not read anything from Reading Crop Books."

"No," he admitted. It was a specialist publisher for over-eighteens. "Not read any of those, but mostly because I found one in my sister's bedroom some years back and she did her nut when she found me with it."

Ruth smiled in a way that he imagined was her thinking of him as a teenager with the contraband book. Then her head dipped as she sipped her drink.

"Well, I was reading this one passage about a guy using a cam-girl site, texting the woman he was watching and getting her to do whatever he wanted."

"Anything I'd find … instructive?"

"Well, the man was a generation older than the girl on screen, because he asked if she still had her school uniform. He commented on how he remembered her wearing it as a child. Remembered the way she grew to fill it out."

She reacted. He wasn't sure if she was impressed or horrified.

"The thing that struck me was that when she said that would cost him extra, he said it wouldn't, then asked what her mother thought of her job."

Ruth hadn't been moving much but now she stilled and spoke carefully. "That could be … motivational."

He'd been thinking more in the way of blackmail, but he couldn't really say that. "Proximity might be an issue, though."

She nodded. It would be difficult for Rhiamon to have killed Raymond in Heolgerrig when she was in a warehouse in Newport. That was a minimum forty-five-minute drive. Then Ruth shrugged, and the way she looked at him changed.

She paused before she spoke again. "Why did you come to Northern?"

It took him a moment to figure out the question. "You mean transferring to Merthyr?"

"As opposed to staying in Eastern Division," she clarified. "Most want to work in Cardiff."

"Oh. Well, there's the fact that I live in Merthyr."

Her look turned cynical. "Don't you live in Cefn Coed?"

She really was a pedant. "Technically," he admitted. "But most people don't know where that is."

"Want to hear something odd?"

He shrugged.

"I also live in Cefn Coed. Closer to town than you. Opposite side of the valley. Now, get back on point."

The smile was unavoidable. "See? You don't need anyone keeping you on track."

"You apparently do." She smiled.

That was fair. "I moved division because it is closer to home and because it's where the sergeant's job came up. I want the promotion to be permanent."

"So, it was nothing to do with Becca Sims?"

Curve ball. It was difficult not to react. Detective Chief Inspector Rebecca Sims. Poster girl for equality in the force, fairness in all, greatly respected. All front. Fourteen years older than him, his senior officer, able to totally ruin his immediate work life and his future career. And Becca decided she wanted him to do her bidding. At first, he wasn't sure about the come-on and tried to ignore it. After all, he was young and keen to get on. The fact that he was married hadn't made the slightest difference to Becca. Then he'd weakened, given in for what was a fairly innocent New Year's kiss. The problem was the innocent part was quickly dismissed and the kiss was soon used against him. He'd felt trapped and out of control. He'd made a fool of himself. It hadn't been more than a kiss, not even a good one. After that came recriminations, controlling, years of it, not to mention blackmail. He suspected Becca was why Mannford hated him. "Why would it?"

"Because I know Becca." The tone was dark and distant. Knowing and liking were two different things – vastly different, if that tone was anything to go by. Ruth had good taste. "I also know she tried to stop you getting the position in Merthyr. Geraint had to go over her head to appoint you."

Madoc hadn't known that and was unsure how to take it.

"But given that trouble, it makes me wonder why you told Ali she could say what she wanted about you."

"Because if Becca taught me anything, it was that truth can be irrelevant. Gossips say what they want. Denials only act like confirmation."

"Yeah. Well, your person is safe with me, and it would be good if we could get you known for your good detective work, rather than … well …"

"Yes. Thanks."

Her phone rang. She checked the caller and answered. "What are you doing working on a Saturday?" She listened. "Oh, okay. Are the others doing that, too?" She waited again. "Shocker." The tone was sardonic. More listening. "Okay, how much longer you going to be there?" Pause. "Okay, we'll call in on the way up."

Their food arrived as she signed off, smaller portions than expected.

"Ali wants us to pop into the office on our way back."

"Did she say why?"

Ruth answered with a head shake, flicked her ponytail over her shoulder, and started to eat.

Chapter 33

Parking in the industrial estate on a Saturday was amazingly easy. There were no cars in the lab's spaces, so leaving the engine running, Ruth called Ali hands-free.

"I'm here," the chirpy reply came. "I'll come let you in." Ali rang off before Ruth could say another word.

She shrugged to Palmer, killed the engine, took the phone from its cradle, and stepped out. Palmer was at her side when she saw Ali opening the door. The younger woman was back to having spiky hair, blue this time. It brought out the colour of her eyes.

"Morning!" This bright and breezy individual was so different from the dull girl they had seen yesterday, Ruth worried about the change. Wild mood swings were not a good sign.

"You seem better. Everything okay?"

"Perfect!" Ali Cat grinned, showing sharpened veneers. "Whatever you said to Mam, it really got her off my case. She even suggested I decorate my room and didn't have forty fits when I mentioned black paint. Hello, gorgeous!" She grinned at Palmer as he stepped into the building, then closed the door and locked it behind them.

"Ali," Ruth advised, "you've already been in trouble once over inappropriate interactions with Palmer, so it would be best for all of us if you lay off that sort of thing."

The youthful face took on a contrite expression. Ruth doubted that would last.

"Sorry. You'd best come through."

"So, will you paint your room black?" Ruth asked as they crossed the foyer.

"Nah. Well, maybe part of the wall," Ali said, as she entered the code to open the lab. "I was thinking of painting one section with chalkboard paint so I can draw or make notes or do whatever, but the rest I was thinking I might go for a pale green. Something fresh."

"Nice."

They were inside the offices now. Ali led them over to a table bearing a light box, a range of plastic bags on it. They were arranged in a sort of grid pattern. Between the first two columns, near the bottom, two samples sat one above the other as if linked. The third column was clumped in the middle of the arrangement. Ruth had to look close to see that there were fibres inside all the clear and labelled bags.

"Okay, so what do you have?" she asked.

"When we pulled the skeleton out from the Heolgerrig site, we gathered some of the mud that was around the body too, to check if there was anything that would help with identification. All these fibres were in the soil. I spoke with your Sergeant Bates. He did some checking for me, and at the point where the body was, the builders had cleared the topsoil, which is about four-to-six inches, but they'd added about six-to-eight inches to correct the level."

"Why make up as much or more than was removed?" Ruth asked.

"Topsoil is more fertile and valuable," Palmer explained. "So, they take that away and put in infill."

Frowning up at him came naturally to Ruth. "How do you know that?"

"Landscaper in the family," he explained.

Ruth nodded and turned back to Ali, who took up her explanation.

"Anything in that layer of ground has the potential to have been a more recent deposit than the body. But anything in the soils we were looking at can only be one of two things: deposited by the construction crew, or in the ground about the same time as the body. Most of these are recent deposits. Some are even natural fibres." She pointed to one clear bag, middle-top, which contained short, fluffy red fibres. "That, for example, is off a red fleece jumper. Something which doesn't match the clothing of the victim, and it's so visible that it's unlikely to be from the murderer, or it might have been seen and removed. But, when I was up on the site, one of the fit young builders was wearing a red fleece under his works jacket, so it's probably from him."

"Did you get Mr Red Fleece's name?"

"No." Ali's expression dropped. "Sorry, I—"

"Ali, it's okay," Ruth said, gently. "You didn't know the red fleece was important when you saw him. I just wondered, if he was that fit, if you got his name for your own purposes."

Ali flushed. "No. That wouldn't be appropriate. That there —" She pointed to another sample and this time Ruth noticed Ali's nails were painted a lurid sunshine yellow. "—is a synthetic fibre in blue, part of the standard Shalestone official wear." Her hand moved on again, this time to a fibre nearer the bottom of the Lightbox. It was thicker, about half-an-inch long and brown-beige, the brown part of which could have been staining from the mud. "This is wool off something like a knitted jumper."

"You didn't happen to notice any fit young builder wearing an Arran jumper, did you?"

Ali gave her a look. "There really weren't that many who'd fall into both the fit and young categories, sorry. But the point is, it's wool, soaks up water and muck, gets runs and pulls really easily."

She stopped, waiting for them to get it.

They didn't.

"Is this the sort of clothing anyone would wear on a building site?"

Ruth honestly had no idea. She shrugged. Then she looked more closely at one bag. "Is that a black dog hair?"

"Possibly," Ali said. "But it could be a badger hair, too. Hair isn't my speciality, so I'll have to research more before I can tell you for certain."

"Where was it?"

"It was in the mud from the trench," Ali said.

"Not from Raymond's clothes?"

Ali shook her head.

"Which means it's inconclusive." Ruth sighed.

"I've gone through all Raymond's clothes, taken tapes. There was a hair on it." Ali pointed to the relevant bag. "But as you can see, it's white, not black."

"God, I thought that was more cotton." Ruth looked to Palmer. "Did the Bevans have any pets? I don't remember seeing any."

"They don't," Palmer said.

"So, whatever the hair is, it's an outside source."

"Then there's these." Another movement, another bag. "These are cotton fibres, so they have to be fairly recent."

"How recent?" Ruth interrupted.

"No more than five years. That's how long cotton generally takes to break down."

"That doesn't strike me as being very recent," Palmer said.

"Well, no, but that's not what makes me think they're recent. Like, day of death recent."

"Then what is?" Ruth asked, aware of Palmer's heightened focus on the girl, too.

"I think they might be a match for the shirt your victim was wearing when he fell into the trench. Only I haven't got so far as to check." Ali's attention returned to the lightbox, to the samples clumped mid-right. "This is what I actually wanted to show you."

Ruth and Palmer both leant in. They were very thin pieces of thread, some quite long. "That looks like cotton," Ruth said. "You know, thread to stitch a hem or something with."

"That's almost exactly what it is," Ali confirmed. "It's actually a polycotton, which is why it lasted longer than whatever material it was stitched into. I suspect a pure cotton fabric, because there was nothing left of what it hemmed. We've got just under two metres of it, all in little bits. Longest one was 18.3 cm. Given the location, at body level, and the sheer volume of fibres, I'd say that this was part of what the skeletal victim was wearing when buried."

"So, thread but no fasteners? No buttons, poppers, hooks, no zip?"

Ali shook her head. "Would have to be some sort of shift dress that just pulled on. Wasn't the missing woman going to a photoshoot the morning she disappeared?"

"Screen test," Palmer corrected.

"Possibly the same considerations, then." Ali shrugged. "When I was in uni, I shared a house with a girl from a textiles course. One of their modules was to put on a catwalk show and she roped me in. She was like a bridezilla without a wedding, you know? Anyway, she was really rabid on the point that we weren't to wear any underwear for a minimum of six hours before the show because there were to be no bra strap marks for the off-the-shoulder dresses. One of the other girls said it was fairly normal for girls doing fashion shoots to be told not to wear underwear to avoid marks like that, but she thought six hours was a bit much."

"Oh, okay. That's something I was never going to think of," Ruth admitted. "If all the fabric is gone, but the threads remain, how long does polycotton take to decay?"

"Anywhere between twenty and two hundred years," Ali said. "So, not much help in this case."

"No," Ruth agreed. "Overall, does that confirm our victim was buried between five and twenty years ago?"

"Give or take for ground conditions and the proximity of a decomposing human which would give extra encouragement for the cotton to rot, then yeah, minimum of five years. That said, I'm not putting that into the report until Daf checks it over and agrees. After all, he's the one who gets to do the expert witness stuff."

Ruth looked her over. "Er, yeah."

"Stop it!" Ali playfully slapped her on the arm. "I'd be a credible witness."

Ruth grinned, glad to see that one of them was back to their normal selves. It helped her re-find herself. "Yeah, right, one with fangs."

"I like my teeth!"

"And that's fine," Ruth said. "They also don't impede how your brain works, so I'm confident that the evidence you bring me, the conclusions you provide, are correct. However, the way most juries' brains work, they'd take one look at them and your hair and write you off as a fantasist. You don't *look* like a credible witness; therefore, you won't get treated like one, and your testimony won't be given the weight it should."

"It's not fair," Palmer added, "but most of life isn't."

Ali looked disappointed, young, and more innocent than she had a moment before, as she looked between them.

"Where's your car?" Ruth asked. Ali had both a five-year-old Fiat 500 and an ancient Mini, a 1972 third series Classic. It had been a rust bucket, but Ali and her dad had restored it, rebuilt it, sourcing spares from other old Minis.

"The Fiat is in the garage getting MOTed. But the Mini!" Ali's eyes lit up with excitement. "It's in the shop at the moment. They finished the last bit of welding. Then it's just the respray to organise. I can't wait for that, then I can put on all the freshly chromed accessories. She'll look stunning at car shows."

"What colour did you say it's being sprayed again?"

That grin widened, showing the pointed veneers and a wicked expression. "I didn't, as you full well know. I'll do a proper reveal party when it's done."

"I look forward to it."

"We'll look forward to it," Palmer added. "If I'm invited, too."

Now Ali grinned up at him. "Of course, you might even be the tallest person to sit in her – if I let you."

Palmer's grin was every bit as warm with reminiscence. "Oh, I've folded myself into Minis before now. No worries there. But driving them can be testing. Insufficient room for my knees."

Why Ruth had a problem with Ali's coquettish little laugh, she wasn't sure. Ruth's first car had been a brand new Ford Fiesta that Paul had bought her when she'd passed her driving test. Unlike most people, she didn't have those amusing stories of bad first cars. She'd always had a decent car; Paul insisted on it. He had always been so considerate of her every need.

She sighed.

"How is it," she said, catching Ali's attention, "that you and your dad can spend years restoring a shed of a car for you to drive, and yet your mum keeps your bedroom like you're nine?"

"Mam sees me in my overalls and thinks I still look like a little girl tinkering in the garage with Dad."

"And you didn't turn into a mechanic?" Palmer asked.

"Engines are too easy. Forensics are much more interesting and complex." The way her eyes twinkled, it was clear where her true love lay.

"I'm guessing, then, that you're going to want a lift to the train station?" Ruth offered.

"That'd be great, if it's not too much trouble. I need a few minutes to catalogue and pack this lot first. You okay with that?"

Ruth nodded. "Is the fridge still stocked?"

"Cold cans re-filled yesterday."

Ruth went to the kitchen and grabbed a drink, holding the door open for Palmer as he followed. A shake of his head set her straight, and they moved to the one table and the hard plastic chairs there.

"Would you take a couple of notes for me?" she asked as she popped the top on a diet Fanta.

His reply was to produce his phone from his pocket and flick it to a new notes page.

"I think we have some new actions. Add confirmation of the last text from Raymond to Queen Ree and see if the timing still fits."

Palmer so noted.

"See if Mike found anyone from *Valleys View* and see if they can confirm if Seren and Rhiamon would have met for their interviews or screen tests or whatever."

He wrote that down.

"Double-check the Seren Rosser file, see if Wendy Rosser suggested any likely outfit at the time of the disappearance."

Palmer didn't look away from the phone as he spoke. "She said she didn't."

"She's saying that now, but when she first reported it, she might not have. Memories can fade. I just want to check."

Palmer waited. Ruth wasn't sure if there was a definitive action she could come up with. At least the five years minimum didn't rule Seren out.

"Oh yeah, can you check with Bridgend if they have the DNA test results yet?"

Another note added.

"Oh, and don't note this, but I must thank Rita for her research into Rhiamon's background. Without it, I wouldn't know that she was up for *Valleys View* as well as Seren."

"Yeah, you're just so terrible with all the bringing younger colleagues on, aren't you?" Palmer said as he looked up from the notes.

Ruth ignored the warmth of his tone and choose not to comment.

"Is there something else still bothering you?" Palmer asked.

"Possibly," she admitted. "Why?"

"Because you constantly flicking that can tab is really annoying."

Ruth looked down to her middle finger. She hadn't even realised she was doing that. "Sorry." She peeked at him. Clearly, she'd have to find some annoying habit of his, just to even the score. "Don't suppose your gut instinct is telling you anything that might point us in the right direction?"

"Only that I'm sure the Naked Lady is Seren Rosser."

"I have a sense that I've missed something," Ruth said at length. "That somewhere in all that we've seen or heard, we've seen or heard the answer. I just haven't recognised it yet."

"Then we'll go back and review it all," Palmer said. "We'll re-read the Seren Rosser file, check the test results, run through Raymond's timeline, check the statements, find someone from *Valleys View*, and review every little fact and find the incongruity."

Wanting to believe and believing were two different things. She felt his foot nudge her leg.

"We'll find it," he said. "Whatever it is. We'll find out who murdered Raymond and who murdered Seren. We're good like that."

His confidence was infectious, but she had to face realities. "You can tell that after five days, can you?"

The serious look worried her. "I can tell you're dedicated to the job, that you care more than you want to let on, and that you're an outstanding detective."

Sardonic humour rose in her. "Don't put me on too high a pedestal."

"Oh, we've all got feet of clay," he admitted. "But whatever else is going on with you, don't let work get you down. I have every faith in you."

And she was starting to have faith in him. Which was terrifying.

Chapter 34

Ruth seemed to perk up after their chat. She was back to the strong, controlled woman he'd first met by the time they reached the incident room. Madoc was surprised to see a uniformed constable among the staff there. Generally, only the civilians worked the weekend.

"Are you trying to earn brownie points with Mike?" Ruth asked the woman.

The young PC turned and offered a shaky smile. She seemed a little in awe of Ruth. Madoc understood that.

"Ma'am," she greeted. "Mike had plans for this weekend, and he was talking about cancelling, in case anything came in on your case," she explained. "So, I said I'd do the weekend as long as he didn't." The PC had visible subcontinental bloodlines, but the accent was pure South Wales. Madoc guessed Merthyr born and bred.

"That was good of you," Ruth said. "Mike loves his tennis. Have you two been introduced?"

The young woman blushed, shaking her head.

"DS Madoc Palmer, PC Rita Jefferies."

They exchanged greetings, and Madoc tried not to acknowledge Ruth's twitching lips as Rita blushed again. Then Ruth handed over the transcript from Lush Ladies. "This is a record of Raymond Bevan's recent activity on the cam-girl site he was using the morning he died. Matches the general times given, so no real surprises. But can you just double-check?"

The PC nodded, and Ruth turned to lead the way back to their office. Then she stopped and swung back to the younger woman.

"Rita, by the way, you were spot on. Rhiamon Drake had applied for *Valleys View*. She says she didn't remember Seren, though, so when we get in touch with anyone from the production company, we'll need to check if they were ever called together. But excellent call, well done."

Rita blushed at the praise.

Back in the MCIT area, they were surprised to see Geraint in. He was looking at their boards.

"Geraint?" Ruth asked moving up to him. "Everything okay?"

Geraint turned to face them. "Fine. Liz has gone on a shopping trip to Cribbs Causeway, a birthday treat for one of her friends, so I thought I'd come in and catch up on the never-ending paperwork. I take it Zach's with his father today?"

"Sorry," Madoc interrupted, looking at Ruth. "Just so I'm clear, Zach is your son, right?"

Those caterpillar brows focused darkly on Madoc.

"Yes," Ruth said, and her tone killed further discussion.

"What about Osian?" Geraint asked. "He with his mam?"

That was vague enough for Madoc. "Yes, sir."

"Right. You two turned up anything new?"

Ruth gave a concise report, but it ended on a sigh. "So, no actual evidence of anything."

Geraint turned to prop himself against the nearest desk, though he kept his eyes on the whiteboard. "So, aside from the hair and the potential *Valleys View* link between Rhiamon and Seren, there's nothing actually linking anyone to anyone?"

"Not at the moment," Ruth said. "We've gone through everything on the forklift, and at the scrap merchants, looked at possible connections with the Prices and the Flacks. But only the Jameses seem to be involved there. We're no nearer knowing who killed Raymond Bevan now than we were when Maggie called it in. In most murder cases, the victim knows the killer. It's frequently the very person who either found the body or called us. Maggie Drake did both. But we've no evidence of her involvement."

"What motive?" Geraint asked. "She might not have liked Bevan, but we've all got colleagues like that. Christ, you and Jenkins practically hiss at each other, but neither of you is about to kill the other one."

"Who's Jenkins?" Madoc asked, again the outsider.

"Inspector Robert Jenkins, works Serious and Organised, deals with a lot of drugs cases," Ruth advised.

"They hate each other," Geraint added.

"True, but we have good reason."

"And we do have something," Madoc added to feel less of a fifth wheel. "We now know Raymond Bevan was paying Rhiamon Drake for sex shows. If Maggie Drake found out about that, she wouldn't be happy. That might be a motive."

"Big if," Geraint said.

"Erm, excuse me?" Rita's voice was very tentative as she approached the three of them.

"What is it, Rita?" Ruth asked.

Rita glanced nervously at Geraint.

"It's alright, Constable," the old man said. "Despite rumours, I don't actually bite."

Rita didn't look convinced. Instead, she focused on Ruth and stepped towards the other woman. "You asked me to look for references to dogs in the various witness statements, and to be honest, there weren't many. There is nothing to corroborate the report that Maggie Drake raced Kohl home between calling us at 04:58 and PC Reilly arriving at 05:20. Oddly, though, Alan James mentioned waiting for a woman walking a black dog to turn the corner before they entered the site shortly after four. Description was too general to be useful: average height, dark trousers, pale jumper."

"Maggie said something woke the dog, the dog woke her. We've been assuming that it was the break-in that woke the dog.

But if the Jameses waited for Maggie to walk past, what woke the dog?"

Rita looked at her oddly.

"Go on, Rita, what are you thinking?"

The younger woman looked nervous. "I was thinking that you aren't a dog owner."

Ruth shrugged. "No, I'm not. I've never owned a dog. Why? Does it matter?"

"Not really, but dogs are odd. Anything can wake them up. My parents' corgi once woke us up in the middle of the night baying like the hounds of hell were after him. Turned out it was a spider. As soon as my dad got the spider out the window, the dog was quiet again. He just crawled back in his basket and went back to sleep. The rest of us had way more trouble getting off again. Anything could have woken the dog; it probably doesn't matter."

Ruth laughed at herself. "That's true. I just don't like loose ends. Thanks for keeping me grounded, Rita." Her glance to Madoc told him this was the 'keeping on track' she had been talking about earlier. "All of which brings us back to insufficient evidence."

"But Maggie killed Raymond," Madoc said. "She must have found out he watched Rhiamon." He picked up a photograph of Seren. His sight blurred and he felt the truth of it. "She killed Seren, too."

"You got evidence of that, son?"

At Geraint's deep question, Madoc realised he was leaning on the table to support himself. He didn't have any evidence. Just the unshakable certainty of his gift.

"It's the best theory I've heard so far," Ruth said, though the look she shot in his direction was a warning one. He dropped the photograph and took his hand from the desk. He had to focus. Focus on finding evidence and not losing his place here. He didn't want to leave the first place he'd found where he could be comfortable with someone knowing his secret.

"But it's still only a theory," Geraint pointed out.

"No. I mean, yes. Sorry, Geraint," Ruth said. "But every instinct I have is telling me it's the right theory."

"Based on what?" Geraint demanded of Ruth this time.

Madoc wouldn't have wanted those expressive caterpillars pointing at him that way. Ruth glanced at Madoc. Was she about to tell Geraint what he could do? Would she? What would Geraint do or say if he found out? The foreshadow of laughter and being told to get out froze him to the core.

Ruth blinked and looked back at her boss. Her expression was almost little girl lost, but there was something harder than cutesy about it. "Would you accept my copper's hunch?" She was covering for him. A relief, but why would she do that?

"Jesus, Ruth!" Geraint sighed. "You know I am more than ready to listen to hunches, but we need to make the case, a rock-solid case to take to the CPS. We need evidence. It has to be unquestionable. Clean," Geraint said.

"We always want 'em cl—" Ruth's eyes widened as her voice trailed away.

Madoc had learnt that when Ruth's voice stopped, it was usually because her brain was running faster than her mouth could keep up with.

"Clean," she said.

Apparently, Geraint was used to her process, and they all waited for the wisdom pearl. Madoc felt more than a little uncomfortable when Ruth swung her gaze to him, dragging the attention of the others in her wake.

"Describe Andy Porter and Maggie Drake when we first saw them."

He frowned slightly, uncertain where this was going. "They were in the PortaKabin they use as an office. Both looked shocked but functional."

"The word that struck me was 'clean'." She was trying to point him towards some revelation, but he wasn't sure he was following.

"They were both fairly clean," Madoc said. "It was first thing in the morning. Andy Porter was in work clothes and boots, mud almost covered the boots, but it was largely dry and flaking by the time we got there. And there was mud on the right knee of her work trousers, where she said she'd knelt down to look closer, stains and dust on her clothes. Maggie Drake was wearing a sweatshirt with the construction company logo embroidered on it, office trousers tucked into her work boots. They had mud on them, too." He frowned. They did, didn't they? He tried to clarify the image. "Yeah, her boots had mud on them."

Ruth nodded. "When we went up there, we walked over to that trench, and you got filthy to the knees. I had wellies on, wellies up to and over the calf. They saved my trousers, but only just. Think about the boots Maggie was wearing."

He did. "They were those pull-on boots. Loads of the construction guys were wearing them. Oh!" Suddenly he saw it.

"Well, don't stop there, Palmer," Geraint said. "Tell the rest of us what Ruth's spotted and led you to."

"Maggie Drake's boots," he said. "They were ankle boots. Only the soles and low sides were dirty. She'd walked to the PortaKabin, the least muddy area, but her statement says she walked to the trench and found Raymond, then reported it, then nipped the dog home, and came straight back. But if she'd done that, dressed like that, she would have got way muddier. Besides, she said she had gone out to walk her dog, and only nipped home to drop the dog off. If that were true, why was she already wearing the works sweatshirt and boots? Who's going to get up before four in the morning and dress in work clothes to walk a dog if they don't start till eight? She'd go for something warm. That's what doesn't fit in the timeline. She was too clean; she must have changed clothes at some point."

"And that means," Ruth added, "that she's got something to hide. Wait a sec." Ruth held up a hand and the rest held their silence. Then she turned to Rita. "You said the dog walker was wearing a light jumper?"

Rita nodded. "That's what Alan James said in interview. A pale wool jumper."

"Good, good." Ruth nodded, drifting away.

"Ruth," Geraint called her attention. "There's probably more than one woman with a black dog in Heolgerrig. This isn't proof."

"It's a hell of a coincidence if it wasn't Maggie." She turned to Geraint. "Ali said there was a woollen fibre found with the body, only half-stained with mud. And there was a hair that might be from a dog."

"But it was a white hair," Madoc pointed out. "Kohl is black."

"How old is the dog?" Geraint asked. "When they get old, even a black dog might have some white hairs."

Madoc considered it. "The dog's probably old enough."

"And if I ended up with dog fur on me just standing in that house, it's probable that Maggie kneeling on Ray's back to drown him would transfer at least one hair to him. If we find Maggie owns a matching jumper, we can put her not just at the scene but in the trench and trying to cover it up by changing her clothes."

"That's a big if," Geraint said.

Ruth sighed. "They're all big ifs." But she was rooting around her desk.

"What are you looking for?"

"The autopsy report on Bevan."

Madoc went to his own desk, then passed the file across to her. She looked through the details.

"Good, yes." Ruth looked at Rita. "Did Alan James give a physical description of the woman he saw? Timmy didn't even mention it."

Rita shook her head. "But I can arrange another interview to ask."

"Please." Ruth focused on Madoc. "How tall would you say Maggie Drake is?"

He shrugged. "About your height, maybe a little shorter."

Ruth nodded. "I'm 165, so let's say Maggie is 163. That fits well with Tom's suggestion that Raymond's assailant was in the 160-170 cm range. There's dog hair in the trench, Maggie owns a dog. There's a pale wool fibre in the pit, a pale jumper on a passing dog walker, within the bounds of the time Maggie could have been walking Kohl. If we can match the dog hair or find a matching jumping, that puts Maggie in the trench with Raymond and makes her the killer."

"Motive?" Geraint asked.

Ruth stopped to consider. "Protecting Rhiamon."

"One unguarded comment from Raymond would be enough to push her over the edge," Madoc added. "Even Rhiamon said if her mother knew what she did for a living, she could kill."

"Ma'am?" Rita said quietly. "Do you have a copy of Mrs Drake's original statement?"

Ruth moved files on her desk, found it, and passed it over.

"It's all still a bit open to interpretation," Geraint said as Rita reviewed the file. "It's enough for a search warrant but might not stretch to an arrest warrant."

"We can apply for both, though." Ruth said. "Rita, did you find something?"

"Did you say Maggie's trousers were clean when you first saw her?"

"Yes," Ruth said.

"Definitely," Palmer added.

Rita passed the file to Geraint, pointing to the relevant passage. He took at moment.

"Get Alan James interviewed, and quick. Then apply for both search and arrest warrants."

Chapter 35

As ever, there was paperwork to do before warrants could be applied for or granted. They needed a cogent, reasoned explanation for the application. Most judges, for good reason, wouldn't accept 'gut instinct.' Working together, Ruth and Palmer got the paperwork in logical order. Another call to Andy Porter helped and confirmed they had resolved the issues from the West Llanelli site. It wasn't clean, but it wasn't illegal either.

Being a Saturday didn't speed the warrant process any, but they got them, got everything organised internally. Then, Ruth led the way out. A team from Uniform who would undertake the search followed them, and this time Ruth booked out a pool car. "I don't want her kicking off in the backseat of my car," she said. "Nor do I want any dog hairs on my leather upholstery."

They were soon at Maggie Drake's door.

The smile slid from the older woman's face the second she saw them. "Oh, what now? More questions?"

"Yes, Mrs Drake."

Ruth gave no quarter as she moved Maggie Drake into the house, showed her the search warrant, and set the uniformed officers to searching. Maggie spluttered at the intrusion, but there was nothing she could do to stop it.

Once the search was underway, Ruth officially arrested Maggie, advised her of her rights, and put the swearing woman in handcuffs. Drake complained the whole way to the station.

Ruth had been called many unpleasant things in her time, but this was the first time she'd been accused of cruelty to animals because she'd insisted that Kohl be taken to the RSPCA for temporary housing to avoid it drooling all over their officers as they searched.

The custody sergeant was unimpressed by Maggie's protests of innocence. This probably had a fair bit to do with the multiple drunks already kicking off, which seemed early especially for a Saturday with no footie or rugby. Naturally, Maggie demanded a state-supplied solicitor and then complained about her treatment as they put her in a holding cell until said solicitor arrived.

"Well, that was fun," Palmer said as they left the increasingly noisy custody suite.

"Yeah," Ruth agreed. "Do you need to get home?"

He indicated not and asked her the same.

"Zach's not home till tomorrow. I'm fine."

"Ruth." He pulled her to a stop before they entered the open office area. "Thank you."

"What for?" She sounded honestly confused.

"Covering for me with Geraint before. Do you not think he'd take my … difference well?"

She hung her head, pausing before she looked back up at him. "Honestly, Palmer, I'm not sure yet how well *I'm* taking it. I'm not ready to tell Geraint or any of the others. I don't know how they'll react. What I do know is that I don't want you or me laughed out of the job."

She moved on again, leaving him to his thoughts. She really didn't know what she felt about it all, and now wasn't the best time to try to figure it all out. They had a job to do.

In the seventy minutes it took for the duty solicitor to arrive, Ruth and Palmer planned their approach for the interview. Confirmation of a muddied Arran-knit jumper found in Maggie's bin helped. Thank God bin collection day was a Monday up there.

"Given that I was her focus of hate on the way here, do you mind leading the questioning?" Ruth asked. "If you don't get a response, I'll jump in and push harder."

His agreement relieved Ruth. That should give her the break she needed to control the urge to punch Maggie Drake. Her own temper she put down to lack of sleep the last few nights. The interview hadn't even begun, and she felt stretched the limit. She had to find her way back to an even keel. Especially with Zach – he was just a kid, her kid, and they needed to stabilise their relationship. She'd have to see what Zach said about his father when he came home tomorrow. And she'd call the doctor on Monday.

"I can't believe you've dragged me in like this!" Maggie stated as soon as they entered the interview room. "I should sue for wrongful arrest."

Ruth wanted to scream, but she just raised an eyebrow in response. She said nothing, started the recording, stated the admin for the case, then handed over the Palmer to start the questioning.

To get Maggie in a more cooperative mood, Palmer took them through a summary of Maggie's statement, and let her agree to it all.

"So, to sum up, you found the body. Andy Porter arrived. You called us. Then you rushed home with the dog. Then went straight back to work?"

"That's right," Maggie said. "Just like I've told you. Time and time and time again. Why won't you listen?"

"Oh, I'm listening, Maggie," Palmer assured her. "I just need to be absolutely clear. You took Kohl home, put him in the house, returned directly to the site."

"Exactly."

Ruth sat back with her arms folded. She wanted Palmer to push more, but all the time Maggie was responding to him, and answering questions, things were going well. So she stayed quiet and let Palmer continue. Despite her fraying nerves. With his relaxed tone and charming smile, he had both Maggie and Tessa Winter, the duty solicitor, in the palm of his hand. She really needed him to get to the point, and lightly tapped her foot against his leg to speed him up. The way his eyes tightened momentarily suggested it hadn't felt as light to him as she'd intended.

"Can I just clarify how long you've known Raymond Bevan?"

"Around eighteen years."

"Since you started at Shalestone Homes?"

"Yes."

"Not before?"

"Well, before then, I only knew *of* him. I didn't really know him before we started working for the same company."

"And you classified your relationship as colleagues, not friends, is that right?"

"Yes."

"So, there's no reason Raymond Bevan would know your ex-husband or your daughter?"

Maggie's eyes narrowed. "I've never introduced him to them. But Rhiamon is my little star. I carry her picture, she's been on some sites with me. It's possible he'd recognise her, but again, I wouldn't say he knows her."

Palmer nodded. "From your statement, you say that you left Kohl tethered at the fence line, then entered the site."

"Yes."

"Then what?"

Maggie frowned. "Pardon?"

"Exactly what did you do after you left the dog and started onto the site?"

This time Maggie shrugged. "I walked on the site. The cabins were locked. The damage was obvious, I could see what had been taken. Then I saw Raymond. As my statement says."

Palmer nodded. "Okay. How?"

"How what?" Maggie asked.

"How did you come to see Raymond in the trench?"

"Oh, I was walking past."

"Walking past?"

Maggie nodded.

"For the tape, please," Ruth said.

"Video not enough?"

"No. I want to hear you say it."

"Fine," Maggie snapped. "Yes. I was just walking past."

"Going from where to where?" Palmer asked gently.

"From the stores to the offices."

"Andy says she never saw the dog," Ruth butted in.

"He's black, it was before dawn," Maggie said. "Maybe she didn't see him."

"All black?" Rush pushed.

"Yes," Maggie said.

"How old is he?"

"Nine."

"That's old for a Labrador." Ruth had checked average lifespan while they were waiting for the solicitor to arrive.

"Yeah, well, he is old."

"Getting a few grey or white hairs?" Ruth asked.

"I suppose he is," Maggie said. "Around the collar and muzzle. So what?"

"A white dog hair was found on Raymond's body," Ruth stated.

Palmer didn't leave a breath, didn't want Maggie thinking her way out of that. "Andy said you didn't leave the site after she got there."

Ruth could see Maggie was getting flustered. Good.

"She's mistaken."

"Is she?" Ruth asked.

"Yes!"

The snap assured Ruth she was getting to Maggie. Good. She wasn't sure how much more of this she could take. "Why was there an Arran jumper in your rubbish bin?"

"I don't want it anymore." She sneered at Ruth. "You want it? Seems your style. Scruffy."

"You walked from the store to the cabins?" Palmer asked.

"Yes."

"Straight from one to the other without diversion?" Palmer pushed.

"Of course, it was terribly muddy."

Palmer nodded. "Indeed, it was. In fact, when I first walked over the site, I wasn't prepared, and mud got up almost to my knees. Even DI Atkins' wellingtons were muddy to the top."

"Yes, I spotted that."

"I'm sure you did," Palmer said as he opened the file and took out a plan of the site. It was the set-up plan, everything marked up for where the PortaKabins would go, where the supplies would be stored. He laid it out on the table and pointed it to face Maggie. For the benefit of the tape, he described what he was doing, giving the drawing number for reference. "Can you confirm that this is an accurate representation of the Heolgerrig site?"

Maggie looked it over. "It is."

"And can you point out the siting of the PortaKabins and the stores?"

For a moment Maggie just sat there, her eyes turned hard.

"Mrs Drake," Ruth said calmly. "Point on the plan to where the cabins and the stores are."

The uncompromising request earned her an icy glare.

Maggie's finger stabbed at the plan quickly as she said. "Here and here."

"According to this," Palmer said easily, "there's a clear and direct route from the stores to the cabins. Comes this way." His neatly manicured finger traced the obvious path, a small swoop towards the boundary of the site and straight to the cabins. "Was that the way you went?"

"It is the most logical path," Tessa stated when Maggie said nothing.

"Indeed, it is." Palmer agreed with the solicitor before turning again to Maggie. "Can you also point on the plan to where Mr Bevan was found?"

Again Maggie, just looked at Palmer.

"Mrs Drake?" Ruth pushed.

The older woman switched her attention. "I'm not entirely sure."

"I see," Ruth said. "How long have you worked on the Heolgerrig site, Mrs Drake?"

"Since it opened seven months ago."

"And how long have you worked for Shalestone Homes?" Ruth asked.

"Nearly eighteen years," Maggie said without hesitation.

"You'll have seen a few of these plans over the years, I'd guess."

"Plenty."

"Yet you can't point out the location of the trench where Mr Bevan was found?"

"I'm not exactly sure of the location," Maggie stated with a tight grin. "It was a shock, unexpected. I'm not sure where it was exactly."

"And the obvious mark Andy Porter put on the plan before she gave it to us doesn't help you at all?" Ruth reached out and tapped the mark. "Doesn't appear to be on the direct route between the stores and the cabins, now, does it?"

Maggie stared at the plan. "I … I was in shock. I … I didn't know where I was heading."

"What shocked you?" Palmer asked gently.

"Finding a body, of course. It doesn't happen to me every day."

"You were so shocked by finding a body, you got turned around and lost on the site you've worked on for seven months, which is how you found the body that shocked you?" Ruth asked.

"Yes!" Maggie said. "Well, no. I mean …"

"What do you mean, Mrs Drake?"

Maggie looked to her solicitor.

"Inspector Atkins, you're confusing my client."

Ruth raised her eyebrows at the woman. "Your client's confusing me. She claims the shock of finding the body confused her into finding the body." The two women faced off. Tessa looked away first, then Ruth swung her attention to Maggie again, relieved to have something to get her teeth into and externalise the stress inside.

"Right. Let's look at something else, then. Earlier you remarked on how much mud Sergeant Palmer and I had on us when we first visited the site. I remember thinking at the time that you were very clean to be on site."

"Well, I'm more used to sites than you are," Maggie said with an air of condescension.

"Which must be why you were so clean," Palmer spoke lightly. "I noticed that as well. Do you remember your state of dress?"

"Of course, I do," Maggie sighed. "I was wearing my site boots, trousers, and my works sweatshirt."

"How muddy would you say you were?" Palmer asked.

"Not very." Maggie shrugged calmly. "There was some mud on my boots, but that was about it."

Palmer nodded.

"I'd agree with that assessment," Ruth said. "Wouldn't you, Palmer?"

"I certainly would."

Ruth smiled at Maggie. "So, we're all in agreement: when we got there, you were clean. Roughly an inch of mud on your boots from walking on site, but your clothes were clean. You'd agree with that, wouldn't you, Mrs Drake?"

"Of course, I would. I don't see why we're going over all this again. I can't see how the way I was dressed makes any difference."

"Don't you?" Ruth smiled.

"No," Maggie said, folding her arms.

Palmer paused before he started. "So, it is your claim that you saw the fences down, tied up Kohl, went to investigate the theft, got confused as to direction on the way back and saw Raymond Bevan's body in the trench. Then Andy arrived. She opened the cabins, you called the police and then rushed Kohl home, and returned to the site in time to meet our first responder. Is that correct?"

"Yes," Maggie smiled. "That's right."

"Is it?" Ruth asked. She took Maggie's original statement from the file. Turned to the sentence Rita had marked. "According to your original statement, and I quote: 'I saw poor Raymond in the trench and was so shocked, I fell to my knees and just stared at him'." She stopped reading and put the statement in front of Maggie. "That is your statement, is it not?"

"Well …"

The solicitor pulled it across and read it.

"Did you lie then, or are you lying now?" Ruth asked.

"I …" Maggie looked at her solicitor. "No comment."

Ruth internalised her grin. A doubtless evil grin the way she was feeling. "You got to site a lot earlier than you're telling us, didn't you, Mrs Drake?"

Maggie looked away.

"Don't try too hard to find an explanation. You see, you were seen. Walking a black dog – Kohl. Wearing a pale jumper. The one you so recently decided to throw away."

Maggie's calculating eyes now showed a little fear.

"The theft was over, but Raymond was already there. He was alive, too, wasn't he?"

She saw the older woman's lips compress, her eyes narrow.

"I checked with Andy and others on the site. It even appears in some of the statements given by your colleagues, that you and Raymond didn't get on. Loudly, sometimes. Some said it was light bickering, some said it was more than that. Was it?"

"That's hearsay, Inspector." Tessa did her job.

"I know. That's why I'm asking for clarification."

"My client doesn't have to answer," Tessa said.

Palmer took up the question. "Maggie, did you and Raymond bicker on site?"

"Lots of colleagues bicker," Tessa pointed out. "You can't build a murder case on that."

"We don't need to," Ruth stated. "Given what we know, it seems likely that you, Maggie, made some accusation over the break-in being Raymond's fault – lax on security, something of that nature?"

Maggie turned to glare at her. "That probably is what happened. He was never good at keeping his mind on the job. Well, not that type of job."

"What type did he concentrate on, then?" Ruth asked.

Maggie made a gesture.

Ruth sighed. "For the purposes of sound recording and in case the video did not pick up that gesture, Mrs Drake made an open fist and shook it. Would you care to define for the record what you mean by that gesture, Mrs Drake?"

Maggie glared at her again.

"Come now, Mrs Drake, if you're going to make the gesture, you could at least tell me what you mean."

"You know what I mean," Maggie said.

"No, I don't."

"He was a wanker!" Maggie snapped.

"Are you accusing Raymond Bevan of inappropriate sexual behaviour in front of or towards you?" Ruth asked.

"Of course not," Maggie spat. "That git wouldn't dare. He was too busy—" Maggie cut herself off.

"Too busy what?" Ruth pushed. Though Maggie turned away, uncontrolled anger seethed beneath her skin. Ruth hoped she was better at controlling any outward display of her own raging emotions.

"When we spoke to you in your home, you said Raymond used pervert sites. Can you clarify what you mean by that?"

Maggie's glare was hotter than a thousand suns, but Ruth wouldn't melt before it. "He liked to look at pictures of girls."

"Pictures?"

"He got girls to do things for him. He paid to—" Maggie cut herself off.

"He paid to what?" Palmer asked softly.

Maggie's jaw clenched. "Watch." She sneered. "The pervert paid to watch them."

"Watch them do what?" Ruth asked.

Maggie didn't look at her, didn't respond.

"What makes you think he did that, Maggie?" she pushed on.

"I know he did."

"How did you know, Maggie?"

"It's obvious."

Ruth tried again. "How?"

"It just was. You know."

"Not really. But maybe I should ask your daughter."

Every inch of Maggie's face tightened.

"How do you know Raymond used cam-girl sites?" Ruth pushed.

Maggie said nothing, but her colour was rising.

"Did you use them with him?"

Maggie glared at Ruth. "Don't be disgusting."

"So, how do you know?" Ruth asked again.

"Did Rhiamon tell you?" Madoc asked.

"Don't be ridiculous," Maggie snarled.

"She could have," Palmer carried on conversationally. "That is how Rhiamon makes a living. She's a cam-girl."

"That's a lie!" Maggie was on her feet.

"Sit down, Mrs Drake," Ruth said, well aware Palmer had tensed ready to defend her.

"My daughter isn't a slut!"

"It hasn't been suggested that she is."

"You should leave her alone."

"But Rhiamon *is* a cam-girl," Ruth stated.

"She is not!"

Palmer pulled a printout from the file and put it on the table. For the benefit of the tape, he described it as a screenshot of Rhiamon Drake, AKA Queen Ree, at work.

"It's a lie," Maggie said, though weaker now. "Fake news." She sank back onto the chair.

"On Tuesday morning," Ruth said calmly, "you arrived at the site much earlier than you claim, and you bumped into Raymond Bevan. You and he don't get on. You said something to Raymond that upset him, then he said something to upset you. I suspect he moved further onto the site to see if anything else had been stolen, and you followed him. You argued with him."

"What did he say?" Palmer asked.

"He lied," Maggie said. "Like all men. Total liars." She glared at Palmer now. "All of you!"

"That's not a nice thing to say to my sergeant," Ruth said. "He keeps defending you. I'm the one that thinks you're a no-good murderer."

"He had it coming!" Maggie snapped. "He said Rhiamon did whatever he wanted on the internet."

"Then what?" Ruth said. "You got angry?"

Maggie's face was puce now. "He said my daughter would 'get her tits out for him'."

"How did that make you feel?"

"He was lying!"

"What did you do about that?"

Maggie clamped her jaw.

"Rhiamon must have enjoyed it. Being paid to be on camera," Ruth said. "Your little star."

"Shut up," Maggie said.

"Your little porn star."

"Shut up!" Maggie said.

"Your daughter likes doing whatever men ask."

"That's a lie." Maggie's jaw was clenched. Her lips back in feral anger.

"She did what Raymond asked her, too."

"No."

"We can get video footage if you'd like to see it."

"No!"

"What did you do to Raymond?"

"Nothing."

"What did you do to Raymond?"

"He's scum."

"He paid Rhiamon, your little star, to touch herself."

"No."

"And she did."

"No!"

"What did you do to Raymond?"

"What he deserved!" she snapped.

"What happened?" Palmer asked softly.

"He drowned," she snapped. "Serves him right."

"How did he get in the trench, Maggie?"

"He was a wanker!"

Ruth concentrated solely on Maggie Drake. All else was a world away. "How did he get in the trench, Maggie?"

"And a liar!"

"Did you push him?"

"I wasn't having that scum tell lies about my beautiful girl."

"Did you push him in the dirt?"

"The bastard deserved it. Deserved the dirt and the muck and to drown in his own filth."

"How did he drown?" Ruth asked.

"Too fast."

"How did he drown?" Ruth asked again.

"He should have suffered longer."

"How did he drown?"

"I pushed him in the trench, jumped on his back, and held him down!"

Chapter 36

The world came back as Maggie fell silent. Ruth saw the sudden widening of the older woman's eyes as the implications of her unwitting confession undermined the house of cards she'd been living in. Maggie narrowed her eyes at Ruth. "Bitch."

Unfortunately, that merely reinforced Ruth's own view of herself. "Your opinion is noted, Mrs Drake." Ruth displayed a calm she did not feel, though the energy needed to cop an attitude was beyond her reach. Maggie had confessed. It was on record, recorded, and they had all the evidence to back it up. Or they would, once all the forensics were verified, and she trusted Palmer's instincts that they would be. This long and emotionally draining day was done.

"So, why did you kill Seren Rosser?"

What? Ruth was painfully aware that the other two women were staring at Palmer. His question had been calmly asked, but it robbed Ruth of calm. What the hell was he up to? It was all she could do not to glare. She had distinctly told him not to mention Seren in this interview. She had to remain professional and smother the urge to strangle Palmer.

Tessa's slight frown was confusion, but the wider eyes, the pale face on Maggie Drake told Ruth that the older woman knew exactly what Palmer was talking about. Then she clamped her loose jaw and folded her arms. They weren't going to get anything out of Maggie on this one.

"Sergeant, my client is here because of allegations about Raymond Bevan. I've never heard of anyone called Seren Rosser." Tessa's tone conveyed calm superiority. Ruth was impressed, given that her client had just confessed to one murder.

"But—"

Ruth tapped Palmer's ankle under the table, though given the reaction, it might have been more of a kick. She concentrated on Tessa and Maggie. "There's nothing more to discuss on the Raymond Bevan case at this point. So, I'm concluding this interview." Following procedure, she finished the necessary recording details and turned off the tape.

Maggie was returned to a holding a cell. Ruth heard her heat, her anger, like a ticking bomb, and time was running out as Tessa stopped her in the corridor.

"Who's Seren Rosser?"

Ruth glanced at Palmer. The way he flinched suggested it was one of her killer glares. For a second, she closed her eyes and tamped down her temper, before turning back to Tessa. "She's a girl who went missing some years ago. Another case we're working on."

Now, Tessa glared at Palmer. "Is he even qualified to be a sergeant?"

"Yes, he is," Ruth snapped back. "I strongly advise that you don't get too comfortable when you get home, because this isn't over." She turned on her heel and stomped away. Tension thrummed through every fibre of her being. Tension, hunger, and exhaustion. It had been a long week, a long day, and now it was going to be a long night.

She heard Palmer trying to get her attention as she hurried up the stairs, but she didn't want to speak yet. Speaking would lead to yelling, and she wasn't ready for that. Fists balled, she slammed into the door and into their office. A glance told her that Geraint wasn't there, which was just as well, given what she was about to let loose. She rounded on Palmer, blood pumping loud in her ears.

"What the fucking hell was that?"

Even blazing angry she could tell Palmer was pushed to his limit, too. The muscle in his jaw clenched, his Adam's apple bobbed. "It was a salient question." Anger marred his tone, too. "She killed Seren Rosser."

"We haven't got one fucking shred of evidence to prove that, and what you did just now gives Maggie forewarning that we're going after her for it. Something I did not want to give!" Ruth rose to her tiptoes and she was still way shorter than him. "You're still in training, Palmer, and fucking stupid mo—"

"Ruth!"

This time she understood why Geraint was bellowing at her as he appeared in her sightline. She shifted so Palmer wasn't blocking her view and realised they were being watched by most of the people on the floor – those not on telephones, anyway. Cold washed through her. Shame at her own behaviour. She could feel her skin changing chameleon-like.

"My office," Geraint growled at her. "Now!"

Madoc could only stare at the place where Ruth's face, the perfect picture of fury, had been. He wasn't sure what he'd done was worth this outburst. He did know he wanted to go to the toilet. Part of the fight or flight reaction. Animals naturally expelled anything they could to run; it improved the efficiency of the effort. Of course, the urge to go might also be a result of his full bladder.

He turned, suddenly aware of the audience behind him and their interest. His heart hammered as he forced himself to walk normally, aware of the slamming of Geraint's door.

The toilets were not a pleasant haven, but they were his only option.

Worries crowded his head while he did what was necessary, washed his hands. Ruth was furious with him. If she took against him now, she knew everything she needed to destroy him. He closed his eyes and leant against a cubical door, slowly banging his head against the Formica of the toilet partitions. How could he have been so stupid as to trust another senior woman with his career?

"Thought I might find you in here."

Madoc opened his eyes and saw John Harris. He didn't know what to say to the uniformed officer. Middle age suited John, softened his muscles and eased what would have been a bruiser's jaw. The air of confidence had grown from self-certainty, supported by years of experience in the job. There wasn't much John Harris hadn't seen or done in his time. Madoc saw a Hierophant, a teacher, someone he could learn from. John knew everyone in the station better than Madoc did, including Ruth.

"I fucked up," he said.

"Oh, I don't doubt that." The man moved to stand before Madoc. "Look, I don't know what you did, but I do know Ruth. For her to explode like that, either you have a very good reason for hiding in here, or something internal to Ruth that you don't know about set her off. I've only seen her explode like that a few times in the thirteen years I've known her, and there's always been a reason for it. But twice there was something else, too, something going on with her that took her to the edge before someone else's actions pushed her over. Meaning, you may not have fucked up as badly as you think."

"Thanks."

"Oh, don't get me wrong, pal. You fucked up. It's the intensity of the explosion that might be out of proportion."

Madoc nodded, sighed, and hung his head. "What do I do now?"

"Depends," John said. "You can walk away, accept the failure, and come crawling back to being a constable, where you'll have to stay for the rest of your working life. Which, by the way, is something some of us are very proud to do. Or you can get your arse back in there, face the scariest pairing in the division, and fight for your right to carry on."

"Do you think a grovelling apology will help?"

The roll of John's eyes surprised Madoc. "No, not especially. Apologise, yes, but I said fight for your right to be here. Explain why you did whatever you did, so they understand your reasoning, and learn from whatever response you get. Geraint and Ruth can be hard to deal with at times, but they both do their level best to support their team. Even when pissed off with them."

Just like Ruth had spoken in his defence to Tessa Winter downstairs and to Geraint when Jacqueline had made her accusations. He thanked John and headed back to the office. Ruth and Geraint were still in the DCI's office. Clearly, their discussion was heated. His approach caught Geraint's eye. The older man jerked his head in that way that commanded Madoc to join them. What surprised Madoc was that he then turned to Ruth and ordered her out.

Her hair was disarrayed, and her skin oddly mottled. Was she crying? Angry tears? She didn't seem the kind to cry for sympathy. Geraint wasn't the type to sympathise with tears. She wouldn't meet his eye. Instead, she slunk around him to sit at her desk. It worried Madoc that she banged her elbows on the table and put her head in her hands. Had he caused more of a problem than he could fathom with one out of place question?

He stepped into Geraint's office, and carefully closed the door when told to. The man was looking at him, steel in his gaze. That look would send a suspect gabbling to confess. But Madoc remembered John's advice.

The sound of paper slapping hard on a desk outside made them both jump and look beyond the partition to where Ruth was shifting paperwork at her nearby desk. Turning back to face Geraint, Madoc felt a surprising calm descend through him.

"Well?" Geraint said.

A well's no good without water.

Great. The passenger was the last thing he needed right now.

It's one of Ruth's sayings. She got it from her mother.

Not helping. He wasn't sure what would help now he faced Geraint.

John's advice was good. Explain, don't grovel.

"I asked about Seren Rosser because I'm convinced Maggie Drake killed her."

The way Geraint watched him without comment made Madoc's stomach cramp. Which made it grumble.

"Do you have any evidence of that?"

The calm tone shredded Madoc's nerves. "No, sir."

"No," Geraint said.

"Bollocks!" Ruth's curse drew their attention out of the room again. The thump of both fists on the table was swiftly followed by some frantic tapping of the keyboard.

Madoc turned back to Geraint. They were, for that second, united in not knowing what was going on. Geraint used silence like a weapon, and Madoc felt it pierce his skin as the pounding of his heart boomed in his ears.

"Ruth tells me that you have great gut instincts."

Oh God, here it comes.

"She says that you're intelligent, capable, and considerate. But …"

Did he have to leave it hanging? Of course, he did. He was probably unused to the idea. How did a dyed-in-the-wool police officer deal with one who was so off the wall? At least Geraint wasn't laughing. Yet. But that spectre stood in the corner, waiting with sacks full of humiliation to dump on Madoc. Could he go back to being a constable? Did he have a choice?

Of course, you have a choice. You can quit. Jump before you're pushed. Or you can take John's advice and fight for your right to be here.

Better to go down swinging. "Look, sir. I've done everything in my power to impress DI Atkins. And you. I know I stuffed up with Ali. And okay, the incident with Tom was stupid, but I'm not the one who commented, all I did was snigger. The only thing I have done wrong is ask one inappropriate question. I don't deserve this level of criticism. I don't deserve to lose my job."

The jump up of Geraint's eyebrows warned Madoc to shut up. Dipping his eyeline he hoped to hide the emotions warring inside him.

"Have I criticised you?"

He looked back up. Swallowed. "No, sir."

"No. Do you know why?"

Er, actually … "No, sir."

"Because, from where I was standing, Ruth was the one out of line. I criticised her."

That surprised Madoc. To the point he wasn't sure how to react.

"What exactly were you expecting?" Geraint asked.

This was worse than a bollocking. "A shit sandwich?"

Geraint nearly smiled. "You're up on management techniques, then. Compliment, complaint, compliment?"

Madoc nodded.

"Not where I was going," Geraint said. "You're not about to lose your job, so stop stressing. You fucked up—"

"No, he didn't," Ruth said as she opened the door and stepped back into the office.

Madoc held his breath. What was going on?

Her skin looked sallow. Shadows under her eyes underlined her tiredness, as if she'd aged years in the last few minutes. The internal screaming remained, but it carried an air of both defeat and discovery. Carefully, she closed the door behind her.

"Okay, yes, that question was a fuck up. It shortened the time we have to prove that Maggie Drake killed Seren Rosser, but after what I just saw, I know Palmer's right. She did kill Seren."

Chapter 37

Silence hung heavy in the room. Ruth wasn't sure she had the strength to stand beneath it. She was exhausted beyond reason, hungry, and the constant ache in her breast was getting worse. She had to stop soon. But first, she had to catch up and make things right. The caterpillars were in neutral, but was Geraint? Madoc? She couldn't look at him; she wasn't strong enough. He must think she'd lost her mind. He might even think that she'd betrayed his confidence.

"I'm really sorry. This is my fuck up, not Palmer's. He saw what I've been blind to. Worse yet, I blinkered him. I told him not to pursue the very line that would have led us down the right path from the start."

Geraint crossed his arms. "Explain."

She did.

She had never got around to reading Seren's file in detail. After she passed it to Madoc, she had just taken an overview from him. He had mentioned that when Seren went missing there were reports of her getting into a blue car with a partial number plate. She hadn't asked about the car. Madoc started the background check on Maggie Drake, and if he'd carried on, he would have found that Maggie was flagged as a person of interest in the original investigation into Seren's disappearance. Back then, Maggie she had owned a dark green Volvo with a reg number that could have been mistaken for the one given. The car had never been checked.

"Do you know why the car wasn't checked?" Geraint asked.

Ruth shook her head. "It was a Missing Persons call. I suspect that they judged the match too tenuous and the likelihood of forensics too low to be worth the expense."

"Mispers have an even tighter budget than we do," Geraint said.

"But there's more," Ruth added. "When we visited Rhiamon Drake in Newport, she was opening the garage door until Palmer showed his warrant card. Then she closed it. The garage, not the warrant card, obviously. But I saw a second car in there, a green one. I didn't register the plate, and don't ask me if it was a Volvo because I didn't see a badge. But it can't be coincidence."

"No, it can't." The caterpillars were crowding together.

She'd messed up with Palmer and now she was pissing Geraint off. This was going well.

"If I'd just mentioned the car to Palmer, he would have made the connection. But I didn't. I didn't think it was significant. It's my fault the connection wasn't seen earlier."

"Good of you to admit it," Geraint said. "But now is not the time for you to screw up. You know the importance of murder cases. They can make or break careers. You're both smart enough to know any of us are only as good as our last case." His focus pinned Ruth. She felt skewered. "Fuck this up, and your reputation could be shot. Pretty-boy Palmer could be scuppered for career advancement. I might not last long enough to retire. This is ridiculous, Ruth. You're off your game. What is going on with you?"

Ruth hung her head, fought back the urge to crumple and cry. Bile embittered the back of her throat. What could she say? For the first time in a long time, she knew she needed help. She remembered the feel of Madoc's hand on her shoulder at Sian's bedside. Even the memory gave her some strength. This was awful and it was all her fault. She looked to him.

Lost.

The way Ruth looked at him told to Madoc she was lost. This was worse than when she'd stood beside Sian.

Then help her find her way.

"This is my fault." The words escaped Madoc before he considered them. Geraint's focus felt like a pin in the chest. Just another moth on the board. "Atkins has been kind about my …" *Oh God, am I really going to do this?* Did he have a choice? "… abilities, but I—"

"No."

Ruth's snap dragged his attention to her.

Her eyes, those brown and green rings, were on fire again. Blazing with anger at him. "No, you don't get to fall on your sword when it's my fuck up. Yes, you screwed up in the interview room, but only because I wanted to keep it back so I can go home, eat, and sleep. Now, I'm going to have work on, get this sorted sooner rather than later. The only thing you are guilty of is one imprudent question because I didn't tell you not to mention Seren."

Only that was precisely what she had told him, and he'd forgotten it in that moment. Why was she lying now?

She huffed out the obvious excess of emotion before she turned to their boss. "Geraint, you're right. I am off my game." Her vulnerability was clear in her shaking voice, not to mention her rumbling stomach. "And I have been for a few weeks now, long before Palmer joined us. Putting me with him was as much a test of my abilities as of his. And this time, I'm the one twitching. The only thing Palmer is guilty of is being too observant. Sometimes, it's like he knows me better than I know myself, and that freaks me out."

Madoc stared at her. She was covering for him. She was saving his job by risking her own. Why would she do that? It didn't make sense.

There's something else she's not telling anyone.

He knew that, but what? "Ruth?"

Not now. That's not a work conversation.

His passenger was especially annoying when right.

When Ruth didn't answer, Geraint spoke. "Ruth, do you know what's wrong?"

Madoc could only sense her internal scream, though this time the tightness of her body also demonstrated pain and suffering. At last, she nodded. "And I'll get it sorted. I promise."

Geraint let out a long, controlled breath. There was a strong sense of frustration washing off the man. "I'll ask Saunders to take over the case."

"No!" Madoc spoke without thinking. It pulled their attention to him, and he had to run with it. "Like you said, murder cases can make or break us. You call Saunders in on this and you're telling the world you don't trust us, which I can live with, but you'd be telling them you don't trust Ruth, either." He turned to Ruth. "Now you've spotted the connection, you have a plan, right? You're not broken."

Ruth straightened her spine. The pain was still there, but so was the steeliness of her nature. "Yes. I mean, no. No, I'm not broken. A little cracked maybe, but not broken." It was a weak joke, but it was more Ruth than she had been. "And yes, I have a plan."

"Good." Madoc smiled at her, hoping it was the support she needed.

Now, Ruth faced Geraint. "We haven't fucked up this case." Her voice was stronger, steadier. "I haven't completely ruined this investigation, and I won't. I know what I need to do next, and I'll get it done, and I can get it done faster than you can get Saunders in here and caught up."

This time, Geraint nearly smiled. "Now you sound more like you than you have for ages. So, go get to work."

Ruth's smile was small and short-lived. "Yes, sir."

She left, and Madoc stepped to follow.

"Palmer?"

He stopped in his tracks. The Sword of Damocles was still on the one hair over his career. "Yes, sir?"

"Whatever confession she just stopped you from making, I'll let it pass this time. But the training you're on is difficult. Fuck up again and there's a good chance she'll have your balls long before I can get there – but trust me, I will get there."

Madoc nodded. "Yes, sir."

Chapter 38

Persuading Gwent to help meant calling DS Andrew Creak and persuading him to call DI Jestin Morris, to get him on the case. She glanced up at Geraint as he left while she was still on the phone.

The call with DI Morris a few minutes later was not fun. Her head was in her hands again, aware of the world working around her, but concentrated on the call, when a plate of pizza slices was slipped under her nose. Farmhouse pizza. She told Morris she understood and said she'd get back to him.

This time, when she looked up at Geraint, she smiled. "Thanks, boss."

"Well, I can't have you passing out from hunger. Bring me up to speed."

Before she could, Ruth sank her teeth into the thick, pointed end of a pizza slice and closed her eyes to savour the taste. She hadn't eaten since lunchtime with Madoc, which felt like a lifetime ago. The sound of pleasure that escaped her sounded almost orgasmic even to her. When was the last time she'd enjoyed that alternative pleasure?

She opened her eyes to see Madoc sitting opposite, also eating pizza. Thoughts she really shouldn't have crowded in on her. She swallowed the mouthful and put the slice down, grabbing a tissue from the box she kept on her desk to wipe her fingers.

"Right, well. DI Morris and DS Creak from Gwent are going to go to Rhiamon's place and seize the car. If it is the one linked to the Rosser case, they'll impound it. They've also agreed to do the initial interview with Rhiamon. I'm going to send them an outline of what I want them to press her for. What they won't agree to is the cost for a forensic team to examine the car."

"You want me to go higher and give someone a rocket?"

Ruth shook her head. "Actually, I was wondering if you could call Daf? See if he's interested in the work. I'd rather it was done here than in Gwent, anyway. I'll call Ali, she owes me a favour, see if she's able to do some of the work. If they agree, I'll ask Morris to arrange for the car to be taken directly to Treforest."

The caterpillars came together for a silent conflab. "I'll ask Daf to pick up Ali and take her to Newport. They might be able to tell us if there's anything worth pursuing. Forensics at this stage may be beyond detection."

"What do we do if we can't get anyone to work on it now?" Madoc asked. "It's late and tomorrow's Sunday. Who wants to work on a Sunday?"

"Anyone I say has to," Geraint said as Ruth ate. He refocused on her, making her feel guilty and gannet-like for enjoying the hot pizza he had provided. "Mind, this could wait till Monday. We've got Maggie for Bevan's murder, so she's going nowhere. But let's see if we can get the job done today. If not, then this rolls into next week."

Ruth nodded her agreement, relieved Geraint got it.

"Okay, so what do we have on Maggie for Seren so far?"

Madoc washed down more pizza with the can of diet soda Geraint had also provided. "Well, we have to start with the assumption that the DNA will come back with a positive identification."

"It'd better," Ruth grumbled, "or we're sunk without a clue."

"True, but we only have to wait till Monday to get the official version," Palmer said, going through what was on the Naked Lady board. "At the time of her disappearance, Seren was living in Ochr-y-Mynydd, and though she could drive, she didn't have a car, so she was planning to use public transport to get to

Cardiff. Which meant getting a bus through Heolgerrig to Merthyr train station. But checks at the time could find no trace of Seren on any of the bus CCTV records. We have a report of a girl matching Seren's description getting into a blue Volvo with a partial number plate. Maggie was highlighted as a person of interest at the time, but the car wasn't checked. That car is now subject to a SORN."

"An off-road notice has to be renewed each year," Ruth added. "That means Maggie knows where the car is, and the only reason I can think of for her keeping it and not selling it on is because she knows there's evidence in there."

"But she's not keeping it – her daughter is," Geraint said.

Ruth let out another Anglo-Saxon expletive. "You're right. This is messy. Maggie claims Rhiamon lives in London and Rhiamon says Maggie doesn't have her Newport address."

"So?" Palmer asked.

"So," Ruth answered, "either they're lying about Maggie not knowing where Rhiamon lives, or …" Apparently, she didn't have an 'or'.

"Or possibly, Rhiamon is signing the SORN and forging her mother's signature," Palmer said.

"Which is an offence," Geraint pointed out. "But why would Rhiamon keep the car?"

Ruth had to think about that for a moment. "She must know there's evidence in there. Why else hide it the second a police officer shows up?"

"Are you suggesting she was involved?" Geraint asked.

"More likely an accessory after the fact," Palmer said.

Geraint nodded, then focused on Ruth. "Is this what convinced you Maggie murdered Seren?"

Ruth felt Palmer's eyeline switch to her. *Damn and blast.* His abilities had convinced him. And her. How to save him falling on that sword now? "*Valleys View*," she managed around a mouthful of pizza.

"Yes," Palmer took up the idea. "Both Seren and Rhiamon were up for places on *Valleys View*. That's where Seren was heading the day she went missing. Rhiamon, too, only Maggie couldn't take her because Maggie was banned from Culverhouse Cross, where the screen tests were held. The production company had hired a studio for the day."

"But what would Maggie's motive be?" Ruth understood that Geraint was asking these questions to test their theory, not them. If they could be persuasive enough, he'd let them follow the path.

"Rhiamon said that Maggie was a total stage mom," Madoc said. "She'd have done anything to get her daughter the job she thought Rhiamon deserved. Maggie killed Seren to reduce the competition."

"Can't see someone going to those length for a TV show, can you?"

Ruth nodded as she swallowed more of the lovely pizza. She felt revived already. "Oh, hell yeah. You should watch the movie *Drop Dead Gorgeous*. Or *Stage Moms*."

"Maggie has this odd attitude," Palmer said. "What was it you called it?" he asked Ruth. "Devoted servant?"

Ruth nodded. She really shouldn't be stuffing food into her face this way, but she needed it.

"Maggie will do anything for someone who loves her back," Madoc said. "And I mean anything. She's also got a bee in her bonnet about men being selfish, so she acts in ways that she thinks are the opposite of that. She'll give up anything to prove her devotion. Besides, just look what she did when she found out Raymond was letting Rhiamon star in his sexual fantasies. Oh yeah, Maggie would have killed Seren for Rhiamon."

"And that devoted servant attitude is the lever we use to get under her skin and get her confession," Ruth said.

"A confession is always good," Geraint allowed. "But the CPS will want more."

"And once we get the forensics from the car, and the interview from Rhiamon, we'll have it."

"Well, we'll need that before we can get an arrest warrant, which means there's not a lot you two can do for now. Enjoy your pizza while I call Daf."

The way Ruth ate with gusto was a surprise and a pleasure; she clearly enjoyed every mouthful. That noise she'd made at first bite had left Madoc grateful to be sitting down to hide his reaction. She looked less stressed now. He wondered what it was pushing her to the edge.

Not now, his passenger warned. *She's back in work mode. Keep to that.*

It was good advice, but he couldn't follow it exactly. "Thanks," he said softly, "for covering for me."

Her focus shifted from the food to him. She even checked that Geraint was on the phone before she spoke. "I'm not covering for you; I'm covering for me. I can't believe I was so short sighted with this. You were right from the word go."

"Without evidence, which you've now arranged to get."

She nodded, given her mouth was full.

"And next time, I'll check with you before asking off-the-wall questions in interviews," he said.

"Oh, don't do that. It's the off-the-wall questions that usually trip up suspects. But we'll have to do better on communicating between ourselves what is or isn't to be brought up in an interview. I should have been clearer. Sorry."

"To be fair, you were. I should have been more circumspect. Sorry."

She smiled at him, all soft and warm. "Oh, shut up and eat."

The interview room, again. Hours and a lot of liaison with Gwent Police later. Ruth had gone over what they had with Palmer and Geraint. They knew they had to get their ducks in a row.

By the time they were back in interview, Maggie looked like she'd been crying and Tessa looked exhausted. They were all fraying at the edges. Only the second arrest was shiny and new.

"We mentioned Seren Rosser in our last encounter," Ruth said after the formal interview was started. "Can you confirm you know who we were referring to?"

Maggie said nothing.

"Shall I jog your memory?" Ruth placed a picture of Seren Rosser in front of Maggie. "Look at the picture, Maggie. That's Seren," Ruth said. "Seren Rosser."

"Never saw her before in my life," Maggie said.

"She's a striking-looking girl," Ruth said. "I'm sure you'd recognise her if you looked at the picture."

"I looked. I don't know her."

"Maggie, lying helps no one here."

"My client has said she doesn't know the woman, Inspector Atkins," Tessa said. "Please stop badgering her."

Ruth nodded, indicating Palmer could put the photo away. "Okay, let's move on to the matter of your Volvo, Maggie."

"I drive a Fiesta."

"Now, yes, but you used to drive a Volvo. A green one."

"Years ago," Maggie said. "Scrapped it."

"When?"

"Years ago."

"Where?"

"Can't remember."

"Any scrap merchant would take your registration documents to advise the DVLA that the vehicle was off road. However, according to the DVLA, the car is still registered to you."

"That's their mistake."

"Then, why do they also have a SORN document saying you have possession of the car? It's signed by you and only seven months old."

"I don't even know what a SORN is," Maggie said.

"It's a Statutory Off Road Notification. One has to be filled in every year and sent to the DLVA to save you paying road tax."

"I don't do that."

Which, if true, meant Rhiamon was signing it. "Where's the car, Maggie?"

"I don't have it."

"You don't have it?"

"That's what she said, Inspector. Can we move on?" Tessa asked.

Ruth looked at Tessa. "Not yet, no."

"Oh, never mind some bloody car," Maggie grumbled. "What about my dog?"

"The RSPCA will take good care of Kohl. It's the car that's missing. If you can't tell me where the car is, who can? Rhiamon?"

"Leave her out of this."

"Sorry, Maggie, can't do that. Let's start with something simple. Where does Rhiamon live, Maggie?"

The glower was dark. "London."

"Nope, she lives in Newport," Palmer said. "We saw her there this morning."

"You're lying."

"We're police officers," Ruth reminded her. "It's not in our interest to lie. And it's not in your interest for us to phone Rhiamon, either, is it?"

Maggie just glared.

"Why is that, Maggie?"

The silence stretched.

"Nothing to say?"

Maggie said nothing.

Ruth nodded. "That's okay, I understand. To be honest, it really wouldn't do any good to call Rhiamon right now. What with her being under arrest an' all."

Maggie's face fell. "No." The word rang with disbelief.

Ruth nodded. "In the custody of Gwent Police as we speak."

"What?" Maggie demanded. "What trumped-up nonsense is this?"

"No nonsense," Palmer assured her.

"You see, we asked Gwent Police to have a look in Rhiamon's garage. Where they found a green Volvo," Ruth stated. "The one still registered to you."

"A forensics team went over it with a fine-toothed comb," Palmer added. "They aren't happy about being called out on a Saturday, so they're making damn sure it's worth it. They're highly motivated to find the smallest bit of trace evidence."

"There's no evidence to find," Maggie said.

Ruth smiled. "Fortunately for us, that's where you're wrong. The forensic team has already found blonde hairs. Since neither you nor Rhiamon are blonde, they must have come from a third party. Like Seren Rosser."

"There are a lot of blondes in the world."

Ruth nodded. "Which is why the CSIs were particularly happy to tell me they can now get DNA from hairs without follicles. They've already started, in fact. So, do you still want to claim that you don't know who Seren Rosser is?"

Maggie looked at Tessa, then back to Ruth. "No comment."

"Good call. You've already confessed to one murder today. Luckily, I can comment as much as I like. So, let me lay out the situation for you. First. You've already demonstrated that Rhiamon is a liar."

"I have not!"

"Oh, so *you* were lying when you said Rhiamon lived in London?"

Maggie's eyes looked stormy. "No comment."

"Second fact. The car still registered to you was in Rhiamon's possession."

"Proves nothing."

"Fact three. A signed SORN shows you accepted responsibility for that vehicle up to seven months ago. Suggesting you did know its location. Meaning you lied to me in this interview."

Maggie looked dejected now. "No comment."

"We have also established, by your own confession to Raymond Bevan's murder, that you will kill to protect your little star, Rhiamon."

"That's not a new development, is it, Maggie?" Palmer asked.

No response.

"We now have evidence of a blonde being in your car. In a few hours, we'll know that blonde was Seren. Here's another fact for you. We have also established that both Rhiamon and Seren were taking screen tests for the same show the day Seren was last seen. That establishes they were rivals. That gives Rhiamon a motive to murder."

"No."

"Yes," Palmer said.

Tessa put her hand on Maggie's arm to stop her retort.

"So, let me tell you what's going to happen now. As Rhiamon had possession of the car, and the direct motive, she'll be charged with murder. And since you signed the SORN, you'll be charged with accessory."

"I didn't sign any SORN."

"Then we'll have Rhiamon charged with falsifying legal documentation, as well. Though, it's fairly minor compared to the murder."

"No! Rhiamon didn't do anything," Maggie said. "She wouldn't. She's a good girl. She's my girl."

"Your little star?" Ruth said.

"Yes. She's my star."

"Accorded to Lush Ladies," Palmer said, "she's a star to lots of men, too."

"You're disgusting!" Maggie surprised them all by spitting at Palmer.

"Just to be clear," Ruth said calmly, thankful that the spittle had only landed on his jacket, "that's now considered assaulting a police officer and you will be charged with that as well."

Now Maggie glared at her. "You're all filthy pigs. You're probably a dyke, too. Wouldn't even know how to dress like a lady."

"I'm not a lady," Ruth smiled back. "I'm a police officer."

"You're trash! Look at you. Dressed like a man, acting like a man, talking like a man. All they ever think about is sex. My daughter's worth more than that. She's an angel. Should be a star. She will be a star. I wasn't going to let a plumped-up, boob-jobbed, bottle-blonde bitch steal my girl's place!"

Ruth looked at Tessa. "Would you like to give your client any advice at this point?"

Tessa quietly advised Maggie of her right to remain silent, and the value of 'no comment.'

Ruth saw Palmer as they listened. He looked tired, too. Hopefully, this wouldn't take much longer. Palmer took a breath when Tessa finished.

"You can, of course, take your solicitor's advice, but we need to know what you know about Seren's death and her burial. If you don't tell us, then we'll turn to Rhiamon for answers, and as the one with the direct motive and possession of the car, she's more likely to be the one the CPS agree to charge with the murder."

Maggie looked at Palmer. She glanced at Tessa, then glared at Ruth. But said nothing.

"Heyho," Ruth said lightly. "Well, just think, while you'll be serving time for killing Raymond, Rhiamon will be serving time for killing Seren. You might end up sharing a cell. I'm sure

Rhiamon would love that." Sarcasm dripped acid from her tone. "Tell me, how will you make her a little star then? To whom?"

"You're disgusting," Maggie sneered.

"I'm not the murderer here," Ruth said. "That's you. Oh, and Rhiamon." She closed the files in front of her, to all intents and purposes preparing to leave.

"No!"

At Maggie's cry, Ruth sat back down.

"It's not fair," Maggie said. "Rhiamon didn't do anything. I did it. I killed and buried Seren Rosser, and the bitch deserved it, too. Getting in the way of my little star."

"What happened?"

Tessa interrupted. "Mrs Drake—"

"Oh, shut up. You're no use."

Tessa, Ruth knew, would be more useful if Maggie would only listen to her.

"I knew Seren would get a bus to the train station."

Ruth watched Tessa roll her eyes at the stupidity of a second confession.

"So, I drove around until I saw her," Maggie said. "She was bouncing down the street, those stupid massive boobs bobbing like a neon sign for some man to go fuck her. No dignity, that sort. All boob, no brain, like. I stopped, told her that the buses were running late, asked if she wanted a lift. She knew I was Rhiamon's mam, but she also knew she needed to get to the station, so she got in anyway.

"I locked the doors as we drove and pulled off onto Upper Colliers Row. She couldn't get out. Tried fighting me. But I pulled the pillow from the back seat and stuffed it over the cow's face. Bitch tried to scram me."

Ruth figured, if someone was trying to suffocate her, she'd do a damn sight more than just claw at them.

"But I got her jammed in the corner, between the seat of the car and the door. She passed out. I kept the cushion over her face and waited. And waited. I didn't let go until I was sure."

Maggie looked away, her eyes on the table between them. She was lost in her memory. "It was getting light by then. There were dog walkers about, but I keep a folding spade in the car, for snow. Seren had this massive bag, a beach bag with clothes and shoes, makeup and stuff. I put the spade in there. I knew there was an old rhododendron on the waste ground, God knows why, but there you go. It had got so big, it kind of hollowed out in the middle. The seat belt gave me trouble for some reason. Then, I dragged her out of the car and into the bush. I decided if anyone asked, I'd say she was drunk and I was trying to sober her up before taking her home. But no one was around once I was on the common. No one saw. No one asked. I dragged her into the bush, it was massive and there were voids in the branches, dug as best I could, and covered her over. She spluttered at one point. I just shovelled more dirt on her face. She didn't do it again."

That, Ruth concluded, was why Maggie had pulled Raymond's face from the dirt: to check he was dead. Didn't want to make the same mistake twice.

"I wasn't to know they'd put a damn housing estate on her. And if that twat of a labourer hadn't put the trench in the wrong place, she'd have been buried forever under a house. Buried and forgotten, like the trash she was."

"Do you remember what she wore that day?" Ruth asked.

Maggie shrugged. "Some sort of shift dress, I think. Lightweight, cotton."

"And her shoes?" Palmer asked.

"Ballet pumps," Maggie said. "I found one in the car after I got home. Don't know what happened with the other one. Probably fell on the road."

"What about the bag?"

"Took it home with me. Threw it and the shoe on the next bonfire I had."

"Your evidence is still circumstantial, Inspector," Tessa said.

"Not so much now," Ruth replied.

"We didn't say where the hair was found," Palmer said.

"But Maggie just explained how it got into the seat belt casing," Ruth said. "Your client will now be charged with two counts of murder."

"But not Rhiamon," Maggie demanded. "You can't charge her."

Ruth almost wished Maggie was right. "We won't be charging her with murder, no."

Maggie looked relieved.

"But she kept the car. That makes her an accessory after the fact. Which we will be charging her with."

As Maggie revolted against that prospect, Ruth took stock. This woman had nearly got away with murder. Twice. If Rhiamon hadn't kept the car, she would have. And why?

Cloying mother love.

Ruth felt sick. She wanted to go home and hug her son, tell him she loved him, and try forever not to be Maggie's kind of mother.

She terminated the interview.

Chapter 39

"Why here?" Madoc asked in the coffee shop above the swimming pool. It was Tuesday afternoon. They'd both taken Monday off in lieu, under Geraint's instruction. They were off the clock, but Ruth had asked Madoc to meet her here.

Thankfully, this week was, so far, quieter and easier than the last. They'd spent most of the day wrapping up the Bevan and Rosser cases. Gwent had discovered that Rhiamon was croupier for some high rollers, and it seemed she dealt more than just cards, hence sufficient funds for the house. Forensics had confirmed the body was Seren's and matched the white hair from Raymond's back to Kohl, who was now up for rehousing. Best of all, they'd confirmed the identity of the girl in Geddings' house. At least that family had some form of closure. And Loren Baxter's case was on its way to court.

"We're here because it's public," Ruth said softly. "The coffee's okay, few of our colleagues come here, and I need to ask something I don't want them overhearing."

His mouth went dry. There was still so much on the line. Her gaze was cautious but deeply curious. She was a conundrum he had no idea how to solve.

"Okay," he said carefully. "What do want to ask?"

That her eyeline dropped and she shifted in her chair surprised him. She could stand up to the Flacks and Geraint, but couldn't talk to him?

"Your, erm, reputation?"

Oh dear.

"The thing with Ali," Ruth said. "That wasn't good."

That's a cop out.

I figured. "Okay, but that wasn't really down to me."

"Yes, it was. You told Ali she could say what she liked. What if that got back to your family? I've seen these things play out in school yards before divorce courts. You wouldn't want Osian getting into a fight over it, would you?"

The point was valid, and slightly painful. "Of course not. You're right, I was part of that problem, but won't be again. I'll do everything in my power for there to be no more rumours."

"Good. I mean, I know you can't entirely control it, but I wouldn't want your wife hearing such things. The trouble it could—"

"It's not a problem. My wife—"

Ex-wife.

Exactly. "—knows the truth. But I take your point. Not sure what I can do about gossip, but I take your point."

"Be faithful. It's all any married man, or woman, can do. Now, I promise that's the last I'll say about your family."

"Ruth, for someone who doesn't talk family, you talk a fair bit about family."

"I don't."

"You do." He smiled. "You even told me your mother is English, that she knows where you live, and your tone suggested you don't want her to. Then there's Sian, who's virtually family. And I know your son's giving you grief, indications being that his father isn't your late husband."

She hung her head.

"You were friends with Sian," he said. "You trusted her. I just want you to trust me the same way."

She didn't look at him as she answered. "I … can't."

"Why?"

I think you scare her.

That didn't sound good, but Ruth had looked up again. Pain twisted her expression. "I can't have the same friendship with you I had with Sian. You're a man for a start, that automatically makes it different. I trust you. I even like you. But you … sort of freak me out."

What?

See? Give her a break. She's trying to be honest, his passenger said.

Ruth looked away again, sipped her coffee. Delaying tactics. Again. What was really going on in her head?

"Ruth, what did you really want to talk about? Because you not being direct is starting to freak me out. This isn't like you."

"Sorry." Her fingers tapped the table.

The temptation to reach out and put his hand over hers was great, but she wouldn't welcome it. At some point soon, he was going to have to tell her he was divorced.

Won't do you any good, the passenger chimed in. **You're a younger subordinate officer. She won't risk a relationship like that.**

By the Goddess, he hated that voice.

No, you just hate that I'm right.

"Look, it's …" She faltered again.

"Is this about my abilities?"

She nodded. "I don't think the others should know."

That was a relief.

"So, we have to be careful. It's not that I don't want to know when you get … Would you be okay to keep referring to them as gut instincts?"

Such coyness made him smile. "Sounds like a good idea."

Her smile of agreement was warming but short-lived. "Right. So, you let me know, and if I see the benefit, we'll follow your gut instincts. Okay?"

"Okay." It was very okay.

"But … look, the rest don't need to know, but I do. I need to know the rest." She pinned him with a look. "I need to understand what I'm dealing with with you. What I might have to cover for."

This was just about the weirdest conversation Madoc had ever had with a colleague, but probably the most important one, too.

"Okay. Well, then. Let's start with the fact that I'm a pagan, what's called a hedge witch."

"A witch? You do spells and stuff? Magic?" Her curled lip told its own tale.

"Not exactly. I mean, I have had some limited success with a casting or two, but mostly it's more … Well, this is going to sound dreadful, but part of me thinks it's more positive thinking and aromatherapy."

"Those things have their benefits."

Their shared smile pulled at his heartstrings.

Curiosity returned to her gaze. "Could you do that scrying thing for a misper?"

Scry to find a missing person? He considered it. "Possibly. Probably not. Though, Aunt Maureen might be able to."

"Okay, something else the others aren't to know about. Aunt Maureen and your religion."

He shrugged. "Geraint already knows. About my religion, anyway. He will have seen from my personnel details that I'm a member of the Pagan Police Association."

Her eyes went wide. "There's an association?"

He nodded. "Just like there's a Christian Police Association and a National Association for Muslim Police."

"Oh. Okay." Her curiosity clearly wasn't sated. He liked that. Her mind was open to possibilities. "You said that sometimes your gut instincts are the emotional equivalent of an out of context power chord?"

"Not quite what I said, but I like that version. And yes."

"Which can knock you off your feet?"

"That's only happened a couple of times, but yeah, they can."

"Well, give me a bit of warning and I'll support you as best I can."

That seemed to be her way. "Thanks."

"Is there anything I should know about? Wards or amulets or whatever? Anything I should make sure never to put in an official report?"

He smiled at the question. "If there's anything non-reportable, I'll let you know. But you'll definitely know if I wear one of Aunt Maureen's amulets. I have no idea what she makes them from, but they stink worse than Dad's slurry pit."

Ruth's smile was almost a chuckle. This was an unfamiliar experience: someone finding out about what he could do and not belittling him as a freak.

"You know at some point I'm going to have to meet this Aunt Maureen of yours."

That made him smile. Two less alike women would be hard to find. "Sure."

"So, is that it?"

"Pretty much. I'm Pagan, I believe in cosmic harmony, Gaia, Goddess of the Earth, and Selene, the Goddess of the Moon."

"I thought Luna was the moon goddess?"

"In Roman mythology, yes. Selene was the Greek version. I just prefer that name."

"Okay."

He paused to check if there was anything else. "Oh, and I read tarot cards."

"O-kay." That dragged out in darker tones.

"You don't have to pull back. It's not contagious."

Her cheeks reddened as she relaxed again. "I'm sorry. But my experience with tarot was getting the lecture of my life and being told I'd ruined a whole family day out, just because, when I was twelve, at some fair, I asked if I could go to the mystic offering tarot readings. Mum went off the head, told me it was the route to evil and that I was a wicked child for even asking."

Now, there was a set up for lifelong issues. "I'm sorry you had an unpleasant experience, and a narrow-minded mother."

"Yeah, well. Life." She sipped the coffee again. "Hang on, the other day, you came into the office smelling of burnt sage. That was at full moon. Was that some Pagan moon ritual thing?"

"I'm impressed you noticed." He grinned.

"Well, I like to cook. Not especially good at it, which is how I could tell the burnt smell was sage."

"I meant you noticing the moon phase."

She shrugged. "I'm female. It's not just the moon that gets full every twenty-eight-ish days. Not that I'm in sync with her or anything, but I keep an eye out."

She called Mother Moon 'her'. Perhaps their belief systems weren't so far apart after all.

"I burn sage to cleanse the tarot cards. I was up that night anyway. It was the night my father-in-law had a heart attack, so seemed as good a time as any to do it."

"Is he okay now?"

"My father-in-law? Yes, thankfully. More a warning than anything."

"Good. That's good. I see, so that's it? You're a Pagan with good gut instincts, aromatherapy, positive thinking, a weird aunt, and tarot reading? Oh god, are you into yoga, too?"

He had to laugh. "Why does that seem to offend you?"

"It doesn't, it's just all a bit too New Age-y. I tried yoga but can't get into it."

"I suspect your mind doesn't quiet down enough. But you can train for that. I'll help you if you want."

He wasn't sure how to read her reaction to that offer.

**Move on.*

"Okay, so to answer your question. Yes, that's sort of it," he said. Honesty was clearly important for Ruth, so he might as well tell her everything. "Though, things might be changing."

Her head tipped to one side, but she didn't prompt. He'd have to find a way to say this.

"Recently, there's been a new voice in my head, and it's not mine. It talks to me like a separate entity. He *is* a separate entity."

Ruth seemed concerned. It made her softer, beautiful. He swallowed that traitorous thought away.

"Is it bad?"

"No, just new."

"Do you know whose voice it is?"

He shook his head. "And I'm not overly comfortable with that."

"Can I ask where this comes from? Is there some occult connection?"

"No. And I'm slightly offended you'd think that."

"Sorry. I don't mean to be insensitive. I just don't know about these things, so I'm stumbling around blind here. Sorry."

"You're forgiven." He took a moment to consider how to respond to her concerns. "It's not occult. But to be honest, I don't know where this new voice comes from, either."

"Okay."

The slightly pained expression suggested she was struggling to assimilate all the information, but she was trying, and he appreciated and admired that.

"Can I ask one more weird question?"

"Sure."

"Did you read the tarot for the Bevan case?"

He shook his head. "Not exactly. The morning I started, I asked what I was likely to encounter and pulled a card. I pulled the Queen of Cups."

She frowned and her eyes searched his. "Meaning?"

It wasn't intentional, but his eyes slid down. She was definitely a Queen in those cups.

You should see her out of them.

The real life tut was sharp. "I'm pretty sure it's not about my breasts."

His grin spread with the warmth of embarrassment. Caught out again. "Cups represent the emotional. Queens represent maturity and nurturing. They are generally read as adult women. When I came in and Geraint told me to work with you, I assumed the card indicated you. The Queen of Cups can be a creative or a nurturer of another's talents, but, if the card is reversed – or fumbled, as I did that morning – it can represent someone who takes that too far."

"As Maggie did. Mother love turned to smother love?"

He nodded.

She huffed. "Yeah, nurturing isn't my bag."

"Rubbish." His certainty on the point clearly surprised her as much as his passenger's duet surprised him. "Besides, Queen of Cups has another potential meaning: the finding of an ideal partner."

Something akin to terror jumped into her eyes, and she pulled back. "Right," she said. "So. We'll use your gut instincts but keep them between us, and any developments with …" She pointed vaguely to her head.

"The passenger."

Now her eyes showed how close she was to freaking out, but she managed to control it. "Right. Remember, we can use gut instinct, but still have to put the graft in, do the work, make a strong case for the CPS. We do everything clean, clear, and above board, by the book. And now I've run out of cliches, but you get the point. Don't you?"

He did. "Yes, sir."

"Good." She drained the last of her coffee and stood. "I'll see you in the office tomorrow morning, then." She stopped herself and turned back. "Oh, and since I forgot to say it last week: welcome to MCIT."

Chapter 40

The moon was waning now, and the sky was cloud-free.

It was warmer, but skyclad still wasn't practical; Madoc kept his trousers on. This time, he wasn't surprised when his phone rang.

"*Bore da, modryb* Maureen."

"Whatever it is you're worrying about, stop."

Easier said than done. Something was definitely eating at Ruth, and he was worried. He owed her after all she'd done for him.

"I have no idea what's going on, but I had a message that the right person has been contacted and all will be well."

If so, then Madoc was relieved. "*Diolch.*" He just wished he had been the one Ruth spoke to. "Aunt Maureen, have you ever heard of Mair Merch Farw?"

She signed. "Given that that translates to Mary's dead daughter, I don't imagine it's an unusual reference, but I'm not aware of any local connection. Got anything else?"

"A possible connection to Llangynidr Moor, maybe?"

He waited while Maureen considered.

"Hmm. Not picking anything up immediately, but I'll work on it."

"Thank you."

"Now get some sleep. Another long day for you tomorrow."

"*Nos da.*"

Acknowledgements

As ever, the first thanks is to my family for their continued support.

Second thanks is to you, the reader, for reading. I wrote the book, but you imagined it, you completed it. I hope you enjoyed it too, and if you could manage a little review, that would be most appreciated, as it really helps others to find my work.

With this book there are more special thanks to give as well. To Tony Fyler, my first editor and harshest critic – by the way that harshness is something I truly appreciate. But also, for brainstorming with me as hubby drove down the M6 and helping me see what Madoc needed to make him whole. And for keeping me going through various neurotic writer moments. Tony, you're a true pal, now go finish writing Hammersmith.

Thanks to Alis Hawkins (great writer - check her stuff out!) for reading and encouraging me to continue when I was ready to give it up. In fact, thanks to all of Crime Cymru and Gŵyl Crime Cymru Festival, having a bunch of like-minded writers to share with helps.

To Vicki Brewster, for the final edit. To Best Page Forward and Ad School for helping me on the marketing side. To Kim and Tanja of Deranged Doctor for the Cover – I absolutely love your work ladies.

And if you'd like to keep up with my work, hop over to books.gailbwilliams.com where you can get a free download and sign up to my newsletter for all the latest.

Thank you!

Other books by GB Williams

Charlie Bell stories
Locked Away
Locked Up (The Locked Trilogy Book 1)
Locked In (The Locked Trilogy Book 2)
Locked Down (The Locked Trilogy Book 2)
The Locked Trilogy (ebook only)
Unlocked

Atkins and Palmer Psychic Mystery Series
The Queen of Cups Murders

Other works
The Chair

The Elain Blake Novels
Breaking Free
Play the Game

Short Stories
Last Cut Casebook
First Shot (a Ruth Atkins story)

Printed in Great Britain
by Amazon

50492104R10192